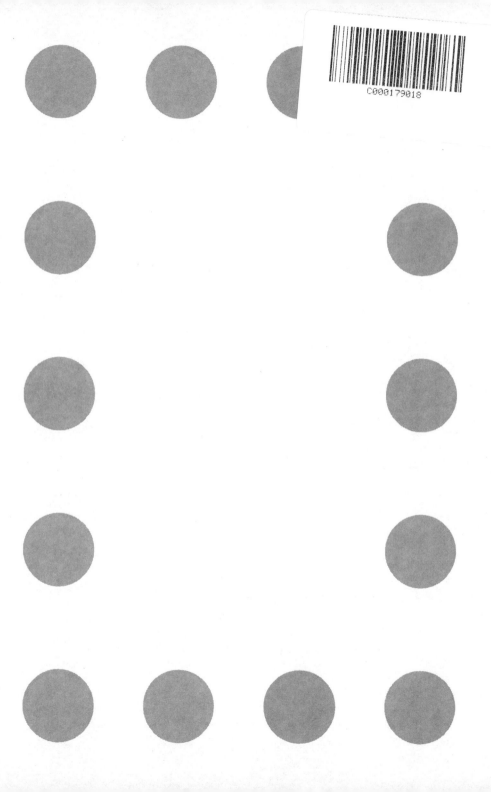

Changes

1: A New Life

Francis Oeser, born 1936 in St. Andrews, grew up in Melbourne, went to UK in 1967 retracing Alexander the Great's tracks from Taxila to Athens. Now he lives on Aigina island, Greece.

He has collaborated with artists and musicians as poet and librettist, published a score of books since 1983 of poetry, art and prose.

Work in progress:
The Seasons, Shakespeare's Songs, Portraits, Time & Memory, Greece, The Language of Social Dreaming.

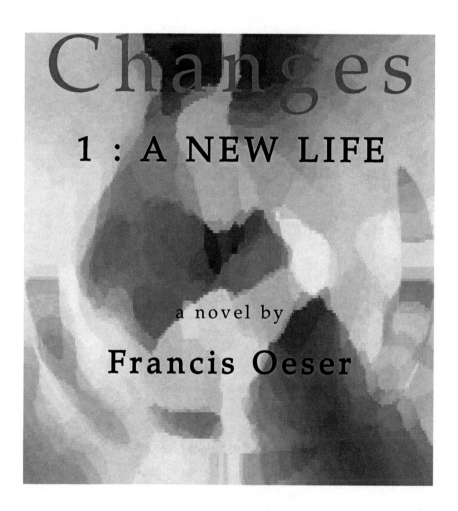

Changes

1 : A NEW LIFE

a novel by

Francis Oeser

Sicnarf Press

London, Melbourne, Ithaca : 2010

Also by F.Oeser & The Sicnarf Press:

O for Love 2 (with Ann Dowker) 2010
Giants, Divas and other stories 2009
Reflections 2008
Orchestra 2008
Outrageous Fortune 2007
Loukoumia 2006
Africa Sung to 2005
After you've Brushed your Teeth (Bunyip Stories) 2005
48 Evening Ragas 2003
Your Whispered Name (with Ann Dowker) 2003
Eyeland (with Akiko Fujikawa) 1997
Scenes from Childhood 1997
But (with Akiko Fujikawa) 1996
Persephone 1996
O for Love (with G. Wickham) 1994
You, Me, We 1993
Social Dreaming & Shakespeare 1992
Bay Break 1991
Africa Sung (1). 1987
Seasons End 1984
Black Notes 1983

British Library cataloguing-in-publication data.
A catalogue record for this book is available from the British Library.

ISBN: 978-0-9552974-5-8

© The Sicnarf Press 2010:
122 Dartmouth Park Hill, London N19 5HT, UK.
Box 708, Aigina Port, Aigina 18010, Greece.
Readings, PO Box 1066 Carlton Victoria, Australia.
Bookery, de Witt Mall, 215 N.Cayuga Street. Ithaca, 14850 NY, USA

Printed & bound by TJ International, Padstow, Cornwall, UK

Mixed Sources
Product group from well-managed
forests and other controlled sources
www.fsc.org Cert no. SGS-COC-2482
© 1996 Forest Stewardship Council
FSC

Foreword

THIS NOVEL is arranged in six sections: Birth, Rebirth, Findings, Watershed, Arrivals and Ageing. It is the first of a five book sequence collectively titled "Chages", and set in Australia, Greece, Venice and a Pacific island. As fiction, it should be enjoyed as such. End notes may be useful to readers wanting background information not supplied by the text.

Acknowledgements

THANKS Priscilla Hall for vital early editing advice (CH1); thanks to Judge Graham Frike for help with the trial scene (CH1), to Warren Simmons for clarifying the law relating to children (CH4). Thanks to June van Ingen for help with German and Italian words in the early stages (CH1&3). I am glad to pay tribute to Angela Matheson for her fine translation into Italian of Ossian's Venice song (CH4), and to the late Tom Matheson for his support, his advice on Feminism, as well as Shakespeare. Pauline Cohen and Dr Frances Gilley were insightful on the interpretation of dreams (CH1&4).
To my forebearing wife who thought, as I did, the tram-stop meeting was to be a small short story, thank you. It's probably my fault.

Birth

1:

A TRAM GRUDGINGLY GATHERS SPEED clanks onward bursting with school children. A dishevelled boy, careless of risk, dashes blindly across the road, throws his satchel on the seat and glares at its departing rear.

In the last halted car a man dawdles. This was his old school. His tram stop. His escape. He is handsome with a sensitive face, sharp eyes and a firm chin. His hands elegantly hold the steering wheel. The car draws level. The boy looks sad. The man stops. 'I'm sorry you missed the tram. Hop in. I'm sure we'll catch it.' The boy clambers aboard, kicks his satchel under the dashboard and settles gladly into the deep plush seat.

'Is someone waiting for you at home?'

'Nope.'

'Then I suppose you just wanted to escape.'

The boy looks up at the kindly face. 'I guess so.'

'I know how you feel. I went to your school ages ago. I loathed it.'

'Mm' mutters the boy enjoying the ride. 'What was it like then?'

A bridge of silence.

'Brutish. Brutal boys, brutal staff, brutal lessons, brutal sex, brutal sports – that culture pervaded everything . . . And now?'

'The same.' The boy grimaced. 'What happened to you?'

'Lots of things . . . I was hunted by my form, set up by a master, a quarry running to rehearsals in the school hall every afternoon. Helpless. Like the boys seized each recess, taken to the grandstand, abused, having hair hacked off. I was beaten up by the boarders, branded as a poofter.'

'Are you?' stammers the boy, flushing

'Then, I was captain of music, a girlish pastime they believed, for "rugby or rowing makes a man of you". Yet musical touching-up is similar - superior I think.'

'Did that . . . you know, that . . um . . kind of thing happen?'

'The coarse groping disgusted me. I wanted someone special, just for ourselves, not crude public displays.'

The man looks at the broad young face grey eyes bright and wistful under a mop of fair hair, the sculpted lips slightly open as if taking in the scent of their conversation, the graceful almost fragile figure. He sighs. 'I once had a friend like you. We used to meet after school; sometimes we met on Saturdays during cricket matches.'

'Did you like cricket?'

'No. We went to the music school. I had a key. We'd be together there most of the match.'

'Playing music?'

'Playing is a fair description.'

'Oh' The boy starts. 'Were you ever caught?'

'Never. It was odd with so much groping at school. Once in class in the front row, a boy kneaded my fly. Nothing was ever said. I guess it was par for the course – after all, boys will be boys. But my friend was special; it's true. Yet it was impossible to face our feelings which belonged with girls. We didn't know how to deal with the mechanics of love so drifted apart. He was fourteen, I was sixteen. Partners for a wonderful moment, nothing more.'

'I'm fourteen,' parries the boy. 'Those things do happen. I'm ignored. They rip off pretty kids' trousers and rub them off.'

'We called that tabling,' says the man.

'We say doing a bummer.'

'Nothing changes.' the man sighs. 'Look, there's your tram. I told you we'd catch it. Shall I drop you at the next stop?'

The boy gazes shyly into the distance. 'Can I go with you to my road? I only live a bit further on.'

The man smiles. 'Of course.' He squeezes the boy's knee.

The traffic lights flush red. The man pulls on the handbrake and turns to confront the boy. 'It's hard being on your own.'

The boy starts. 'I've never told anyone these things.'

'Nor have I.' The man sighs. 'Are you OK?'

'Yes.'

'How do you feel about them?'

9

'Everyone does it, I know that.'

'But you told me they hadn't got you yet.'

'No one's interested in a little runt like me.'

The man trembles as he steers them towards the boy's home.

They make their way up the front path. In the shadowy entrance hall the man takes the satchel and places it on the floor. He clasps the boy in a gentle hug. The boy submits to searching lips. He gulps the foreign tongue while exploring with his own. His hand is positioned over the big crotch while his rough school trousers are caressed. Gradually the boy's shirt is unbuttoned. Sharing the need to be in touch they cling awash with pleasure. The boy blushes. 'We've got two hours.'

'Let's shower?' says the man.

'It's down the hall.'

Questing fingers slip and probe in soapy play. They stumble flushed to the boy's room, unwrap towels and lie on his bed. The boy is overwhelmed by the man's desire. He kneels, long-ing, unsure, accepting teasing kisses and fingers. The man begins to move into him. The boy fills. His body opens to skilled caresses. Tightening with excitement, new sensations burst, then pain to the man's urgency, his indrawn breath, wilting withdrawal.

'Fuck, that hurt.'

'We came together,' murmurs the man.

The boy looks in wonder at the drops on the towel as pain is overruled by freshening pleasure. 'Was I good?'

'Quite amazing. Great beauty inside matching your outside.'

The boy is aroused. He clings, kissing nipples and their wisps of hair until the exhausted man rolls over and takes the erection into his mouth, rolling off the foreskin, teasing its naked head with a restless tongue and massaging its length with a sticky hand. The boy gasps. 'AH. I came. Sorry, I should've said.'

'I love your taste,' whispers the man in a dream: he is six, or sixteen. He'd wanted such joy all his life. He is deeply grateful, sharing rich beginnings with a shadow-self: the end and the begin-ning entwining with this boy.

They talk about the boy's lonely life with his working mother and her new workaholic husband, he is a nuisance left to fend for himself, never up to scratch. They lived for shopping malls. School is an extension of his agony. No escape either way.

The boy lies watching the man's chest rise and fall, echoing his own. 'I'm all over the place. I don't know where I'm going.' He is fascinated by the life this man leads: far away, working and boating and travelling, what an ideal life; and does he have other boys, and is he good, or as good? Each admits this first time.

'I, you – giving me everything – I'm so happy.' the man stammers. 'Can we meet again, I want . . all . . you . . so much.'

'If you like.' the boy says softly.

'Could you come for a weekend? We could book a motel and go sailing down the coast, I'll find us something.'

The boy only nods.

'I'll meet you at our tram stop on Friday. Just bring shorts, togs, a tee shirt and a toothbrush, oh and a hat for sailing. We could ring your parents that evening, when it's too late to say No.' The man brushes a velvet flank. 'And I'll help you with your homework. There must be a decent time for work and play.'

'Yes, all right. Wow. Can we really go?'

Parting, the man kisses the soft mouth. The car glows as it slides away and across the hazy city, which they now share.

2:

THE CAR WAS WAITING beyond the tram stop. The boy threw his satchel onto the back seat and clambered in. (Would it be OK? Could it be fun? He had been sore the next day; was he safe?). He looked steadfastly ahead seeking answers written on the white lines guiding them. He had never been so angry or disobedient, never had a soul-mate to share his troubling needs. Inexorably the lines kept coming, dictatorial and mute.

The man glanced at him. 'Hello.' He waited, and tackled the silence. 'Shall we stop at that milk bar?'

'No, not that one, it's full of kids.'

'Of course. Let's go further away into the country.'

'I agree.'

They began to find each other. The road spun out before them. Their plans unfolded. Some distance along a country highway, they stopped for petrol. A garage with loitering battered gum trees leaned against the harsh afternoon light. In the store they examined a pair of shorts and matching tee-shirt . The man grinned. 'They'd be perfect for sailing'.

The boy fidgeted. 'Aren't they too posh?'

'Nonsense, you look great.'

The man selected thongs for him. The boy rudely sucked his milkshake. 'So, which thongs do you like?' the man asked gently.

'I don't mind.'

'But what do you want?'

The boy faltered. 'I like the black ones with colours.'

'Then you shall have them. Black gets hotter than anything else, just throw a towel over them when you're swimming. Now, put them on and we'll get going.'

They sped a short way, coming to rest under a shady tree.

'Come here,' said the man softly. He took the boy in his arms and kissed him until the boy curled up on his chest, hearing a heart beat like his own. Intimacy dissolving their pain.

They drove on through rolling countryside to a peaceful river inlet and hired a catamaran to negotiate the sand bar across its mouth and on to the open sea. 'I'll show you how we sail over that in the morning,' promised the man as they made for their motel.

The phone call to the boy's home was uncomfortable, as they knew it would be. Sweating, they hung up, sauntered back to their room, moved the beds together, took a long soapy shower and lay in the darkness calmed by musing crickets and the boom of distant surf. 'Do you want to go first this time?' the man whispered. He turned on his back, lifting his legs. Pleasure wafted them into sleep.

And then dawn, and the boat. The boy was clever. He quickly picked up crewing skills as they flew over the ocean swell to a stiff breeze beyond the breakers. The boat responded to good handling. The boy was elated. They crashed through smoking tops, drenched in spume, cut through the glass-clear water their double wake curling behind. The sun gilded his body, flashed in his eyes. He was flying – well, it felt like that. The sea cleansed him. Sucked by the breeze, laughter gushed from his throat. The sails stiffened and bulged as the catamaran leaned over until the boom almost brushed the running waves and the three of them – the man, the boy and the boat – hung god-like in watery haze.

As the morning passed, their teamwork failed less frequently. The first capsizes were scary. 'Cats are hard to bring about,' the man explained. They thrashed around in the water, turned the sloshing hull until, standing on the submerged keel and facing the breeze, managed to right the boat, clamber aboard, talk through the mistake and go on.

'The sea's a tough master.' laughed the man.

'So's the wind.' shouted the boy. 'Let's go.'

They became one with the boat. Revelling in their skill. Sure of themselves now, they drifted way out. The man peeled off the boy's trunks and lovingly pushed him overboard. 'We're too far for anyone to see.' he sang. Naked and holding a rope they splashed beside the boat. They grasped and fondled, free in their own world, hauling themselves panting onto the canvas deck slung between the two hulls sprawling naked, reinvigorated.

Elated, they sped back through the surf, over the bar and beached the boat. They swam in the calm river, duck-diving, basking and floating finally to shore. And at last, back in the motel, weary and content, they lay, drifting towards a candle-lit dinner.

They ate hugely, spoke of dreams, dislikes, pain, even pride, drank much; afterwards stumbling back, the boy needed support.

Showering amazed them. They dared extremes. The man lay in the bath, the boy crouching over his erection.

'Go down on me. You're full of shit, push it out.'

'On you?' The boy wavered.

'Yes, of course.' the man said.

Warm slugs plopped onto his stomach washed by urine; the man smeared the young flanks. The world reeled. The boy lowered himself, staked like a sacrifice.

'Push out more,' breathed the man drunkenly, and erupted. The boy farted out the shrinking member and collapsed in tears.

They struggled out of the mess. The boy was hosed down and unsteadily carried to bed. The man, apalled, peremptorily cleaned himself and the bath. It was like the beginning of the world: God seeding the primal shit. But life then followed, he thought. To have fallen from our celebration of love to these depths is frightening. He hated himself for pushing this precious boy into hell, life was deathly enough. This could topple him.

Light from the abandoned bathroom dimly illuminated their beds. The boy lay sleeping, slightly curled up; unblemished by shit, sex or adult interference, his beauty fresh as the ocean. But tears trembled on his lashes. Was he dreaming?

The man bent and licked the damp salt. These drops announced the end, the pearls of the dead. Surely his beloved would live? He would make amends. But could anyone save him now? Life was entwined with death, as he around this boy. What treachery!

The man fell into an uneasy sleep waking as dawn paled the room. The boy had moaned and turned half-smiling through sleep, softly kissed a stubbled cheek and snuggled into his chest purring in the security of a hug. Dreaming, until the sun burned them awake.

The boy was sore but unbowed. Curious, he insisted on hearing of their drunken orgy in detail. Faced with the truth he laughed. 'I'm sorry for shitting and pissing on you. Did I really come in my own shit?' His face fell. 'You hurt me inside. Did I really kiss you in the night?' He grinned. 'If that was love I'd hate to make war with you.' They showered, and ate. Then homework was tackled.

Making amends, the man heroically dealt with a puzzled student, teasing thoughtful work from him. Together they explored his ignorance, honing the boy's skill. Both were glad to escape to the sea. Later, carefree, they headed home.

'You're a Greek god.' The man said in wonder.

'So were you with nothing on but a foreskin.' The boy's laughter had filled their weekend like a healing song.

'Could we really have found such happiness, an old man and a young boy? We aren't Adam and Eve, but it feels like the Garden of Eden. I could never forget you.' the man muttered.

The boy sighed. 'I'm glad we came.'

They rehearsed the boy's homecoming speech, and wondered how they might meet again. For soon the man must go. They planned a longer outing. The plan was audacious and danger-ous, it could be undermined. The boy seemed secure from the high flak from school and home but vulnerable to low sniping; as vulner-able as Ned Kelly in his body-armour whose heart was protected while his legs were shot away.*

---

*   See notes at end.

3:

AFTER SOME STRETCHING of the truth, the school accepted the boy's absence for a day and a half so they left the tram-stop at lunchtime on Thursday. The boy was to return the next Monday. His parents assumed he was staying with a friend. Jollity resounded as the car sped into the country.

'Why not take your school trousers and underpants off?'

The boy giggled. 'You'd better keep your eyes on the road.' He coyly changed into his new shorts and shirt, and was admired. By mid-afternoon they had found a room in a farmhouse at the edge of a lake and borrowed a *Lazer* sailing boat. Stowing a plastic bag with water and nibbles they pushed it out from the landing stage, sailing towards a small island clad in high reeds and a few trees. They ran the boat onto a sandy beach, dumped their clothes and waded into the water to float under majestic clouds in the summer bronzed landscape.

They returned to the beach, drying and falling into each other's arms. Release was triggered when exploration brought each to that imperious point. Mirrored needs mirroring exploration and release. Afterwards they lay watching the water shake the image of the sky on its placid face, something restless from a calm majesty. Surer, they explored the lake until dusk. The farmer's wife cooked them a huge meal. Held by the silent landscape they slept together in their own truth.

Next day they drove straight to the coast, to a wildness of sand, ocean and sky, the beach marked only by birds' wanderings.

'It's like Treasure Island.'

'You can be Boy Friday.'

'Because it's Friday, I agree.'

They dashed naked into the rearing ocean buffeted and slapped. They surfed back to the beach, sand in their crevices and hair, grazed chests and knees. The breeze laughed with them, whisked untidy streams of urine far along the sand. It was virginal. Beyond time. They were shadowy dreams in a nascent world, the first humans. The power of the sea held them; the spumed waves, streaming into a vast sky reflected on the wet beach. Dry sand streamed from the ridges of dunes, manes combed by the breeze. Rocks glowered like monstrous animals. The two, hand-joined specks in the vast wilderness.

Towards evening they found a pub made entirely of wood in a bare country town. Their first-floor room faced the dusty street. It was off a corridor to many others. Although the night's activities were audible through the flimsy partitioning, the row from the public bars beneath obliterated the chorus of cries from energetic neighbours. They had rolled to bed comfortably filled with T-bone steaks and chips and awash with enough beer to feel lascivious and free, but remembering to lock the door and switch off the light.

They stood by the window, gazing through untidy trees on a deserted street. Then a light went on next door, gleaming through a hole in the wall, eyeing their darkness and drawing the boy into voyeuring a prostitute there. The spy-hole was strategically placed. A large, man stripped of his trousers revealed the biggest penis in the world, a naked fist on an arm – so that's what a real man has! The woman teased him softly, feeling down its length, measuring the pleasure and the pain it represented. She peeled a condom over its hugeness and lay back on the bed, talking all the while to her customer, enticing him to enter her. She wore nothing under her skirt. The boy glimpsed a triangle of pubic hair, and the man pushing and thrusting to climax as the woman held him.

The big man was replaced by a wiry one with a slim, long penis who argued until the woman accepted another bank-note, peeled on his rubber sheath and knelt on the bed to be entered from the rear. The boy started – this was his scene. He was transfixed, but couldn't associate the brutal encounter with his own love-making. Then a much younger lad entered, pushed in by rowdy mates in the corridor. He needed coaxing. The woman undressed him and ran appraising hands down fair skin and into his sex until it reared up. She softly wooed him onto the bed, crouching over him, bouncing up and down until suddenly he finished.

The boy had never witnessed love-making before. Its bestiality disgusted him. It looked nothing like his feelings, yet it was exciting. Now he pounded with desire and demanded attention, everything for himself. Their bed creaked along with the others. They gasped with ejaculations ferrying them to a sleep as restless as the rise and fall of the all-night carousing below. No one seemed to care the boy was under age. They had drunk and eaten, and now moaned, made love-messes; in the morning they would leave unchallenged. The protective isolation of the coastal wilderness had seeped into this country town.

They reached the city by lunchtime. It was a smart hotel with an immense atrium, their spacious room with an enormous triple bed. The man looked around at the Jacuzzi, the worktable with computer terminals. 'I'd be happy living here in the cupboard.' He insisted the boy get out all his school books and make up the time lost on the journey. They studied hard for some hours until the man kissed the graceful neck. 'You've earned a break. Let's case the joint.'

Hand in hand they sauntered through thronged streets at the harbour end of the city with a mix of old buildings and modern steel-framed giants. They discovered a cosy Thai restaurant in a tiny brick house for their last night together, agreeing to take it easy with the grog to avoid grossness. 'I'll piss on you any time, if you want,' teased the boy, radiant from basking in the landscape of their journey and in his friend's admiration. Footsore, they stumbled back to shower and make love. The day waned, myriad lights festooned the city as they changed for dinner.

Following the gentle fun of the meal they ventured into a gay club. They pacified a door-keeper and slid into chairs in a barn-like bar where men danced in provocative clinches. They joined in, swaying gently in a dim empty corner, pressing together, feeling the push of excitement and taking sweetness from each other's lips, moved by the music, clinging together affirming their partnership, cementing the promise of a sailing holiday in Greece, ignoring tomorrow's parting and fears about coping alone.

'Tell yourself you *have* changed, in spite of careless judgements that you're an idle, dumb, wilful kid; tell yourself this over and over. Stay in touch. If things get bad, tell me. Try to remember everything we've done. Try to keep me inside, so you feel stronger. But write and tell me everything, I promise to. And we'll meet soon on my boat.'

They danced blindly.

'You'll have to leave. Pronto! This is a men-only club, regulated, above board.' a bouncer barked.

Ablaze, they fled, dawdling along the harbour edge back to the hotel. They swayed to imagined music before the bay window of their room, floating over the jewelled city, abandoning clothes, falling onto warm skin, wet lips and openings responding to the slightest touch. They prolonged this coupling, teasing out pleasure in minute ways so as to go on, go on delaying, until as lights were dowsed over the city and quiet reigned, the boy, in a flurry of love, fountained into his friend. Then he turned to be flooded. They were engulfed in one sweet dream.

4:

TIME PASSED. Snails went faster. And then they were reunited in Greece. Summer there reminded the boy of home. He had brought his sailing clothes – they were all he needed. He was surprised all his earlier sailing experience was essential, and there was lots more to learn. He delighted in helping manage the large boat, particularly in and out of crowded harbours, tying up securely (he was often praised for that), or in secluded bays, second-anchoring to the shore with a long line he usually swam in with and secured to a rock or tree. He gloried in the warm water, being naked, and wanting a man around.

Love-making continued. But grew less frenetic with time. Sharing the boat all day was a satisfaction softening desire. And the lad was getting older altering their needs. But sharing the messages mutely expressed by their bodies still mattered.

After a week at sea they had moored on the east coast of Odysseus's island, Ithaca, off a white marble beach so steeply shelved the boat could lie within a few meters of the shore, an easy wade. The place was empty. Both the beach and its hinterland of scrubby olive groves were uninhabited. The deep shade beyond the blazing white of the marble beach released the boy's extremes: anger boiled out of contentment. He seemed to adopt both shade and brightness, from uneasy calm to dark moods and fire.

The boy slumped over the rail, his head churning. 'You're always pushing me around, telling me what to do, touching me up, never thinking what I want. You don't own me.' Tears came.

The man approached humbly. 'I'm sorry. Sometimes it's hard being skipper as well as friend. I'll try to give you more space. You're quite right, I lunge for you without thinking. You are right.'

The boy lightened. A hand lay on his own – soft, entreating, generous, which somehow drew down the veil of anger until he could turn and put an enervated head on the strong chest. He shivered. 'I'm shit. Why do you bother?'

'Do you feel that bad?' the man whispered as the sun cut them into thin strips of shade and brightness. 'You shouldn't let the people who anger you get inside. They'll damage you . . . like me. You should push us all away. Nobody owns you.'

'I don't want to push you away. I get so mixed up.'

'It's hard being skipper or crew.' The man smiled. 'I guess we struggle because it's a matter of life or death.' He hugged the boy. 'Let's swim, you'll feel better.'

Together they balance precariously on the ship's rail and then spring, arching through the air to splash deep into the clear green water, alarming fish seething in the shade of the hull; down, down into eerie silence, washing cares away, their feelings held by the fullness of the sea, until two breathless heads burst into the air and cheerful cries like invisible balls bound over the restless surface.

With a new ease the boy beachcombed and built a cairn of white marble stones, his claim to the virginal beach and a memorial to his spirits. The man dozed between studying charts and tidying up (the boy threw his stuff anywhere). It was bliss, and they would stay. The boy hunted fish with a spear-gun, returning triumphant with a small catch which the man gutted. They collected wood for a barbecue that evening.

The boy laughed. 'I've never cooked in the raw.'

'Don't singe your stick, you need it, well, I need it . . . if and when your majesty agrees.'

The boy grinned. Reefs negotiated, they drifted into calmer waters. The impartial natural world brought them solace with ways to share pain and pleasure. Open space was their elixir.

'How love transforms us.' the man mused to himself. 'How the boundary is blurred between my feelings for nature and feelings for another person; all the wonder, humility and hope mix until I fuck the landscape and am fucked by it, or is it my fleshly lover? I can't tell. Love transforms everything. The song says it: "When you're smiling, the whole world smiles with you". Hurt and pain distort us and the landscape. We are dealing with that. It's worth it with this boy. We're both arid landscapes filled with storms that somehow bring greenness.'

It seemed impossible to add to the boy's beauty, yet that evening firelight flickered an immeasurable allure over him as he sprawled with unconscious grace beside the fire, his twisting shadow dancing on the white pebbles, the coals glowing in his eyes, a mystery of shadows refining his nakedness, his hands masterfully turning the fish in the wire grill until his unsteady voice proclaimed supper. They feasted: fresh food, fresh feelings, faces for each other. The dark hemmed them, the sea sighed on the shingle, a sickle moon hung over this Bethlehem as frankincense and myrrh rose in the smoke spinning upwards into starred space. Lastly, in a loose satiated embrace, cradled by the boat, they slept.

5:

LIFE FELT NORMAL AGAIN. They avoided further conflict, enjoying the voyage. But there was a preoccupation, a nagging resistance between them: The boy was not a girl; and although they exchanged roles, this confused rather than clarified them. A balance became increasingly fraught as the boy matured. The man turned to Greek myth celebrating paradox.* Tale after tale he told, in sun, under the stars and snug in the cabin. He and the boy looked for answers apart from separating, which neither wanted.

'Persephone belonged *both* above and below the earth; the pull was both ways. That's me,' said the boy. 'But can I really be male and female?' He groaned. 'Maybe I'm gay.'

'Maybe a complete man is both. Like Tiresias, or Dionysus, in spite of the rules of the world,' said the man. 'Just think, a woman

---

* See notes at end.

has a miniature penis in her vagina, the clitoris, and we men have replica breasts of no earthly use. Men and women share origins. We start in the collision of sperm and ovum, so carry remnants of each, both physical and emotional, as we've found. Persephone represents the male and female duality in our genes.'

Sunlight flickered into the cabin. The man reached out and smoothed the frown of concentration from the boy's face. They rested. Later the light withdrew. The man tenderly brushed matted locks off the boy's forehead and mused, 'You know, we're changing. We float between being mother and father – sometimes I'm father to your mother, sometimes you father me. That's how it is. We're lucky, we balance out, we can play the range, use our whole natures. It scares us at times – I know. That's when rage happens, and the rejection and guilt. At least I've been a man in my life. But look at you, on the brink of manhood. Asking who you are is much more unsettling, I admire your bravery. I love you so much for allowing me to find my place in our floating world, for turning my life into such an adventure; giving me back what I'd lost.'

'Oh no, you have everything.' The boy blurted. 'I went with you because of that, because I had to. I'm not angry with you. It's been great. Everything. I don't mind the sex. I'm better at school – you were right, I've got to sharpen my mind too. If I'm gay, I'm gay,'

The man, trembling, touched the boy's Adam's apple. 'Don't let anyone decide what you are. You must do that.' His vehemence startled the boy. 'Who you are is another set of extremes we'll deal with. Don't let guilt about being different punish you, don't give yourself false titles. I know you deeply now. Inside and out. There's a stirring in you, your male sex drive. You've been questioning yourself every time we kiss, every time we do wrong things like being fucked. But look how you share all the tasks of sailing – you're discovering what men do in the world. After all, yesterday you were a child. These changes don't happen only in words but go on in us as we drift towards the choices life is full of. You are changing, although often don't see that. I know you know you're not a girl. I'm so lucky to be with you exploring what sort of person you'll be. It's like looking into a gloomy cave, often I glimpse a fine, beautiful, and clever young man, who needs a little help to step out into the light, whose bravery astonishes me.'

The boy's gaze dropped. He lowered himself onto the man's

knees racked by doubt and pride. He faced the old phallus, bent his head low, his cheek slipping on a firm thigh. He wallowed in its spicy scent. 'Yes,' he said softly. 'It's like looking into the dark.' At that moment, recalled much later, he understood he was loved. The sex, the laughter, the play, the work, the fury, fear and cover-ups had all been leading to this insight.

He knew now he wasn't alone. He gazed up at his skipper. A kiss stopped further talk. Perplexities settled. Cold beers then time to dive: gulping air to get down to the sea floor, as if swallowing their journey to reach the destination. Held there by the benign sea was confirmation.

6:

THEY LAY GASPING on the wet deck after diving when the boy asked, 'Who was Tiresias?'

'I'll tell you about Dionysus first, you're just like him. He was brought up disguised as a girl and surrounded by females in order to hide him from the wrath of Hera – he was fathered by Zeus, Hera's brother, her king, her husband too. (Well, your stepfather is not too fond of you either). Then he was discovered. To save his skin he was sent away on a journey around the world.

'I think of that girlish bit of you. All boys have it, like the young Dionysus. He was a crazy uncontrollable teenager – a boy changing into a man. He struggled to find himself and his place in the world and grew into a wilful god of revelry and lust. He was the master of the Felt, irrepressible, unreasonable. You're going to get there too. You'll grow into a wonderful man, I know it for sure.'

The boy laughs, grabs the man's hat and throws it high over the ship's rail. It lands like a spinning UFO on the sea, waterlogging, slowing. Together they follow, fighting to recover the sinking shape before reaching the stones on the bottom decorated in a breathing net of sun-patterns. Naked glee. Everything chuckling. Two figures, one crowned in a streaming melting hat, burst from the disturbed water, clamber up the ship's ladder and collapse like seals into the cock-pit.

'You think you're Zeus, thundering after breakfast'

'Dear boy, Dionysus, crowned, wilful and ravishing.'

'A girl?'

'No. Maybe girlish. Now, I promised you more. Like Dionysus, Tiresias began as a girl and grew up to be a woman who later became a man. Some time afterwards there was a dispute between the two ruling gods, Zeus and Hera, about who had the greatest sexual pleasure, men or women. So they summoned Tiresias, who had known both. He prevaricated. Either way he'd offend one of those mighty ones.

'In the end he told the truth: "Men have the noblest of experiences, but women enjoy the deeper pleasure". Zeus went berserk – males had to be better at everything – and he blinded Tiresias. Hera got back at him in her own smug way – she gifted him prophesy. So that's why Tiresias saw into the future. A poet called him "Tiresias of the withered dugs" - half man, half woman.

'Here's another paradox – he was blind but had insight, he could see. This is another thing we've engaged with: your getting inner sight. We struggle through ecstasy and guilt and doubt. No wonder we fight. We're battling up out of an abyss. I just hope we'll always be able to help each other.'

The boy sighed. 'That dark cave. Looking inside is terrible. I see monsters, not the future.'

'Maybe the future seems monstrous.'

'It's best now. Being here. It's fun but serious. I like that.'

'Well now, serious fun is a Persephone sort of contradiction. Think of Persephone, she *is* important. We keep trapping ourselves in opposites, in the either/or, in the male/female, the black/white, friend/foe, sane/insane, right/wrong. The truth never lies all on one side. That's why we need bridges, Persephone Bridges – they link the opposites so we can negotiate the chasm of fear between.'

'Between straight/gay?'

'Exactly, the mix we're exploring. Persephone was loyal to two worlds. She belonged to the light, to life above the ground – what you see, that reality. She also ruled the dark underworld of feelings, of intuition and of death. Many would say she's two-faced; I think she expresses true loyalty – what is a life of light without its shadow? your objects in the mysterious cave-gloom? What is our male life without its female part? Persephone was loyal to both, as you are to the boy and the girl in you. Aren't we learning to defend true loyalty?'

The boy winced. 'It's hard as shit!'

'Of course it is. But worth it?'

'Um, I suppose so. Yes.' His brow uncreased.

'It's tough on the bridge. Don't worry about what it looks like to others, explore! We must feel our way to understanding. It's scary. It takes time. But if we don't do this we're blind and lost semi-people. I cry for you when you say you're gay. That's glib. Don't be fooled, you're much more than that. You're looking around already – you'll get to know yourself all right, and come to rely on what you've found. And believe me, there isn't a label in the world that's big enough to describe you.'

The boy gazed seaward. 'The waves are nodding.' he said to himself. Happily he watched the skipper unhook the canvas shade over the boom, roll it up and put it away. Perhaps I don't need a shelter from brightness or dark anymore, he thought. We are playing with our bodies, our thoughts and the boat. It's rewarding. New for me. Making me someone, at last.

7:

IT WAS LATE AFTERNOON. The sun was sinking into the blazing horizon. Overhead, long, livid pink clouds stretched across the tissue paper blue. Some of the boy's brilliance was fading with the day. He and the man would soon become shadows below decks, sheltering from the freshening wind. They laid another anchor to ride out the predicted storm.

They ate outside in the cockpit. In the gusty dark the stars grew distinct. The moon rode through low cloud. The wind stiffened. Below, they had petted and slept. The boat tossed awkwardly. The man sprang up and struggled up the companion-way. The rocky shore was perilously close. He fell back down the steps, pulled on wet-weather clothes, calling, 'Wake up, come on, quick! The anchors have dragged, we're being blown onto the rocks.'

They hurried above decks to start the engine, winch in the main anchor. The boy struggled forward to battle with straining ropes, pulling at the second anchor, buffeted by a black wind.

The man shouted. 'One hand for the boat, one for yourself!'

Try as he might, nothing gave. 'It's jammed.'

The man yelled: 'I'll steer the boat over the anchor so you can pull it up. There now. Try again.'

The boy panted and strained, pulling against the whole weight of the buffeting boat and the roaring air, slipping on the deck awash with spray, screaming at the line stuck fast under the heaving water. 'It won't come.'

'Try again.'

The boy struggled and slipped, until letting go the pulpit rail, with a mighty two-handed wrench he freed the line. The boat bounced free. He fell, pulling in the encrusted chain. Length by length it piled up as he knelt in streaming water, crying out his struggle and his victory. 'OK. OK.'

'Well done.' shouted the skipper. 'Hold tight. I'll take the boat to the other side of the bay, it's calmer. We'll be safe there.'

The darkness howled around them, The shrouds shrieked with wind. The boat bucked rolling, pitching, slowly responding to engine and tiller. Like a sleepwalker it nudged towards nothing visible, to a blind target drawn on skilled memory. Gradually the indistinct shore loomed, a still silhouette above the turbulence. They eased towards it, the sea calmed. It felt safer. The winch was started and the main anchor grumbled out and into the heaving sea. The boat was still drifting.

'Throw your anchor out.' yelled the man.

'OK.'

The boat seemed to stop.

'Take up the slack and tie up.'

Perhaps the anchors were holding. Trying to sight something on the shore, they watched against the mast, rail stanchions, any fixed points on the boat, to see if the coast had steadied. The boat still bucked but it seemed safely anchored now. The man gingerly winched out more anchor. The boat fell behind towards the beach until the depth gauge showed a jumping 1.6 meters, just above its draught in the choppy sea.

'Can you take a line to the shore? I think there's a rock you can tie to. Put the chain round, not the rope, so it doesn't fray; secure it with two half-hitches, or make that three. The chain should hold. I'll pull in the slack. Wear your thongs. If there's a problem in the deep water call me. First connect a line to the boat so I can pull you back, if . . Be careful!'

In the cold gloom buffeted by wind and sea, the boy waded with the line and then swam back. 'Will you check it?' His voice grew urgent, imploring. 'Please, please, check it.'

'No. I trust you,' the man called into the wind as he edged the bucking boat into deeper water. He struggled, tightening every line until the boat lay secured.

The boy looked on, wet through, shivering with exhaustion and fear. They stripped their drenched gear off at the foot of the companionway and stowed it in the heads. In the cabin light they surveyed the damage. Both were bruised, the boy's knee was badly gashed, his hands were a bloodied mess where the anchor chain had ripped them.

'Shit, I meant to say "Use the gloves",' the man groaned.

'I did. But they blew away while I was trying to sort myself out,' the boy muttered.

'Gloves don't matter, your poor hands, they must hurt a lot.'

'Yes,' The boy, shivered.

In the saloon the man dried him, got him warm clothes, wrapped him in a blanket. The boy allowed his knees and hands to be coated in antiseptic and bandaged. Then wearily accepted a mug of hot milk and honey with a dash of whisky. Warmth flooded him.

'We did it. You were great. Impossible without you.'

'It was still impossible.' the boy croaked.

'Yes, but we did it, somehow. Here we are, safe and sound.'

'Are you sure?'

'Listen, at worst we could be washed to shore. Our lives are not in danger now. There's a small risk we might drag anchor if the wind blows from another quarter. But I think the stony bottom here will hold us and your shore line will steady us.' He felt the boy relax.

They moved to the triangular bunk at the front of the saloon, sprawling ready to save the boat. Tenderly linked, uncomfortably rocked, eventually they dozed. Hours later they woke to weak sunlight and a sea heaving with the aftermath of the storm. Then the boy slept deeply.

The man pottered, checking gear, fixing the canvas shade over the cockpit. 'Let's mooch about for a day or so to recover and to check the boat,' he suggested when the boy emerged blinking into the light. 'Look, your shore-line is perfect.' He petted the boy towards excitement but the storm was still in them; it needed time to still. In the growing heat, they ate breakfast. The day complete.

8:

THE WEATHER TURNED. Long days filled with breathless sunshine. The boat seemed caught in a motionless haze in a glassy sea only disturbed by their swimming. The boy sometimes took his *Walkman* to the back edge of the beach where the fields started. There he rested under a gnarled olive tree. Stiffness and pain eased.

One afternoon they sprawled, restless on the beach. The boy stood to pee.

The man smiled, 'Why not do it on me.'

'Like before?'

'Yes, but no shit. That was disgusting. Do you remember how I rubbed it all over you?'

'Yes.' The boy grinned. 'Do you mean it?'

'Come on!' The man lay on his back on the shingle. Streaming urine warmed his chest and legs. 'My face too.' His hair was drenched and some ran into his mouth. The boy sniffed. The man was aroused. 'That felt great.' He smiled as the boy sat down. 'Now it's my turn.'

He straddled the boy and struggled with his flow, pinched off by his arousal. He tickled the sides of his bottom for release, directed a trickle onto the boy's lap to dribble through the wisps of pubic hair and through his legs. Then he wet his hair.

The boy shook his head as some ran into his mouth. He rose and spat it out. 'Yuk.' he gargled. 'It tastes like almond vinegar.'

The man kissed the wet from the boy's face and awakening penis. 'If we were shipwrecked, we'd have to drink it to survive.'

'It was disgusting.'

'You shower, so what's wrong with warm water then?'

'It wasn't water'

'Anyway, when you suck me off urine's mixed with semen. You don't get fussed about that.' It hasn't made you sick has it?'

The boy shook his head, 'Why do you like it?'

'Because it is from deep inside you. In that clean, wonderful place giving such incredible pleasure. Anyway, you make urine like you make ideas. I love all the things that come from inside, even your shit. Well, shit is pretty gross, even your shit.'

The lad let himself be held. Fish on gleaming fish flowing.

'You're really very beautiful, you know; inside and out. All of you.' the man murmured, licking a wet ear and holding velvet testicles, as soft as shoulders are bony.

The boy struggled free and leaped up. 'Let's swim.'

The man laughed and joined him, surging into the clear water, calling and swimming into the centre of the bay, heaving and splashing until the softest ripples reached the shore, to whisper into the shingle. He swam up to the boy. 'Let's get away in the morning if there's any wind. Or we can stay here until it cools and then do an all-night sail. It's very special at night.'

'Dangerous?'

'Not at all. There are fewer boats about. Only the professionals with radar and steersmen. I'll show you all our equipment.'

'Let's go tonight.' the boy pleaded.

They flopped about, swam and snacked, waiting for the wind. The boy caught some fish they grilled on the beach, feasting in farewell before setting off.

As dusk settled the boat nosed out into the open sea. The chart table glowed. The satellite navigation and radar screens recorded their passage. Beyond the coast a breeze sprang up. The sails were set the engine still ticking over. The small navigating lights at the masthead mimicked the stars whose faint reflections winked in the sea, their shadowy boat following an invisible thread.

'The moon comes up in several hours. Magic.' the man said.

They dressed in warm clothes under kagouls.

The boy offered to take the first watch. 'I want to be in

charge. Oh, please, I'll be fine. It's only four hours.'

'Wake me if anything at all bothers you. Anything!' The man ducked wearily down to the saloon and his bunk.

Six hours later he woke with a start, blundered into his clothes and struggled up the companionway. The boy was hunched in the cockpit humming softly to himself, measuring the moonlight snaking over the water. They snuggled in contented silence, enjoying the night. The vast starry dark arched overhead. That was the outer limit of the world, a band of dark water transporting them. Unseen powers nudged the boat this way and that as it rose and fell over the long swell and rolled dreamily into troughs as dark pleasure seeped into the two sailors.

A large dolphin followed the boat for a while until, bored with the lack of reciprocity, it rolled over, flicked its forked tail and vanished. 'Wonderful,' the boy breathed. The man slid a hand under the boy's shirt to feel his warm heart beating. The boy swivelled round into the man's chest to kiss him and push exploring fingers into his shorts. Silvering moonlight.

9:

NEGOTIATING A RASH OF ROCKY ISLANDS, they reached port in the early afternoon. They moored at the long crowded quay, took in water and fuel before lunch in a small taverna, sitting upstairs away from the throng and where they could see the boat. Tired yet relaxed, they talked over the last few days' adventures. It was a cheerful meal but missing fruit. An inquisitive old lady at the next table asked them back to her house for fruit and coffee. It was a steep climb. The boy struggled with his sore knee. But they soon arrived at a stone two-storey house overlooking the harbour.

She lived alone, her husband dead and her children having moved on. The house was filled with mementoes of her family life. She had watched the two over lunch, enjoyed their intimacy and happiness now bringing a warmth to her house as she offered them little cakes, fruit and coffee.

The boy looked like a young god – exceptional even in Greece where many of the young are god-touched. Stiffly she reached up to take a large book on Greek art from a shelf in the living room, and showed them a picture of a statue he clearly resembled. 'Except those young men had more curls on their foreheads,' she mused, 'and wore rather less than you.' She had a white wool jacket that might fit him. With the boy in tow, she went deeper into the house to investigate. He returned magnificent: a high collar framing his generous face, bringing out the bronze beauty of his skin. The old lady smiled. She didn't press them to stay. Raising her arms in blessing she embraced the boy, and the man too, as they left.

They trudged down the street, heading for the boat. They moved to a quiet bay nearby. In the soft evening light the man made the boy pose in his jacket, open to show his bare torso; then insisted he stand naked with hands outstretched pouring an invisible libation, like the statue in the picture. And yes, they said to each other, they would send prints to the old lady. His mop of soft fair hair shone in the dying light, his youth and nakedness far more beguiling than marble.

'Come on!' The boy urged the man, 'You too. Strip!' They posed together, arms linked, bare and smiling in the evening light. Later the pictures would cause a storm, the boy's apalled parents berating his 'totally unacceptable behaviour with that stranger'.

How touching the image was: the youth and the man, the blond beauty and the greying bear, Ganymede and Zeus. On the blazing white beach the boy's solidity had been eaten away, the sun reducing him to an emaciated stick figure by Giacometti - the antithesis of the fleshly cup bearer in the evening photo.

Yet neither image represented him. The man held a portmanteau of impressions: the perfect skin above his groin, exquisite almost clear nipples, the grey depth in his eyes, the unsteady voice coloured by involvement and doubt, the way his penis expressed feeling, how he fell away after coupling, or poised for diving. His body expressed the person inside, only visible if one looked with great care; like Praxiteles who saw an invisible figure in a block of stone, who bared the form by chipping away the excess so others could see it; similarly, intimacy stripped away the layers liberating the core reality.

Theirs was an abnormal (pathological?) relationship. Their

coalescent sex was an individually driven working-through of longing. Hopefully its denouement could be personal flowering rather than some hopeless linking with denial and death.

Intimacy involves risk. Acknowledgment of this is the only way forward. Perhaps it's sick for a boy to hunger for a man, and sicker for a man similarly to hunger. Yet it continued to sustain them while isolated by their sailing life.

It was the boundary between their private life and the everyday world where damage would be inflicted. The old lady had seen in the boy an image of a young god and had appreciated the warmth of feelings between them (maybe she saw, but turned a blind eye to more). She had responded gently. But like the sea, the world could be a cruel place. Usually, one waved or drowned, for staying afloat involves great skill.

Blame can not be attached to the destructive sea. But humans should behave better. Objects, as well as justice, are not only what they seem. Beyond the above-ground aspect, is another underground sense, giving them ambience. The pictures of that heavenly boy and the greying man must be both 'seen' and 'felt' to be judged sanely. Happiness shines in their faces as nobility.

Did love put them above the law? the man worried. Would the boy in spite of, or because of being abused, live his own life? Or debased, would he founder? If he had damaged the boy, then reparation lay in loving acts of healing ('uncoupling', whatever that entailed). This creative transformation, like that from queen to daughter-Persephone, is surely life supporting? How should the everyday world judge them? There they stand waving in the picture. Should they drown, be drowned, or given a lesser banishment?

They considered and skirted these questions during the last days of the holiday; part of the ritual of separation prior to re-crossing the boundary into the every-day world with values so different from theirs. But in the midst of the running sea and the fun, and their final port emerging through the haze, it was hard to anticipate future trials.

10:

SAILS FURLED, fenders hung over the side, ropes coiled at the ready, they slipped into the last harbour keenly inspecting the mooring options. They chose the quietest quay beyond the bustle of shops and restaurants shaded by ancient pine trees, protected by a breakwater of tumbled rocks. They tied-up uneventfully with perfected team-work. There was enough time for ice-creams and cold drinks before port duties needed to be attended to. They leapt off the boat onto the stolid shore and slouched along the quay thirsting for icy fare, vital now it was available.

After dining that evening they sat in a bar on the noisy quay sipping fruit juice in frosted glasses. It was early. The crowd was not expected for an hour or so. They wanted to dance. They slunk to a dim corner at the back in a space uncluttered with tables and rocked to a sultry south american beat, until involuntarily they pulled closer, feet glued to the floor, their bodies swayed as one, groins locked by lust, lips brushed, faces ablaze. Rock music blared stopping them. They ambled back to their table now occupied by a group of students. 'Sorry! We'll move' said one of the girls. 'It's OK' replied the man. 'There's lots of room.' The students, from a diving club holiday, entertained each other with raucous stories which fascinated the boy while irritating the man. 'Another drink?' he enquired. The boy nodded.

The man returned from the bar. 'Here you are. I think I'll go now' he said quietly 'Don't be too late.'

The youngsters settled down to more guffawing and stories. One brazen guy's girlfriend (sensing her girl-friend's interest in the boy) asked if he'd like to come with them the next day.

'Please come.' crooned her eager friend. 'It'll be great.'

'I'll have to find out if we're staying '

'It's not for kids.' someone simpered.

'Where are you staying?' the girl enquired.

'On our boat'.

'Oh, I saw you – I'm sure it was you – coming in this afternoon. You're moored over there?' The girl pointed across the harbour.

'You're not with that poofter?' demanded the brash boy.

The boy flushed and looked away.

The girl countered, 'Shut-up you wanker. He's a better sailor than you'll ever be. And probably a better diver too.'

'We'll see about that in the morning'.

'Let's go and find out,' suggested the girl breathlessly. She wanted this fabulous boy. He looked too young, yet moved with sure grace. He glowed from weeks in the sun, his unkempt shining hair crowning his face. His talk was not the usual bravado of most of the boys; he radiated a physical sureness she had already noted in the quiet way he spoke as if he was used to thinking deeply and, she hoped, feeling deeply too.

They wandered along the quay. She said 'I watched you enter, case the joint and moor; everything ready and then straight in, drifting to a stop just before the wharf. The way it should be done.'

'My friend uses the stern anchor line as a break to stop.'

'You don't hang about!' She laughed. 'I saw you leap over the bows with a line like a flying monkey.'

He grinned. 'Do you sail?'

'All my family do. My dad's got rather a lot of cups.'

They sat under a lamp watching lights snake over the water 'This is my first holiday in Greece'.

'I can see you've been out for a long time. You're so brown'

He told her about the beach of white marble shingle, the swimming, beachcombing, his fishing successes, then described the storm, explaining his limp and why his hands were tender. She took his hands in hers, turning them over to inspect them.

'Oh, you poor thing' she crooned (such fine hands) she kissed them. 'Does that hurt?'

He gazed with wonder at her shapely neck bent over him and hair softly cascading onto his bare knee. Her touch confused and excited him. His penis stiffened; his body always awoke when he was gently touched. She looked for his arousal. She needed a sign (men were so impassive). This wonderful boy is a dream come true. She trembled. Still holding onto one hand she drew him along the quay pausing under the pines in front of his boat. 'I'll wait here while you ask.'

Shortly, he returned. 'Come on! He wants to speak to us.'

The man liked her. She was soft, intense and carefree. 'You must be careful. Look after one another. Drink very little alcohol – stick to fruit juice or something soft. Avoid the drunken riot'.

She nodded.

The boy was bemused by the promise of caring. So, it was agreed, tomorrow was to be theirs.

'Now I think you should walk her home' the man concluded. He watched them saunter along the quay. 'They're so young, so beautiful, she has his shy captivating wildness. Both bursting with life.'

The two youngsters left the port and went to her hostel to check-out wet suits and lay them out for the morning. Then she accompanied him back down the steep track skirting a gash in the rocks allowing uninterrupted views of the sea. The moon was up making a glittering path to paradise. The breathless evening drew them together. They walked the last few meters in silence. At the junction with the harbour road she spoke, 'I'll go back now.' They stopped, as one. This closeness was tantalising She leaned over to kiss his lips. He started. Held her and planted a long kiss until sharing tongues and faces and torsos, they merged in a longing embrace. Time stopped. Long afterwards he flew down to the happy harbour while she trudged up the steep hill warmly blind. Their kiss was everything.

The diving day was a success, heightened by their companionship. His obvious prowess – and fitness – soon stifled the ribald comments about 'cradle-snatching' and 'baby-face'. They all returned festooning the diving boat after a triumphant day. While the others drank and rolled about like noisy buffoons, she sat with him on the top of the wheelhouse roof watching him watching her, fascinated by the power of her feelings and her helpless infatuation awoken by their kiss. He seemed unperturbed, expectant rather than doubtful, leaving her breathless: he was bashful but surely experienced? Hesitantly she confided her double room would be free all that afternoon.

They trudged dutifully up to the hostel to return the heavy wet suits, then hurriedly retired. The diffused light through shutters bathed them in milk. He gasped at her breasts brimming and full and was a trifle confounded by her vagina which reflected nothing of her passion, unlike his sex. She admired his sun-bronzed body and longingly mused on the naked freedom of his holiday, mixing his beauty with his landfalls as dream blended with sensual delight.

She found a condom that wouldn't roll on; she knelt to help. Inadvertently turning it over so she sheathed his erection. Coupling was a huge pleasure. The rubber took an edge off his sensitivity but that was all to the good as, to her delight, he laboured deeply and long until both were blown away, held tired and tender in the fading light heralding supper.

Later, they danced the night away until reluctantly dragging to separate beds. Yet early in the morning she tripped down the boat's companionway into the saloon waving his togs he'd left under her bed, waking him with a teasing, 'What were you doing last night?' He lay tousled and sleepy, delighted to see her.

'I'm going to do some shopping before we go. It may take some time.' The man smiled. 'Close the cabin door for privacy. There're condoms in the rail under the porthole.'

She pulled off the sheet. He was stark naked, beautiful beyond words. Trembling he peeled off her shorts and tee shirt and flung himself at her pushing his erection against her panties soon damp with their want. She helped him pull them down and lay moaning as he buried his face in her mound of hair and licked the lips of her vagina until it gaped. He stumbled across a ridge (the clitoris the man had told him of). Frenzied delight.

Bursting, he fumbled again with a greasy sheath. This time it rolled on. He took her deeply, spurred by her cries, filling with the tingling shrinking his balls, making everything burn until he exploded. Overcome for a little, they then hugged and dressed, sheepishly emerging to find the skipper making tea.

She brought such delight with her: such soft happiness pervaded the boat. She represented something of the mystery of opposites the two males had tried to confront. Afterwards, beyond this island, they agreed life was founded on the paradox of man/woman. (No wonder he ached for her). Out of difference grew life itself. From this coupling of opposites babies were made, also daily life. For however essential the man and boy's love was, life involved 'the other': the other sex, the other idea, the other future, the other land where life would coalesce and where happiness fed other hopes and dreams nurturing change.

11:

THERE WAS REGRET in their next love-making: missing female softness and sensing the farewell looming. The man hungrily teased the boy, caressing and licking him in his sensitive places until he was bursting with desire 'Fuck me' the man implored putting lube under the young foreskin and along its stalk.

The boy entered him and began to thrust. His excitement grew. He was nearly beyond the point of no return, flushed and panting. 'I'm sorry I've nothing better.' gasped the man.

' It's the best.' the boy cried. 'I love being naked in you; you touch me brilliantly. I love your tightness as I push in. Feeling you in me is fantASTIC.' (he came).

He felt a different sense of authority – was it from having had his first girl? And the man's demand now contained an entreaty. Were they more equal now, in love, in leave-taking?

'Many would say you have been in hell this holiday' the man mused. 'But maybe hell's what you're returning to. I am sorry. I won't be out again for ages, so we MUST stay in touch. You MUST write or ring me. I certainly will. But you must promise me!'

The boy nodded. 'I promise.'

12:

THE BOY flew half way round the world back into misery. Over succeeding months his letters and phone calls faltered into a silence broken eventually by an official note from a rehabilitation hospital:

> *Re TIMOTHY MACKNIGHT:*
>
> *I thought you would wish to know that Timothy*
> *was admitted here after serious drug abuse.*
> *He shows great improvement. I am seeing him*
> *daily. He talks of you. He tells me you are a*
> *friend who has helped him a lot, and there is*
> *no one else he wishes to see. He is adamant.*
> *It has been agreed I should write to inform you.*
> *Timothy will probably be discharged in about a*
> *fortnight but will need help in his rehabilitation.*
>
> *Yours sincerely,*
> *M.Dodd.   Senior Social Worker*

Immediately the man telephoned Tim's parents: 'I'm coming out . . . Would like to help if I can . . . No, the hospital contacted me. Oh, just tell him I'll see him soon, and give him my love.'

13:

A BALMY SPRING MORNING, nature holding its breath. The man rang. The multi-chimes played tunes until the boy's mother opened the front door. 'You're early, but come in.' she said. 'He's still asleep. Sit down, I want to talk to you.'

The man perched on a hard leather couch facing the bleak manicured garden. She looked squarely at him from her chair. 'I don't know what happened in Greece. And I don't want to. But it didn't do Tim much good, did it? Well, the hospital says you might help. We don't see how. But my husband – Tim's stepfather – and I have finally agreed. We are at our wits' end. You made the mess. So you can try to get us out of it. Anyway, it really doesn't matter, because at the end of the term we can take him away from the school to start in my husband's business – in stores – then we'll see how it settles him down.'

The man sat still; his fury reflected only in his trembling hands. 'I'd be very glad to help,' he said evenly. 'Maybe I could get him up and take him out. It's a stunning day. Give you a break. I imagine you'd like to get back to work rather than hang about at home baby-sitting.'

'Well, I do have things to do.'

He was careful not to scowl. She stood up. 'I've left his breakfast on the kitchen table. If I go now I'll catch the 8.30 bus. Yes, it would be helpful. He must take his medication with meals; now and at lunchtime. I'll be back late afternoon.' He nodded. With some effort she added, 'Tim's room is last left, along the hall.' She went inside. Time passed. The front door banged. He got up stiffly and went down the hall. It still smelt the same. He opened the boy's door and slipped in. The curtains were drawn; even in the dim light he could see the place was a prison (the rigid order imposed on despair, he thought, recalling the joyous mess the boy had made on the boat). He tiptoed to the bed. The boy was asleep. Haggard. A sheet over the body, shrouding his loveliness.

The man gently shook his shoulder. The boy winced and drew himself into a fearful crouch. He blinked awake submitting to a long hug.

The man felt him gradually relax. 'Come! The bathroom.' In institutional striped pyjamas, the boy dazedly shambled off the bed. In the hall the man pulled the pyjama cord to loosen the pants, and pulled the shapeless top over his head. 'You're not a convict any more. You're my lovely crew. From now on I'm in charge.'

'What about Mum?'

'She's gone. Now, first, a shower – can I join you? I've come straight from the plane.' The boy nodded. 'Second, breakfast. And third, we hurtle off in the car to somewhere nice and quiet where we can walk and have lunch together. I wondered whether we might go up the river to a restaurant there with a path along the bank.'

They showered. There was relief in bodily contact. They both began to relax. But soaping wasn't as sweet as it once had been. Drying off with towels was no stimulus. The boy seemed dulled, as if in a far away dream. The man inwardly wept but let him be.

They found the river restaurant and decided to walk a little before eating. 'Anyway, I'm not hungry,' muttered the boy. The river was burnished by sunlight. They stumbled over roots and stones on the rough track into a pleasant wilderness. The mood lightened. When they were alone the man halted and said. 'Can we sit down?' Gingerly he pulled the boy onto his lap to lie staring ahead stiff with shame. 'It's great to be with you,' the man whispered. 'I missed you terribly. Terribly.' He caressed the shaven head and ran an appraising hand along his limp arm. 'Have you done any sailing since you got back?'

The boy shook his head. After a while he murmured, 'It's not your fault. Although that's what they'll tell you. They hate us.' He turned to look disbelievingly at his friend. 'You'll leave again soon.'

'No. I'll stay if you want me to. Stay until we sort things out. It's really up to you.' The man fell silent, not sure what else to say.

'Take me with you. It's terrible here. Everything.' Tears welled up and the boy cringed with unhappiness.

The man relieved by his outburst, caressed a wan cheek.

The boy sniffed. 'Anyway, it doesn't matter. I leave school at the end of the term and go to my stepfather's business.'

The man heard the mother in his words. 'But if you passed?'

'But I don't want to go on. I don't.'

'But if you did?'

'It's impossible. But I suppose I'd go back to school. But

that's impossible!' cried the boy. He let himself be kissed, 'to dry your eyes' as the man had always said to him, and then their lips melted together, the feeling of joinedness, the remembrance of that far summer sail, of other possibilities. Their bodies once again might help, if the tyrannies of distance, drugs and age allowed. It was a small beginning. At that moment they were both withdrawn.

'Listen to me,' the man said. 'You are very bright. No, don't look so disbelieving. You picked up all the physical aspects of sailing, mostly after one lesson, then you mastered all the electronic gear, route mapping, everything. And remember, we only had a few hours to sort out your homework when I was here before, and you did brilliantly.'

The boy said nothing.

'There are ten or twelve weeks left in the term. Together we could do two years' work in that time. Together. But only if you agree to work hard and play hard. We've enjoyed that before and we can do it now. If you promise to work your arse off.'

The boy patted his bottom still tender from injections.

'Yes, that too.' The man's face softened. 'But you'll have to make me a very serious promise. It's the only way.'

They wandered back. Lunch was enjoyable. Both were hungrier than they'd expected. The boy began describing how he'd ended up with dope, drugs and booze. He skated over the worst sexual encounters and all the shameful repercussions, but his loss of self-esteem and hope were clear. He managed a faint smile over ice-cream dessert, recalling the delicious expectation stepping ashore for one after a long hot sail.

Soothed by the quiet of the river, they dallied until the man said he should go and find a hotel, one near-by so they could meet easily. His sheer practicality cut through the boy's despair. The man really cared. Suddenly it all became real for the boy – he'd do anything to keep him near. That was all that mattered, not the grand plan to recover, that was impossible. So he promised to work and play if only the man would stay and help.

They found a hotel in a shady street and let themselves into a room with a view of trees and tiled roofs, flooded with light. The boy dumped the suitcase on a rack beside the door and yawned. The man gave an exhausted sigh. 'Shall we rest for a bit?' Removing shoes and outer clothes they pulled off the bedcover, and lay down.

The boy was sitting on the end of the bed staring blankly out the window when the man awoke. It was morning.

The man groaned. 'You must telephone your parents.'

The boy gave a long wince and took up the phone. There was a terrible silence as he confronted his mother's fury. Numbly he passed the phone to his friend.

'You. You have no right, keeping him out all night.' she screamed. 'He's sick, and no thanks to you.'

Firmly the man explained about their day walking and dining beside the river, looking for a hotel, and how they had both collapsed and slept right through. 'I'd meant to rest for a little and then take him home. The medication he's on makes him dopey and I hadn't slept for two days – I came straight to your home from the airport . . . Yes, it seems inconsiderate but believe me, we woke and rang you at once. I'm very sorry . . . Yes, you must be worried sick, as you say . . . Yes, of course you worry . . . Yes.' (he lied) 'Tim told me of the hospital appointment today, but not the time. I'll take him, if that would help. And if you agree, let me look after him for a few days so you both have a break. It's a big double room . . . Yes, it must have been awful . . . Good. Let's meet up on Saturday afternoon, OK?' So, he had the boy for the rest of the week.

The boy clung to him, some of his agony melting.

Tim seemed better that day. Maybe it was less medication; he was more alert and responsive. Intimate care also seemed to help. At the hospital the doctor supported these ideas. 'Yes, try slightly reducing the dosage, keep an eye on him, but drying out takes time.'

They wangled a medical letter stating Timothy should not attend school for a while but light schoolwork was acceptable during his rehabilitation. Thus armed, they visited the school. Tim's form-master had clearly lost faith in the boy and accepted the letter in that spirit. Study materials were found: the year's curriculum, all the textbooks and a bundle of past exam papers. The boy didn't even try saying goodbye to anyone. He was almost cheerful as he ransacked his locker. The two drove through the school gates to freedom. They would not return until the boy's exams, for him a figment in the future.

But the man was serious. 'Listen, it's going to be tough.

There's more than a year's work. It means six days a week, maybe seven – of course with swimming and sailing and whatever in between – but it will be tough. Believe me. You have to do the work, I can only help. But I'm clever at exams. I'll help you with pass-techniques. remember Tim, you promised.'

There was no reply. As the school receded behind them, the man glanced at the boy's fragile face. Tim's eyes seemed more focused. They drove on in silence. His body still slumped, yet he was turning his head more. Time, it just needed time. They would go gently from shop to shop to shop buying the textbooks, and fancy pens and writing books, tapes of his favourite music too. And a couple of books on Greek myth to share again after their discussions on the boat. Textbooks of hope.

14:

THE MAN HAD A FRIEND at Eliza Beach, well beyond the city. It was agreed they could live there, and work until exam time.

The Saturday meeting with the parents was awkward, frosty. Swayed by the medical letter and the school's response, they agreed to the plan. Yes, it would give them the break they needed; the schoolwork plan was futile; they would pay for any reasonable expenses if required; they should be informed of the boy's condition. He packed a few things, including some treasures, his friend insisted, for the months ahead.

They returned to the hotel. Next morning they would drive to their new base at the beach. Then would come the long hard labour, and the exams – a huge heady idea, scary, maybe brilliant, would it work? That evening they ate at a small French cafe, savouring pepper steaks and wine (strength for the boy) and a rich chocolate mousse. 'This reminds me of Greece.' the boy said suddenly, 'I'll have another one of those.'

Their room breathed welcome. They showered, more easily. 'You must grow your hair.'

'You're lucky to still be brown all over.' They roughly towelled and blushing, fell into bed as if they were in Greece, renewing tenderness, relief and increasing talk.

'Do you shave under your arms?'

'How thin you are.'

'You've got to exercise that tummy away.'

'Happy?'

'Mmm.'

'Sleep well.'

They woke cheerfully. Sunlight bathed the bed.

The man stroked Tim's velvet cheek. 'You enjoyed last night? But do you mind sleeping with me, Tim?'

'Does it feel like it?'

'It's just there's a reluctance now, as if you're somewhere else . . . thinking of something else. It's OK if there's someone else – there should be – but tell me. You're growing up. Our affair can't last forever, we both know that.'

'There's no one. I'm so crazy after doing it drugged to the eyeballs. Really screwed up. It's not like that with you. It matters.'

Haltingly Tim recounted some of the sexual exploits he and his friends had tried when high on dope and drink. 'We did multiple penetrations – a boy in a boy in a girl, busy with her mouth. Someone pushed an effervescent pill up my bum and fucked me when it was bubbling. 'It was like being raped by an elephant. And we tied our penises with tight rubber bands and tried to ejaculate; one of the guys got up someone and pissed in him; that kind of stuff.' The boy whispered.

'Tim, was it fun?'

'It was at the time but it made me sick. At the hospital they said I had a distended anus and asked awful questions about sodomy, and what was I revolting against. I didn't answer them.'

'People who have heavy and aggressive anal sex loosen up, in the end they can grow incontinent. But you're too young to have indulged much. You'll recover, you probably have. Our lovemaking was gentle and safe.'

The man kissed him and turned him over for inspection. Ah, what a delicious crinkled entry, tight and neat. 'It's still perfect.' He slid down licking it, pushing his tongue in. 'But we must look after it. We both need it.'

'I was happy yesterday; what we did.' Tim grimly smiled. 'We broke the rules and got away with it: left school, hospital, home. We can do whatever we like. Oh Chris it's still OK with you.'

The man hugged him, yet grew pensive. It was true about the rules, well almost. But there was a price to pay in having to keep secrets, having to behave differently in public. And would the boy suffer ill effects from a relationship involving someone much older? What chance of him ending up with a full and happy life? And what did Full and Happy mean anyway?

Chris sighed. 'Remember Persephone. Maybe we broke one set of rules. But we must respect the other, of love, honour, integrity and fairness. Those are the things our life rests on. We must learn to live not only with our dark inner selves, but by the light-expectations of other people. After all both make-up, whole, the world.'

With his precious snuggling boy beginning to whisper about out-facing the storm and mythic paradoxes shared long ago, Chris quailed. It was hard to go on without his voice trembling. 'That's why you really must put everything into your schoolwork. Your honour's at stake, so is your future.' Chris held the boy closer. 'Think of work as making love – how wonderful to give everything.'

Tim nodded ever so slightly. He glanced up and outside to leaves waving darkly against the sky.

'You lose everything but get more than everything back.' Chris stroked his lean thigh. 'Remember?'

Tim almost nodded again, leaned up and kissed the mouth to silence. Just now being together was all any boy needed.

Re-birth

1:

THE JOURNEY TO THE COAST was filled with glee, the rush of wind and pop music bursting the car. They arrived relieved if careful. The house, of friendly rustic mien, was perched on land falling to cliffs overlooking a small beach. The front entrance was at street level; the slope allowed back rooms underneath, facing an overgrown garden and beyond to the watery horizon.

An aged woman greeted them with intense warmth. Nina was frail and bent, with piercing blue eyes and a voice of authority despite a slight quaver. She lived alone, her family dispersed, her husband dead.

'I have prepared the guest room for you. How lovely you've come to stay.' She directed them down the inner stairs and there it was, a generous twin bedroom, with attached shower room overlooking the garden; the sea beyond.

'It's perfect!' they both blurted.

'I trust it will suit you' Nina said, 'Now, let's have a bite to eat. Timothy, you open the wine; and Christopher will help carry the food from the kitchen.' And for her, from the very beginning, that is who they were. 'I despise the shortening of names, it's like lopping off a limb.' Christopher and Timothy were delighted.

They felt at home. Nina insisted they discuss the plan of work with her. She approved. 'No boy should be without education. Those popinjays who think they run the world need curbing. Only an informed citizenry can do it.'

Tim warmed to her power and passion. He realised Chris was like that too. The animated talk flushed out his darkness; little by little his physical grace returned. His growing contentment was watched with relief. Chris and Nina didn't say a word, even to each other.

They were anchored by the household routines from the beginning. The men cleared and washed up morning and evening. Nina rested more than they.

'We'll rest too.' Chris said.

In their room they grabbed one another and fell onto a bed.

'It's great to be here,' Tim said a few days later. 'She's nice.' But he was restless, wanting to explore. So while Chris slept he ventured into the unkempt garden – so much more beautiful than his at home – and found the broken gate at the far end and the path to the sea. He stood at the top of the cliffs facing the breeze, so full of happiness he had to yell a lung-emptying 'Wheeeeee.' Sea gulls overhead screamed rudely back.

The first morning they met in the library lined with shelves from floor to ceiling. They worked at a huge desk in front of the generous window; long use had polished it to a deep redwood mirror. They made timetables for every subject. Chris helped with planning and work methods, aghast at the technicalities of geography and science.

'And I shall help with English, when Timothy's read the books,' Nina declared. She examined the timetable. 'Ah, I know some charming young teachers at the local school who will have to help us.'

Tim enjoyed sharing his life this way far more than he'd expected. He and Chris rose with the sun, and read for an hour. If the day was sunny and still, in that unpredictable spring, they traipsed down to the beach for a swim before breakfast and then maths in the library. Work was divided into one- to two-hour slots, some shared, others for Tim to slog through on his own. In between, the two worked in the garden or helped around the house.

Lunch was usually ad hoc, depending on whim, weather or circumstance. More often than not, the two of them were on their own, sprawling on the grass sheltered by trees in the garden or with sandwiches on the beach after bathing. Free time began around two in the afternoon when the Oldies liked to rest, when there was a chance for everyone to be alone, which Nina regarded as essential.

Work resumed about four until supper at half-past six. In the early evening a couple of hours was usually spent discussing and reading – there was much to catch up on. Then the three would lounge in the upper living room to gossip, discuss books and plays, often related to Tim's curriculum, or sit quietly reading, studying or listening to music.

The first few weeks of work were tough on the two friends until they got used to the daily rhythm. But it was a delight for Tim to be with older people who backed him wholeheartedly day after day. How different from the niggling criticism at home, the disdain at school; here, they could share or just stay comfortably together. His enjoyment in being a part of the household grew. His appetite for sexual antics returned. They coupled, discreetly. Sometimes it was hard to drag themselves out of bed next day, but unfailingly they got up and got on. So much was different, so much, new. Tim's delight blossomed.

2:

THE TWO had finished reading *Jane Eyre*.*

'And now I propose Timothy and I discuss it,' said Nina firmly, and led him off to the library. They sat together at the desk, light on their faces, and she began. 'So, what's it about?'

'We think it's about love, and prejudice in the class system.'

'All very well, but the thread leading us through the book?'

'To the fire?'

She smiled. 'Ah, indeed. The mysterious noises, the comings and goings, Rochester's unexplained absences, his daughter, the interruption to the wedding, the fire; none of which fits together because . . . ' She paused for him.

'Until we know about his wife.

'Because of the secret he kept,' said Nina gently, looking steadily at the boy. 'The secret leading to the fire and his blinding.'

'Which made him see better.'

'Yes, of course. But I want us to think carefully about the corrosive power of secrets, as well as the power of the everyday world to destroy or remake old conventions when a secret is uncovered.'

---

*   See notes at end.

Tim was startled. This touched on things he and Chris discussed about their shared life. It was private. Not for exams. 'Do you think the secret kept them apart?'

'Do you?' Nina smiled encouragingly.

'Yes. But secrets can bind us together too.' he stammered. 'And the secret did not change Jane's love for him.'

'But had they dealt with it earlier, Rochester would not have been blinded, and the book might have ended with a whole man and woman united, living happily ever after.'

He was rattled. 'You don't approve of secrets.'

'Of course I do. But it's essential to share at the right time.'

It was an opening gambit. He knew it and was not going to play. She knew that too, and persevered. 'Now, let's discuss yours. How much do you love him?'

His young face was caught, reflected in the polished top of the desk: a dim image gazing longingly from the shadows out into a brighter world. He feared this sort of interrogation. He glanced at the kindly old face, felt an understanding hand on his arm.

'I think we both do, don't we,' she said resolutely.

He had no words but blazing, nodded, 'yes, yes, yes', his leaden head falling onto her old breasts as somewhere to hide.

'I thought so,' she murmured and stroked his salty hair. 'I have to say I'm a bit surprised. He was always so charming; always a bit of a misfit, now I think about it. He was just beyond your age when he first came down here. Yes, it makes sense. I'm so glad it's you and not some pansy-boy. Do you know, to have love in the house is always wonderful.' She stopped. He was looking at her in admiration as she whispered. 'A lot?'

He nodded, smiled and breathed, 'A lot!'

'Then let's continue with *Jane Eyre*.' she said. 'Think of it as a sort of mirror –your own reflection, if you like. In your case, you probably realise Christopher will be the equivalent of blinded if your secret comes out. You're only fourteen? fifteen?– underage. He would be branded a criminal, you know that, don't you? He'd be dragged through the courts, thrown into jail, and both your lives would be ruined.' The boy nodded his head in disbelief as she continued. 'So secrets involve great risk but also great rewards when you share them – I see you understand that. Your love brings responsibility with it. You must protect him, as well as yourself.

Otherwise madness will take over, and the house will burn down. You see how *Jane Eyre* applies here.'

He dropped his gaze. Us, in this book? the boy thought.

'I agree with you however, the class system and the rules attached to it stultify life as it should be lived. It's man's law condemns you for being lovers – you are, aren't you? And it's love blessing and binding you as Jane and Rochester were bound.' She regarded this bright, fragile boy. 'Do you see how precious books are, how they illuminate and dignify our lives?'

He shook. Gratefully he nodded.

Then she enlarged on the stifling eighteenth century from which their own had emerged, about rules and dreams, risk and reward. He nodded. Embracing silence they gazed out the window into the garden. Gnarled old trees, blown by the relentless coastal breezes, bent over to protect the green spring slips now emerging. Tim felt sheltered, learning now engaging his whole being.

'Well then.' She drew herself upright in her chair 'Dinner in an hour. You will set the table by then, won't you. Now go to him.'

Chris had been reading. A book lay beside him on the bed where he lay dozing. The boy sat beside him reeling, now confronting the man who had broken so many rules to get him here. It had been impossible to acknowledge to himself he loved; now it really was out. In the library not only thoughts and feelings were uncovered, but their physical coupling. How liberating to admit that to himself, and to share the secret.

As never before, he began to know the depth and the power of Chris's love for him. He touched the haggard face softly, awakening a smile which vitalised as strong arms took him and pulled him down.

'She knows about us,' the boy muttered.

Chris sat up startled. 'You told her!'

'I had to. We talked about secrets and she just came out with it, "Do you love him?" What could I say? But she knew all along.'

The man was stunned. Suddenly the world was out of control, they were careering towards destruction. All his carefully made plans. Yes, Tim couldn't hold his tongue, he was too young to understand. He patted the boy's shoulder with infinite sadness.

Tim knew it meant Chris needed to make the next move on his own. With courage enabling him to lead his life Chris laboured up the stairs. Hopefully his old friend could find the leeway for a new plan to help the boy. Maybe not.

Nina smiled at him. 'Where's Timothy?'

'Downstairs.'

She took his hand gently in hers. 'I forced it out of him. You see, I knew. Could you hide such devotion from me?' Her calmness steadied him. 'I wanted to find out whether it was mutual – the young are so accepting, and I don't want you hurt. I wanted to hear what I read in his body. He's not just clever, but very brave.'

Chris had no words for a reply. Her voice grew more tender. 'The poor dear, it was hard to utter what he did, hard to allow his feelings out. He's so young to love in this way. I saw just how devoted each of you have become and how vital your friendship, and how fortunate I am you let me share in it.'

Weeping, Chris took his dear friend into his arms. He shook.

'Let me help you. I'm old but not beyond it yet.' she said, 'And I'm worried about you. You seem very stressed. Try to relax. It will be all right, I'm quite sure about that. Be careful. It's a jungle out there. You and Timothy must be prudent. There's a lot at stake.'

He nodded.

'You know your secret is safe with me.'

Her words reached the boy hovering in distress at the bottom of the stairs. I must look-up Prudent. Ah, such dear friends, he thought. The odd word Fortitude came into his mind. It seemed to fit the household. It had to include him. 'Maybe I could pass the exams. If that's what they think, they must be right. The work is very, very hard but they make it stimulating.' And he was happy. He loved being here in this warm wooden house leaning like the trees because of its lifelong buffeting.

'This is a house of love and I'm at its centre,' the boy thought stepping lightly up the stair. Then, without more ado, he set the table.

3:

THAT EVENING Nina telephoned two teachers from the local high school who agreed to help one half-afternoon each a week. Max would take physics, chemistry and maths, and Janet, geography. They were daunted by the volume of work.

One evening Janet traipsed down the cliff path for a swim with Tim and Chris. The sand was warm and the bloodied sun dripping below distant hills as the three splashed and shouted in the sea still chilled by spring. Tim's laughter had a joyous energy. Janet, whom Nina had briefed about the boy, was touched by his pleasure and interested in this man who stood waiting on the beach, watching the two in the waves, as steadfastly as his support of the school-work. His intense relationship with Tim made her yearn more sharply than she had since her boyfriend left six months before. She felt drawn to the boy too, in ways she would probably have resisted had they been in school. He and Chris expressed a freedom she happily fell into, initially only aware of the pleasant mix of social, intellectual and physical life. But the richness of mood stirred feelings difficult to bear. She changed the routine. Tim went to her house instead, where she had all the books they needed, when he occasionally shared the coaching with a girl called Sophie from Janet's school who knew embarrassingly more than he.

Three weeks went by before Janet invited Chris for an evening meal. 'Why are you worried about Tim?' she asked. 'You seem so tense about him. But he's working well. Max and I both feel sure he'll pass. He'll probably do quite well.' Shyly, she carried on. 'I shouldn't get involved with him but you and Tim were so carefree before, and now you're both quite moody.'

Had she guessed they were lovers? The question shrieked inside him. 'Yes,' he said hesitantly, 'Nina spoke to me. She's arranged for Tim to see her doctor. Maybe he's having withdrawal symptoms after his treatment. I'm going for a check-up too. I am rather exhausted; it's been nerve-racking, sorting out his muddled life. Maybe I'm working him too hard.' He sighed. 'Thanks for your concern.' He squeezed her arm. Blushing, she drew back and hurried to open the wine.

It was a splendid meal. The evening took off, got light-hearted, and next thing they knew they were in the darkened courtyard taking off their clothes and slipping blithely into the spar-bath. With stars above and the night-whisperings around them, they regaled each other with stories from their past. Bathing seemed enmeshed with their growing up.

She laughed. 'I first made love in the sea with a surfie I had a crush on. It was uncomfortable but exciting, with me just fifteen and him a man or so I thought. My life became a series of mistakes like that, choosing men who weren't what they seemed.'

'Same here,' he confessed. The answer delighted her. She skittered over close to him until their shoulders touched suddenly desperate for him, feeling up his leg for his erection. 'I'm drunk, crazy, lost the plot,' she told herself, as she was pulled over to straddle his body and opened to its relentless push, a luxuriating penetration, clutching him. I want you, oh, drive out my loneliness fill me – the pang of it shook her but it was utterly true. She rocked on him, surprised at how long he stayed and how tenderly he held her until he gasped, 'I'll come if we go on like this.' 'It's OK,' she moaned, 'Oh. oh o o o . . 'They thrashed towards climax. And then they were floating in quiet water. They hardly spoke when they got out and dressed, but their farewell kiss lasted long afterwards.

The next morning he was awakened very late by the boy, tousled and damp from swimming. 'Were you bonking last night?'

'Um, yes.'

'Was it good?'

'Um, yes.'

Tim snuggled up to him appealing for his morning kiss. 'I knew she fancied you. Are you in love?'

'I don't think so. We got rather drunk. Sex was a celebration of a wonderful evening.'

'It's always a celebration.' The boy pressed into the man supping on the lingering warmth of his lovemaking. 'Now it's our day of love after your night love. I'm like Persephone, sharing in both.' He paused. 'Can we go on with *Gulliver's Travels*?' *

---

*   See notes at end.

52

4:

CHRIS AND TIM arranged a second visit to the doctor to discuss their blood tests. Doctor MacKay was a shrewd old man concerned with people *and* medicine. He had looked after Nina and her family for years, seen her husband deteriorate and die, and been consulted by several odd-balls who had stayed in her house over the years.

The boy amused him. He was a mix: sure and fragile like Nina's second child. He just needed a little medication to ease his way back to a completely normal life, a mild antidepressant to lessen the mood-swings. But the man was run down, clearly a worrier. Talking with him confirmed the view – he was far too involved in supporting the boy, who was old enough to look after himself. So, pills and care: the two medicines, were appropriate.

'Now, I'd like a chat with Timothy, alone,' said Doctor MacKay. Chris withdrew and Tim was waved back into a chair. 'I think I understand something of the difficulties you have experienced, and how your friend and Nina helped you. But I feel I should tell you he is not well. He's doing too much. I wonder whether you could find ways to help him rest. Otherwise he could become seriously ill.'

The boy fidgeted with anxiety. 'Is it my fault?'

'No, not a bit. He's a worrier, that's all. Sometimes we need our friends to help us over hurdles, as you probably realise. There's nothing at all to worry about if he eases up a little.'

The boy nodded emphatically. 'Yes, I'll see to it.' But he was fearful. Never having questioned Chris's strength, he began to think more deeply about the life they were leading. It reminded him of a voyage. Was it time to share the skippering? Was this another Persephone duo, with them in the middle of a bridge between leading and being led? Should it be like their love-making?

Through the next week he noticed how much Chris and Nina strove for him. It resulted in how much he did. He would try to help them more he decided. Now he was going to pass his exams there was time. The idea balanced him: the boy in him would take his turn being a man. And he was excited: he wanted to help sail their ship on its fantastic journey and with the two most wonderful skippers in the whole wide world.

Over dinner one evening they all argued delightedly about *Gulliver's Travels*. 'Oh, it's a parable on life, just like *Animal Farm*.' Nina said, getting Timothy the book from her bedroom.* 'You should read it. But what else does size reflect?' and she hushed Chris with a wave of her hand.

Timothy's eyes blazed. 'That being little doesn't stop the Lilliputians being in charge of the giant.'

'Bravo!' shouted Nina. 'People with no rights – and that includes children – can wrest authority from those in charge and become responsible for their own lives. But it does mean they must change in order to resist being exploited. Change is the key.'

Chris laughed. 'But co-operation between Gulliver and the Lilliputians was the key to them all surviving.'

'Ah, but Gulliver turned out to be a gentle and dependable giant, unlike some who should be done away with,' cried Nina happily, 'like bad schools and bad parents.' She looked tenderly at Timothy, ruffled his hair, and ambled away to bed with a flourishing 'A very good night, my dears.'

Tim touched Chris's arm. 'Go down. I'll clear up.'

Chris kissed him. 'Come on, let's do it together.'

Contentedly they cleared the debris, filled the machine, washed pots and pans, and set the table for breakfast.

'Tomorrow, I think I'll have a go at fixing the veranda steps,' said Tim. 'If I get stuck, will you help me?'

Later they showered. Tim fondled Chris. 'Fuck me,' he moaned. He gasped as the big cock slid in. He yearned to be overpowered. He tucked his hips upwards to accept all of the man. Overcome, he gave up his body. His own penis stiffened and pain like a knife seared his innards. They laboured on, the phallus in his guts tearing him to climax.

'We came together,' Chris said weakly.

'Yes . . . Did we? It hurt like our first time.' the boy moaned, grimacing as the man withdrew. Even skippers, he realised, sometimes need to be overwhelmed.

---

* See notes at end.

5:

THE EXAMS were getting closer for everyone. Janet held a history and geography day one Saturday afternoon for a bunch of her students, suggesting Tim join them. 'One of the boys is staying over, so it would be nice if you did too,' she said to Tim. 'And give the oldies a break.'

He enjoyed the afternoon, especially on discovering he now understood a great deal. The boys and girls were friendly, so much nicer than the grim all-male groups at his school. He shared a bedroom comfortably with Ian, the other boy. Ian was self-conscious for this was his teacher's place. But Tim hugged the secret of Janet and Chris's midnight bathe like a warming cloak; it blurred the barrier between pupil and teacher, haunting him willy-nilly after years of neglect at school. Tim realised Janet had become a friend and a teacher. He enjoyed being her boy at home and being a bridge between Ian and her.

When Chris arrived next day, Tim had already gone off with Ian's parents. It was late afternoon.

'Come in for tea?' Janet asked tiredly. They searched for some of their earlier intimacy as they sat in the courtyard. Evening softened the day. 'Let's have a spar, it'll help wash away your work.' he suggested.

They sprawled in the water, excited but conscious of the last daylight and the flimsy fence of the neighbours. The dusk deepened. At ease, she looked him over with a new candour and decided he had a nice body, fine limbs and eyes and a beautiful sex. She had always relished tight sexy bottoms like his, but seldom admired men's genitals – they were usually rather ridiculous. He stroked her hair and her generous face. Her breasts swelled enticingly floating free. He spied her little mound of love modestly clad in hair.

Memories of lovemaking stirred. Wrapped in towels they skipped inside. In her shadowy bedroom they fell to exciting each other until contented they rolled apart.

Janet broke the sleepy silence. 'I can't take any more of your money for lessons. Yes, I know it's what we agreed. But the boy must be costing you a fortune. And I don't really need it. And . . . '

She tailed off.

'And?

'And I think I'm falling in love with you.' Her voice was quiet. 'It's all right, I know you have others. I don't care, as long as we can meet sometimes. We've each got our own lives. I know it's impossible. Please don't speak. Your life is elsewhere. That's OK. Just let's be friends. Please let me help Tim as a friend now, a friend to both my dear dear men.'

Much later he was leaving. Holding each other tenderly they kissed long and deeply at her door in a silent contract. The day had enriched them both, had stilled some restlessness in each.

6:

JANET HAD ARRIVED AT NINA'S for a teaching session with Tim. She was flustered by a busy day, and the summer heat was upon them. Chris smiled. 'Would you like a swim first?'

The three scrambled down the cliff path to the sea. They fooled about on the beach, free as silly turtles, then Tim headed into the surf. Chris and Janet stood watching him. Janet spoke first. 'Have you thought about next year?'

'It worries me a lot.'

'Tim should come to school. Max and I were talking about it. Would you like me to ask the bursar? I don't see any problems.'

'Please. But you know I can't stay beyond the holidays.'

'He'll miss you. So will I.' She took his hand. He swung back and put his arms around her in apology just as Tim came up, shaking his wet hair on them like a dog and smiling, 'No sex in public, please, children' and began his leaping ascent up the cliff path to the house.

They plodded after him. As he flitted over the top, they paused. Chris panted, 'I've not faced next year. It was hard enough getting Tim sorted so he could go on. I don't know where he could live or how to arrange support for him. I guess it'll sort itself out in the next short time.' His pain was clear.

Janet kissed him fervently. 'I can take him in the holidays. Would that help?' She felt him relax, felt his penis press through her thin bathing costume.

'Let's speak about it again.' Thankfully he held her.

Tim had finished showering when they reached the house; the place was awash. 'Don't be too long,' he cracked. 'I'm off to the library. I'll shut the cabin door for privacy.' Chris chuckled and told Janet about Tim's girl in Greece. Showering, she was aglow, being with them: the boy and this sane lovely man mattered, she mused, lifting her vagina so his penis pushed in, and they stood rocking in the shower until pleasures burst.

Afterwards in the library she flushed under the boy's straight gaze. Most kids would not cope, she knew; but Tim was a special child, maybe a bit too advanced for his years. The extremes of his life had made him grow up quickly.

'You don't mind?' she whispered.

Mischievously he grinned.

7:

OVER DINNER Chris voiced his concern about Tim's future.

Nina shook her head. 'And I agree with Janet. He should be in school. In fact, why shouldn't he go to our high school? She's already offered to take Tim for holidays.'

'Maybe there's a family here who'd take him in term time.'

'I think Timothy should stay here.' Nina said briskly. 'He feels at home' - Tim nodded emphatically – 'and I love having him, having you both. Also, I don't think I can do without him. He's become a wonderful help around the house. I feel with Maria here maybe another half-day and Timothy, I could stay on living here for a while longer. His labour is more than equal to any cost. It really would help me out.' She leant over and patted Tim's hand.

The speechless boy looked from one to the other, upset his glass as he leapt up, and gave her a flailing hug. Suddenly Tim felt that anything was now possible. It was like the storm which so terrified him, but they outfaced it and saved themselves. He understood fear but it did not immobilise him now.

The three of them had experienced the small miracle that Tim, although seeming much the same, had really changed. Dinner became a celebration of change.

Max had arranged a couple of extra laboratory sessions at the school for pupils who needed more lab work. He invited Tim over as his assistant, giving him practical lab experience.

Tim, in a new white coat, shyly followed Max around, listening to the discussions. We're in the footsteps of the pioneers, he thought, Hook and Pasteur, all those great experimenters. It's hard to break through tradition to see things in new ways. I like working here, and with Ian and Sophie and the others.

He yearned for a year doing science for its own sake, but the cold fact was exams had to come first. He was already summarising his work on sets of cards and doing some of the old papers. Chris coached him in exam techniques – mastery of those silly speed tests, they agreed. Tim laughed at his racing-form tactics of surveying all the past questions and spending more time on ones that might recur. They joked about the odds, but underneath they knew the exams were vital, and very close.

The weather grew hot. They swam two or three times a day, and sometimes at night when, on their deserted beach, they went naked and then fondled themselves up the cliff to shower and bed with spirits only dampened by the approaching exams.

8:

THEY RETURNED TO THE HOTEL near Tim's home the weekend before the exams. It was to be their base. When they went to Tim's house to collect his school uniform, his stepfather remarked, 'Of course, as soon a school finishes you'll be coming in to work.'

'What if I pass?'

'Hmmph. We'll see about that.'

His mother sniffed. 'You got a nice tan lounging outside while the rest of us worked. Is that what the hospital prescribed?'

Tim sweated but stayed silent.

In the car clutching a bundle of his school clothes the boy sadly nuzzled his friend, so in need of his comfort. 'Timbo, you're OK, you know that. We're all proud of you. I do love you so much.'

'I feel so angry. They betrayed me.'

That night they talked and talked. Lying in his dear Chris's arms, Tim ruefully announced. 'That's not home for me anymore.'

The exams were far less threatening than Tim expected. Facing one manageable question after another, he grew in confidence. Eventually the results came out: not only had he passed, but he was rated within the top ten. In English, maths and science he had come top. It was impossible. But it had been checked twice.

The English master was handing back the papers to the class one by one. 'Lastly, Macknight. I've never seen a paper like this.' The class hooted rolled their eyes and mimed shooting-up. 'Quiet, please.' He continued. 'This is the best paper I've ever seen. A first-year university student would be proud of this.' A disbelieving titter came from the back of the class as he handed the paper back to Tim. Unperturbed, he added, 'At last, here is a boy who reads and also thinks. Something few of the rest of you will ever achieve.' He glared at the back row. 'Now get out.'

The boys headed for the door. 'Stay a moment, Macknight,' the master called. Tim came back. 'You've been sick, haven't you?'

'Yessir.'

'Been working at home?'

'Yessir.'

'With a bit of coaching?'

'Yessir.'

'Have you been to Greece?'

'Yes sir, I went sailing there last summer.'

'Mmmm. I enjoyed your commie comments about *Jane Eyre* although I don't agree entirely. And your inclusion of myth interests me. You've got a lot to say. Well done.'

The boy reeled out of the classroom. Nobody at school had ever said such things to him. Chris was not going to believe it – top! And the science and maths papers were OK too – they had been tough, no one really starred, but his preparations had paid off.

Afterwards the form master, Mr Adamson, took them, still dealing with the exams. He shouted at the boys, 'Listen, you lot, if Macknight the drug addict passed, why didn't you?' He turned to Tim. 'How did you do it?'

'By not being at school, sir.'

The master reddened. 'You. Get Out! Go and stand on the Headmaster's mat and take an hour's detention, which I will supervise myself. How dare you.'

Tim strode out of the classroom and over to the Head's door. In fury he knocked.

'Yes, come in, Mackenzie.'

Tim went up to his desk. 'Macknight, sir.'

'Oh, yes, you've been sick, just back. What do you want?' He heard Tim out, and was about to respond when Tim added, 'It's an insult to me, sir, and it has to be withdrawn.' The head winced.

'Go and ask Mr Adamson to come and see me. Wait outside.'

Tim was shaking as he followed his form-master back to the Head and waited. The two men talked for ages. He could hear them just as a murmur through the door. Then he was called in.

'There does seem to have been a misunderstanding. The best way to deal with it is to shake hands,' said the Head. 'There, shake hands and let's forget the matter. And may I complement you on your exam results.' Tim didn't care. He had decided to leave anyway. He shook hands and stalked back to class. Such a challenge to authority, and no consequences! Tim was a hero. They flocked round him afterwards (some, plotting to strip him for bummer-display on the table) but Tim longed to be back in his beach-house with Nina, Chris, Janet and Max. At the end of the day he pushed through boys seething at the ranks of lockers. He pulled out everything and stuffed his satchel full.

Chris was waiting. Tim looked drawn. 'I'll never go back.' He slumped into the car seat as he had in their very first meeting.

For Chris, this could mean only one thing. Tim had failed. His mind ran ahead. This was not a disaster, just a setback. But nothing could be done in this hellish place. Wordlessly he drove out of the gates.

They went up-river sat on the bank where they had been reunited after the hospital, quaffing drinks and pastries. Chris dug for the news. 'Now, tell me everything.'

'I passed everything. Well. I came top in maths, and science, and English.' He flung himself into Chris's arms. They wept and laughed and hugged while the ducks waddled around them wagging delighted tails and munching on abandoned pastries.

Then came the saga of the form master. 'Oh, I'm so angry,' Chris yelled. And then, more gently, 'I'm proud of you. You stood up to him, you were valiant.' He got up. 'Nina will approve! We must ring her.'

They would collect all the text books from the hotel the next day and return them to the school which could send Tim's report to his parents, and to Eliza Beach. 'That's your home now.' Chris said.

9 :

TIM IS CHANGING. thought Chris that night as they lay satiated and sleepy. 'He feels tougher, sinewy, more manlike.' This tender boy was slipping away. Soon perhaps their love wouldn't do any longer. The boy in himself Tim had nourished would have to stand on his own feet. 'Love changes, so relationships change.' he mused, 'We're all growing up.' Lovemaking that night had engulfed them. Lingering. Passionate. Fulfiling. All a celebration could be.

For Tim the dream continued. First the party of celebration at Nina's house – at his house! Oh, the laughter, the pride and satisfaction – all the love that had changed him flamed again. He was bursting, like a rocket about to soar into the space of his future which his friends had fuelled. Janet, Max and his wife he would see next term; also Ian, his new school friend. Nina, a sort of godmother, beyond explanation. And his other half, Chris, who had tormented and loved him to death. He pinched himself, saying, 'This is my new family where I belong. There is a way out of hell. I'm here, and I'll stay.'

10:

CHRIS LEFT. It was school holidays, so Tim stayed with Janet. Both were lonely. They decided to host several barbecues, inviting first Ian, who slept there again, and then Sophie. Sophie Dean lived near Nina. Janet hoped she would help Tim settle-in when school started, and Sophie was ready to try. They'd also vaguely agreed to see a movie sometime at the end of the holidays, 'When I'm back home,' as Tim put it.

So they went. The movie was a love story, with a surprise ending. Far from being bored, as boys usually were by love, Tim pondered the film at length. Afterwards, they caught the bus to the bottom of the road serving their knot of houses along the cliffs. Nina's was one of the original timber bungalows, built at the turn of the century in what had then been bushland; Sophie's was more recent, with a swimming pool. 'Oh, it's still so hot, come and swim,' she said. 'There're spare togs in the changing room.'

Modestly they changed and then stood in the shallows. And of course eyeing each other – his well-hung fullness in the shorts, his tight arse and broad, straight shoulders, her swelling breasts, small solid waist, and a few hairs which curled from the crotch of her swimsuit. Fooling about with a waterlogged ball, they tussled and laughed and showed off until they clambered out panting and lay in the dying sunlight.

Sophie eyed him through half-closed lashes. 'I thought boys weren't interested in lovey-dovey films,'

'It wasn't lovey-dovey, it was real love.'

'Do you think love is interesting?'

'It's the best thing in the world.' His voice trembled.

'Have you ever been in love?'

'Yes.' His inner world shadowed his face. She regretted prying and was silent. They both welcomed the quiet.

Later her mother raised an amused eyebrow. 'Who was that gorgeous boy I saw in the pool?'

'Oh, Tim. He's moved in nearby. He's going to school next term. He'll be in my year. He's clever. I met him at the history and geography sessions. He's a brilliant sailor.'

'Daddy will be interested.'

Sophie nodded. 'That's what I thought.'

'So, let's arrange lunch for next weekend.'

Sophie grimaced. This could be rushing it. But she telephoned him and he sounded pleased.

It was a swim barbecue with the gas grill set near the pool the Dean family milling wet around the food. Something in Tim seemed to prime Sophie's young brother Jeff. The 13-year-old's flare for sexual innuendo coloured the conversation; everyone joined in. Sophie was alarmed.

Tim enjoyed the attentions the Deans relished on him. But why? he wondered. He tried seeing himself from outside. He must look pretty good – muscled and tanned from swimming. He felt at home with everyone, and surely they must feel the same about him. They seemed to glow in his company, and Jeff's admiration was open. It was fun, Tim acting the elder brother. They clowned about in and out of the pool amusing the family. It got rougher, Jeff pulled Tim's bathers down, everyone laughed. But the game was stopped.

Mr Dean got to his feet. 'Well, what a time we've had. Come on, you two, may as well get changed.' The three males went off to shower, emerging later, a well-bonded trio. Tim had accepted an invitation to go out in the family boat – 'It's for next Saturday, just Jeff and me. Oh. great.' He gave a happy whoop.

'The girls are lousy sailors,' Mr Dean put in. 'So it's just us men.' Sophie, nettled at being left out, was glad to be walking back to Nina's house with Tim. Tim hummed contentedly, and she felt more at one with him than ever.

'Your pool's brilliant,' he said, 'but we should go

swimming down below the cliffs sometime.'

'We could go now maybe.'

'Or after supper, when it's dark? I love it at night,' he said shyly. 'No one's there. The sea whispers. Have you heard it? It's like listening into a huge shell.'

She was charmed. 'No, not really. All right, let's go tonight.'

Back at her home, Tim appeared to have become a household god. Sophie announced they were going off for a night swim ('and just the two of us'). The idea was not even questioned. 'Of course. Have a lovely time,' her mother crooned.

He led her down the rough cliff path, helping her as they stumbled in the dark. The beach was still warm. They kicked off flip-flops skidded their feet along so the sand moaned underfoot. They stood stock-still in the balmy night, listening, rapt. The sea whispered longingly.

His throat tightened. 'Shall we swim with nothing on?'

'Do you do that here?'

'At night, always. It's great in the waves though sometimes I get scared about sharks.'

'Your not-so-high voice tells me you've not been bitten yet.'

They giggled and stripped off, splashed into the waves, and floated back into the shallows. It was so dark, they could hardly see each other. Slowly their eyes adjusted, and they looked around.

'Look at the stars!' He was entranced. 'They remind me of Greece. One night we sailed by starlight. It was magic. I stayed up all night, I couldn't sleep; it's fantastic just how uninvisible starlight makes everything.' He turned to her. How tangible she had become now his eyes had grown accustomed to the night. His penis hardened. She can see it, he thought. It'll put her off.

She touched his chest with the tips of her fingers. 'I'm glad you came today,' she told him quietly.

The night became strange then. There was nothing more they needed to say, but they both felt unsure what to do. They wavered back to their towels and began rubbing down. 'Can I help?' he asked softly, daring to gently tousle her long damp hair. She stood before him mute, with beating heart. She felt the warmth of his body, his breath on her cheek. She turned to take his arm, pulling them together, aware of the pressure of his erection up her tummy as he bent his head to kiss her.

It was a full connection. They floated, with the sea whispering on, wave after wave. She explored his back, running shy hands down the indents of his spine into the crease of his bottom, keeping away from his nagging erection. His yearning fascinated her. His frankness of need alarmed her. It was gigantic, new yet not exactly unknown, like a long distant dream surfacing as skin touches skin, so she trembled; and he did not press her.

They stayed close for a long time. Chilled, they finally dressed and stumbled up the tortuous path into Nina's unkempt garden. A dim light from the house lit their wide eyes, the softness and muscled tension of skin, the youthful lightness each had held on the beach far below. Speechless, hand-in-hand they wandered from Nina's house to her's, Sophie blushing with content.

Tim turned and hurried away. He let himself into Nina's house. In the shower he soaped himself and masturbated, then fell into bed, his body still hungry. Sleep only came after he jerked off again; his dreams filling with the lascivious whisperings of the sea.

What the Deans had was a speed boat that bounced over the waves – not as graceful as sailing - but the two boys enjoyed their turn at steering, and flinging the boat into a tight circle until it was caught in its own wash to buck and heave over the unruly water. Mr. Dean stopped the boat for a swim. 'Bathers off.' he ordered stripping himself and tackling the boys with deft grabs, adding 'It's too far out for them to see' and dived in. The boys moved forward. Jeff admiringly watched Tim's penis begin to swell, his also stiffened. Tim looked at the lad's small, hairless wand feeling a surge of desire. Jeff was so young, so tender, unaware yet of the pleasures Tim yearned for, yet aware enough for sexual camaraderie. They clinched and jumped as one into the sea.

The boys were the first to hoick themselves back on board. They were sitting on the side, feet overhanging the water, when a wet hand grasped Tim's ankle and pulled. He arched and then slipped into the sea into Mr Dean's arms. Tim read the lust in his eyes but couldn't avoid the kiss. He was not surprised, only uninterested. He gasped a lungful of air and dived under the hull, coming up spluttering on the other side. Jeff cheerfully bombed him, water and laughter cascading over both of them.

There the boys stayed, larking in the deep water. Tim encouraged Jeff to try a dive under the boat. 'Don't be scared. Go under at the prow, where it's narrower, not the middle where I was,' he suggested. 'Look up when you're under, the hull looks like a whale surrounded by breaking water. You go there, I'll go back the way I came.'

They met triumphant on the shore side, suddenly aware just how far out they had drifted. 'Time to go.' Mr Dean shouted. The boys clambered aboard streaming with water. He roughly dried them both as if nothing had happened, and let them perch on the forward deck on the way back. Jeff's rolling about on his stomach with a hard-on, thought Tim, amused by the 13-year-old's antics. He's a nice kid. Why don't they let him be, he wondered.

They drove back to the house, where Mrs Dean and Sophie had prepared lunch. The meal was filled with boat talk, future swims and fishing trips for the boys. The young savoured these last days of freedom before the school term shackled them.

While he had the time, Tim said he wanted to finish sorting out his garden. Sophie offered to help, so after lunch they walked back to Nina's house. She was surprised his caretaking was in return for rent and food, astounded to learn how he'd left home and passed his exams, going from the bottom of the class to the top. She had guessed at his ability and strength, but now she had an idea of the support he had in that house.

Nina looked fondly at the two youngsters snipping, raking, talking non-stop. 'How perfectly beautiful the young are,' she mused. 'I'm pleased to see Timothy with another friend. He'll be lonely here with just an old crock like me. Ah, Adam and Eve.' She laid aside the book she was reading and dozed. A smile flickered across her faded face, she enjoyed Eden.

11:

TIM WAS SETTLING into his new school, He finally admitted to Nina that he had been terrified at first. 'It was tricky. In some ways it was like my old college, same lessons same smell in the classrooms. But all the people are nicer – the staff and the kids. They treat you like a human being.'

'Well, my dear,' Nina studied his fresh face. 'You are a lovely human being. But I must remind you of your solemn promise not to drink in public and to avoid all drugs. Remember what Doctor MacKay said. Now come here and promise me again.'

Tim rose from dinner and stepped over to her. He hugged her tenderly. 'I promise' He beamed. 'I'm far too happy to get into all that shit again.'

'Dear Timothy, please, please be careful. I never told you about my second son. He slipped into drugs, it was many years ago now.' Tim sat down near her, holding her hand as she told him how her boy could not escape the drug scene and had died in agony. 'It killed my husband. It would kill me if that happened to you.'

When Tim looked back, that evening was a watershed for him. It was not just about staying off drugs. It was not even about loving Nina, which he increasingly did. A new fierce longing grew in him to live fully. He realised this one day, hearing his new friend Ian play his clarinet. The low notes, rich and woody, entranced him. Oh, to make that sound. 'Its low notes are a reflection of my secrets, and the sound Nina's richly polished desk would make, if turned into music', he said to himself.

'Come to our music bash this Saturday,' Ian said. Tim was delighted. It was to be held at Simon's, the music master's house, and very informal. A range of ensembles played, Simon accompanied some soloists. People listened, performed and talked all day long. Everyone had brought something for lunch, and spread it all out on a large table in the garden. Tim held a violin for the first time. Its fragile delicacy fascinated him – so tense and yet so light, with its sound peg hidden within, supporting the bridge and carrying the music into its florid body. Tim knew then, he contained the raunchy moan of strings.

It was nearly the end of the day when Simon asked Tim to join in an impromptu singsong. Shyly, with his unsteady voice, Tim let Simon test his range, singing the notes played on the piano. 'You've got a lovely alto voice' remarked Simon, 'and you sing in tune.' Patiently Simon rehearsed the alto part with Tim before they all gathered. Singing, all together, his own voice merged with the others into one rich sound. It was the unity of love. Tim felt embarassedly happy. 'Don't push it,' shouted Simon over his baton, 'the inner parts really can be heard.'

Simon wanted Tim to sing in a choir he ran. Tim agreed to some coaching. Ian was delighted they would perform together. Tim was impressed Ian had clarinet obbligatos in a number of songs; his friend, the soloist! Then, to his horror, Simon asked Tim to do a couple of alto solos. 'Don't worry.' said Simon, 'Ian and I will coach you. Are you free next Wednesday? Then, come here after school.'

At the first lesson Simon took him into the living room, and sat at the piano and ran through the music. It was all new to the boy, too much to learn in one try. The resonance in his temples and upper cheeks. The smooth open passage of his throat. His supporting diaphragm, so near his sex. His mind floundered. Again and again, the man held his head, his back, his neck and pressed his stomach teaching support. Was this what happened at singing lessons? Yet the man continued moulding Tim's body, talking and talking, always about the singing, until the boy trembled and a mound grew in his trousers.

'You're managing' said Simon. 'Are you all right?'

'Sorry.' Tim found himself unable to speak clearly.

'What about?'

'That.' Tim glanced at his bulging fly.

The man covered it with a palm. 'It's real music.' He pressed it. Tim sweated, yearning to get away~to stay. 'Are you and Ian screwing?'

The question was a shock. 'No, we're just friends.'

'You look like a couple. Aren't you that sort?'

Tim retaliated. 'Are you?'

'Of course.' The man was smirking. 'And you?'

Tim was scared now. It wasn't just the question. This was

exposure in public. This was a test of his love. He stood silently beside the grand piano in the wilderness of the room, tensing against the question teasingly thrown at him. 'This is a small storm.' he told himself. 'I can weather it.'

'You've fucked, haven't you.' It wasn't even a question.
'Yes.'
'I thought so. You see – I can tell. Boys?'
'And girls.'
'Ah, finding your feet.' Then *sotto voce*, 'So very young.'
'I guess so.' It was all very awkward. He was gently pulled close by a strong arm until he resisted.

'OK.' The man was whispering. 'I won't hurt you.' In a level voice he continued, 'Now, let's get on.' He turned to the keyboard. In relief, Tim sang through all his parts until the man stopped them with, 'You have a lovely voice; we must look after it. You have learned quickly. Enough for now. Well done.' And he looked Tim blandly in the eye.

The boy cycled home soberly. What would have happened if he'd said Yes? He'd said Yes to Chris, when he was young. But he knew it wasn't that, and it wasn't Chris's age either. He went through it again in his mind. Each shared a deep need. Each had said Yes. That's why they coupled, even in ways that had frightened him. Fallen into a vortex of lusty love, yet protected by joy and regard.

He hated thinking about the singing lesson and about Mr. Dean's watery kiss. He'd felt exploited. They'd just wanted him and bugger his agreeing. 'I've been overlooked most of my life', he told himself sadly. 'I've had it with uncaring people. Forever.' His thoughts flicked on. But Chris cares. He's taught me to care about myself, as well as others. That's what I love most about him. Anguished longing swept through him, and still burned in him during supper. All Nina felt she could do for him was to say, 'You miss him tonight, don't you.'

His face trembled, very quietly he said, 'Yes.' She saw his wry smile, his determined effort at conversation. But later in bed he yearned again, pushed a greased coke bottle into his arse, and wanked himself into a troubled sleep.

12:

DURING THE FIRST SCHOOL HOLIDAYS at Janet's house, Tim asked her if Ian could stay over. This was agreed for an evening when Janet would be away. After supper the two boys watched a video, then slipped naked into the spar-pool outside. Ian was smaller and softer with puppy fat the more wiry Tim was fast losing. Both were eager for intimacy. Offering his in response, Tim shyly touched Ian's swelling penis. It was neat and bare.

'Are you a Jew?'

'No, are you?'

'How could I be, with my foreskin.'

The boys inspected each other's equipment. Although smaller, Ian had more hair, even some peeping from his armpits. Tim pushed a wet finger into Ian's anus. 'Have you done it that way?' he whispered.

'No. Have you?'

'Yes', Tim confided, 'It's terrific if you're careful.

'I tried it once and it hurt a lot.' Ian's voice was small.

'Who with? Was it Simon?'

'No. With another boy. Has Simon groped you?'

'Why?'

'He's gay, didn't you know? He lives with his boyfriend. I'm sure they fuck. I found Goo in their bedroom.'

They were getting close, Tim knew. But wanting sex and keeping this friendship worried him. 'Can we go inside?' Damp, nervous, the two fell on Tim's bed. 'Shall we take it in turns?'

'Be careful.' Ian said nervously.

Tim reached under the mattress for a jar of *Vaseline* and primed Ian's bottom. Snuggling-up, his arms were trembling. Ian presented his bottom, its secret ring hidden in the gentle crease. Ian was broached. He shivered with fearful pleasure as Tim slowly thrust and slightly withdrew until a panting rhythm rocked the bed. Ian's spasm glued them together. Ian groaned as Tim burst and fell, gasping 'We came together.'

'It really hurt,' Ian cried. He fingered the wet drops on the bed. 'Did we?' said in proud relief. Tim rolled over and pulled him into his arms and lightly licked his salty lashes.

'You're too big,' Ian whispered into the heaving chest.

'No, when you came, your arse tightened. I had to go on to bring you off.' Tim felt the wet bed. 'Wow, you came a lot.' He sensed remnants of desire seething in Ian.

Tim lightly touched his soft body and licked his lolling penis, building ecstasy for him. Tim knew Ian had not imagined such pleasure, or pain. Generosity, drove him. Tired as he was, Tim offered his lubricated bottom and juggled his hips so Ian could push in. Then Tim prompted, 'Now fuck me all you want.' It was Ian's turn, and it liberated him. He struggled, plopped out several times until he'd mastered the thrusting. In a flurry of feelings he fountained. Both were wrung out.

Janet found them entwined when she returned. Their angelic sleep and the messed bed were eloquent. She was awash with jealousy at their bliss, ashamed these boys fucked in her house, fearing what parents would say. Deeper still, had Tim learned this from Chris? Loving Chris, she had grown to love Tim also – that's why Tim was here. Her heart spiralled down as she thought further, 'Maybe Tim misses him as I do, loves him as I do. Maybe Tim has found a new love now.' Sadly she went to bed. In the morning, when she entered the living room, there was Tim demurely asleep, or seeming so, in the bed made up on the couch.

They had a huge breakfast. Then the boys made for the spar. 'You left the cover off last night,' said Janet. 'Where are your togs?'

'We didn't use them.' And Tim gave a hoot.

'That's the way. Off you go then. Let's see some bare flesh.'

From the house she watched them laughing and tussling. Ah, the beauty of their youth. They settled. 'They're touching each other,' Janet decided. They went still in turns, then slouched into the water to their chins. 'Their recourses are endless', she decided, and nearly laughed as she went to dress. The boys emerged with a careless lightness. So much horsing around, so much nonsense. It's puppy love, she thought. Did Ian get it from his music? she wondered. The gentleness, the joy, without the competition stifling most boys' lives? Whatever was going on was part of a growing friendship, a stage she would not betray.

Later, she ruefully acknowledged the men she knew had

never learned to love. Maybe these silky, sweet, tail-wagging, wet-nosed boys were finding ways to become better adults. All the same, she reflected, Tim should mix with girls. Then he would be in a position to choose. She would support him whichever way he went.

But she still had doubts. She needed to talk with Nina, went to visit her, and hesitantly told her about the boys. As ever, Nina was wise and caring, 'I agree with you, only in a general sense. I am wary of interfering in his life or any others. Life is so very intricate.'

'Full of intimate affairs.'

Nina smiled. 'Yes, that's Timothy. Affairs seems to be how he's working on the challenges of growing up. It's a good way, because he can feel, act on, and confront the mores that imprison us.'

So she agrees, thought Janet. 'We stay mum, let the boys grow.' Nerving herself, she said 'I was wondering about Chris's involvement.'

Nina gently reached for her hands and held them. 'What do you know about that?'

'Oh, very little.' Janet said, too firmly. Gradually, details came. They had included her in their intimacy (Why doesn't she say love? Nina wondered) including study, action, talk. Lasciviousness.

Such danger here, Nina saw, a breach of ethics if a teacher got involved with a pupil's guardian. Suddenly she recalled the boy daring to tease Janet after a lesson, and she knew. 'You and Christopher became lovers.' Janet was silent. Nina paused respectfully, but had to say, ' You and Christopher – is that so different from Christopher and Timothy?'

Janet was nettled. 'He's a boy.'

They needed to think. The two women went to sit under a scrawny tree in the garden, sharing unease and concern in silence. It was a long time before Nina said. 'I do believe children have as many rights as we. On the other hand, we do sometimes withhold responsibilities which is probably wise. They make more mistakes, of course; that's inevitable. But in blundering they have scope to find living values in the labyrinth, however shocking the process seems at the time.'

Janet looked drained, so Nina elaborated kindly. 'I also had doubts when I discovered how complete their intimacy was. But you know, my dear, I saw the boy on arrival – nervous, stripped of any status, awash with drugs and pain. A ghost. Then he began to revive and live. It was their bond that enabled him to do so. What shook me was realising their love shone through my house, its wonderful power.' She saw Janet nod, and grew exuberant. 'They felt and acted upon their love with great resourcefulness regardless of convention or risk. And I saw mutual adoration. It supported Timothy in working for what he believed was a futile goal. It supported Christopher in carrying out his dream of salvation. I looked on, of course, in stupefaction – oh, I did admire them – contributing when I could. Well, Janet, so did you. We now have a delightful boy engaging with his life, getting to love it.'

She sighed, stirred, and burst out again. 'My dear, we must simply hold him (not onto him) trusting our hearts and his. He'll keep making a mess, he's bound to. I don't think that will matter. And it doesn't matter what he decides or becomes. The only thing, the sacred thing, is his integrity. People with integrity – and you're one of them, Janet – help us survive the ravages of the rednecks, who will certainly destroy everything unless we challenge them.'

She was in full spate now. 'I would cite a Greek myth Christopher often quotes, how Gaia helped Persephone break laws so as to link dark and light, thought and feeling: many duos. And life and death, of course. I think that's why these two lovely men are so alarming; they're playing with life and death. The risks and rewards are great, and usually all we'll be able to do is look on. And love them, of course.'

Her voice was dropping. She summoned it back. 'But I do approve your plan. And you should know that. But let me tell you, Timothy has a number of friends who drop in here, for instance a girl nearby, Sophie, I think. She and Timothy are very close. He's met her family too. They walk on the beach and she helps him tidy my garden. Delightful. They're all delightful, the children growing up hereabouts. So very young these days. We must give them time.'

She sighed, failed to get up so Janet lifted her and helped her up the steps, one by one by one, back into the house.

13:

A CHILL WIND messed the first fallen leaves. As autumn deepened Tim swam in the Deans' heated pool. Young Jeff, on the threshold of adolescence, was often there, overjoyed by nakedness, intrigued by Tim's body. It was all very rich for Tim, who liked Jeff despite his corncrake jokes, enjoyed the intimacy and being so frankly admired, and through everything felt the buzz of being close to Sophie. Occasionally in the changing room the boys collided to touch each other. Jeff was thrilled by the swollen power of Tim's erection and his heavy sacs; It dizzied Jeff to hear, 'Yours is beautiful, bigger than mine when I was thirteen.' Once Tim masturbated the youngster, thrilled with the discovery of such keen pleasure who soon softened. Tim stopped Jeff's caress by turning hurriedly to dress, to lessen yearning.

And every morning Mrs Dean spied on them under the guise of preparing breakfast. Spellbound she watched when Tim stood on the pool edge like a young god; when the two stood, arms akimbo, her son an immature reflection growing fertile like this achingly lovely boy, when they pulled themselves giggling into the water like frisky lovers. At such times, she found herself trembling.

Sophie was not good, early in the day. Still, she often dragged herself out of bed to join them. Sometimes the boys were naked, sometimes, dressed. How strange of her, Mrs Dean mused, she doesn't seem interested that their flimsy trunks show everything. Surely she and Tim aren't intimate?

The boys were clad when Sophie swam with them. There was a pleasant balance: the nonsense expressed by the boys along with a seriousness Tim and Sophie shared; and the common geniality. The parents saw only the harmony Tim brought, for which they were grateful; the lift in spirits was more uneasily acknowledged by them. But everyone revelled in the friendship.

14:

SIMON HAD ORGANISED a music weekend. The choir and chamber groups were bussed to a distant youth centre. Ian and Tim were allocated a small room in one of the huts scattered around a lake, huts housing most of the activities. All arrived on Friday afternoon for the induction and a meal, and then a huge bonfire where everyone cheerfully settled for singing, silly sketches, games and hot faces, ending with steaming cocoa from a cauldon on the fire.

Afterwards it was hard to settle down. Long into the night, guffaws and shrieks rang out, keeping everyone awake. Nervous and tense with desire, Tim crept to his bed holding a cold tube of goo nursing a lump of a toilet roll under his pillow and an erection pushing at his pyjamas. He waited. The high jinks went on and on. Ian seemed asleep. Maybe he doesn't want it, Tim thought, and I'll die. Footsteps pounded past their door, which opened flooding the room with torchlight. 'Good boys.' said Fran, a bassoonist. 'Good night.' And then, 'Pipe down, you lot, or there'll be big trouble.' Gradually peace prevailed.

Tim was masturbating when Ian slipped in beside him. They hugged one another. Ian snuggled down and enclosed Tim's hard in his mouth. Tim grimaced. 'Ouch, don't bite.' 'Sorry!' Ian whispered, cupping a hand under deliciously full sacs and squeezing them. Tim stiffened, pulled his face up and kissed him passionately. 'I'm nearly there,' he breathed. 'Leave it for a while. I thought you'd never come.'

'It killed me having to wait.' Ian whispered excitedly.

The boys nestled and caressed until their penises oozed. Ian's resistance broke first. 'Can I . . . ?' Tim crawled off the bed pulling down pillows for his knees and laid his chest on the bed, spread his legs so Ian could squirt goo, lubricate him and gingerly enter. It was blissful, no fear at all: this was not Chris's mighty tool. Tim strained backwards to enfold pleasure while Ian laboured pinioning him. Wilting he fell away. They changed places. Tim thrust hungrily. His storm broke. They crawled into bed and lay as one, dead beat with pleasure, and slept.

It was such a rush in the morning. Stuffing erections into

their tracksuits they arrived almost too late for breakfast. Simon was amused. 'Come on, you two beauties. Rehearsals in half an hour.'

The cacophony began. In the thick of it all, Simon took the singers one by one or in small groups for voice training and music practice. Tim sleepily rested in the autumn shade awaiting his turn. Summoned, he went in, and Simon turned and pulled him gently until Tim felt the man's erection pushing at his waist. 'You owe me for last night.' It was teasing, and it wasn't. Simon was caressing his face. Tim parried. 'What shall I sing?'

'T H A N K Y O U as a scale, one letter at a time in B flat minor, if you please, the key of Bach's great Second Suite. I'll play along with you. Going up, starting with T and down starting with T.' Tim carefully followed the piano up, and down, and up again. 'You sound even better than usual,' Simon said. 'I find that sleeping with one's friend lubricates one's voice too, wouldn't you say?'

But Tim was unable to speak. His painful blush rebuked Simon as he tried to make amends. 'I'm sorry, my dear, I didn't mean to upset you. Here, sit down.' He made room on the piano stool. Tim sat beside him, sightless from the banter, mutely screaming to himself love wasn't an entertainment, it was sacred and private. In tears he slumped into Simon, who embarassedly patted his wild mop of hair and stroked his limp velvet arm, 'Gee, dear one . . . here, hold up. Don't take me so seriously. Timothy. You must know how much I really really like you. There, there. Here's my hanky. Blow.' Tim filled the immaculate handkerchief with slime. Simon took it politely. 'Gee, I'm sorry, forgive me. Timothy?'

To cover the boy's silence and whatever it meant, Simon regaled him with a description of Bach's Second Suite and then played bits of it, expertly singing the solo flute part. He showed the boy how Bach had set tunes against themselves, how some were turned upside down as the bass 'lovers facing one another in perfect harmony.' Simon was starting to chirp again. 'Do you like it?'

Tim smiled wanly and nodded. He preferred Simon talking about the intricacies music. If only that were all. Simon's sort of sex belonged in a creepy, appaling world he did not wish to enter.

'I'll lend you a CD when we get back, OK?' Simon was crooning. 'Do you know, your voice sounds better in the country. It's a fabulous, soft, rich sound. Are you up to another scale?' Tim sang, his voice growing stronger as he settled, defter as Simon guided him. They ran through his solos and bits of the songs they were to perform at a future concert.

Then it was time for the next pupil. 'Yes, yes, come in, Amanda,' said Simon evenly. He pushed the piano stool back and gently hugged Tim and murmured, 'Today you were wonderful.' Tim let himself out into the sunlight. The warmth melted the numbness in his gut. All he could think of was seeing Ian, getting back to what they shared; yet he was muttering, 'Oooh, I miss you, Oh, Chris!' as he stumbled through the open glare near the shining lake back to his shadowy room.

Ian lay on his bed smiling. 'Had a good morning?' Tim shook his head, clambered over, and lay face down beside him. He pushed his hand up Ian's shorts and kneaded his responsive sex. He rolled on top of him and hugged him fiercely, then fell back saying, 'God, I need you.' He knew his hunger amazed Ian, knew Ian's own had grown with each coupling, now he'd begun to yearn, he would understand.

'What happened?'

'It's Simon. He arranged for us to sleep together so he could ask me to thank him.'

'He's a gay shit. Why can't he leave us alone?' Ian eyed him. 'Did he hurt you?'

Tim shook his head. 'I hate him groping.'

The boys sprawled until Ian wriggled saying, 'You hurt me last night. I couldn't sit still during rehearsals. It's great having a flaming arse.' Tim fell on him with blown-out desire. Needing to be held (Oh, Chris). Needing comforts which boys are loath to give (Oh, Chris, Chris) yet lightened by Ian's gentle presence and his awkward concern. They lay in each other's warmth until the gong sounded for lunch.

It was a free afternoon. Tim sauntered towards a distant hut where a string quartet was playing. They smiled expectantly, happy to share Haydn, and played on. It was a simple work, in a way, a conversation of instruments. Its eloquence shook Tim, the gentle swells of support by the viola, the two violins playfully swapping places, lovers, mimicking, vying for brilliance, uniting in the end. Tim yearned for the knitted relationships Haydn had made, the difference celebrated by each part, just as Chris had allowed him

77

to be himself.

He sat unaware of the tears on his face until the players stopped, anxiously, and asked, 'Are you all right?'

'Oh, Sorry. It's just so beautiful. Haydn is talking about such difficult things. I'm sorry. I'm OK, really. Go on, please.'

'Amanda said you had a bad time with Simon. Don't take him seriously. He's just a harmless windbag.'

A grateful smile flooded his face. They grinned encouragingly and continued.

Later, he held the viola. It had a solidity compared with the violin, like holding Chris's penis rather than his own. He loved the way the cello was embraced between open knees; like a lover.

He'd promised Ian to come and listen to him playing in a wind group, and found them huffing and puffing the witty elegance of Mozart, full of immoderate conversations wheeling about delightfully ambiguous, with lovely climaxes. The group sounded like a happy family: the bassoon's almost broken voice was rich in male amusement, senior to the younger clarinet and oboe, and supported in a motherly way by the booming French horn, while the blithe flute floated free over them all. Yes, definitely a good family, without menace or pain, with immortal relationships delicately caught, and endlessly reworked.

And Ian was terribly good, Tim realised. But it was Fran on the bassoon who entranced him. How she savoured the long-necked mouthpiece and, stretching for the keys, her breast brushed the bulky wooden tubes – *fagotti*, bundle of manly sticks and a spangle of silver keys. He flushed with the depth of its reach inside him. He knew she had heard him sing and praised him to others, that at times now she glanced his way, sharing the musical interest with him. When the music making was done, she called him over. Would he like to try out her bassoon? Yes, a large and heavy instrument, but he looked fit enough to manage. Diffidently he draped the holding cord around his neck and she hooked the instrument on. Wow, it was big. The bulky reed filled his lips. She helped put his fingers on the keys one by one attentively adjusting stretch and shape, intimately without fuss. He blew long and strongly. To her great surprise, a decent stream of notes emerged.

'I played the recorder for a while when I was a kid,' He worked the keys finding a bumbling tune.

She was so impressed. 'Do you like it?'

'It tickles my mouth. I love the rich farty sound,' he stammered, and sat down suddenly giddy.

'So do I.' She smiled. 'Oh, that's just hyper-ventilating, you get used to the breathing quite quickly.' Adding 'Would you like to learn? You seem to have a flair for it. If you like, I'll come to your house and we can experiment before you decide, and then we could speak to your parents. We need bassoonists.'

She was amazed at his address. 'Oh, but that's Nina's place, isn't it? Yes it is. She's lovely. She's a friend of ours. My sister spent such happy times there. Oh, of course, You must be the boy Nina told me about.' Tim shrugged. 'I remember now. You are the brilliant boy from Greece. Well, that settles it. Shall I come next Tuesday?'

He floated from the room. 'God, I love her.' he declared to himself laughing.

That evening there was a complete run-through of the concert programme. Simon was getting flustered and harangued the children as they struggled with everything: notes, time signatures, bar lines, repeats, dynamics. There was so much to remember, so much to get wrong. He was completely ratty by the time the choir started. They began tentatively and were soon lost. He raged as they'd never seen before. Tim was unnerved, and faltered when he was waved in for his solo; and then, of course, the whole choir collapsed. 'Stop!' Simon yelled. 'What's wrong with my pansy alto this evening – too much bed and not enough sleep? Sing as you poke, my love, or shut up.' Tim reddened. Again they messed up. The third time things wobbled a bit, but they managed raggedly to the end. Tim's voice was hoarse. 'We'll do it again. Until we get it right,' Simon shouted.

Tim raised his hand. 'I can't, Simon,' he said croakily.

'Then get out,' Simon screamed. 'You're another incompetent wasting my time.'

Trembling, Tim left the stage, to the audible sympathy of the choir. Fran saw the boy white with despair. She went to him, put a friendly arm about his waist and shepherded him outside, then gently propelled him to the lake. Tenderly she pushed him onto the grass and sat beside him. Then the bitter and sweet extremes of the day cut him up. How was it possible to cope with all this? It was not.

What a mess. Tiredly he laid his head on Fran's warm lap, a mix of dewy grass and her intoxicating musty perfume. 'I can't cope,' he whispered into her womb.

She caressed his soft hair. 'You'll be OK on the night. But you must treasure your voice. Simon should know how fragile it is at your age. And remember, try to keep a sense of the beat in your own head. Don't rely on others, particularly conductors. Knowing where you are is the first secret in playing.'

'And in life.' He could hardly say it. Shyly he put his arms around her. She did not respond. He became set on her, mad for her. Because she was unresponsive he lifted his head to read her face and then surged up and hungrily kissed her mouth, clinging to her to claim her, spirit and all. His passion was not denied, was even accepted, but throughout their infinite pause she seemed as one dedicated to giving him courage and calm. She disentangled herself, sadly saying, 'Feeling better?' He had to keep his hands away, had to say Yes. Light from the huts cruelly cut the black surface of the lake into shivering segments as if goaded by the fury driving the rehearsal that evening. He day-dreamed of sailing across the water to a place where he would be whole, with her.

Everyone revived around the late-night bonfire. With relief they watched the cheerful red sparks fly up to the stars. They sat in the glow and sang songs of nonsense and love and betrayal, thankfully reunited at the end of such a long day. And then it was time for bed. As the crowd moved off with mugs of steaming cocoa and the last hilarity, Ian and Tim stumbled upon Fran in the darkness. She held Tim's waist, stopping him with, 'OK?' 'Yes,' he breathed, reeling at her contact. 'It was a great sing-song.' He looked at her, the firelight dancing in her dark eyes and making her olive skin shine with life. Her breasts, so soft, so full, and the shadowy mystery between her legs, that musty scent. And how her touch burned. 'Thank you' was all he managed. But she understood, he was sure. She leant towards him sighing, 'Good night, Tim', and kissed him on the cheek; and then 'Good night, Ian', and let them pass. They wafted into the dark beyond firelight, warmed by her.

Simon burst unannounced into their room later as Tim, balancing on his rumpled bed, bare but for underpants, was trying to fix the skew light shade. Simon ran his hand up Tim's bare leg and onto the soft bulging underpants teasing, 'Ian, the most beautiful legs in the world. We are privileged.' Tim jumped down defensively. Simon sat beside him on the bed. Ian, smouldering and challenged, looked on.

Simon held the lad with a light caressing arm. 'I've come to apologise. I've been ordered to. I'm sorry, my dear. I did not mean to hurt you.' He eyed the two boys. He's wishing he was with us, Tim knew. He's wishing he was one of us. To him, we're the pure ones, with real feeling. But Tim had nothing to say to Simon, nor did Ian. Their blank glances excluded him until wild with yearning he rambled out of the room.

The boys grin in relief and anticipation. The rest of the night is for them. They hurry out into the dark and try to urinate against the hut, battling their erections, then scamper back to one bed, desire goading them on to acts of ecstasy. Ian is exultant, Tim relieved; both are exhausted by the music of the day and the music being played in their bodies.

At a bleary-eyed breakfast Fran asked them if they'd like a lift home. She was leaving early to drive back. Remembering the fun in the bus delayed the answer, 'Yes, we'd like to go with you.'

'See you in the car park. Oh, and Tim, there're some things I want to do at my house. We'll go there first before I deliver you to Nina's.' And that's how they went, dropping Ian off on the way.

It was Tim's first entry into where Fran lived. While she was checking for phone messages, he inspected everything. She found him examining a set of photos on the mantelpiece in the music room. 'Is that you?' he asked. 'No, it's my sister.' Tim stared. 'Yes, I know, we are alike. We were identical twins.'

It was all getting close, coming too fast. 'Play me something on your bassoon.' he asked.

She loosened all the clips of the case and assembled the parts carefully. 'This is the beginning of the *Rite of Spring* by Igor Stravinsky.'

He had never heard a lament that haunted him even while the notes sounded. 'Play it again. Play it now.'

She did, then told him about a tribe dancing at the end of winter, sacrificing a virgin so spring would warm the world and life continue, babies, green shoots, all the abundance of the earth renewed. The intensity of his gaze troubled her. And why had she chosen the *Rite*, of all things? He's undressing me, she thought. 'This music is an entreaty for life. There is a spiral of need and desire. It can be in the seasons, or a life span, or between two people in a single moment. We all know this, but Stravinsky makes us feel the immensity of need and longing.'

Her voice, her mind, gave him the breath to breathe, 'Do you think we have to sacrifice in order to live?'

'It's impossible to avoid loss or sacrifice.' Her tone seemed blurred and low as she turned away to disconnect her instrument, pulling a cleaning cloth through and nestling it into its case.

'Oh,' he whispered, leaning towards her. 'Oh, I believe you. Maybe people don't care, if it's what they want to die for.' He had said too much, more than he intended, far more than he'd ever expressed before.

Fran shook her head. 'But to kill a girl so spring will come. That's extreme.'

'Taking someone's live body, doing what you want with it?'

She was silenced, and he had not expected that. He had to carry them on. 'Do you love?' He gulped.

'Do you mean "Have I" or "Do I"?'

He looked blankly at her, disabled by her question.

'I'm not in a relationship just now. But yes, I have loved, and do.' These were not things to say to the boy. Why should he care? Why ask? Why tell? 'And you?' Suddenly she needed to know about him too.

Something trembled across his face, yet the grey of his eyes blazed 'I do love.' His whole body tensed with memory. 'But Chris is in Greece.'

'Ah yes, you came from there.'

'No. We were sailing there, it was the best time of my life.' They were tied in silence.

'Did you meet there?'

'No. We met here outside my old school.'

'Is she my age?'

'No. Older.'

'How old were you?'

'Fourteen.' He sensed her shock. 'It was . . . It was not like that. We wanted each other from the very beginning.'

'And you really loved, then?'

'I still do. I love Chris more than anyone in the whole world.'

'You miss her still?' she gently probed.

'Miss. Yes. I miss him all the time.' He shook his head, trying to get the loneliness out of his hair. His agony overcame them both, and she took him to her bosom. Awkwardly he embraced her and then sought her mouth. He throbbed against her; his erection nudged her thighs until they opened slightly. Decorum had to return and accordingly she stepped back, dismayed by her own greed, and by his. 'Come on, I'd better take you home.' It seemed the only decent way to behave.

Back at Nina's, Tim remembered her last words about starting him on the bassoon and saying, "I'll see you on Tuesday, after school", which now had no clear meaning. He showered in a daze. With a sudded hand ejaculated; his *Rite*.

He lay in bed, exulting in all the music he had discovered, and far, far more than that, the lyrical bliss now filling him so sensually his body buzzed and everything around resonated.

15:

TUESDAY, AT LAST. The school day finally drew to an end. Tim got home for Fran and the bassoon lesson. She showed him over the instrument, talking through music matters between short bouts playing her own instrument. Her voice and his first playing made him so light headed it was difficult to think or speak. Did he want to continue with lessons? He'd have to set aside time to practise, 'So you have to be really interested. It is perfectly OK to say No, we could still be friends.'

Anxiously he asked about payment. Chris had left him pocket money for things like this. But Nina had earlier told her enough about his circumstances, so she generously countered, 'No money for this term, we can talk about that later. But in return you've got to work hard, OK?'

He looked adoringly at her. 'Yes. I do want to go on.'

She showed him the playing posture and how to support the

notes with his diaphragm as Simon had. But her cool touch stirred him. 'I recommend you play these scales,' she went on, writing them out in a manuscript book she'd brought, 'and just fool around playing as you did at the camp. Sing! Playing is an extension of singing. Everything you do must be done seriously, with thought. It's important to develop your ear, and your body, swimming helps. Stop if you're giddy: breathing takes time to master.'

He savoured the hour, and then she was leaving. 'I'm sorry the instrument I have for you is being overhauled. It won't be ready until later today.'

'Can I come and pick it up?'

'No, it's a risk carrying it on your bike. I'll bring it to you after supper,' she said. 'Unless you'd like to come with me to the repairers. The workshop is fascinating, precious wood, sets of silver keys, oil and leather smells, bamboo and racks of sculpted tools.' He blazed with delight. 'Then I'll pick you up in a couple of hours.'

'Oh no!' He groaned. 'We eat then.'

'You can have a bite with me, if Nina doesn't mind.' And of course, Nina didn't.

While Fran got busy in the kitchen, Tim studied a piece written out and propped up on the piano. The writing was hers, in the notation and the title: *In Memoriam – Fiona – for two bassoons*. He tried singing it but it eluded him. During supper Tim asked her about the music. 'It's a sonata, in three movements,' Fran answered. 'I'm having trouble with the centre slow section.'

Later she sat at the piano and played parts for him. To her surprise he quietly sang back one of the themes. 'Let's do it all,' she said. He sang along as she played until he had it more or less right. Gradually she began singing the other part. The duet began to work, the last try without piano. His voice was clear and sensual 'It's beautiful and sad,' he murmured.

She smiled at him. 'You know, you sang a wrong note here, and here, and here.' She pointed to the score. 'That's A-natural; you sang A-sharp but it sounds much better, can I use it? I'll call it Tim's A-sharp.'

The lamp bathed them in gold while the night gathered outside. They had forgotten time. 'Do you know, I think it's finished. Thank you.' She breathed out and smiled in happy accord as he grinned at her. 'Who is Fiona?'

'My sister.'

'The one in the photo?'

'Yes.'

'What is Memoriam?'

She blinked, looked at him with tenderness and put a hand on his knee. 'It means "In memory of,"' she said sadly. Startled, at a loss with her grief, he gazed at her, kissed her hand, hugged her as best he could. 'I'm sorry,' he whispered.

It was then she knew she wanted to take him to bed. Yes, it was a sort of thanks, but mostly she was sure it would feel like an extension of the duet they had just sung, meeting each other on equal terms, when he had shared happiness and pain so generously.

'But look at the time.' she cried. 'We must go. Get your bassoon. Where did I put the car keys?'

She dropped him outside his darkened house.

'Can I come for supper again?' he pleaded.

'OK, some time next week?'

'Fantastic. Thanks.'

'We'll speak. Don't forget: practise!' she called as she left.

It was almost all he wanted to do now. He lay sweating in bed massaging his penis and whispering, 'I love you, love you, love you,' then fountained into sleep.

Nina woke the next morning to strangled sounds from the bassoon and Tim's singing. It has a more broken voice than he has, she thought, and chuckled. The pooping continued, then silence and he was gone, off to the Deans' swimming pool and school. Thankfully she tidied the mess of books on the library desk and put his abandoned trainers at the top of the steps to his room. Maria can take them down, her mind ran on. It's working out well. He is wild. But happy, I think. I must write to Chris – he'll be relieved.

It was a long, painful time for Tim. The phone didn't ring. He looked hurt as Fran began their lesson a week later, played carefully and talked in monosyllables until Fran said, 'I'm sorry I haven't rung but I'm playing a concert on Friday and I don't have time.' Such relief there was another reason and she wanted to explain. 'Would you like to come?' she went on. 'We are playing Stravinsky's *Petrushka* , one of his great ballet scores – like the *Rite of Spring*. You'll have to get the train up, but I can bring you back.'

He blushed with pleasure. 'Ooh, yes.'

'I'll leave a complimentary ticket for you at the box office. Come to the artistes' lobby afterwards. We'll be back late.'

'Um, can I stay over?' Even his arms were throbbing.

'Probably. Let's see. Come over after tea today. I'm teaching then, so I won't have time for you, but I'll lend you a book about *Petrushka*.' He would see her again. It would be brief, not enough, yet Heaven.

16:

NINA APPROVED OF HIS OUTING. 'Yes, it is sensible to stay with Fran after such a long a day for both of you.'

On the way to the station he got money from an ATM. The train journey was over an hour. He watched his invisible friend (whom he had invented as a tiny boy) skip along the wires and fences demarking the track, mirroring the train and joyously riding the catenas of the wires in switch-back fashion or jumping the uneven gaps in the fences as they rattled past.

'Having a night out on the town?' a man asked.

'Yes, I'm going to a concert. My teacher's playing in the orchestra. It's *Petrushka*.'

'Stravinsky. Great ballet. Have you seen it?'

Tim shook his head.

'It's wonderful. From the very first note you're plunged into a Russian Fair. The music is filled with the shouts and dust, the gaudy stalls and thronging crowd, cries from the stall-holders, and the man with the puppets.'

'Which come to life.' Tim said.

'That's it.' said the man.

'It's sad Petrushka dies. I wish his love could save him.'

'Love isn't everything' said the man, 'It's only a folk story.'

I thought that art told the truth, Tim pondered. In that case, love is not invincible, so how am I here? He looked out the window. His tiny friend had gone.

The train terminus was thronged. Tim pushed through and on to the concert hall. In the basement bar he perched on a stool ordered sandwiches and a glass of orange juice. 'Would you like a 'Bucks Fizz, deary?' said the barman, 'It's orange juice, with a dash. It's on the house.' He smiled. 'I'll disguise it in a tall glass for you. There, bottoms up.' Tim sipped. It fuzzed up his nose. He sneezed. 'Oo, here's a napkin' The barman gently wiped Tim's face. 'What are you doing afterwards?'

'I'm meeting my teacher who's taking me home.' The barman moved away, Tim knocked back all the drink and weaved his way to the toilet. He blundered into a cubical and, unusually, sat to urinate and realised, 'That bastard spiced my drink.' His thoughts careered back to his days of doped sex. 'Fuck. It's that easy. I must be careful.' He emerged, splashed his face with cold water and shambled into the hall. But he was all ears by the time *Petrushka* started. Yes, the opening is the fair. He was there with all the gawking motley jostling and open-mouthed: The Giant, the Fat Woman, jugglers, the man with two dicks. The puppet show absorbed him. He suffered with Petrushka, hated the Blackamoor and despaired of the Princess who should have followed her heart and Petrushka; she was not worth dying for.

The ending, a return to the fair – as dream or puppet story – mixed comfort with pain; the familiar cloaked the painful truth Petrushka had died because no one cared for him. Tim wept. 'It's true. I'd have died without Chris defending me, and there was Nina and Janet. The man in the train was right: Love is not enough. I'm not Petrushka anymore. I love Fran. I must have her or I'll die. Fuck the Blackamoors.'

Fran met Tim in the lobby reeling from the concert. His eyes shone. He bounded up to her babbling about the shimmering woodwind, the screaming strings, the cruel brilliance of the trumpets, all the wonders of the fair, the unnecessary death of a dreamer. They exulted in Stravinsky making such mysteries tangible. Suddenly, without reserve she loved him. He talked and talked.

Silence settled as the car sped home. 'Please stay with me tonight' she said brushing his fly, 'Keep it for me.'

Tim blazed. 'I love you, Fran.'

'Oh my dear, dear beautiful boy.' He sat very still holding his reality. 'Thank you Petrushka for helping,' he breathed as the night glittered past.

Teasingly they made hot drinks and took them to her music room sharing the long couch demurely until he said, 'I hate you in black.' She kicked off her shoes and he began to peel off her white blouse and black skirt and tights. He fumbled with the clip of her bra until she felt behind and released it so that it fell revealing her breasts. She gently undressed him down to his underpants. Their last flimsy barrier to the risk lying beyond. He began kissing her neck, eyes, ears, then feeding off her mouth as she found his.

'Your lips have sores.'

'I guess the calluses from my bassoon reeds.'

'Will I get them?'

'Of course. All reed players have them. It's our secret trade mark.' She chuckled against his exquisitely smooth lips.

He suckled her nipples. She arched her back demanding more. He gently moved downward, leaving a snail track of saliva to her navel and onwards along the crease where her thigh joined her body until he found her spicy scent again. She trembled with delight as he kissed the mound of hair and with a firm tongue split her and entered that wet cave, exploring the silky, glistening skin and the ligament of her clitoris. Fran's body tightened. She floundered in waves and shivering fell back into the couch. 'Oh, my love,' she whispered drawing his face up to kiss it again and again. She leaned down and lifted his underpants over his erection. It reared up, slightly to one side, marbled skin sprouting from skinny loins, and sparse pubic hair, without veins, its fleshy foreskin slightly parted by the engorged glans whose purple crown broke through.

'It's beautiful.' she whispered. (It's perfect, smaller than Danny's huge fisted arm; different to Viv's, his is stubby with huge pendulous balls). She fondled Tim's sacs, so delicate, filled with a tangle of tubes and fruit. Here was the centre of his softness under-lying his phallic desire and his bony body. In those sacs nestled the warm flood she now craved. She pursed her lips, pushed back Tim's foreskin and engulfed it. He burst, flooding her mouth with smooth faintly almond-flavoured seed. 'Oh, oh, oh, oh I've come. I'm sorry. Oh oh, oh No. I wanted you so much, inside.'

Then she began to kiss him as he had never been kissed before, softly, urgently, until he quivered, his skin glowed, and his penis grew again. 'Come on, let's go to bed,' she whispered.

They stumbled through gloom and flung themselves onto the bed. She lay under him as his slight sinewy body spread-eagled over her. 'Put your legs on my shoulders' he pleaded. Quickly, cleanly, he entered her and deeply plunged in. She gasped and lifted her hips to accommodate him. It would soon be over, so sweetly silky and virginal, so strenuous. But he held himself fully extended, almost still, pulsing deep so her womb responded with little waves taking her breath away. She clutched his tensing bottom, felt the luxurious feminine smoothness of his back, watched the dancing hair crowning his beloved face.

Little cries proclaimed how deep and how fully she was being taken as wave on wave erupted, driving her further and further away from herself, further and further into his arms his thighs, further and further, trusting, merging, merging. Now she experienced Hilda, the glamourous head girl at Girls' Grammar, her first love for three star-struck years; and Amy, the man-hater who had usurped and then violated her. And Fiona her twin, her mirror until she died and the men whom briefly she'd loved. They clamoured as this boy stormed beyond anything she had known.

Unstintingly she offered up all her treasure until she screamed 'Now.' Blinded by bliss as orgasms overwhelmed her, oblivious as Tim began his last effort, arching tensely above her his arms pressing into the sheets, his toes the locked foundation for stiffly spread legs, his stomach hard as if he were diving far far into deep water, taut as he drummed on her own tight flesh. They ran with perspiration which sucked as skin met. Another song belched from her bloated vagina as he drove in and out with long sweeping thrusts, they whimpered and cried aloud. With three or four spasms, he collapsed, Fran wept.

'Oh, God,' Tim cried out. 'What's wrong, have I damaged you? Are you all right?'

She sobbed, 'Oh, Tim, oh my dearest. You're wonderful. I love you so much. I'm so happy. Oh Tim.' She held him, her warmth invading him deeply. 'Me too!' he managed.

Liberated, heart beating with heart, they triumphantly slept.

In the morning he took her again. She revelled in his ferocious lust seemingly endless. It's the same way he devours everything, she mused, a dying man desperate to live before he snuffs it. No wonder he already plays the bassoon like a child who's been learning for a year.

She sat him down to watch a video of a ballet performance of *Petrushka* while she went shopping. He was transfixed by the marriage of music and images. The dancers wordlessly told the story; the dancer-Petrushka became the puppet. The music was saying, 'See, it's only a silly story, don't weep, it's make-believe.'

'The puppeteer is a magician who tricks people into thinking myth is reality.' Tim declared helping Fran in with her shopping.

'But equally, it's saying that life and myth are indistinguishable' Like Persephone, he realised, as Chris had said. He hugged her saying, 'You see, life is myth!' and demanded she milk his bursting cock bouncing pleading out of his pants for a love duet.

It was lunchtime. The day was pressing but doubts nagged her. She took him into the living room. 'I must ask you something, something important.' She paused. 'You said you loved Chris more than anyone, is that right?'

He nodded.

'Who is Chris?' she asked, gently taking his hands.

He slumped, his face aflame, sweating, tense, speechless.

Oh, now he's cracked, she thought, a helpless, lonely wreck. Why didn't I leave him alone? She was ashamed. He was crying. She felt his tears dripping onto their clasped hands. She drew him to her. 'You don't have to tell me' she whispered, 'I don't care about anything just as long as we're friends.'

'You know, he's a man.'

'Did he teach you how to be such an incredible lover?'

'Yes.'

'He helped you to come down here?'

'Yes. He saved my life.'

'No wonder you love him. He's given you life, happiness, love.' She sobbed with him. 'Dearest Timtim, don't run away.'

They clung in silence. She stammered, 'Can I tell you? I have a secret like yours: I worshiped Hilda at school who lured me into sex. We were overrun by Amy, another one. They made me a servant, a faceless slave. My own needs were ignored and shamed. That's the reason I got into music where I could feel and respond. I was nearly destroyed during those years. Music saved me. Then again, yesterday. We not only shared music, but you allowed me to completely want and to get everything, for the very first time. I've never given-up so much or got so much in return. I've never been loved that way. You make me feel very special. He melted into her until she whispered, 'Will you take me to bed now?'

Their coupling was blundering blubbering and sweet. Then they talked. Secrets poured out. He described the ways men couple, of being penetrated – they agreed to try it sometime. 'I suppose it feels like the power when I'm entered' she murmured. She showed him a double dildo Hilda had got her, 'I'd better wash it thoroughly before we use it.' Tim mentioned his Greek discussions, about the mix of man and woman in everyone. She was shocked the mix of girl and boy so turned them on.

She laughed. 'You're a Goy'.

He patted her bottom. 'And you are a Birl'.

Liberated and entranced, he wanted anal sex. He shyly kissed down her crease and onto her anus softening as he probed with his tongue. 'I like that,' she called through her open legs. He coated his fingers with grease and gently pushed them in, one, two, three, until she dilated. He snuggled close, she admitted his erection 'Now do a long fart' he commanded .

Fran relaxed.' Wow It's exciting.' Fingers fondled her breasts, her hips, found her weeping vagina, her clitoris. She moaned. 'Go deeper, Tim, I love having you inside, flood me.'

Stimulated, exultant, he was quickly overwhelmed. She felt his force, the sinew-breaking tension as he strove, and the whimpering joy at ending. She was deeply intruded upon, pounded and stirred, her sensibility abused by this little beast, yet she gloried in his abandon, throbbed in hidden places, exultantly.

Shrunk, he plopped out. He lay on the bed and fell asleep. She was burning. I should wash, she thought, watching over him.

He lay, arms outstretched, able hands opened flat on the sheet, of water? She kissed the poetic line of the knuckled spine, still damp, the pet. Such fragrant skin, hairless and vulnerable; he could be a girl. Yet her arse proclaimed, her whole body proclaimed, here was a boy of such beauty she literally ached. Gently, so as not to wake him she lay beside her statuesque swimmer drinking the perfume from an arm pit. He turned slightly, his penis limply marking the fallen skin of his testicles; a few strands of pubic hair crowning it, whispering potency. She saw it as an offering, as a focus of his need, the vulnerability of his body; she floated away in its beauty.

The afternoon dimmed. They wakened and gazed out.

'Better?'

'Yes.'

'I'm sorry.'

'I was scared.'

'Scared of losing you.'

'I want you to love.'

'I do.' She smiled. 'Let's wash.'

They ran naked through the house.

'What a wasted day.'

'All this time, losing and finding ourselves.'

'Was it worth it?

They kissed frantically, mouthing, 'Yes, yes, yes, Oh. Yes.' He took his untouched over-night bag and bounded to the car. She drove to Nina's house and waved him goodbye; the world returned to normal, she was his teacher again.

More weeks passed, busy and engaging. Tim and Fran coupled to salve an ache echoing in lessons and outings. Each of them felt stronger; she was more resolute; his fraught extremes lessened. 'He seems calmer.' many commented.

Tim began doing odd jobs to save money for a bassoon. Nina had broadcast how good a handyman he was. Friends and neighbours hired him. He had four jobs in the Deans' road, one was working in their garden. Jeff often wanted him to play, but Tim worked on until Jeff joined in. 'Mum, you pay me too. If we're fast, Timbo, it'll soon be done.'

'It's better with two.'

'Yes, more gets done, if we don't fool about.'

'If you pull your finger out.'

'Fingering is fun.'

Tim grinned. 'Keep your mind on the job.'

'Time's up.' Mrs Dean called, 'Give me your clothes, Phew. I'll put them out to air. You have a swim. Just as you are, there's no one about. The money's under your drinks. Never mind me.'

Tim's reticence about stripping there effected Jeff who was growing awkward teasing his sister about Tim. Some things, he decided, were better left hidden, or unsaid.

17:

MAX TELEPHONED one evening asking if Tim would again be his lab assistant after school the following Tuesday.

'I don't think so, unless I can change my music lesson.'

'I'm glad you're musical.' said Max, 'What do you play?'

'I'm learning the bassoon.'

'Well I never.' said Max. 'My neighbour played the bassoon, I went to some of his performances. See if you can come on Tuesday. I need you.'

Fran made a plan delighting them both, 'I've a rehearsal here on Saturday afternoon, so after your gardening, why not ride down for supper? Bring your music but not the bassoon, I don't like it on your bike. You can borrow mine. We'll eat and have a lesson in the evening, or on Sunday, when we wake up.'

Tim whooped and whispered, 'I miss you.'

'Dear one, please wait for me.'

'I don't think I can.'

'Well, don't make the sheets too wet.' she laughed, kissed him down the phone and hung-up.

In the laboratory Max welcomed Tim, 'Fran says you are doing well, so I spoke to my neighbour who is happy to show you the instrument her husband played. He died several years ago and it is littering the house she said.'

'Oh dear, I haven't got much money yet'.

'Perhaps I could lend you some; you pay me back bit-by-bit'.

Tim brimmed with gratitude; he shone as a white-coated assistant, helping Max clear up and to prepare for morning classes.

That Saturday, with Tim hovering, Fran rang the old lady. 'Yes, next Tuesday. I'll pick Tim up from school and we'll come on to you.' She hung up, turned and kissed his smiling face. Immediately he dragged her to the bed. They made love, then ate, coupled again and then blissfully slept. The lesson had to wait.

Fran had arranged a complicated piano and bassoon exercise based on Fiona's *In Memoriam* slow movement tune with Tim's A-sharps. This she explained to him after breakfast. 'You know all the notes, we have sung and played them now. But notice the length of the notes changes – watch very carefully indeed. Alone you should have no problems, if you count the beats. But when I play with you it'll mess you up as I've put in many little tricks of time and harmony to throw you. My love, it's not to tease or to hurt you. I want you to begin to understand the difficulties in playing with others, remember your trouble in the choir. Everyone depends on our bass line, so we must play firmly.' She pressed Tim's fly saying, 'You know how to be firm, Tom-tom Tim.'

He giggled, licked his reed and struggled through.

'Good. Again. Better. Once more? Good. Now I'll play your line with you on the piano . . . one, two, three. ' They were absorbed. Tim with the exhausting mechanics of blowing and moving his fingers correctly, Fran nurturing him, remembered Fiona, her twin.

'Now each of us on our own parts.'

He stumbled angrily and stopped.

'Well done. It's tough, isn't it. Do you want to try it again?'

He nodded.

'Do you remember in the choir how, absorbed by all the harmony around, you sang without hearing yourself yet you felt the beat and the pitch?' He grinned. 'That's how you must play: guided by your inner voice, the one that says, "I love you." You have a splendid inner voice, just ask it to help.' They struggled for an hour until Tim's arms ached and he was dizzy and Fran, at the end of her patience. Complexity mastered, the mess cleared, the polyrhythmic tune each was playing merged and hovered into a unity.

Tim sighed. 'Fiona would have enjoyed that.'

Fran's face crumpled. She swept him into her arms and hugged him. 'Oh. Yes. My Timtim, you're fantastic.'

'Fran, It's amazing how you changed sound and sense'

'It's partly rhythm (remember Stravinsky) but also the power of harmony. After we've rested I'll play you some Gesualdo, a Neapolitan murderer who wrote the most extraordinary madrigals in which the colour changes like light on shifting silk. Let's have a hot drink. But please kiss me Tim. I need you, now.'

He was startled; it could have been him asking. He kissed her gently all over the outside of her lips and face, as if washing away the stress in tender thanks for stretching him almost beyond endurance and for being with him all the way.

Fran put the Gesualdo CD in the machine and excused

herself, 'I have to telephone and organise rehearsals and pupils. I'll be some time.' Tim found the music hard to follow; it changed mood and key, shifting about unexpectedly, reflecting the words; but he enjoyed being surprised. When the CD had run, he replayed it, jumped up reeling and sliding round the room like Petrushka.

He was hovering, arms outstretched, folding and unfolding them over his head, dipping his square, slim shoulders mimicking a rocking boat and screwing his hips in lascivious circles, when Fran entered. She was entranced. Her body knew his: its tight ligaments, bony bits that had pushed against her; muscular swellings bringing grace and strength to his long limbs; the neck growing from set shoulders; able feet and hands balancing and holding; the neat, bunched cheeks of his bum dimpling when pushing his sex into her and cheekily flexing as he walked; his flying hair following the bounds and twists of his sweet frame, as he twirled round like an entranced dervish, and saw her. Caught but not vilified. (He lived in a culture in which dancing was sissy and expression ridiculed, so he'd learned to hide). But Fran was not like that.

'Oh, my Tim, you dance like an angel. I love these Madrigals; and every time I hear them I will remember how you danced them into such beautiful and expressive life. Your body says so much. Don't stop, you aren't shy in bed. Dance more, my love.'

But he grew wooden with an audience and soon dropped panting beside her on the couch. Later, practising in Nina's library he turned his meagre tunes and exercises into dances pushing the bassoon beyond decent sounds until it both barked and sang, squeaked, rasped and fog-horned to the tap, tap, tap of his foot.

Nina, reading in the living room, chuckled. 'My, your old bundle of sticks is almost talking' she told him over dinner.

'I was trying to make it dance.'

'It protested; perhaps it's old, like me.' Both laughed.

There is always something of interest happening in the house with him here, Nina mused. They cleared-away together, after which she habitually retired to bed to read. She hugged him tenderly and kissed him saying, 'Good night, dear Timothy. I am so happy you seem contented and that you are here with me.'

'I am happy. I think. Well, sometimes. I love being here so much. Now, it's home.'

'Of course it is.' she called as she left the room.

18:

ON TUESDAY Tim walked to the Deans'. After larking about with Jeff he dinked Sophie to school on her bike. 'Left my bike at home. I'm meeting Fran later. Are you all right? You're so quiet. Yes, it's a pity it's too cold to go to the beach.' After school Tim rushed delightedly out, waving to her jumped into a car and left with Fran.

Max's neighbour was called Mrs Brandt. She was small and thin with white hair hanging lank around her face as if it had fallen asleep. Her blue eyes lit up when she grew excited. Fran reverentially took out the worn bassoon and assembled it. She had her reed with her and began to play. 'It's a really beautiful instrument.'

'Let's go and get some tea while she tries it out.' said Mrs Brandt. In the kitchen she pushed the switch of an electric jug. 'Now, tell me Timothy, how much money do you have?'

He looked bashful. 'Um, I've only just started working . . . but I have five hundred dollars in the bank, and I can borrow more.'

'From your parents?'

'I don't have parents. No, from Max.'

'Max. No parents. Mmm. Is that really everything you have?'

'Yes, everything. But I can . . .'

She waved him silent. 'My dear boy, you can never pay more than you have. To give all is a very high price indeed. Now, you will pour hot water into this teapot and carry the tray.'

'It needs an overhaul, oiling, some new pads and a new vent key which newer bassoons have these days. But it is a fantastic instrument, you probably know that.' said Fran.

'Good' said Mrs Brandt. 'Anyway, Timothy and I have made a deal already, if you think it would suit him.'

Fran looked troubled. 'It's not a student's instrument, it's better than mine.'

Mrs Brandt's eyes sparkled. 'Then you take it and give Timothy yours.'

Tim watched the seriously sparring women with alarm.

'I can't afford it.' said Fran.

'But Timothy and I have already agreed all money matters.'

'How much?'

'Five hundred dollars, you said you had Timothy?'

'Yes Mrs Brandt.'

Fran was baffled. 'It's worth five thousand, probably much more.'

Mrs Brandt handed out tea and crumbly biscuits. They supped quietly, her bright eyes held them. 'When I was twelve, I was being shipped to a concentration camp in distant Poland. The train was shot-up by resistance fighters and by some chance the side of our cattle wagon was damaged. I fell off the train into a deep trench covered with brush. I lay there stunned. The train, with much shooting, rolled away. I had only one possession. So precious. My mother's pendant. She had been shot dead not long before. That week I traded it for a slice of bread and guidance to the boarder where I escaped. You see, I gave up everything to walk the tangled woods to freedom, and to my life here. As a musician, you must know that in music, as in love, it is not the cost; the value is all that matters. Like me, Timothy gives up everything. I see about music he is serious; and I hope he will also be, when he falls into love.'

Fran reddened. 'He is serious about both almost everything.'

The old lady sighed. 'My dear, this was Hans's first love. I cannot 'sell' his - our baby. If Timothy had had only two cents I would have agreed that sum: everything for everything, try to understand.' Mrs Brandt looked severe. 'But, handsome Timothy, you must promise both of us you will work hard and care for your instrument.'

Fran had tears in her eyes.

Tim hugely nodded. 'Mrs Brandt is terrific. She is wise and good. A true person, like Nina and Fran, and Chris,' he told himself. 'and she makes miracles happen.'

'Timothy, would you like to inspect the garden while I persuade Miss Fran to take my sheet music away?'

Tim pushed at a sagging door and stepped onto a patio leading into the tangled garden. Fran leafed through a treasure chest full of music. Later he helped her to load up her car and carefully placed her 'new' ancient bassoon case on the back seat. Tacitly it was agreed, she should have it.

Leave-taking, Tim hesitantly said, 'I do gardening and odd jobs. I could come and sort your garden out. For free, of course.'

The old lady's eyes gleamed, 'Oh Timothy, what a nice thing

to do. You can see I'm not a very handyman. Hans has not cut its hair for such a long time. ' Her face softened. 'You see, my dears, how everything transforms everything.' Then she drifted inside.

Fran sat still behind the wheel for a long moment. Then turned and took Tim in her arms. It was so intense the windows began to fog. Then, without another word, she drove him home.

In the morning Tim practised and then bolted for the Deans' pool. No one was about. He rolled back the pool cover then let himself into the changing room, stripped and then dived in, swimming as many lengths as he could under water, he had to improve his lungs for playing his bassoon. He showered still panting. Jeff shambled in sleepily and dropped his pyjamas. 'It's too cold to swim.' His erection brushed Tim's thigh. His hand found Tim's. They played each other.

'Do you do this with others?' whispered Jeff.

'Boys? Yes.'

'Do you ever go the whole way?'

Tim ran his fingers down the young boy's back, through the velvet crease of his bottom and onto his anus. 'You mean there?'

Jeff nodded.

Tim considered. 'Yes. Do you?'

Jeff pleaded, ' I've tried with friends . . . does it hurt you?'

'No. But sometimes it can. You have to grease-up.'

'We use spit.'

'No wonder it hurts. Grease and tongue and fingers.'

'I wondered.' Jeff sighed. His masturbation was attentive.

Tim was growing excited. 'Can you come?'

'Not yet.' admitted Jeff, 'Is it good?'

'It's the best. I'm getting close, do you mind?'

'Shoot away.'

'Shit, I'm close . . . Now.'

Jeff admired the streams of fluid running down his thigh. Tim leaned into him collected the sticky seed with two fingers and pushed them into Jeff's mouth. 'It tastes good.'

'Is it OK to swallow?'

'Of course. It makes you strong.'

Tim then pulled Jeff into his chest, took the pencil penis in a cupped hand and began expertly to rub it. 'Keep it really stiff.' he coached. 'Feel everything go down there. It's not like pissing.'

Jeff tightened his bottom, strove and wilted. 'It felt great.'

Tim bent down and squeezed the softening penis like a tube. A tiny silver droplet formed at its tip. 'Look, you're nearly there. I guess soon you'll come like me.' He slid a finger over the slit in the glans and offered it up. 'Taste it, is it like mine?'

'I can't taste much, is it salty?'

Tim crouched and sucked the flaccid flesh. 'That's the semen. The sperms are milky.' He fondled the sacs holding exquisitely small apricots and soft tubes. 'Doing it will bring yours on.'

Jeff flushed. 'I'm not sure I like the taste. Can I feel you there?' He weighed the big pendulous balls in his hand feeling the skein of firm tubes and the plush swell of Tim's maturing gonads. He longed for such a sex, so full of life. And Tim was so clever, so lively and so loved. His head fell on Tim's chest.

Tim grinned. 'It's hard work, coming, isn't it.'

'I feel great.' Jeff said. He clambered into his pyjamas and raced to the house. 'Hurry, or we'll be late for school.'

Mrs Dean watched them breakfast. 'Now, boys. Easy, easy. You're on your own. Sophie's not feeling well and is staying home.'

'Oh. I'll bring our assignments over after school, so she doesn't get too far behind.' said Tim.

Mrs Dean was delighted. 'Do stay for afternoon tea.'

'Thanks Mrs Dean.' He and Jeff sped down the gravel drive, the ghosts of the night blowing away.

After tea that afternoon Sophie took Tim up to her room.

'What's wrong with you?' he asked.

'Nothing. Just women's matters.'

'Tell me.'

She found reassurance in his dove-grey eyes. 'I've got my period. Sometimes it gives me terrible pains and I feel sick.'

'Nina told me it keeps you really healthy when you bleed because all the yuk come out, leaving you clean again.'

'Do you really talk about such things?'

'We talk about everything.'

Silence. (The centre of sharing).

'You're lucky, Timmy.' she murmured. 'I hate my body, the smell and the bleeding and the pain . . . I never knew it was a cleansing process. Tim, you're lucky to have such a lovely body.'

Tim took her hand. 'So do you, Soph.' He kissed her lightly.

She looked pale. Her head fell on his shoulder as she wanly hugged him. 'Not really. Sometime, will you talk to me again?'

Tim stammered, 'I miss our night swims. Being together.'

A tear welled. 'Oh, Timmy, so do I.'

'Let's get on, eh?'

'Let's.'

'And let's share homework like this once or twice a week.' They worked cheerfully until the shadows lengthened. She saw him to his bike and burst out, 'Are you in love with your bassoon teacher? She's very beautiful.'

Tim blushed deeply. 'It's a secret, even from Nina. How ever did you find out? Nobody knows.'

'I saw you both leaving school yesterday. You both looked very happy. So you are.'

'Please don't tell. Please.'

She shook her head dumbly. He pedalled away. He turned, saw her still standing at her front gate. He waved. She tentatively waved, it seemed to Tim, a farewell.

19:

WINTER WAS PASSING but some unruly remnants remained. Sleet lashed the children, harried the postman and shook the trees in Nina's garden. Yet the grey world was tinged by buds on trees and bulbs from the earth. Winter and the term were nearly over.

'Persephone is emerging from Hades to join Demeter.' Tim decided. He enjoyed a shift from death/darkness/feeling he was discovering in Fran (and Sophie), to the life/light/thought in himself. Myth and season were his mirrors.

Tim's weekends were a riot of wanton joy. He arrived at Fran's bursting for attention. His sexual energy, dammed for a week, overwhelmed them. She provided immediate gratification calming him and extending the play preluding ferocious coupling later. He willed her to pull away from their embrace just inside the front door, find and caress his arching cock, kissing him everywhere.

Sometimes his pent-up energy burst at the first contact. Sometimes he would drag her to the couch in the music room and ravish her. Once during dinner he crouched down and skittered under the table, pulled her nickers off to kiss her vagina.

Tim was totally involved, unthinking about his demands or the way Fran responded. Glorious, calming. They enjoyed anal sex more often; gradually he unburdened details of love-making with Chris, at last adding, 'Now, can we try the dildo?' He thrilled as she pushed it in.

'This is the power men feel' she gasped.

Tim cried as she thrust deeply. 'No, don't stop. It's OK. Oh.' He gripped it so she could thrust over its length until her excitement blossomed. 'It's like being with Hilda.' Then she fucked him. 'Is it the same as Chris?'

'It's not often like that. God, it hurts, coming while being fucked. It's not as exciting as the real thing which grows bigger and stronger and anything might happen, like it exploding, or ripping your guts out or setting you on fire, something cataclysmic.' he paused. 'It's better lying on my back, I can see how helpless he is afterwards, reassuring when you're pinned down. Are you afraid when I fuck you?'

'Once or twice I was disconcerted, never fearful. Tim, I love your beautiful penis. I clamour for it. I utterly trust it when you take me. I have seen what you described in Chris: how your power withers at the end, how my perfect god shrinks into a wee worm, leaving me filled with its life. It's just as well I'm on the pill. I throw myself at you careless of everything but union. There is a moment, you have it too, when we are one gasping being. I struggle after that moment with all the love I have.' She hugged him.

'Don't you mind that I'm gay?'

'Timtim, I love all of you, the straight and the gay, just as you are. You have shared the girl within you and allowed me to find the boy in myself. I worried about my ambivalent sex since puberty. Yet perhaps we are more whole being both girl and boy. Our "goy and birl" contains a truth don't you think? I must say Timtim, I don't think you're gay, just a fuller man. Think of Simon. He'd run a mile if a woman opened her legs for him.'

'That's what Chris always said, even when we were fucking every day.' He sighed. 'But we changed places: sometimes active, sometimes passive, like Tiresius the blind seer. Like you Frani, I need it both ways. Ever since Chris took me I have longed for a penis, maybe more than I longed for a vagina.' He gulped, 'I'm still fooling around with boys . . . I feel bad.'

'But do they want you as well?'

He nodded.

'Then why worry? With their appetites boys have to shoot somewhere, and girls are not ready or able to cope. I certainly couldn't've. If it's mutual, anything is acceptable even among children, provided it grows from love and not destruction. It is rare in such circumstances that lasting damage is done. Hilda and Amy harmed me but not for life. It was my way into adulthood debilitating though it was. What permanently harms us is after-guilt arising from destructive, conformist judgement.'

'Chris also says we don't know how to stand on the bridge between male and female; we rush to one end or the other forced by gender rules, so there's no bridge, only the chasm between keeping apart bits of male and female we hold inside until we grow into split incomplete people.'

She took his silky sacs and kneaded them tenderly, feeling stiffness grow along the length of his penis and its root into his anus. 'Timtim, you built a bridge for me which I have edged along until I feel both sides and the chasm beneath. I am far less fearful now, nearer the centre.' She wriggled a finger in his anus.

His face suffused with pleasure. 'You built me one. I will never forget how you dealt with my shame about being fucked by Chris. I thought you'd throw me out . . . Shit, that's great . . . I suppose I had edged a bit further than you, but it was such a private place until you made me see you were there too, and that . . .' he stopped. '. . . that you loved me regardless. God, I need to come.'

She rolled over and pulled him into her. 'Come, my dearest!'

With a cry of delight he exploded. He lay in her arms, on the bridge, looking both ways, wholed and contented.

During a lesson Fran said, 'In the weekend after next there's a party in the city with musician colleagues. So, I'll be staying over.'

'Can I come?'

'No, my darling. Sometimes I like to see my friends by myself. We work and relax together. It's only one weekend. OK?'

'I suppose so.'

'Darling, there's next weekend, together.'

A weekend filled with pleasures. Yet by the end of the following week Tim was feeling abandoned. On Saturday he mooned about the house seeking comforts, masturbating in vain. On Sunday he wandered along the pristine beach as gulls wheeled screeching overhead. Angrily he scuffed the sand filling his shoes with chaffing grains. He perched far out on damp rocks, watched the sea rise and suck at seaweed, fill pools with swirling froth and then withdraw like a disinterested lover, until a surging wave wet him, driving him back to shore.

After lunch he decided to work in Mrs Brandt's garden. 'Perhaps it will connect me to Fran.' He attacked a section of unweeded bed near the back door until she called, 'My dear Timothy, that's enough for now. Come and have tea with me.'

She regaled him with snatches about her gypsy life; much of it, involving loss and escape, chiming with his present feelings. She talked of her musical life, how it had liberated her in so many ways. He was unsure at that moment whether in his case it was liberation or imprisonment. But he was interested in the thread of Han's bassoon and her piano enabling her to travel so extensively.

She had unearthed a metal music stand folded into a small neat cross-legged bundle which he accepted gratefully. 'No one else cares for me.' he muttered. He tied it onto the carrier on his bike and rode away to Fran's house. 'She must be back by now.' There was no answer to the bell. He kicked the door angrily and puffed up the hill to the Deans'. They were out. He ripped off his clothes and fell into the pool. With a finger on the rail behind his head, he floated looking up at the fluffy clouds. 'They look like my balls after a hot swim,' he mused. 'They move in the same slow way telling me things I don't understand. They rain like my spunk.' His prick stuck its head above the water. He floated keeping it arching upwards, letting the water flush his balls about like hands through his open thighs.

Mr Dean tiptoed over, stripped and, sporting an erection, slipped in beside Tim, swung in and kissed him, capturing his penis, slobbering over his face. 'You are the loveliest boy in the world.'

Tim let go the rail. They sank under the surface. In an airless embrace he managed to struggle free, thrash to the steps and rush into the changing room where he damply dressed just as Jeff bounced in. 'Don't go Tim, come in again with me.'

'Hi, Jeff. No. I'm off.' he took his bike and pedalled home.

At dinner Nina felt Tim's silence. She regarded his drawn face and the pain his body expressed. 'Is it medical or emotional?'

'I don't feel well.'

'Yes dear, I can see that, is it medical or emotional?'

He looked down at his plate his anger and disgust boiled. 'I . . . I don't know. I feel awful.'

'Timothy, we have struggled with you and your feelings a great deal; I'm sure if you would look into yourself you'll be able to answer my question. Only then can we find a cure, my dear.'

'Please Nina. Not now. I'll be all right.'

So he feels that strong, thought Nina. Perhaps it's time he coped. 'Good.' she said. 'But to get you to sleep tonight I propose giving you half a sleeping tablet. Sleep is the best healer. But don't tell Doctor MacKay.'

Starting the week, he stayed at Nina's in the morning. After practising he raked the debris off her garden. He ate there before setting off for school. The day dragged; he excused himself from Sophie's work session and slunk home to surround himself with his own affairs. Tuesday restlessly passed; he pedalled as if up-hill all the way back to his bassoon lesson in the library. Dourly he played for Fran, grunting at her questions. 'Come on Tim,' she cried. 'Put some spunk into it.' He stonily ignored her until she cried, 'That's enough. Tell me, what is going on?'

His rage erupted. 'Leave me alone. Pick, pick. Always picking. "Try harder Tim, you're not good enough." You don't care about anyone but yourself.' He slammed the bassoon down and stormed out into the garden. The door slammed shaking the house. He stalked over to a tree and flopped down glowering.

Nina stepped gingerly down the steps to find Fran, white-faced. 'I imagine you understand what is troubling him. Is it possibly your absence last weekend?'

Fran trembled. 'I don't know. He accepted it when we talked.'

'He still doesn't always connect with words. You know he's fallen for you?'

Fran nodded.

104

'And you?' asked Nina gently.

Fran took a deep breath. 'Sometimes I love him more than anyone in the world.'

'He demands that, doesn't he, the pet.' Then Nina told Fran something of Tim's past. About his breakdown under drink and drugs, of the enormous struggle to re-start his life and wrench him away from his disinterested home. 'So much depended on the ferocious love between Chris and him (yes, he had confessed to Fran about that). A love that still propels him. Now I understand what you call his "remarkable progress". For you see, he responds to life driven by his feelings. Nurtured by his love for you he's wolfed all the music you've thrown at him. But it's too emotional a situation for his own good. Or put it another way, his achievements are at a huge cost to himself.'

'And at huge cost to others.' Fran whispered. Stiffly she put her instrument away, collected her possessions and made to depart. 'Nina, I'm at my wits' end.'

The old woman struggled to her feet. 'My dear, let's you and I sleep on it. He's a very precious boy. We'll find a way of taming his wonderful enthusiasms, won't we.'

Fran drove off. 'I've lost him.' she sobbed.

But she telephoned the following evening to ask him if she could pop in and see him.

'When, now?'

'If you like.'

'If you insist.'

Nina had retired when she arrived. They sat in the living room quietly until she managed, 'Tim, I'm sorry I went away. I didn't think it would matter that much. If I'd known I wouldn't have gone to the party.'

'You were fucking some guy, weren't you. I know because you never came home.'

'Perhaps we both fuck around, you told me you do.'

His winced.

She relented. 'Tim, I had a good time. But I didn't have sex with anyone. You are everything to me, you know that. I came home wanting you and wanting you to be there. My empty house and then you, punished me for being away.' She was trembling. So was he. In agony they sat. She timorously hugged him. He fell into her lap.

She patted his wild mop of hair and stroked his velvet cheek until their trembling died. He lay against her for a long time. Then he whispered. 'I get so . . . lonely . . . I'm sorry.'

She bent and kissed him. 'So do I, but you *must* believe however long and dark the tunnel is, I'll be at the other end waiting for you.' Then she rose to go. He shadowed her to the front door.

They agreed to reinstate their weekend ritual until the coming holidays. But how would they feel now the spell was broken? He flung his arms about her and hugged her breathless. They kissed. She stumbled to the car and slowly drove away.

After locking the house Tim fell into bed. The dark whispered around him. He clutched his balls while his erection matured. Ferociously he rained on his bed, eventually drifting into a troubled sleep from which (as Nina had said) he emerged feeling able to face the day. But not the Deans. They would take longer.

'OK, you've been busy. But you're not busy now, so plea-ea-ease come back.' Sophie and Jeff chorused when they all met at the bike shed at school. Nervously Tim cycled home with them. Mrs Dean, beaming, flew about the kitchen preparing special treats. Tim, torn by the conflicting pressure from brother and sister, and fearing the father's return, offered first to swim with Jeff (Sophie could join in if she wanted – she did), then study for a while with Sophie. 'And Jeff, you've got to promise to leave us alone.' she chortled.

Mrs Dean watched her children romp with this fabulously handsome boy. She stood absentmindedly polishing golf trophies, gazing at the waves splashing out of the pool transforming the paving into a gleaming sheet of happiness and the three children into water sprites straight out of her own childhood.

Suddenly she sagged. 'I love you Tim. Oh, how easily the children love you.' She hid her face as they trooped in and bustled upstairs laughingly settling to their tasks.

'. . . Fuck off, Jeff. You promised.' Then Jeff's gale of laughter as he pounded into his room and happily slammed the door yelling, 'Wow, I'm glad he's back.'

20:

A NEW TERM HERALDED SUMMER. Already Tim was working outside without a tee shirt. He loved the long warm evenings, star-kissed swimming, these days of wearing very little. His body felt enlivened by the breath wilting the fleshy plants, shimmering above the roads, turning him to gold. Life was dampened by preoccupation with his lusty needs. Even the sun dimmed in comparison.

His voice settled as desires unsettled him. His body filled out. Was he taller, or did he now see further? Gradually his life became complicated again. This time not from isolation, but from his passionate friendships jostling, whispering and tempting him in ways which giddied him. He had so loved Fran, yet that too was changing as they faced the demands of separate lives. 'However, she'll always be there, at the end of the tunnel,' he told himself.

His growing up took another bolt one afternoon at the Dean house. The children had gone out. He had swum, left his togs to dry on a chair, wrapped a towel around himself, and drifted for a drink into the kitchen. Mrs Dean was busy fussing over her sink. Tim, reached up to a high shelf to get a glass. His towel unwound and dropped to the floor. Mrs Dean darted forward and crouched proprietorially over it gazing in stupefaction at the perfection of his nakedness. Like Botticelli's Aphrodite balancing in an unsteady shell, he raised a protective hand to shield his sex. But Mrs Dean's hand had already found it.

He stood abashed as she fingered him. His erection reared up as she fondled it pulling the foreskin on and off the shining tip clasping its swollen length, caressing his naked flanks, as she blushed with desire, as they both sweated and moaned and yearned until he burst over her face and dress and she cried, 'Oh, my darling, my darling.' Rising unsteadily she turned and fled crying out her shame, lust and all her broken childish dreams. Tim looked at his mess on the floor, wiped it away then slipped back to the changing room to shower and dress. No one saw him out.

Sophie now often spent summer evenings with Tim. They began either working in the library or in the garden, then sharing supper with Nina, listening to heavy big records on her ancient

107

gramophone – he explained about Vivaldi's *Four Seasons*. The shimmering summer meadows, the glassy icicles in winter, all the glories of the year the music celebrated. Sophie was entranced. She didn't like *Petrushka* much, but hung on every word as Tim described the action climaxing in the death of Petrushka and the weakness of a love unsupported by action.

Sophie worried over how much of the passion he radiated grew from the affair with his teacher which had never been broached again. Sometimes they sat quietly breathing in the dusky scents of the garden before stumbling down the cliff to the empty beach with towels around bare necks where they stripped and swam. They lingered longer each time they dried, sometimes clasping each other in a heart-beating embrace she cherished, but left him in a lusty whirl.

The school year was drawing to a close with exams in a few weeks. Tim shrugged off the anxiety falling heavily on them all; he found solace in his music and occasional couplings with Fran. They both worried about parting for the long summer break. She was tutoring at a Music Camp that year; it would be some time before he should apply. 'I'll tell you when you're ready,' she promised. 'We can be together. Will you work if I'm away, will you stay happy?'

'I'll be OK this time,' he said. 'But ring me.'

Janet confided in Nina. 'Tim and Ian must be lovers. I found a jar of *Vaseline*. Surely they are getting too old for that?'

'Do you think they're happy?'

'I'm sure they are, that's not the . . '

'Trust them; happiness is too precious to tinker with.'

'Well, Nina, at least Sophie is staying while I'm away at a union conference. The Deans are very cooperative.'

'We shouldn't meddle Janet. Remember, it's their life. Trust them with their own dreams and choices.'

Tim slouched around the garden, sweating when he worked, sweating when he rested, yet contented being there with Nina and swimming two or three times a day.

Occasionally he took the bus into the village to watch a movie or to put gardening money into his bank account, shrunk having paid Mrs Brandt. Playing Fran's bassoon, it was as if he hugged her, and in taking the tongue-like reed into his naked lips, it was her passion that flowered.

Nina told him it was Shakespeare who began *Twelfth Night*, "If music be the food of love, play on." which he thought wonderful because it was true. They read the play together. Tim found the video in the village shop. They watched it three times.

'Nina, it's confusing. Men fall for boys, women for girls, the fool is wise, the manager foolish. Is everyone blind?'

'Timothy, it's the confusions we've often discussed. The mix of boy and girl, also the seeming and the real. The quality of love. Don't you think love is blind?'

'Um, I'm blind.'

'To all your loves?'

'Blind . . yes, blind to all my loves.'

'Being in love, my dear is being blind. That's why you must be careful, otherwise you easily stumble.'

As the Deans stumbled over me, he thought.

Nina raised another theme, Tim's escape from stupidity – well that's what his old school and his parents had called it. What did Feste say about Malvolio being a greater fool than he when the tables were turned?

He grinned. 'The fool's right. Here the themes are twisted. Not only blind, the paired lovers are fools, denying the obvious.'

Nina smiled. 'Denying the reality of gender plus the possibility sister *and* brother had been saved from drowning.'

Tim nodded. 'The truth was uncovered by seeing the "Two apples" together (Fran and Fiona?) clarifying everything.'*

Nina nodded. 'As did Malvolio's letter. The play mirrors our uncontrollable drifting. Similar themes exist in our labyrinthine lives, such as foolishness, love, pride, skill, honour.'

'Hate and fear.'

'Yes of course; as you know, in our blindness of passion we can see only by risking everything.' Nina rose. 'You were very brave admitting to blindness just now. I am proud of you Timothy. Music is certainly your food of love. And my dear, you are nobody's fool.'

Tim adored this frail intense old woman who stood with him and railed against the world, showing what dignified quality a committed life had.

---

*   See notes at end.

Findings

1:

THE BACK SEAT OF JANET'S CAR was covered with Tim's things: clothes in a soft bag, books, bassoon, music-stand, CD's, photo albums from Greece and his bike.

'It looks as if you will be away for a year.' smiled Nina who came out to kiss him goodbye.

'I'll be back before you miss me.' She looks old and bent, should I be leaving her? he mused.

'And, you'll be back before you miss her.' said Janet laughing. Their easy relationship soothed the upheaval. Respect had grown during the tough times. In the car Janet said, 'I've begun to redecorate your room. Let's finish it together.'

During the painting they cheerfully tussled about finish and colour. Tim slept in the living room until the painty smell lessened.

At night they sat outside in the spar and talked until skin wrinkled. Tim was wary. Janet, sensitive to adolescent self-consciousness, left him to decide whether to wear his togs. She was naked. Eventually he stripped and sat with her, grateful and excited they could simply be together without the innuendo plaguing him at the Deans. It's easier to talk like this, he thought after admitting some of his sexual encounters with boys.

'Is it love?' asked Janet.

'I don't know.' He was embarrassed. 'But I like them a lot. I couldn't, otherwise.'

'Same with my growing up. Liking is on the way to love.' She told him bits from her youth. The parties in the bush, the goings on in the scrub beyond the firelight, a house party where she'd been caught by her lover's parents, 'We were only fifteen. They literally pulled us apart. What a row. Why don't people leave children alone. You know, it was *coitus interruptus*. I still hunger for him.'

'What's that?'

'It is an interrupted intercourse. What a man does if he hasn't a condom – you pull out before ejaculating. We were a long way from that.

'I've never done that. I use condoms.'

'Do you use one with Ian?'

Tim froze. She knows! Silence.

'Tim, I'm sorry. I shouldn't pry, but I found *Vaseline* beside his bed and wondered.'

'It's difficult to talk about. Um. He's a brilliant musician. We met at rehearsals . . . Yes, it started here. We both wanted to. Then we slept together at a music weekend. It was great. Both of us were happy. When he was here, last time we needed to, um, each other.' He squirmed. 'I love him.'

'I see. So you use condoms with other boys?'

'Other boys? No, it's unnecessary. I meant to say I used them with a girl I met in Greece. It was great.'

Ah, boyish experimentation until he settles it, thought Janet. 'Do you mind Sophie is coming for a week so you'll have company while I'm away?'

'You know we're friends. Of course I don't mind.'

'You'll have to sort out sleeping arrangements with her. Will you or she sleep on the couch.'

'I don't mind. I'm sure she won't either.'

Janet lay still. The spar bubbled. The stars winked accusingly. The telephone rang. She splashed out leaving a trail of footprints to the house. She came to the door. 'It's for you, Tim.' He climbed out. The light spilling from inside threw the contours of his body into relief. Janet inwardly gasped, 'He's really very handsome.' Clutching a towel to his crotch he brushed past her. It was Fran. They talked and talked. Afterwards Tim snuggled happily into his duvet. He slept like a baby.

The next morning the house resounded to his bassoon practice. He always started on Fran's manuscript book with her warming-up exercises. Her voice was in her handwriting. It nagged. His lust grew. He couldn't help it. Lovingly he played scales and some of the twisted little pieces she had given him to overcome finger and breath problems. Then he took Fiona's slow tune and played it in all her variations until the house rang with its sad longing. He struggled to keep his emotions under control so as to be able to pitch and to finger it delicately. He was bursting by the time he finished. Janet saw the struggle in his face. ' Well played. Take a break, Tim. What about . .'

'I think I'll go for a ride.'

'Fine. Be back soon. I've a surprise expedition for you.'

Later Janet took him to a computer shop in the village, which had up-graded an old computer. 'This is for you.' she said.

'My own? Oh Janet. For keeps?' Happily he loaded it into the car and they trundled back to the house where he spent the rest of the day connecting all the cables, reading the inexplicable handbook and installing Janet's software. He played the games and found he could connect to the telephone and send Chris e-mails. He supplied a bassoon preamble to supper, reread *Twelfth Night* until Janet called, 'Spar time!'

He bounded outside to join her. 'How happy you are, when you're happy' she spluttered shaking her head from the splash. He excitedly rattled-on about his new toy. 'Gee, thanks.' flinging his arms about her. She put a hand gently on his taut smooth back to steady them both. Feeling his erection she gently pushed him away.

'I'm Sorry.'

'Don't be ashamed of desire my dear.' Janet said softly. 'It is a great compliment.'

He moved away.

'Let's try to be friends. I would feel uncomfortable if it were any other way.' she said gently. 'I know you are bursting, but I don't want that kind of relationship. I like you very much as my handsome clever pupil-friend. I'd like to keep it that way. I think we need that kind of friendship, don't you?'

He crouched in the water. 'Yes. I suppose so. I'm sorry. I can't help my feelings.'

'I understand perfectly. I love the way your feelings propel you. It's one of your endearing charms. You've nothing to apologise about. You have a beautiful body and a good-looking sex. Be proud. I feel OK with my body. I feel comfortable with you. No, I lie. I enjoy being naked with you. For then we talk about things usually kept hidden, things needing airing, particularly when growing-up and dealing with the unruly world. I think that's important.'

'Me too. But my feelings get in the way.'

'They won't if we accept them. Let's face our bodily excitement, being naked together. And agree it won't become a prelude to a sexual relationship. Then we can sport erections and enlarged nipples and enjoy the look of each other. What do you say?'

'Er, I'll try.'

'I know your hunger, I can read you. But find other outlets.'

Tim shifted shyly. 'Do you have someone else?'

'Yes, but it's not a regular relationship Do you?'

'I had a regular relationship.'

'You miss him/her. Which is it?'

'It's been both. At different times.' he whispered.

'Was it love?'

'Yes.' He slid deeper into the water, folded his arms on the wooden side, and dropped his head onto them.

She slid close to him and put a reassuring arm around his shoulders. 'Tim, oh Tim, I've upset you. I'm sorry.'

'You haven't, no.' he sighed. 'Talking about it makes me sad and happy; I've no one to talk to and I love being with you like this.'

'You feel the need to talk?'

'Yes, it helps a lot. It was great last night. I get so confused.'

She turned him round into her arms. 'Never mind about *that* just now. I'm glad it helped. I also enjoyed last night. Talk should be meaningful. Let's keep it that way. I need to talk too. You'll have to put up with my silly little secrets in return.'

'Do you think I'm gay?' he stammered.

'Why, do you think you are?'

'Maybe. I love being around boys. And I really need a woman. I'm such a mess.'

'Well, I don't know what you are Tim, but I like you just as you are.' She stood. 'Shall we shower? Who's first?'

'You go.' he said. She clambered out and paddled inside. Tim lay almost relieved. He rubbed his penis – enjoying the watery resistance – soon it unleashed white strands which floated around him. The far strands of stars twinkled acceptance.

The days were busy. Tim enjoyed exploring, cycling his old routes to the shops where he went for provisions. There was a small piece of untouched land. He liked the tall grass with an untidy clutch of scraggy trees guarding this unkempt spot. A nest clung to the top of one. Magpies fiercely dived on the boy attacking his neck. He waved his cap at them. They were defending their chicks. They ignored him when he dismounted and crouched in the grass pretending to be a stone. Nearby lay a muddy pool where Tim joined other children who were larking about or fishing for yabbies with meat tied to a string. Over the various holidays they'd got to know each other. Sometimes he joined them in games of football or hide-and-seek. Everyone felt free in that forgotten place. 'The magpies keep the wrinklies away.' became the club chant.

One windy evening Janet asked Tim whether he would tell her about his experiences with boys. 'When did you start?'

'I was fourteen.'

'With another boy?'

'No it was a man . . . Does that shock you?'

'Yes. I can't imagine how a boy could cope with the size. He must have hurt you.'

'No. He prepared me carefully. It was gentle. But I remember. It was very big. I was frightened. Couldn't stop it.'

'Why did you go with him, was it rape?'

'He touched me, then only wanting mattered. He held me and filled me up. I felt loved. He needed me. We came everywhere.'

'Was it important to feel filled?'

'Yes. And later to dominate his arse in return.'

'So you weren't only the passive partner?'

'No. It has never been that way. Chris says it's because we are the same, having equal rights. I realised with Jeff I had always been frightened. It's an uncontrollable power. It splits you and blows you up. It's a great sensation although it's scary.'

'Is it different with a girl?'

'Vaginas are succulent and alive. I love lying deep and feeling all the rippling sensations, and being able to come together. The arse has to be conquered, dominated, exploited. Most often you just kneel or lie inert, let him fuck until he's done. The best and the worst times is when I come with him. The pain cuts like a knife. Afterwards there's such deep love.'

Janet was suddenly clear how Tim and Chris were lovers. My God, all the time he studied here. And now Sophie's brother initiated at the same age. How does the pollution spread? There must be a network of boys with such leanings, or did everyone indulge? What a murky current runs beneath the seemingly naive surface of these teenagers, she grimaced. They look such nice boys. Pity help the girls.

Her silence prompted Tim. 'Have you had anal sex?'

'Not really. I tried it once and found it uncomfortable and a bit distasteful.'

'Fran and I do it. It's great. I've stopped seeing anything as dirty. But I am ashamed afterwards, sometimes.'

Janet shivered with the audacity of the boy. His sex drive is strong. He drives himself hard in every department. No wonder sometimes he looks washed out, she thought. She asked as neutrally as she could, 'Do Fran and you love one another?'

'Yes, we do.' He was stern, 'She saved me. Just like Chris. You wouldn't believe what a mess I get into.'

'So, sex is a way of' (she paused) 'understanding, a therapy?'

'Yes, I suppose you could say that. I'd say sex drains me of all the shit people pour into me, and allows me to share what needs changing so I can grow up. You see, without it I would have crashed again. Using drink and drugs was a pretence all was well, but really, I had no life and no confidence. No one believed in me not even myself. Could you do therapy and change me the way Chris did? I don't think so. It's much more than therapy. It's both of us sharing the same boat, the same mess, hatred, arseholes, terror, helplessness, laughter, life. Then you help each other out of the cess pool and crawl onto dry land – I call it love.'

'And Fran?'

Tim flushed. 'She picked me up and gave me herself and it contained beauty and womanhood, and dancing, and music, all the sounds of the universe, all the dreams hidden from me. She gave me all the other people I contain but denied. And a bunch of real people who do not compete but share and make music and love and beauty – all that matters to me now.'

'What you seem to be saying is sex is the vehicle connecting you. It is the basis of being with others who then help you.'

'That's part of it. Sex is also getting the me out. Sorry to be crude, but I shoot-off into the space beyond, in the arse or the vagina, the mouth, tummy, the floor. It's me shot out, the loss a strengthening.'

Janet was lost. It made no sense. It sounded depraved: adults using a boy for sex while pretending to help him. She wavered, 'Does Nina know all this?'

'Most of it, I think. Try to understand, Nina trusts me. She trusts Chris and I think Fran. She thinks it will work out in the end. That's why I'm there. Do you think I'll fail? and if so, why am I here?'

'I don't know! I thought I could help.'

Tim knew anguish and wiped his fingers under her eyes to collect her tears. 'Don't send me away. You help a lot. You have, since the beginning. Don't be hypocritical, I know about you and Chris – I know you love him. That's why I'm here, isn't it?' She wept, her head spun. She felt an ague seeping into her heart. Her stable world was slipping. Chris's love had destroyed her and Tim. Suddenly nothing seemed possible. She had so carefully prepared her life and now it was out of control. Words and resolve lost.

Tim touched her. 'Janet, we have agreed how to live here. We promised each other. True promises. These are my secrets. I have never told them to anyone. Please take them. It's all I have. You said you didn't care who I was. Perhaps you do?'

They sat still and silent. The wind scuffed the surface of the water and whispered in the trees. 'Now you must tell me your secrets.' he said. 'You'll feel much better.'

'Oh dear, no more now. I'll shower.' Janet stiffly stepped out onto the chilly paving, 'Tim, you're right to chide me. I did loose faith for a moment. But I don't care what you are labelled. I will love you in my own peculiar way because I do care for you and for Chris. You are a sort of extension of him in many ways. But I won't try to compete. You're right about competition. You'll always be welcome here, with whomever you bring. I don't know what your relationship is with Sophie, but please don't hurt her. She is another precious person.'

What's this to do with Sophie? he thought. 'Sophie is my best friend. Why should I hurt her?' Silence, and the lick of the wind. 'Oh, you mean sex. Well, she doesn't want sex with me. I know that. It's OK. She's just a girl. I've had enough chances, but of course I wouldn't hurt her. That's obscene. So, you really think I'm only a fucking machine.'

She slapped his face. 'How dare you air your filthy values here.'

'They're your filthy values. Leave me to love in my own way. It's just as good as yours At least I don't lecture one thing and act another.'

Janet staggered against the wall shaking, weeping anger and confusion. This kid doesn't understand, she thought.

Remorsefully he came over. He hated fighting. It was the nightmare of his home before he escaped it. 'Janet, I'm sorry. I know you care.' He took her off the wall, turning her to face him, his strong young arms pulling her into an embrace engulfing her, to which she opened to him, longing for peace. Wildly he held her.

'No, Tim, no,' trying to pull away, trying to cling. 'What a fool I've been. Oh Tim, forgive me.' She struggled. 'You promised.'

He fell back and let her go. He stood fully aroused, and masturbated. Fluid spattered the wall. He was angry. But he respected her determination. There was a line. She had a right to draw it and to keep him on one side. The conflicting messages which she (and he) gave was a sort of "Persephone's Bridge"; he vaguely saw this as their struggle to find a place on the footway. Sex would get us there quicker, he thought. But she's like Soph. They don't want to play dangerous games.

When he went inside, Janet had shut the door to her bedroom and gone to bed. He showered, soaped himself and exuberantly came. Curled like a foetus under his duvet he heavily slept.

They woke later than usual, both bleary eyed. Janet fumblingly made a pot of tea.

'Is there time for my practice?'

'Of course. You look sleepy; why not take a spar first?' Tim nodded. Janet threw him a towel and he wandered out onto the terrace blinded by the light. She watched as he pulled the stiff cover off, pulled off his XXL tee shirt, he wore nothing else in bed, and stepped into the spar. Sunlight glowed on his shoulders and struck down his back highlighting its contours, sculpting the swell of his pert bottom. She murmured, 'What beauty. So at odds with his ferocious appetite: the smiling face of the sea masking monstrous things below. I need a reinforced diving suit.'

Time drifted. They decided on brunch. Janet said calmly, 'I'm sorry, Tim. I shouldn't have pushed you to tell me so much I couldn't handle. We blundered about upsetting each other. Please forgive me.'

'It depends on how equal we are. Now it's your turn to tell me. Then we're square.'

'It's not like same sex. Life involves balance not uniformity. I don't feel the need, and I don't think it helpful for you to be told.'

'I've a right to know.'

'Not if I don't want to tell.' She swam in his grey eyes. 'I am having an affair with a married man, the father of a pupil. You see, we both break the rules.'

Tim's eyes danced. 'I can go for a very long ride on my bike if you want him here.' But he was hurt she didn't seem to trust him.

Later, Janet left a note on his bed,

Dear Tim,
John Donne says it better than me:

PLATONIC LOVE *

I have done one braver thing
than all the Heroes did,
and yet a braver thence doth spring,
which is, to keep that hid. . . . . .

So, if I now should utter this,
others [because no more
such stuff to work upon, there is]
would love but as before.

But he who loveliness within
hath found, all outward loathes,
for he who colour loves, and skin,
loves but their oldest clothes.

If, as I have, you also do
Virtue attired in woman see
and dare love that, and say so too,
and forget the He and She;

---

*   See notes at end.

and if this love, though placed so,
from profane men you hide,
which will no faith on this bestow,
or, if they do, deride:

then you have done a braver thing
than all the Heroes did,
and a braver thence will spring,
which is, to keep that hid!

Tim murmured. 'It's as shifty as *Twelfth Night*. Is he saying it doesn't matter how you love or behave whether like a man or a woman (the He and She apple)? Should you keep this secret, why is only the woman clad in virtue?'

Janet gently shook her head. 'I think it explains our difficulties. Donne is saying there are two ways to love. One is carnal, of the flesh, what is seen, our "oldest clothes", the other is to see qualities, invisibles, within the person one loves, "Her/his virtue"; that there are two ways of declaring one's love, firstly by proclaiming it, secondly by feeling yet keeping it to one's self. Donne suggests this is "a braver" way to love. He also says that "virtues" are to be found in men and women "forget the He and She". Look beyond the obvious, the skin, clothes, rank, other outward characteristics.'

Tim nodded. 'But Donne seems to believe it is either "oldest clothes" *or* "virtues". The old cliche, either/or, which Persephone challenges. I think love is made up of both inner and outer.'

Janet smiled. 'Maybe Donne is saying to love a person for his qualities, and be silent about this, is superior, a braver way.'

Tim blazed. 'I think to love a person for his qualities and to know him carnally and be quiet is even braver.'

'I think you and John Donne are right. It is brave to love a person for their "virtues" regardless of whether they are male or female (I think that's what you are admitting to). You seem to love Ian first for his qualities; well, the way you told me about your affair. That you have kept your carnal experiences so private is both a sort of bravery – I do agree – and a sad reflection of the "profane" world which cannot see things as richly or as impassively as Donne. Would you agree you have loved in order to satisfy some deep need; that you took love wherever you found it, responding to your need and, I suppose, your lover's needs; that you have done this regardless of the sexual nature of the relationship?'

'I'm not sure. I was so desperate for Chris, and for Fran, firstly in a sexual way, then other needs grew. That's why I think I must be gay.'

'My dear, I think you trouble me because you demonstrate we all need both male and female: in friendship, sex, in partnerships of a variety of ages. It's troublesome because it challenges much I have tried to live by, both personally and professionally. It disturbs me that perhaps I want you as much as you show need for me, which I keep pushing away. But I suspect it is your "oldest clothes" of youth and energetic beauty I hunger for. It's not that you don't have virtues, rather, yours don't particularly fire me. Do you know what I mean?'

Tim slowly nodded. 'I need your love,' he whispered. 'That's why I lunge at you. It is thoughtless.'

'I love you the more for lunging. No Tim, it's just, our love better fits John Donne's description of a less proclaimed, more hidden, a platonic love. I have no doubt it is both brave and true. I hope it will serve us both.' She held him. They calmed. 'If only it was as clear and simple as Donne explains.' She knew it was difficult for her to unburden, how courageous Tim had been telling her so much. It was the risky way he led his life. It was probably Chris's fault. His influence had seeped into them both. I'm becoming far too rash, she thought. 'Tell me, Tim, do you think I'm a rash person?'

'You? Rash? You control everything.'

Janet was silent. Tim was right. Her problem with him was deeper than her surprise at his secret depraved life. It lay in the distance between them. Between her control and his abandon. He had been right (again), Chris was their link. Her love for him had spurred her to helping, when normally she would have kept well away.

'Do I control you?' she asked.

'Yes, but I don't mind. I know you think I'm wild, and sometimes it feels cruel. But I am very happy here and I need you to calm me. I know you care. You must have worried about me and Ian all this time and never punished me. I feel you probably um, love me.'

She nodded. Blushed. 'Yes, it is love, and gratitude. I feel alive with you. If it stems from the depravity of our sharing, then I must alter my values. For you evoke happiness.'

Her trip to the city was drawing near. She was apprehensive about Sophie's visit. Making a strange elliptical balance, she asked Tim to take his "long bike ride" one afternoon so she could enjoy her lover. She took her pleasure expecting the two children would take theirs during her absence, showing Tim a way out of his gay impasse, and Sophie into the adult world.

Sophie came gladly. Glad to be somewhere new. Glad to see Tim. She preferred term time when they swam, cycled and studied together. Life was empty without him in ways she could not articulate. Having nothing to preoccupy her, the freedom of holidays became devalued, Jeff had accused her of "being a pain".

Janet organised an unexacting roster of house duties, allowing lots of time for outings to the yabbie pond. Its grassy banks encouraged settling together, despite the dive-bombing magpies. Daily they rode to the shops for provisions, hanging out in the Milk Bar with the local teenagers. Tim showed Sophie his new computer – almost as good as hers – on which they played and surfed happily. Or they would lie out in the spar, demurely in togs, tickled by bubbles and nonsense. Mornings would start with Sophie and Janet having a cuppa listening to Tim's extraordinary bassoon practice.

Janet found it difficult to fathom the girl; she clearly enjoyed Tim's company, was interested in his life. But there was a settled silence about how she really felt; little indication of a sexual interest Janet had expected, an unspoken probity about their relationship (could Janet call it mature?) which intrigued her. Now it's up to them, she decided, leaving a packet of condoms near Tim's toothbrush.

She told them she'd be gone for two days and would telephone from the conference. The children gleefully waved her off.

Then, the house became their own play place. Filled with food-snacks, computer goings-on, all night films and naked dips in the spar. Each fell into separate beds just before dawn and slept until midday.

After breakfasting they cycled to the Milk Bar but, irritated by the banality of the chatter, returned unsettled to the house. The computer didn't hold them long. Restlessly they made cool drinks before agreeing to take a spar. They padded out to the pool, undressed (a trifle awkwardly in daylight), threw their towels away and clambered in, sinking deep into the misting water.

As usual they sat opposite each other, the flow of talk dried-up. Tim began splashing Sophie. Under his water barrage she fell off the seat into the middle and skittered into Tim's open legs, grabbed his waist. He too slipped. They struggled upright. Sprawled side by side, gasping, they clasped each other, invaded by excitement.

Sophie felt Tim's desire. He shyly took her hand and placed it on his erection. She felt it swell when she moved. He sighed with pleasure and put his arms around her, turned and kissed her hungrily. Her mouth opened. He plunged his tongue into her opened, wordless 'yes'.

Soon he was floating over her as she lay seeking lips and the weight of his torso; their legs locked in embrace, his hands holding either side of her head, hers clasping his straining neck. Everything was bubbling as the day faded.

'Will you? Touch me there again!'

She folded a hand around his sex. He pushed through it thrilling with urgency. 'Oh, Soph I'm coming. Oh . . . Oh, yes. Oh Soph.' He collapsed.

'Is that better?' she whispered kissing his neck over and over again. 'You look beautiful, coming, I've never seen it before.'

'Don't you mind?'

She clambered up to squat, her bottom on his hips, her knees gripping his ribs. 'Why should I mind? I loved how the power whooshed out of you. It got so stiff. You really strained. Was it good?'

'Mm. . . It was . . . Soph.'

'You needed it.'

'Yes. I need it.'

Sophie took a deep breath. 'Do you miss Fran?' She watched the struggle in his face.

'Yes.' He whispered.

'Will I do?'

'Yes. You? No. Are you sure? I'm a terrible mess.'

'So am I.' She ran a tentative finger along his eyebrow arches and into his wet hairline; leaning over, her breasts nudged his chest.

'Soph, I'm no good for you.'

'How do you know?'

He shook his head, hunger battling caution. The dark shapes of trees nodded in the dying light. 'Let's go in, then.' he said softly. He stared as she stood up water streaming down her comely body and through the neat mysterious triangle of pubic hair, the focus of her thighs, and he trembled with embarrassed admiration that she could want him. She was not a girl; he must be blind, but when had she changed?

She set the program. 'Shall we eat first?'

Later, in the bedroom Sophie gently undressed Tim. He stood warm, beautiful and aroused before her. Then he expertly peeled off her clothes. Breathing audibly they excitedly inspected one another.

They lay down and tentatively kissed. For a long time, shyly amazed, they teased and explored, until some of Tim's seed bubbled onto Sophie's face. Then Tim skillfully kissed her breasts, kneading her nipples so she cried pure pleasure. He began kissing her stomach and moved down into her thighs. The fragrance of her vagina thrilled him. He ran an exploratory tongue down its neat fleshy lips through its protective folds seeking her clitoris. He licked its taut length.

Sophie moaned. Her body shook. Gusted by waves of orgasm she lifted her hips. So that's what it is all about, she realised. She fell back, recovering in a long luxurious moment, to ruffle Tim's hair and pull him pleadingly to kiss her again until their faces were running with saliva. Tim held her, open under him nearly bursting. He reached under the pillow for a condom and fumbling rolled it on.

He lay between her thighs searched for her with a few gentle hip movements until he felt her pushing the sheath back. His bursting glans slipped in. He began shallow thrusting, easing into her a little more deeply each time. She moaned and shivered.

Tim realised Sophie was trying to suck him in deeper while at the same time trying to escape. He floundered in contradiction.

Tim sweated, struggling to come; he had played too long, blunting his sensitivity and drive. He was panting. Then his gasps grew into a cry of victory as he thrust to finish. He sighed contentedly, rolled over and fell fast asleep heedless of the murmur of awakening birds.

Spasms wracked Sophie. She lay gasping and crying with the magnificence of the pain throbbing in her as deeper orgasm flooded her. Almost blindly she turned gingerly onto her stomach nursing painful ecstasy. She was amazed by the power of his passion – it was irresistible – and she held a sense of infinite capacity, both to hold him and to hold the wonderful enormity of herself. She was Mother Earth, Eve, a goddess called Sophie. 'I heard childbirth was painful. It must start like this,' she mused. She gradually floated away on diminishing pleasures into an enriching sleep.

Janet found them on her return. She quietly shut their door. She sat pensively drinking tea at the kitchen table. The garden looked dry. She needed to turn on the hose. She felt dry also. Sophie stood at the door, shy, embarrassed, 'Hello, um could I have a *Tampax*? My period's started.'

'Is it due now?'

'No. Not for two weeks.'

'Are you bleeding at the moment?

Sophie fingered her vagina. 'I'm not sure.'

'Let's go to the bathroom. I keep them in the cupboard.'

Sophie took the sop and pushed it into herself. The two went back down the hall towards the kitchen just as Tim emerged from the bedroom holding a bloodied sheet and looking stricken. He stood and gazed foolishly at the two women. The guilt of his night's debauchery proclaimed by Sophie's blood.

Janet smiled. 'My dears, let's all have a cuppa.' Then she talked them through virginity. Both were relieved. Each vowed if they were to start regular lovemaking they would visit Doctor MacKay to discuss pill-contraception. 'Boys don't always have a condom handy, and anyway, condoms are not that reliable.' counselled Janet.

Tim helped Sophie straighten the bedroom. He was abashed. 'I didn't know either. And I'll leave you to heal.'

'Don't worry Tim. I'm glad it was you. I wanted you from the first . . . all this time. It was the best night of my whole life.'

She hugged him wildly and kissed his frown away. 'I know how to help you until then.' She patted his shorts. He displayed his erection. She undid fly-buttons and slipped clothing down his firm slim legs. Nestling into his opened thighs she swallowed his penis. He showed her how to finger his balls and explore the firm tube leading to his anus. 'Is that where boys go?' she whispered without rancour.

How does she know? My secrets are not very secure. Tim thought. Does every one know? Does she know about me and her parents? But the pleasure she evoked swept all such thoughts away.

'It's so smooth. No wonder babies are soft.' she whispered.

'You don't have to swallow it. Here's a tissue.'

'I have. I like it, it tastes of salty almonds.' She rose up to his mouth to kiss his smile.

'Soph, don't you think it's vile, doing this?'

'Why should I? Just because everyone says I'm a slut, doesn't make me one, or you a sex maniac. I love feeling your excitement and the power when you shoot. I'd rather have you inside. But I can wait.' She was silent for a moment. 'I never knew how fantastic our bodies are. I've been sleeping all these years and only now you've woken me up. My body tells me what we do is all right. Maybe pain is not. But you had to break into me. If what we do feels good, then it is good. Don't you agree?'

Tim was flabbergasted. He had lived with guilty pleasure for so long. 'What about boys, or girls, doing it together?'

'If they're happy, why not? Did you feel it was bad when you did those things?'

He was embarrassed. 'Um, No.'

'Well, there you are.'

He needed her gladly during her last days. She eased his want, adoring the contact and the lessons she took from his body. Time passed in a dream. He licked her clitoris into orgasm in return for his release. Often they had to stifle their cries. She gloried in every carnal activity culminating in an undisturbed afternoon of love-making in the spar and afterwards on their (as it had become) bed under which Janet later discovered several bloodless condoms oozing quantities of his seed in ugly proclamation of the joyful journey through the last "shadow-line" of childhood.

Content filled the house. Janet was awed by their tenderness. Guilty as well. 'Did I bring them together? Would Nina approve? What on earth would the Deans say? Well it's hardly their business, now,' she mused.

Sophie stayed several days longer than planned. On her return home she seemed dazed, and proprietarily confronted by Jeff:

'You and Tim are fucking, aren't you?' Absently she almost nodded.

'I knew it.' His voice suddenly rose and broke.

What a funny tough, tender little boy he is, she thought. Then she slipped away to telephone the CD shop to inquire whether they had any bassoon disks, 'I must have one for a friend, right now.'

2:

THE SUMMER TERM BEGAN. Homework, even lessons, were challenged by thoughts of swimming, picnics and other outdoor pleasures. Sophie and Tim mixed gardening and swimming with sexual exploration. Tim was demanding, Sophie compliant, but when aroused charmed him. Knowing they were to meet calmed them.

Tim irregularly made love with Fran, now in easy familiar ways. He and Ian coupled occasionally. Sex was an extension of music making.

Sophie half-knew of Tim's other liaisons seeing them as reflecting her inability to satisfy him. So patiently she studied him, trying to respond more fully to his needs. Tim's habit (defence) of silence over feelings lay between the two so the hell of his past sometimes haunted them.

One evening Nina called out to him, 'Tim, a visitor for you.'

Jeff's puffy ashen face shocked him. 'Hi, Jeff. Come to my room. What's wrong?'

Without a word Jeff followed, and stood stiffly immobile just inside the door, clutching a rucksack to his chest as if holding a corpse. 'I've left home. Can I stay with you, until . . .'

Tim drew him down onto the bed. 'What's happened, Jeff?'

'I had a row with Dad. I'll never never go back. Ever.'

Tim trembled at the replay of his own flight. He pulled the boy onto his lap and bent over him protectively while Jeff shook. This lovely boy, so cheeky, so lively who gamboled through his life, was disintegrating. Their secrets, naked swimming, sex, larking about, their growing-up, all howled in derision. Who was crying in whose lap? He? Chris? This little-brother? The love bond was the same for them all, the needs too. Their world was the same jungle. The despair was his. Unthinkingly he rocked to and fro to still the weeping boy. 'Of course you can stay here. Look, there's a spare bed here for you. Nina will understand, OK? Jeff, this is terrible, You must tell me everything.'

Jeff looked gratefully up into Tim's lustrous grey eyes and hesitantly said. 'I was home with Martin. No one was there, so we had a joint and took our clothes off and were fooling around and wanted to fuck, so we did it on my bed. I was on my back – have you done it that way? You too – and Martin was up me. In the middle of it all, Dad came in. He went berserk. He ripped Martin off me and thrashed him into the corner. Then he really beat me. He was screaming. I shat everywhere. He said I had to go to a borstal home where boys with problems were sorted-out. He said I would be there for as long as it took (probably forever). He said sex and drugs were killers, and he knew I did both. He locked me in my room and dragged Martin home. He said he was going to the police and we were in real trouble. So I packed my things and escaped through a window and down the tree. I'll never go back, Tim. Never.'

Jeff sat up frightened. Tim began to quiver and cried, 'Oh, no. Jeff. You can't leave home. It's the end, and a borstal won't solve the problem. I know. I've been there.' He spoke about his own past. Drugged despair, the hospital treatment, caged by hopelessness, leaving home. He skipped over his love affair but described how Chris and Nina had helped him to make a new start even against his own expectations. 'You know Jeff, what an incredible friend you are, also Sophie. Jeff, you are my family. Listen, it's hard at home but that's OK, nowhere is perfect. We must stay together. Would you go back if Soph and I were there, like before, and if your parents gave you space for yourself?'

'No. It's impossible.'

'But if they promised and if we were there with you, could you agree to go back? Would you give it a go, for a short time?'

'Only for a short time. Only if.'

Tim melted. He hugged the taut body, kissing the small, mouth into silent acceptance. They lay, settling.

Then they showered, Tim cleaned him up and bathed his

bruised face. The orphans clung together. Jeff crawled into Tim's bed and hid there while Tim went upstairs to speak to Nina .

'Timothy, I do not want you hurt in this quarrel.'

'I'll be all right, Nina. Really. I'll leave if it doesn't work out.' He telephoned Sophie and told her to cycle over at once and bring clothes and school books. She arrived breathless shortly afterwards. Tim told her she would be staying for several days, took her down-stairs to watch over her brother, then cycled to the Deans' house.

'Where are the children?' asked Mrs Dean.

'They're not coming home until you sort Jeff out.' Tim said.

'Why, what's happened?'

Tim was telling her about the fracas between Jeff and his father when Mr Dean stormed in. His fury quelled them. In a lull, sweating with anxiety, Tim spoke up. 'You're going on about sex as if it's a criminal offense. It may be when adults interfere with children, as you have. If you don't agree a way of having your children back, I'll go to the police and tell them everything, as you say you are going to.' He rallied his courage. 'Feelings often push us into sex – what happened between you and me. Kids need sex as much as you, and only learn it with each other until we grow up and are allowed to pair-off. Your problem is you never finished exploring. That's why you're so hung-up, that's why you make sexual innuendos and want to fool about with boys like me.'

The Deans trembled.

Tim shakily continued. 'I know all of you want to be together. I want this too. Jeff is the little brother I never had and Sophie is . . . a sort of sister who shares so much of my life. You are the parents I dreamed of, I feel like your son.' Then he cried. 'I love you all so much. Don't you see? I lost my parents and my home, and myself. I can't lose you again.' He fell on Mrs Dean's lap.

'Oh, my dearest dearest Tim,' cried Mrs Dean. 'I don't want to lose any of you. You are all I have. There's nothing else.' Shakily she put out a bangled hand saying brokenly, 'Len, we must try.'

Mr Dean saw the abyss of a broken home and shuddered. 'Tim, I want the kids back. I'm sorry . . . I love you in good and in bad ways. Sorry? It's just that. He is. You all are. What can we do?'

Unsteadily Tim began. 'Nina has a rule if a door is shut it probably means Keep Out, so we can share and live separately.

Would you try that? Soph and Jeff need to have their own space as well as needing to share. You do too.'

The parents nodded.

'Some of their friends will be good, some bad; but we can't say which. They must be allowed to find out for themselves. I think it would be better to be more open about friendship, to encourage them to bring their friends here. What's happening out there (he pointed beyond the house) is sick. Kids will behave much better at home, even if they're doing sex. Jeff has got a bit lost. I'll have a word with him about drugs and get it sorted. But you'll have to allow him the friends he chooses. Maybe he'll turn out to be gay. But he'll still be bouncy, cheeky Jeff; surely that's what really counts?'

The parents brokenly agreed.

'Better to make mistakes now, than illegal ones later. They're great kids. I'd trust them if I were you. They need you too.' Sobbing overwhelmed him. He had dared everything. The storm would burn him to cinders; a storm more lethal than the Greek one which had threatened Chris's boat. His hands, and more, would be in ribbons.

Mrs Dean cradled him on her lap. 'Len, help me.'

Mr Dean gingerly put his arms around them both. 'I'll do whatever you think best, my dear.'

Mrs Dean looked gratefully at him. 'Let's try the door thing. And the trust. And having friends over. I like that.' She sniffed. 'And fill the house with young people like Sophie and Jeff and Tim. Maybe we can learn from them and help them with their messes and their successes.'

He nodded, growing into the Big Chief, 'Provided,' he growled menacingly. (They both looked at him in surprise). 'Provided Tim promises to stay in the family.'

Such joy radiated from the boy's face both parents felt blessed and terrified. Was such beauty allowed them, was their love forgiven, nay reciprocated? Mr Dean almost whispered. 'Is it possible from nothing, such riches can be found?' Tim remembered Mrs Brandt: 'When you give-up everything, much more returns.'

Mrs Dean nodded. 'It'll not be easy. But I hope we'll manage; all of us Tim.' She leant over and kissed her husband. 'Now, what about a cup of tea?'

Over tea they accepted the children would stay with Nina for the next school days, and during the weekend they'd move back.

'Let's have a swim barbecue.' said Mr Dean.

'Yes, and I'll make my salads and sweets.' caroled Mrs Dean.

'Just like the old days.' said Tim.

Mrs Dean gave Tim a bag of Jeff's clothes and treasures. 'To tide him over until Saturday.' She kissed him profusely. He left wheeling Jeff's laden bike promising, 'I'll get them to ring you.'

Nina put Sophie in the spare room and gave Jeff clean sheets for the other bed in Tim's room. She was relieved Tim seemed to have sorted matters out with the Deans and a few days cooling-off had been agreed. Sophie promised to help Maria cope with the extra work. Jeff wanted to help Tim around the house. 'We're a good team.' he chirped over dinner. 'You'll see.'

Well after lights out Jeff crept into Tim's bed and snuggled his erection against the beauty Tim sported. 'Can we do it, please.' he whispered. Jeff lay back and presented his arse to the beautiful big cock. Although it hurt a bit he gloried in being stretched and filled. Soon Tim stiffened and pinned him to the bed. Then Jeff finished. He wallowed in power; its sweet discomfort stayed him the following day.

They slept sprawled on the bed, separating in the morning before collecting Sophie to stumble down the cliff path to swim in the deserted sea, all shyly abandoning clothes. The free, restless sea repaired them.

Then, Jeff faced Doctor MacKay's stern lecture about drugs. He accepted a strict regime of swims and jogging, a body-building diet, and contritely promised to keep to it. Tim had offered to pace him and to help him avoid trouble. He was happy Tim was part of the cure.

Thus, Jeff re-entered his volcanic life, reeling through the complexities of the school day. He looked forward to returning to the quiet dignity of Nina's house with his sister and Tim, where he felt accepted, helping Tim with his tasks and sharing house chores so Nina was not burdened. The glories of nightly intimacy shimmered by day. Nina saw it as hero worship and approvingly thought, Good. Tim is a decent hero for this frivolous youngster.

The three children swam early every morning. The beach was empty. The boys began their training session by running up the steep cliff path and then jogging around the block before returning to shower and breakfast. Tim practised while the others cleared away. Then they cycled to school. Some afternoons they followed the routine in reverse, finishing with swimming when Sophie joined them. Eventually, when Jeff and Sophie returned home, Tim would practise and then cycle over to their house to swim and jog and breakfast before setting off for school.

Sophie had withdrawn a trifle because she respected Jeff's need to bond with Tim, an escape from the fracas with his father. She was disturbed by the extreme ways men coped with each other, by either loving or hating. She was curious, how had Tim managed to reunite them all and in far more comfortable ways than had existed earlier? She wondered if Tim's sexual power existed in the social world as another form of power. Did each aspect grow from and support the other? Although she missed intimacy, she was close enough to catch some of his intensity. Comfortably she waited, as she had always done.

The children seemed the same but were changing. Uneasily life returned to its equilibrium. The unease grew from the duality of considering one's own needs in tandem with another's, in negotiating a balance, so everyone could live. The Brandt maxim held for Mr and Mrs Dean. For in giving-up so much for the children, they stumbled upon greater riches in sharing their lives, finding a line separating them, beyond which lay remarkable freedom. ("You have done a braver thing," John Donne put it so well).

Doctor MacKay's rigorous training sessions bore unexpected fruit. They became so fit they were picked for the Schools' Annual District Sports Day. Both starred. Tim coming second in both the mile and half-mile races, and Jeff running a glorious first in the five hundred meters. The general admiration buoyed them. Joy at home covered the scars of the row. Happiness prevailed.

3:

TIM WENT TO A PARTY one evening in a house further along the coast. The parents had gone out leaving it to the teenagers. Music boomed through darkened rooms. Junk food was piled on tables and sideboards. There were crates of beer and spirits. By the time Tim arrived everyone was wildly dancing. Because of his promise about not drinking in public he insisted on fruit juice. He was entertained by a group of girls until Mandy took over (it was her house). Teasingly she talked and then incoherently suggested dancing. She provocatively rubbed up against him snuggling provocatively into his body, holding the firm cheeks of his bottom, locked to him, brushing his lips with her bitter tasting pout until he was aroused. In the dusky corners throughout the house couples were entwined. In Mandy's bedroom they disturbed a couple making love.

Mandy dragged Tim into the master bedroom. She pulled down his trousers and lunged at his swollen penis. Hurriedly they stripped. He fell plunging into her. She gasped. As his climax approached he felt her shiver violently. He pulled out, ejaculated on her body and collapsed.

'Great pull-out, you're better than most. Hey, it's every-where. You needn't've, I'm on Mum's pills. She hasn't noticed I refill with Aspirins. That was lovely. We all thought you were gay.' breathed Mandy drunkenly. 'Wait until I tell the girls. We're your fan club, you know.'

Tim was disturbed. Sex was simply a display to Mandy, something to proclaim (which she did for weeks afterwards). He was a fashionable dress she'd donned. He felt crushed reduced to an object. Whereas he used sex as a way of expressing himself albeit wordlessly, receiving vital messages in return, Mandy made it insignificant. It was like his drugged couplings, fantastic at the time but of no meaning later.

But the word of his exploit got out, the awesome boy had a fabulous cock. Stung by Sophie's terrible anger, he was unable to tell her how much her friendship meant or how beautiful, clean and real their love-making was, how polluted he'd become in Mandy's arms. He retreated in frustrated despair to Ian and Jeff or his pulsing hand.

One night Tim traipsed into the village to see a film about the Argonauts. He just missed a bus. It was an hour until the next one. He loitered at the bus shelter. A car drew up. 'Do you want a lift, Son?' Gratefully he clambered aboard. There were three men in the car. They offered Tim some cookies and drove into a service station spending an unconscionable time on the car. When the car set off again Tim had become strangely disconnected.

Suddenly the man beside him pushed him flat onto the seat and held him down. The car speeded up, arriving somewhere Tim couldn't see, and drove into a large shed where he was bundled towards an iron framed bed. The three men gagged him and stripped him naked. Tim struggled and fought viciously as the three, gasping with exertion and excitement, tied him akimbo to the end frame of the bed, folding him face down onto the smelly mattress to present his bottom for their use. Tim already had no doubt what they intended, drugged though he knew he was. He twisted and strained nearly overturning the structure. Two of the men had to steady it while the third greased Tim's anus and rudely pushed at him. Tim fought with all his might, groaning and rolling, keeping his anus tightly shut.

'Here's a untamed beauty. Give us t'cone, Stan.' rasped one.

He forced it into Tim, stretching him until fingers held him open and a cruelly large penis drove into him. His gag was soaked with spit, tears and his bloody nose which coursed down the boy's face as the men tore at him. Seed and shit and blood oozed from him.

'Your turn, Stan. You get his period.'

The second man was bigger. He numbed Tim's rear. The jerking rhythm cruelly heaved the boy hard onto the iron frame.

'Where's the vibrator, Jack?' someone asked. It was placed between his shivering legs which shivered more until Tim vaguely sensed he'd ejaculated into someone's mouth. His arse throbbed painfully as the third man began. The vibrator was pushed in with a penis shivering with orgasm.

'Come on Alf, don't lick the blood. Time to go.' someone growled. Tim was nearly unconscious. They dressed him, bundled him into the car, dumped him at the bus stop and disappeared swiftly into the night.

A patrol car picked him up and took him to the Police Station where they pieced together the story. A police doctor examined him, took swabs from his anus and pushed some pills into his retching throat. Did he want to ring home?

He telephoned Sophie. It was 2AM. Mr Dean angrily got his sleepy daughter to deal with 'one of your bloody young friends. Never again.' From the silence came a slight croak, It's me, Tim . . .' She gasped, 'Tim?' Beyond himself, he handed the phone to a policewoman who reported the boy's mishap. '. . . So, will you come and pick him up?'

Sophie howling like one possessed smashed her fists into the wall until it seemed the house would collapse. Mr Dean managed to get enough details. Jeff, with wide frightened eyes, pulled everything off the other bed in his room strewing debris everywhere. Mrs Dean shakily prepared it. Together they waited downstairs Jeff fearfully clung to his mother, threatened by shadows everywhere.

Mr Dean had pulled on some clothes and, shadowed by an insistent daughter, raced through dark deserted streets down, down, along the coast road and up the short rising crescent to the police station.

They gasped at the crazed dishevelled boy and gingerly lugged him to the car, drove fearfully home and carried him indoors.

'They said we should wash him and put him to bed.' Father croaked. 'Do you want a shower?' Tim blindly nodded.

Sophie found hidden strength and undressed him (to her father's astonishment) and, pulling off her outer clothes, held him under the warm shower and washed his damaged body, weeping over every welt. The dried blood and shit in his thighs frightened her so much she cried, 'Daddy, help me.'

Mr Dean was equally apalled. They gently sponged him fearful about his anus pouting as if pulled from inside.

'They said their pills would help but he must see a doctor in the morning.' Mr Dean stammered.

They washed his hair in fragrant lotion, scraped the mess out of his crotch and gently bathed his bloated face, then lovingly dried him, covered him in her biggest tee shirt and ferried him to the bed in Jeff's room.

Mrs Dean held him tenderly as he sipped a mug of hot milk and honey (which she knew he savoured). Jeff gave him his favourite cuddly toy he still secretly hugged in bed. They tucked

Tim up. Warm, safe and cleansed. A troubled sleep fell upon the household.

Doctor MacKay, called early in the morning, paled at Tim's condition. He sent everyone out of the room and examined the boy brimming with a slow-burning anger against the thugs who had defiled such beauteous youth. Then to everyone's surprise he asked Sophie to join him. (He'd earlier been consulted by the bashful pair about their love life). 'Sophie my dear, Tim's damaged anus needs nursing care.'

'Of course I'll do it.'

The Doctor showed her how to coat her finger in a generous quantity of ointment, insert it into Tim's bottom and coat all the orifice in healing anti-biotic. 'Twice a day, or after defecating. Until the swelling goes down.' he coached. His eyes twinkled, 'For this penetration you'll not need a contraceptive. But as I've said before, "wash afterwards", at least, your hands.' The two wanly smiled.

He was a wise old bird; he saw a healing power as effective in their smiles as anything he proffered. 'I will want to take a blood sample tomorrow, when the lab opens. Come to my rooms first thing in the morning. And, when you return to Nina's, I would urge you to get down to the sea. It will help the healing. Stay put today. Moving about will be very uncomfortable for a while.'

Tim had two visitors that day. A rakish policeman called with 'his Statement, which needs signature.' Mr Dean insisted it wait. 'We'll get it back to you in the morning,' he promised. But he decided to read it.

The cold, precise, officialise descriptions made him retch. He vomited over the lounge carpet. The hellish extreme of his own longing for the boy accused him; but the damage done was beyond any feeling or thought he could muster to confront the act. Weeping he clutched his trembling wife. Together they cleaned-up the mess. Mrs Dean refused to read the Statement. She had read it in Tim's ashen face. Fiercely vowing to protect her three children so they would never, never have to face this sort of hell again, she hurried to prepare a wholesome lunch.

Nina was Tim's second visitor. She came in, went straight up to him and held him in her frail old arms, kissing his face and hands. She held him while he cried and until his trembling diminished, cooing, 'There, there. It's over. No one can hurt you now.' After he had calmed down, after the others had ventured back into the room Nina spoke. 'Dearest Timothy, Doctor MacKay suggests you come home tomorrow after you have visited him. He thought your nurse' (looking at Sophie) 'should accompany you for several days until you are feeling stronger. She can have Jeff's old bed and take you bathing frequently.'

'But it's school tomorrow.' chimed Mrs Dean.

'I'm staying with Timmy until he's better.' Sophie said so resolutely there was no further challenge.

The news was soon all over the school. The police had come to warn the head teacher. Jeff told the children what had happened. There was a hush in every classroom as a notice of warning was handed them for their parents. 'Poor Tim. Let's send him a card. Let's visit him.' to which Jeff resolutely cried, 'No. Leave him alone. He needs quiet right now.' Most of their friends understood. Some shivered in dread. Some cried. Then everyone missed him. Mandy reflected all their mood. 'It's like there's a hole in school which Tim used to fill. It's awful without him. Give him our love.'

Tim struggled down the cliff path. He was so stiff and sore it took all his efforts to get to and from the beach. They waded through the surf and bobbed about beyond the breakers until their goose pimples drove them shoreward where Sophie carefully dried him, examining his wounds as if her concern would heal them. But Tim seemed far away. Sophie felt the deep tension but was unable to reach in and pluck it out. Nina understood saying to her, 'Just stay with him. Some of the healing must come from within. We can do no more than be here.'

Sophie knew how to stand by Tim. Her gentle presence supported him in his blackest time as he fought the destruction of that night challenging it with every memory of every love he had ever known. So, with growing frequency he confronted an inner her and Nina and all the others. One night Sophie was wakened by Tim's crying about a bad dream:

'I was trapped in a box. It was dark. All these knives were pushed in. They punctured me. The box was full of my blood and guts until I was empty. I drowned in blood and no one knew.'

She slipped in beside him, pulled the duvet protectively over them and hugged him back to sleep. After that they always shared the bed. And when Tim's life returned and his desire grew, she let him ease in, let him shake inside her, let him cry with pain or achievement. Then they both knew she would give him everything she had, and being together made the world complete, and they had negotiated the invisible yet tangible line between his death and their future life.

At this time Tim told Sophie the story of the *Rite of Spring* by Igor Stravinsky, which starts with a mourning bassoon; he felt he had danced so the world would blossom, would continue in its serene and canabalistic way, leaving him to die. 'But you danced with me, in a last dance of sacrifice as I was pulled back into the darkness. But together we are too strong. We have danced a life-dance so the world will blossom and we will gather all the flowers and give them to Nina and Chris and Janet and Jeff.' ('and Fran', prompted Sophie archly) 'Yes, and Fran, and Ian and' ('Everyone we love' she whispered). 'Yes, everyone we love.'

They were lying on his bed. The afternoon sunlight lengthened across the garden and poured in over them. Tim peeled off Sophie's clothes then his own and pushed into her. They overflowed. Slowly the pleasure subsided. Sophie wept with Tim. They didn't know why. Was it the first rain of spring proclaiming their dance had triumphed?

But they soon discovered although Tim could cope with those he loved, the rest of the world now terrified him. At school he was withdrawn, he could no longer venture to the beach or anywhere else on his own, the world outside was filled with menace. The police and social workers tried to provide distress-aid, but the wounded boy clamped up. Nina understood Sophie's distress. 'The problem is, Timothy has deep and passionate relationships out of which he has grown. Somehow we must lead him into such a tried and trusted relationship in order to entice him back into the world. My dear Sophie, it will involve you in the greatest trust, I fear.'

Sophie clutched her hand. 'Anything, to have Timi again.'

'Do you feel you have lost Timothy?'

'I know he's there for me, in a way. But I wish for the old Tim, there for himself and not needing to hide.'

'By that do you mean a complete person?'

Sophie groaned. 'Yes. Complete.'

'So, we are agreed. I felt something had died in him after the rape. I have been thinking over of ways to help him. I can only think of one. This lies through his music making, and with Fran.'

Sophie blinked, then looked into the kindly face and whispered, 'I agree.' A tear splashed onto their clasped hands.

'You may loose him. But not forever, my dear.' Nina said gently.

Sophie sobbed. 'I don't really have him now. It can't be much worse.' Her tears of love burst. Sharing her anguish softened the pain.

'You are a brave girl. Like Timothy.' Nina said warmly.

Fran had been struggling in Tim's music lessons, trying to fire the muted boy to connect with the feelings from which his music stemmed. But to no avail. Nina's suggestions about some concerts and chamber music sessions sounded worth a try. So after a lesson Fran asked Tim if he'd accompany her to a chamber orchestra concert the following week.

'If you enjoy the first, we could go to the series. We'll go in my car. I'll stay with you, see you home, or whatever you like.'

'Mm, I suppose so.'

The program consisted of works from the twentieth century. Bartok's piece for strings, percussion and celeste which rippled and caught the tensions bound up in the boy. Are these my feelings? he thought. The glittering surface is how I laughed . . . before . . .

The group then played a concerto by Arthur Honneger for strings, flute and cor-anglais sweeping him with its auburn serenity. 'Like Janet's hair, her friendly warmth, and the spar. The flute sings my brooding, all the things I tried to play on my bassoon.'

He walked speechless with Fran during the interval in a small paved garden overhung with trees whose high walls protected him, just as Fran did, so his feelings dared release. He connected with the broken boy within. They stayed there during the second part of the concert.

'No, of course I don't mind missing it.' Fran murmured.

They sat on a stone bench. In the silence the indistinct sounds of the concert chivied him to let more of his pain out. He took her hand. She felt his relief. Later at Nina's front door he waved gratefully as Fran drove away. He decided to share the next programme with her.

The concerts became a bridge from inner death to life out-side. Haltingly he began to talk to Fran, as he used to, about the associations the music uncovered. She felt an allogamy between his feelings and the music, each colouring the other. Feelings choking the music, the music allowing an expression of the unbearable, the unsayable. She began to see the engulfing confusions lying under his frenetic, all-demanding lovemaking, remembering how after his orgasms he seemed freed, as if some of his inner boiling had been released. 'I love him because he has poured so much of himself into me,' she mused. 'He trusted me with his treasures and grew free – I remember his expressive dancing.' she smiled.

Some time later Tim attended a Saturday chamber music event in Fran's house. Ian was there. Fran had asked for his help. To start with Fran played the bass parts. Then with the excuse of tea-making she left so Ian could plead with Tim to replace her.

'We can't go on without the bassoon.' they all chorused.

'You'll be all right. Anyway, I'm no good.' grunted Tim.

But he was persuaded to 'have a go'. He had played the part before yet he played unresponsively until he began to forget his pain in the demands made by playing together, so by the end of the movement the ensemble sounded better.

Fran listened behind the door. Warmth and pleasure and intimacy were growing. She wept as the bassoon grounded the caroling upper parts giving and taking snippets of themes, sharing the various moods, adapting to changing texture and tempi. 'Ah, my Timtim, you are making love, such glorious sounds, responsive, joyous tensions, the delight in cadence' ends, just as we shared our bodies . . . my dearest, dearest one, you are returning, at last.'

On the following Sunday, for the first time since his rape, Tim cycled alone to the Deans to be welcomed and feted. The children swam, wolfed lunch and then lay on towels on the grass talking and planning. Mr and Mrs Dean gave Tim and Sophie a swatch of driving lesson vouchers. 'It's time you both learned to drive. Then you needn't wait at bus stops.'

Such astounding care surrounded him. A care which awkwardly he began to take into himself. Life was returning to him.

The police caught the three rapists. Their committal proceedings were set for several months' time in the Eliza village courthouse. The first day was marred by milling reporters intruding on a local community worried about the safety of their children, and uncomfortable as their deepest feelings about love, security and territory were paraded before the Nation. After the prosecuting police outlined their case and had read out Tim's statement they invited the boy into the witness box, asking him to expand aspects of it.

Afterwhich the leading Defence Counsel impressively rose. 'Is it not the case that you are a drug addict.'

Tim remembered Mr Adamson. 'No.'

Counsel expanded. 'Were you not in a hospital for rehabilitation for sexual and drug-related problems. Remember, you are under oath.'

Tim was stunned, what had this to do with his rape? 'When I was young, I had a problem fixed at a hospital. It was a long time ago. I don't do drugs now.'

Counsel coughed dismissively. 'Are you living at home with your parents?'

'No, I'm living with friends.'

'So, your parents find you difficult?'

'I find them difficult.'

'I suggest you willingly got into that car, you are free and easy about such behaviour, and knowingly took the proffered drugs, perfectly aware of what they were, after all it's your idea of fun, you offered to go with my clients provided they took you back to the bus-stop afterwards.'

Tim shook his head in disbelief. The court was hushed. The abused boy was being turned into the guilty cause. The local people seethed, 'Is there no Justice?'

'Shame on all of you!' rang out from the public benches as an old woman rose to her feet brandishing her walking stick. 'You have no right to allow this. The child – every child – has a right to the protection of the law and of this court. You have heard how Timothy was abused. You sit like stones and let him be abused here. Shame!'

'SILENCE IN COURT' yelled the Clerk.

'You should have said that hours ago.' the old lady said. 'How dare you treat our children with so little respect.'

There was a general growl of assent.

'REMOVE THAT PERSON.' Yelled the Magistrate.

Ushers appeared, hurried towards Nina trying to push through the crowd of bristling locals.

'Leave her alone.' shouted Tim, leaping like a deer from the dock, over the Barristers' tables and into the public fray, pushing aside the perplexed ushers to shield his friend whom he angrily escorted from the court. Flushed in Nina's car the two surveyed the anxious faces of the Clerk's staff who pleaded that Tim return.

'You are the main witness.' they whined.

'Over my dead body.' quavered Nina as Tim shook his head. 'I'm taking Timothy home, where he belongs.' she cried fiercely. 'You have his statement. You can defend that. Shame, shame on you all.' she cried and backed the car into a flower bed.

The ushers and staff retreated.

'Nina, let me . . .' said Tim, going round to the driver's door and motioning his protector into the passenger seat. Very carefully Tim manoeuvred the ancient car out of the bruised flowers over the pavement and onto the road. Nervously he drove them home. 'A little extra practice to add to my driving lesson vouchers.'

'Thank you Timothy. I couldn't stand it any longer.' said Nina. 'They have no idea how hard you worked to make a life for yourself. They don't see real change, only shadows from the past, not the bright wonderful person you are today. To try to turn you into a wily teenager rather than an innocent victim is unforgivable.'

Tim warmly hugged the frail bristling old body until the shrill whistle from the kettle proclaimed tea.

In the courtroom the public seethed with anger. Nina had spoken for them all, spoken their inner feelings of concern about their children, the safety of their neighbourhood and a belief the Law wherever it emanated from would, when necessary, support them all.

Old Doctor MacKay reported to the court he had never seen injuries as brutal during his career as the family doctor. Again the Defence Counsel was belittling, saying he was only an out-of-town practitioner. To which the bent old man replied severely, 'I've dealt with accidents on the road, on the beach, in private gardens, with birth and death, with extremes in most households in the vicinity, with all the fears and trials life involves. Do not trivialise my patients' lives. And do not try to turn Timothy into a monster; he is a fine young man whom we all honour and love.'

Then, Janet was called, giving Timothy a character reference much as Doctor MacKay had given. Senior Counsel rose ponderously to his feet again and asked, 'You have stated the boy spends vacations with you. I understand you bathe naked with him in your pool. Doubtless, he'd confirm his pleasure at such easy goings on.'

The Counsel for the Prosecution rose flustered and complained. The Magistrate accepted the evidence had a bearing on the reliability of the main witness and said he would allow the questioning to continue, but on the following day. The court then rose for the day.

Max had discovered the police had been forbidden by the Defence's legal team from taking DNA samples from the three rapists so they could be measured against samples taken from Tim's anus on the night of the rape. He spoke to the Sergeant in charge of the cells where the men were being kept, suggesting Police provide new electric razors for each man and then send the hair samples to the laboratory for testing. No one would savvy the remnants of the morning shave would finish up in the lab. Permission for disposal of such 'residue' could be 'overlooked'. The prosecution team would have to try to delay the court proceedings somewhat, until the laboratory could furnish the results. So Janet's reply was delayed with legal argument and procedural quibbles all the next morning.

Finally she stood again to answer the charges of misconduct and sexual licence with a minor. The situation had a smattering of familiarity. In her worst dreams she had defended her life and values as she now had to do. She stood with dignity. 'Timothy is a special case. He is both pupil and ward. I have never had relations with any of my pupils. It is my personal and professional belief in the respect underlying our duties as teachers I have always honoured and upheld. Yes, Timothy and I have bathed together openly in my pool, dressed as we each felt comfortable with. We have never crossed the line of propriety. We are friends. There is nothing in my life, and nothing in our relationship I am ashamed of. To misrepresent our friendship as you have, is shameful, without a shred of compassion for the ordinary dignities of life.' She waited. 'I must also protest about your accusation he would invite those men to perform such unspeakable acts. He is a decent ordinary boy growing through the usual turmoil of adolescence and has never, never been the depraved addict you accuse him of. I think this court has a duty to protect our children. Not to accuse them of crimes unimaginable to them, and to us.' The Eliza Beach community roared its support.

'SILENCE. I WILL HAVE THE COURT CLEARED.

SILENCE.' cried the Magistrate.

But the crowd roared its approval and support and protest. Knowing that the papers would again scream with headlines of "TEACHER HAS SEX WITH PUPIL" (no names, bringing anonymity, as well as generalising all teachers and all pupils) accompanied by their 'debate' about 'the lewd teenager who stops cars at busstops for free sex and drugs, and what is the world coming to.' With colour photos of the village bus stop where Tim 'operated from'. With letters pages brimming with 'bring back whipping' and 'outlaw sick teenager behaviour, put them in army camps', 'sack sleazy teachers'. plus more 'serious' questions about 'whether neutering should be a legal option'. But there were hints elsewhere the Defence Counsel and the Magistrate had a personal interest in obfuscating the case, that there was a tenuous connection with a sex-ring in the city. But the untreated pain in the local community numbed it to most of the media circus, leaving the agonised question, 'Who will help us? There is no one!'

Many parents shepherded their children to school, running the gauntlet of the knot of press and cameras. Nina insisted Tim stay home. She was bitter, frightened the boy might lose his youthful confidence again. Helping to rehabilitate him after the rape itself had been almost impossible. She feared the present situation would compound his suffering and push him back into the distress she had witnessed when Chris first brought him to her.

Nina was wild in her protection, passionate in her loyalty and determined to guard her cub against all marauders. 'My dear Timothy,' she said gravely, 'I will *not* have you facing that rabble. You will stay here, as we used in the beginning. You will work – you have so much to get on with, don't you – and you'll run up and down to swim. And I'll go over your English. And you and Fran can play to us after your lessons. And Janet and Max will come. And your friends will visit. They are always welcome.' Tim looked at her admiringly. This sort of return to beginnings focused him, toughened him. She reassuringly patted his arm. 'And when it is all over. Our life will return to normal.'

Jubilation reigned in the local community when the Prosecution announced the DNA samples matched the remnants of semen found in the boy the night of his rape. Their feelings of outrage and retribution were unchallengeable. No one could ignore the evidence.

Yet arguments over the legality of misappropriating shaved hair, the irresponsible way the police had overlooked Tim's age (he should not have had to endure the exigencies of the court), all the challenges knotting up court procedures took time to resolve.

In due course the visiting Magistrate committed the three men to full trial and praised the police for their vigilance. He implied this was the end of an 'isolated case' over which no one should worry further. Then everyone went back to the city looking for more engaging issues, and relative calm prevailed.

Eventually the three were charged and sent to prison, by which time a few invisible scars such as the inadvertent withdrawal of breath at shadows threatening nocturnal streets, or an anxious response to innocent questions from lost motorists or a reticence, however slight, which Tim now exhibited in his dealings with strangers, were all that proclaimed damage.

Eliza Beach had changed.

Watershed

1:

TIME PASSED. Tim and Sophie faced their matriculation year, the last school hurdle to university. There was, eventually, general agreement about a break beforehand: there'd be no harm in their hiking in the mountains based on a young peoples' holiday village. Mrs Dean would drop the two at a main station where they caught a train into the country.

Jeff rowdily protested, but cheerfully kissed them goodbye – for he and his bosom-pal Martin had their own holiday plans. Sophie and Tim wanted to be alone. Each was expectant. Tim wanted peace and quiet; Sophie wanted Tim.

After a couple of days in the village they packed their rucksacks with a tent, provisions, maps and equipment for the bush hike. Jan, one of the supervisors, saw off a slim boy his mop of hair frothing under a wide-brimmed hat, his muscled legs brown from swimming. Two similar pairs of legs: hers, shapely long and tanned swelled attractively from her bottom. Both in thick sox and stout boots (against snakes and the rough bush). They could be boys. Jan enjoyed the way Sophie's pack straps emphasised her breasts. She didn't hide them like many girls, and Tim seemed to enjoy looking. His shorts swelled at the front. He was well hung. No wonder she looked at him that way. Jan smiled appreciatively as they walked away. 'Have a good time.' he called. They turned, waved and tramped onward. The bush soon swallowing them up.

Silence claimed them first. Only the crack of sticks underfoot and the wind matching their breathing. They struggled up slopes to sight the compass and move off slanting into valleys filled with the scent of wattle and eucalyptus. The ground underfoot was untrod, wilting in the heat savaging everything. The rocks radiated the fire of high summer. Lust drove them. The joy of being together.

Freedom in a wilderness of dancing shadows, mottled tree trunks, and bathed in a sky so vastly blue it left everything breathless. The rigor of the mountains infused them. The two resembled trees, flexing limbs and trunks, but moving; the sun beating on their and the other trees' shoulders. All day they strode onward, sweating and resting and talking softly. Losing inhibitions, losing themselves in the warm and breathing bush, becoming its progeny. Lizards lay and watched the two stamp past guided by invisible lines of compass and thought, until late in the afternoon they halted on a treeless saddle deciding to camp there.

They struggled assembling all the bits of the tent. Then collected wood for a fire (made in a pit Tim dug to prevent a bushfire). Sophie collected armfuls of bracken to cushion their sleep, before making supper. The light faded in the valleys far below and left them in dusking light slowly revealing its tresses of stars. Cooled by a light breeze, they crouched wolfing fodder off plastic plates.

Tim hesitantly began to sing to the evening. Sophie joined in. They sat, the fire dancing on their faces until Sophie hugged him. 'Tim, take me to bed.' Hurriedly they brushed their teeth and scrambled into the tent where they lunged at each other. Quickly Sophie was moaning. 'Tim, come, now.' He thrust. She gasped, 'Fill me, Tim, fill me.' She cried, screaming to the bush, screaming her passion, her wonder a celebration of everything as Tim furiously plunged and pushed and threw himself into her until, gasping victory, he wilted. Sleep was deep. A starred moon-rocked over the hills, the dark wept dew on the tent and on the grass which pricked his feet when he slipped out to pee.

As dawn grew they made love again. He kissed her everywhere until she moaned longingly pulling him up to her open mouthed, delighted face. He drove his erection in. She gasped and shook and lost herself in his pulsing, sharing desire as her centre shivered with fiery showers so intense she forgot. Forgot where, and when, and if, and who, and why and how. Forgot everything but her/his pounding buoying them to heights never realised (but forever known).

It was ingrained in their fibres; a meeting of the primary powers driving them. A meeting carrying them beyond themselves and into each other. Lusty energy, a crude striving without gender or place or style, binding them.

The sun drove them out of the tent.

Tim was bashful. 'Sorry. Was it all right?'

'Perfect.'

He uncomfortably kicked a grass frond near the tent.

'Tim. It was perfect.' Sophie murmured. 'I want everything.'

'I was too rough.'

'No. Oh no. Tim, I love it wild. That's all I want, really.'

'Like me. Do you mean it?'

'Like you, yes.'

He smiled. She laughed. Perhaps nothing had changed. This was love and war, wasn't it wonderful! They enjoyed breakfast differently. They kissed and washed-up. Happily each saw the other wet and shat in the grass. They packed-up, got into their heavy packs and stomped along a way which took them further and further from home, nearer and nearer to themselves.

During that afternoon they stumbled upon a meagre creek of linked pools deciding to camp near the biggest one. Gleefully they stripped and splashed in. The sun sparkled on wet skin and hair. The water frothed as they gamboled. They came to rest with their backs against an angular rock which channelled the water in the wet season, judging by the debris necklacing its top. Sophie watched as Tim's penis grew. It reared to her touch. He showed her how to rub it keeping the foreskin folded over its tip.

'Is this what boys do?' she asked.

He blushed. 'Of course.'

'Do you and Chris do it?'

'Yes.'

' And Ian ?"

'Yes.'

' . . . and my brother?'

Tim uneasily nodded.

'That's why he loves you.'

Tim tensed. 'I'll come unless you stop.'

'Come then!'

'It's messy.' Tim squirmed.

'I want to watch. I love you excited with seed.'

Pushing back with his hands, he lifted his hips off the bottom until his waist was above the water. Streams of milky fluid spurted out over his stomach into the water. 'Now rub very slowly. Yes, Soph! Oh.'

Sophie put her fingers into her mouth, 'I'd forgotten the delicate taste.' She watched milky strands floating in the pool. 'Tim, don't hide these things. I want to share everything.'

'Are you sure, Soph? It's not much fun for you.'

She pulled close to him to suck his nipples. 'I don't mind. It's being with you. Please teach me how to love you like the others do. And let me be your boy sometime. I think I know what to do.'

He reached over and fingered her anus. 'You mean there?'

Sophie nodded.

'Are you sure?'

Her nipples hardened. 'I want you to play in me everywhere, and you must teach me how to play with you, like just now. You look fantastic, excited.'

'People say I'm beautiful then.' he muttered.

'You are.' Kissing him, she opened his lips. His penis hardened prompting her to say, 'Will you do it to me like a boy?'

They scrambled out of the water and prepared a nest of clothes and towels. He lifted her legs and began to kiss her anus and poke it, first with his tongue and then one, and two greased fingers. She enjoyed his arousal, fired by the oddly stimulating feelings he awoke in unseen parts of her body. Dutifully she knelt. He nudged up to her and placed his swollen glans in the softened ring. 'When you feel me, do a fart, not a little puff, but a long, strong one so you blow up your arse to fit me.' She thrilled with pain as he entered. It was nearly unbearable. Feeling her shiver he gently withdrew.

'Try again.' she said over her shoulder.

'Remember to fart.' Holding her hips he pressed. Her anus relented. He felt her relax. He inched in.

'Wow, it's big in me.'

'Am I hurting you?'

'No, go on moving. I like it.' She rocked back and forth. He arched against her, thrusting, suddenly froze, and finished. Later they washed the towel and threw it over a warm rock to dry then cooled off in the pristine water.

That evening Sophie kissed Tim's anus, sensing his yearning for what she imagined must be a penis. She now understood his desire. 'So men need to be fucked, too.' she said thoughtfully.

Tim turned away. 'Soph, you are the only one who's touched me there since . . . that night.'

She kissed his flank. 'It's my first patient. I must look after it.' They snuggled, idly exploring skin with growing pleasure until they drove each other further than ever, and careless of everything in the unity of their breathing, they slept until a frosty dew drove them under their bedding where they dozed until morning.

The penil shadows shrank as the sun rose over the ridge. The children stoked the fire for breakfast and hung bedding out. Wearing nothing but hats, enjoying the seclusion, they wandered over rocks, already warm to bare feet, to collect drinking water further up-stream from the camp, agreeing to stay and explore.

Wearing boots, hats and lightly clad carrying a small pack with towels, drinking water and snacks, they threaded their way downward along the winding course of the creek. They found a flat face of rock over which the water dropped into a pool a meter below. The rock was hugged by slippery smooth moss down which they careered to splash into the pool.

Sophie watched Tim skidding along, arms outstretched, feet up, his strong back curved in pleasure. His sex flapped loosely between taut thighs, his bottom took on a green tinge, his neck emerged from well-set shoulders and was crowned in a face wreathed in laughter as he splashed in. She was more demure, sliding down in a more compact stance but with matching green bottom and smile.

Trees overhung the pool beside which the children rested. Sophie explored Tim's sex, watching it grow, the balls lengthening in the heat. She gently pulled back its skin cloak and peered at the purple glans with its Polyphemus eye and thread of skin connecting it to the shaft. 'It's an eye that spies on me inside.' They laughed. She inspected the shaft, fascinated by its eloquence; its unblemished skin, smooth as marble, its emergence from his mysterious crotch crowned by a tuft of pale pubic hair; his feelings leaked out as it responded to her caress; his sacs were soft wrinkled tissue paper ('to allow them to grow' explained Tim). Amusedly they watched them move in a slow pulsing uncontrollable motion with which the organs of the body behave. 'You're a contradiction, soft and hard.' She mused.

Then she turned him over to inspect his bottom again,

hoping this time Tim would not be distressed. She liked the pert bunches forming the hairless crease where his anus lay. Sophie picked strands of green moss from his crease and ran an exploratory finger round Tim's neat ring. 'It seems darker. Perhaps it's from that night. It looks beautiful Tim, your perfect little lips.' He sighed contentedly. Sophie slobbered on a finger and very gently anointed him (as if with ointment). 'How's that?' She waggled it.

Tim stretched, allowing it deeper. 'Good. It's enough for now.' He pulled away.

'Tim, can we find a way it can re-learn about love?' He half-nodded, rose and clambered over the rocks up to the slide. 'Soph, are you coming?'

She shook her head. 'Later maybe. You go.' She watched him play. Boyish, manly, utterly beautiful. Damaged, free, more available. She glimpsed his laughing face as he flew, green-arsed through the air and into the pool. The more she knew him the more precious he became. Feelings exploded, she wept.
'
'Sophie. Crying. I've upset you. What is it?'

'No, no. It's just. Tim. It's. I'm so happy.'

He grinned. 'I'd hate to see you sad.' He brushed the tears from her cheeks. She settled. 'Sad? Happy? Sophie, which is it?'

'I was thinking, Timmy, about being here. Just us. It is everything.'

'I've thought the same, and after you fingered me, better now. All our times.'

They sat watching the pool settle in tune with their breathing, watching the shadows dance and the lean grass shiver, listening to the birds, their own hearts. Then they returned to camp.

After eating they went to bed. In the last light they sought hidden places. Sophie lay Tim on his back, opened his legs and fingered the dark ridge of skin, like a sewn seam, which ran from his anus along a tube between his legs, separating his balls and continuing along the underside of his penis to its slit.

His penis arched. She slipped fingers around its swelling base. 'Soph you're amazing. You touch me so well.' he said.

'Help me to know your body,' she whispered. 'I love being with you this way with so many feelings.'

He pushed her onto her back. He ran his tongue around the delicate sculpture of her ear poking into its waxy interior and running questing lips down its curled edge to her floppy lobes, smelling the damp incense in her hair. He licked her eyes, as he had been licked, his tongue sensing the rolling eyeball under its soft lid. He was abashed by her brown eyes which so often regarded him with compassion, shrewdly followed him everywhere, yet swam with ecstasy. Her face shone. What a beautiful face. He kissed her cheeks, nose, chin, slid teasingly across her lips and fell on her breasts. She shivered as he took each nipple into his mouth and ran his tongue around the ring of textured flesh at its base. He cupped the soft swelling in his hand, delighting in its sense of plenty. He ran fingers from the triangle at the base of her back from which the crease of her bottom grew. Soft fullness enraptured him. He parted her cheeks and brushed her anus with the pads of his fingers in the caress he so enjoyed.

'I'm a bit sore.' she said.

'I didn't mean to hurt you. You should have said.'

'I loved it Tim. It's because it was my first time.'

'Like my first time. It was with Chris. It hurt like shit when I came with him, but afterwards and all the next day I glowed. I was only a kid; he was very careful.'

Tim dribbled globules of spit onto her, wet his fingers pushed them in. He wriggled them. 'Is that nice?'

Sophie shifted position, opening her thighs, inviting his other hand into her vagina. She shivered with pleasure. So many intrusions. 'Oh Tim, oh, I never knew my body could be so . . . so alive. Yes . . . oh Tim . . . Oh.'

She tore herself away, turned to grab this magician, for everything boiling inside him. He filled her. They thrashed and sweated, cried in a frenzy of desire and burst. An ordinary hurt, which collects in us each day, leached away. They lay, replete, children of the Bush. They were lying together as the stars emerged. They were asleep when the moon rocked over the ridge.

Next day they journeyed again. Following compass, map and GPS up over high ridges swept by wind in whose sunless hollows a little snow still lurked. Then down into silent valleys strewn with trees and rocks. They picked their way stamping noisily to scare any snakes. The low tough brush whipped bare legs, occasionally faces, as the two wended towards their next camp site.

It was an arduous tramp, engaging with the unexpected.

When they rested she might caress his bulging shorts when desire rippled over him. Sometimes it was enough just to firmly hold the bloated member. Sometimes she took his juice, enjoying his softening face.

She was usually content with waiting. The kisses he planted on her breasts and mouth would suffice until dusk. It was enough to be with him, to respond and explore him. She felt he was growing towards her; she unravelled each strand of his need, freeing him.

Tim smiled. 'This is like playing chamber music, except I wilt when I come - we stay frisky after musical orgasms. Here, we relate in much the same way – your vagina songs to my bassoon cock.' He lifted her tee shirt and kissed her breasts. 'Making love, rather than music, involves even more of us, I reckon.'

She was gladdened by his talk.

After lying on her gurgling stomach he would find the energy to struggle into his pack and go on through the wilderness fired by companionship and the unquenchable music of the Bush.

2:

THEY TRAVERSED THE RUCKED MOUNTAINS until, descending from a high twisting ridge, they found themselves at the edge of water, one of the upper fingers of an extensive reservoir. The expanse of pale brown water welcomed eyes narrowed by the glare of rock and sky. It lapped its rocky edge. Beckoned by sinuous reflections from dead trees sticking out of the water, the silver tombs of a drowned forest, Tim and Sophie stripped and tiptoed over the rocks to find a place from which to swim. He looked at her trim body, so streamlined, so enticing his penis raised itself as he stood hungrily eyeing her. Knowingly she laughed and slipped into the water gilding her shoulders and neck. He stood with shadows chasing over his skin highlighting the glory of his unruly hair, his muscled trunk and gentle open face; below, his sex arched above loose-hung balls, able hands lay against his thighs. (She wanted them to hold). Grey eyes as soft as dawn, teeth she longed to suck like sweets, Sophie floated motionless in wonder, her desire uncontrollable, held as the water held her, in a fluid embrace touching every part of her.

He waded in. His firm body melted into watery indefinable shapes, only his head remained, teasing her. Ripples ran far out into the lake and bounced against the rocks. The children played before deciding to set-up camp. They chose a soft hollow just above the shore where Tim erected the tent. Sophie went scavenging for leaves and brush for a mattress inside. Tim dug a trench for the fire on the breeze side of the tent so the smoke would deter mosquitoes. Then they fossicked for wood, prepared a feast, finishing as dusk settled.

Hurriedly they put water into plates and cups, brushed teeth and scrambled into the darkening tent where they deliriously undressed each other pushing garments to the bottom of sleeping bags while licking and kissing mouths made sucking sounds as inaudible as the water whispering beside them. Tim was overwhelmed by Sophie's desire. It drew from him a long and lustful interlude in which she was born on waves of pleasure as all the private bits of her body glowed with his attentions until shaking she drew him into her. She had already learned to leave his glans alone so as not to bring him on too much. She felt the engorged head move into her, pulling out waves of orgasm, until sounding like wounded wild things they climaxed and fell beyond themselves into that floating wonderland finishing love. In the morning she realised she had forgotten to take her pill.

After breakfast they emptied their packs and set off on a long hike to a settlement down the lake where they bought supplies. Sophie selected a bag of carrots matching Tim's erection, and shyly bought a purple pack of condoms to clothe them. She hoped to add to his pleasures. They returned to camp in the late afternoon, dropped their things and swam far out into the water beyond the silvery ghost trees as if only distance could wash the sweat of the day and the influence of the settlement off, and freedom return.

Sophie shyly showed Tim her bag of penis carrots and the sheaths.' Do you think I'm sick?'

He kissed her. 'Oh, Soph, you're amazing. Of course not. I want you there. Only you.'

She shook. 'I'll be very careful. Tell me how you like it. Tim. I probably need you in the same way.'

'Can we do it now?'

She smiled, selecting a smallish carrot. Oh, you are so beautiful, she thought, I want all of you, the bits you give to Chris, to Fran, to Ian, to my brother, to . . . all the others. I want everything.

'I'll have a shit.' Tim ambled into the trees returning shortly afterwards naked, highly aroused and holding his clothes. He spread them for his knees, knelt, and parted his buttocks. Fingers teased him open, he filled with condomised carrot. Tim sweated. 'Be careful Soph, it hurts. That's better. Yes. Oh God it's great, go deeper. Now fuck me with it.' The fearful thrill swamped him. 'Rub me too. Bring me off. Please Soph.' He was awash with lust. 'Yes . . . Yes. I'm coming. Keep going. That's great . . . Oh . Now. Ahhh.'

He was so tight Sophie could only jiggle the carrot in short jabs as milk spurted from his penis. He fell in it. She left the carrot and lay quietly beside him until he turned and hid in her arms. Shame and relief jostled him. Now, without the nagging pain and terror he was free. Her cure was completed. They lay changed. He the vessel she the implement, sharing the need to be trustfully filled. What glimmered was an infantile sense of being fed from both ends.

Gradually the softening day bled into them; both shivered. Shyly they rose; she helped him clean up then they dressed and made supper. Filled with unspeakable feelings drawing them together, they huddled by the fire as they sang a round in a minor-key which Tim had taught Sophie:

> Hey, ho, nobody at home;
> eat nor drink nor money have I none,
> still I will be ha . . appy,
> Hey, ho nobody at home;
> eat nor drink nor money have I none,
> still I will be ha . . appy,
> Hey ho . . . *

Unscathed after visiting hell, their round danced with the firelight on rocks and trees. The water, still in the windless dark, distorted the firelight into sinewy demonic figures. The children left the embers and snuggled together in the tent. Tim, with wondering

---

* See notes at end.

154

tenderness, kissed Sophie good night. Demon-protected, they slept deeply until stirring bird-song and a pale east heralded another day.

They were swimming when a ranger appeared. He stood by the tent examining their camp. His wide brimmed hat shaded a stern face; he wore a khaki shirt and shorts from which hairy legs emerged. His big Boots crushed the few leaves underfoot – Tim had cleared most away to prevent the spread of fire the Ranger noted approvingly. The children landed together. They hovered at the edge of the water demure and naked, the Ranger stood threateningly between them and their towels. He gazed speechless at the pair ('Adam and Eve belong in the Bush,' he decided).

'Hello.' said the boy, moving past him to retrieve a towel which he flung to the girl who hurriedly wrapped it about her body (what a pity.) while the boy, even more god-like at close quarters, squeezed wet into a pair of brief shorts bulging provocatively, his hairless legs glowing, droplets coursing down his broad face onto boyish shoulders and chest.

'How the hell did you get here?' growled the ranger.

'We came over the ridge.' said the boy pointing up the rock-strewn slope.

'There's a fence and notices to keep people out. And fines.'

'Not there.'

'That's true. It stops below the track.' the Ranger pointed.

'We found it yesterday.' the girl said in a bell-like voice, 'when we went into Stringy Bark Hollow, shopping.'

'Yes, the storekeeper told me.' The ranger took off his hat and scratched his wavy hair. 'This is a drinking water reservoir, you shouldn't camp in its catchment area in case you infect it. You'll have to go.' The children looked so crestfallen the ranger relented. 'All right, I can see you have made a decent camp, a safe fire and have dealt carefully with rubbish, but you'll have to move out of the area in a day or two, otherwise I'll be in trouble.' Gratefully the children nodded.

The ranger advised them to make their way around the top of the reservoir to where an old road, usually underwater, was now exposed. 'It's not on your map. I'll show you if you like.' He squatted down, took out a pen and marked the map, sweating with pleasure as the youngsters pressed against him. It seemed a good plan to follow, then hike down into the wide river valley to a train to take them on the first leg of their return to Eliza Beach.

'There're lots of camping spots along the river, and access through the farms irrigating from it. Ask permission if you meet anyone or pass near a farmhouse.' said the ranger.

He delayed his return for three days. The camp site was deserted; the children gone. The Ranger stalked about, impressed "nothing was left, but thanks" (as Baden Powell admonished), a pressed pile of leaves had been their bed. His boot nudged the pile. Nestling underneath was a purple condom case. 'My God, they fuck.' He flopped on a rock. 'Paired like everything else.' He gazed across the water, empty but for stiff ghost gums riding their sinuous reflections. The deserted camp echoed his own loneliness. The ranger hallood. To fill the emptiness? To protest? His yearning swallowed up by the silence of the Bush.

3:

THEY FOUND THE OLD ROAD with difficulty. The vague strip of levelled ground under the detritus left by the receding water led them around the top of one of the finger valleys from where they climbed up the steep flanks of a ridge they anticipated towered above the valley of the river they planned to follow.

That night they camped on the ridge between two large rocks sheltering from the breeze. The reservoir had refreshed them. They strode more purposely. Merrily they pushed-on through the dense brush carpeting the forest floor disturbing flocks of coloured birds which flew screeching into the leafy distance. Liquid bird song enhanced their reverie. Regularly they stopped for a snack and drink, glad to drop their heavy packs and stretch. Tim reviewed progress scanning his map and the GPS. Often Sophie would sit stock still beside him, or lie on her stomach on the leaf-strewn ground watching the minute life which teemed below the grass-line, delighting in the colour of a beetle or the antics of ants, calling, 'Tim, come and look at this.'

'It's like our inner thoughts,' Tim said. 'There, if we bother to look. But most of the time we deny their existence.' Often he would whisper, 'Touch me.' Sometimes that was enough. Sometimes Sophie would massage his penis, fan his pleasure and watch his seed fly, he gasping as if his soul were leaving his body. She enjoyed his delight as the minuscule drops spewed out. Such tiny signs of so great an eruption of feelings. How much more lay behind larger acts such as smiling or sweating or holding hands.

These acts were the landmarks of their journey. They felt on top of the world. And in a sense they were. Some mornings they watched the clouds, nestling in the hollows below, herded by the wind like sheep to rise fluffily upwards to disperse.

'We are the gods on Olympus.' Tim said. 'Look down Goddess Soph and see the world of mortals far below.'

She smiled . 'Will they learn to worship us?'

'They do, already.'

'Of course. Because we're untouched.'

'Then we must be gods.' They danced in the stiffening wind before humping their packs along the next leg, with a minute insecurity high up on those windy peaks which pared their actions into a sense of being temporary visitors in these high ethereal spaces. They began to look forward to being back on the ground.

As the ridge began to rise towards the next peak, Tim decided they should turn down its flank towards the river valley. After the heights' sparseness, it was tough going pushing through denser scrub, if shady. Occasionally they stumbled across a clearing where packs were dropped, swigs taken from dwindling water bottles. They were sticky from lack of washing; sometimes they would stretch out on the ground and gaze upward at the leaves dancing before the backdrop of the intense blue sky nurturing them, like an eye. When armies of ants seethed over their skin they resumed their decent until silence was replaced by the grating hum of machines.

The children stumbled onto a rough-hewn track. 'It's not on the map.' Tim declared, but they decided to follow it, emerging into a clearing full of logs, a ramshackle tin roof over a circular saw bench and a rash of small huts. It was a logging camp, the track, for timber jinkers taking logs to distant saw mills. The workmen, rough and unshaven, welcomed the two youngsters with mugs of tea and ant-infested biscuits, and gladly let them fill their water bottles from a big tin barrel held up high on a scanty steel structure. Everyone was glad of new company. The men drooled over the sexy girl, 'Half the boy's luck.' they joked. Surreptitiously they spied on the two washing in the bush shower lustily agreeing, 'They're fantastic kids.'

Ginger, one of the burly drivers, was leaving with a full load. He offered the children a ride to where the highway crossed the river. They accepted. It was a more interesting way of covering the last kilometres devastated by machines and logging.

Ginger stowed their packs in his sleeping space behind the cabin seats. The three squeezed onto the front bench, Tim straddling a nest of gear levers. The road was narrow, rough and precipitously steep. They careered downward, behind them thirty tones of gigantic tree trunks chained onto a long, many wheeled trailer, threateningly obscuring the rear window. Half way down Tim spied an empty jinker groaning up the track a few bends away. 'No problem.' grunted Ginger, double-declutching as he roared onwards. The children pressed feet to the floor as they lurched to the inner side of the bend, the wrong side. Collision was inevitable. They rounded the corner, the ascending jinker also on the wrong side. The drivers waved familiarly and passed in clouds of dust.

Ginger guffawed. 'Frightened you, did I? We have our own rules up here. If I'd stayed on the outside I might've slipped sideways and crashed into the bush. No fun, I can tell you. It happens, no kidding. It's timber ways here. All us drivers know 'em. With thirty bloody tones of bloody timber behind you've got to be bloody careful. Pity help some city picnicking car caught up here. It would be strawberry jam all over the bloody track.'

It grew to a comfortable silence. Ginger saw a relieved smile pass between the two youngsters (They too had 'wrong-side' rules).

Sophie laughed. 'You might have told us. But I don't think we'll try it on our driving test.'

Tim moved his leg so Ginger could change gear. 'You guys are right. The law is OK at ordinary times. We should invent our own rules for unusual situations, that way we'll survive.'

Ginger grinned. 'Is that what you two do?'

They nodded. 'We're trying to.'

'Good on yers.' Then Ginger told them of his teenage larks in the country. And they, being caught by the Ranger, and finding the water slide. They were still laughing at the bottom. He dropped them at the bridge. They shouted thanks over the roar of the engine. 'There's yer river' Ginger shouted and pointed along its gleaming length. The bridge trembled as he thundered away.

4:

PEACE AND QUIET RETURNED. They trudged beside fields under the tangle of trees edging the river. They spied a sandy bend down stream, deciding to camp there, found a grassy shelf for the tent tucked beside an arc of sand washed by the water as it turned from stony banks, and swam there. Tim found he could stand, the sand pleasant on feet; he yearned for Sophie and called her over. She knew. She felt under the water for his sex, feeling it grow. He held her breasts. They drew close and kissed. He wriggled into her, thrusting urgently; she opened grasping his thighs in hers. Buoyed by the water she could be held. She moaned with the pleasure he pushed in. Quickly he came, his erection waning, his thrusts diminishing. They clung until it slipped out. She kissed his face, feeling calm return. If only I had him like this, always, she thought.

The routine of setting up camp was easy now. The evening filled with eating and drinking, singing and then the gentlest lovemaking. Somehow, by finding the wrong side, in sharing sex-roles, they found a more relaxed love plateau. (Was it also a lack of abstinence?). It marked their emergence back into a populated world.

Yet Eden existed along the river. For several days they happily dallied along its snaking path. One afternoon they left their lightened packs on the grass and flung themselves into the water. A figure in trousers and bush hat crested the bank. They splashed to shore and shyly donned towels. It was a woman with a tired gentle face. 'Yes, I'm the farmer's wife.' she said. 'Yes, you can camp here.'

During their chat the woman appraised them. 'Do you want work? We could use you for a week or so. They're all away with the sheep. My son and I remain. It's really too much for us, he's a grand nipper but there's the whole property to manage. I'd pay you both the official labourer's wage.'

The children calculated there was time before school began. They should ring home and forewarn them.

The woman welcomed them with iron handshakes. 'I'm Agnes Bayne. Hi Tim, Sophie; good to have another woman around.'

They squeezed into their clothes, collected their possessions, dumped them in her dusty utility and bounced along a faint set of wheel tracks, through many gates (which Tim opened and shut) to eventually reach the farmyard. Tim and Sophie were allotted one of the many vacant workers' rooms in a block behind the main house.

'Move the beds around as you like. The men's ablutions are under the house. Sophie, you'd best use the bathroom inside. And after you've settled, come over for bedding and a cuppa.' Mrs Bayne pointed across the yard to steps up to the house.

5:

'Oh, Tim , our own little house.'

They surveyed their new domain. The room was entirely of wood, with a small back window overlooking odd bits of machinery and oil drums precariously stacked against their wall. The door opened onto a veranda, the length of the building. After moving the beds together, they unpacked their meagre possessions onto shelves on the wall. Sophie picked some flowering weeds and arranged them in a glass jar she set on a table under the window beside the beds. They hung their musty tent, ground sheets and sleeping bags over the rail of the veranda and hugged one another. 'Now we're real workers. But let's not go on strike today.' Then they ventured into the farmhouse.

They quickly decided that Mrs Bayne was nice. She talked passionately, but was an attentive and thoughtful listener. She took a motherly interest in her new workers, offering to wash their bush tanged clothes. 'Can't have the sheep complaining.' she teased. 'I'll find you something to wear while they dry.'

'Er, we don't wear underclothes.' Tim murmured.

'Goodness, I'm not shocked. I've seen all sorts through here over the years. Each to his own life, I say.' She and Sophie went fossicking for shorts and shirts. Sophie enjoyed the company of the older woman. That's the sort of caring I like, she thought as Mrs Bayne talked about her scattered family.

'Sheets and towels.' Mrs Bayne said. 'Come on, I'll help you.'

They walked across the yard. Mrs Bayne felt weepy when she saw the flowers and the way the children had sorted their room. 'It looks lovely dear, 'I hope you'll be happy here.'

'Oh, I'm sure we will.'

'But the work's hard. It's a long day, seven to two.'

'We'll be all right.'

Mrs Bayne was relieved. She had assessed their fitness. It was working out all right. In contented silence they prepared the beds. The iron roof creaked encouragement as it cooled; a flock of starlings chorused noisily in a gaunt pepper tree overhanging their room. The rumble of a tractor buzzed in their ears.

'That'll be Don,' said Mrs Bayne.

Don was just fourteen. A shy, softly spoken boy with a thatch of dark hair springing from his head like an untidy Cossack hat. His eyebrows were in a slashed line separating his clear brow from angular brown eyes, a nose which broadly expanded to shelter his strong mouth and a trim triangulated chin. His slight figure reminded Sophie of a younger Tim. Energetic and sensitive, they could almost be brothers. Sophie and Tim helped the boy unload a cart and put everything away.

Mrs Bayne paused on the top step. 'I'm glad you're all getting along. You're a team for now. Don'll tell you, there's the irrigating, collecting wood, the sheep the darn rabbits, the kitchen garden . . . We've got a mountain to do. Supper in two hours. Now, what about showers? Sophie, come along with me. Don, show Tim the men's section, and hang your towels up afterwards.'

The basement consisted of a rank of changing cubicles, showers and laundry facilities for the seasonal crowd of shearers and crop-gathering men, a barn of a place. Don led Tim to a bench and threw their towels down. Tim sat and pulled off his boots, undid his shorts, stood, let them fall to his ankles, and pulled his tee shirt up over his head. Don watched transfixed, desire and admiration swept him. Tim recognised his arousal as feelings he had had for Chris. This love-urge was shameful yet Don was radiant. Tim knelt and removed Don's boots, grinning as he unbuttoned his trousers and revealed bulging underpants.

'Off with your shirt. I don't wear underpants. Let's have yours.'

'Nowadays mine's always stiff. They hold it back.'

'I hate being covered up. Come on, where's the shower?'

The steam cloaked soapy bodies. Harsh jets tingled skin. They skipped breathless back to their towels. As Tim dried him, Don yearned. To feel naked, alive. To feel. What? Connected? He took a towel and carefully dried Tim. Wonderingly he felt the solidity of his sex, its power, his power as Tim's hand explored him until, blinded by steamy desire, Don drove the big cock to burst. He wiped the magic potion into his skin. He yearned when Tim kissed him, then all his body and his sex until the pangs broke. Ecstasy lingered. Tim again sought his mouth. 'You taste really nice. Here, I've kept you some.' They sprawled on the bench purged. Don felt fingers press his anus. 'Is that what you do, Tim?'

'Sometimes. . . would you like to?'

'Aa, all right.'

'Next time? '

'Is it as good as . . ?'

'Better. Love makes it fantastic.'

'Wasn't I good, just now?'

'Perfect. That's why I want everything.'

Don sighed. ' Me too.' Yes, it was perfect. Tim was perfect. He too. And love? He wiped his flaming face. They dressed. Don kicked his underpants under the bench. Yes, freedom felt better.

Although Don hugged his delight tightly inside, his radiance warmed supper that evening, charming the children, bringing a wan smile to Mrs Bayne's face. Is it possible we are in for a fortnight of happiness? she mused watching the three rumbustiously clear, wash-up and set the table for breakfast. Don dragged himself to bed unhappy to be parted from his new friend. The others sat quietly enjoying a last cuppa.

Sophie and Tim, to Mrs Bayne's astonishment, kissed her good night, then crept down the dewy back steps to cuddles in their own little house. Sleep came as they lay listening to the soft brush of pepper tree leaves licking the corrugated iron roof. In their embrace Sophie caught a whiff of the love he had made. She thought sleepily whether to ask him, but drifted away until light and the invasive dawn chorus of the birds woke them for what promised to be a challenging day.

First thing, the boys hastily gulped a mug of tea and hurried out, Don on the tractor, Tim, proudly driving the 'ute' ('You can drive? Good. Anyway, you don't need a licence here.' Mrs Bayne had said). They bumped over the dusty fields arriving at the river where Don hitched-up the flywheel of an ancient tractor to a belt on a quaint water pump to fill the irrigating ditches networking the paddocks. 'We'll leave it all day.' Don said. 'Let's go for breakfast.'

But Tim grabbed him. 'Are you all right?'

'Fantastic.' Don invaded Tim's shorts.

'Ah, it's awake. Hey Don, no underpants?'

'Like you.'

'I want you a lot.'

'Me too, Tim. N o w.'

Don reciprocated, felt the older boy stiffen and freeze. Both Softened. They bounced back for breakfast to face the rigors of the day. They were inseparable. Tim felt manly, drawn-out by the spirited farmer's lad. Don couldn't take his eyes off his older friend. The way his tackled everything was inspiring.

'It's as if he's in love,' his mother told herself. 'And no wonder, what a fine young man Tim is. I'm glad. Don needs a brother, and a sister come to that. The family I always wanted.' The three were washing-up after breakfast. Mrs Bayne fondly swept them all into her strong arms, like the heavy bales of hay she often carried, and hugged them. 'Oh my dears, it's good to have you here.'

Don grinned. 'Too right, Mum.'

It was late afternoon when they met at the house. It was well beyond the two o'clock deadline negotiated. The chores had been tackled willingly, passion was laced with work, a sense of family lifted them all.

After gobbling hunky sandwiches and swilling tea, the sweaty kids dragged Mrs Bayne across dusty paddocks to check the water pump and then to swim in the sluggish river, naked. 'All right, I agree. And how lovely to be with three so very beautiful people.' she shyly murmured.

The late haze of summer filled with shouts and laughter, cries and splashes as the water fountained and smacked gleaming flesh. Later they sprawled on the grassy bank. Birds swinging through the trees sang liquid songs. Mrs Bayne drove Sophie back while the boys unhitched the water pump and lumbered home. While the women were busy in the house the boys went to shower.

Don fell against Tim willing a caress, awed by desire. Made ready, he knelt, then, fingers followed by the big prick filled him. He was so scared, so yearning, so obedient. 'Now fart, long and hard. Yes, great.'

It was good, the wild pleasure and the discomfort. Tim pulled him so close it hurt. He felt a shrinking, a delicious withdrawal. Tim brushed him to life. 'Now it's your turn.' Don sparkled. He edged towards Tim's anus engulfing pleasure.

Kneeling on the floor, his chest on the bench, Tim shook with the spectre of his rape, fighting it with his longing for Don, with memories of Chris, and Sophie's gentleness. He nervously wriggled his butt until the little stiffness slid in. It caressed him. Tim tutored, masking his fear, 'It's all yours. Go for it. Isn't it great?' He felt the boy labour behind him and fall back.

They showered, dried and collapsed on the bench.

'Tim, was I all right?'

'You were perfect. I love you.'

Don cried.

'I know how you feel. It was like that for me. Such a mess of gladness, love and fear, the weakness of being a poofter, of glories in the heights yet disgust at how it's achieved. Do you feel good and bad all at the same time?'

Don dropped his head. 'You said I love.'

'Yes, Don, I do. It saved my life. Can't you feel it?'

'a n . . . n and I love . . . it's the best thing . . . I've ever done.'

'You see, love doesn't have gender. Probably I'm sick, but I take love from, um, both.'

Silence. Hearts beating.

'Sophie and me?'

'Oh, You understand.' Tim kissed his damp cheek.

Don shivered. 'I'm different now; I've left and come home.'

'Why, of course Don. That's right. What a fab day. Leaving and coming home. I know what you mean.'

Fiercely they gripped each other, angry, greedy, confused tenderness. For what had tripped them up lay seething in themselves, there was no other blame. The indignity could only be dealt with by falling, falling, into sin, into feelings, into love. Love would uphold them. It is one aspect of human experience giving the a-personal mystery of life a meaning. Tim and Don sat on the bench unwilling to separate. Sophie discovered them huddling there naked. They started-up as she crooned, 'Come on, you two love birds, it's supper time.'

After supper they dawdled in the living room, unwilling to end the day. Mrs Bayne put a jazz CD on and gathered Tim to her, dancing with him around the room. Sophie inveigled Don to dance. The music slowed, its pulsing beat invited gentle rocking. Both the boys tried to hide their erections, both woman pulled them close. Mrs Bayne fluttered a hand across Tim's bulging shorts before drawing him into her. He trembled at being invited into her body. He sensed a yearning he tried to push away. 'Things are perfect. Don't spoil them.' he told himself. Then everyone had a last cuppa and hugged good night. Teeth were brushed, lights dowsed. The warm, star-twinkling night enfolded them. Tim made gentle love to Sophie, their little house bathed in the dim glow from a smelly paraffin lantern making their shadows dance all over the room.

They were watched by Don who, unable to sleep, had sneaked outside and climbed onto the oil drums under their window. He saw Sophie kiss Tim's luminous body, watched his erection spring into life (as it had for him); saw Tim kiss her, bury his head in her thighs until she moaned and hungrily pulled him up into her. He was bursting, he longed for them as they moaned and strove. He knew now, and yearned, beating himself, beating, beating want and loneliness, desperately in tune with the lovers until she cried, 'I'm coming .' as he sobbed with release, as Don's fluid spattered the wall and he wavered on the unsteady drums, lost his balance and fell in the dust.

Just after dawn Tim crept out of bed, sleepily wriggled into his clothes and stumbled across the yard. The farmhouse was quiet, everyone asleep. He filled the kettle and switched it on. Then he went into Don's room. The boy was fast asleep. His pyjamas and his bed were coated in dust. Tim gently shook him awake. 'It's time to get to the pump.' he said softly. The boy, hardly awake rolled onto the floor and stripped. His side was bruised and dirty. Tim gingerly touched him. 'What happened?' Don winced, and pulled his shirt and jeans on, found his sox and sat fuming on the floor pulling them on. 'Nothing.' He stumbled into the kitchen where the kettle was whistling just as his mother emerged. 'I'm taking the ute. I'll go alone.' he growled and stomped outside.

His mother was surprised. 'Very well, then Tim and I can collect the eggs.' She gave Tim a wicker basket.

Tim took the back steps in one leap and waited for her. They fossicked about finding enough eggs for breakfast, throwing handfuls of wheat for the ruffled birds and filling their water troughs. Mrs Bayne discovered the mess of oil drums. Together they righted the yard. Tim spied drops of cum on the wall under the window, (So, that's why Don is dusty and moody).

'I've heard drums can explode in the heat.'

'Or children upset them.' Mrs Bayne smiled. 'There, that's done. Thanks Tim. Now you'd better wake Sophie.

There was blood on the bed. Now it was light he saw it. Sophie groaned, 'It's my period. It's due now. Tim, please ask Mrs Bayne for *Tampax*. I use medium size, please Timmy. This extra holiday has mucked things up, I planned to be home by now.' She bent over with pain. Tim hurried to the house and bashfully requested help. Mrs Bayne gave Tim a packet without fuss. 'There's an applicator inside. And take these pills to the dear girl, I use them for the pain. Bring the bedding over and we'll wash it.'

Tim found Sophie curled on the bed. He laid her out and stripped her bloodied clothes. 'Let me do it, Soph.'

'Put one in the applicator. Just push straight in, pull the applicator out. Oh, Tim, I'm sorry about the blood.'

'It can't be worse than my arse.'

'It smells pretty bad though.'

'There now, is that right? It's a bit small. Here's some water.'

'You're gentle Timmy. Thanks.'

He helped her along the veranda.

'The pain is the body protesting at all the babies unborn from love-making.' Sophie sighed.

'But I don't know why we women have to suffer it.' Mrs Bayne said, sitting Sophie at the kitchen table. 'Now eat. The pills are death on an empty stomach.' She strode away to fill the washing machine.

Don returned and stalked out shouting, '. . . any way Tim,

you don't give a shit about anything.'

'It's all right. I'll deal with him.' Tim rose from the table went into the yard. Don was crouching under the old pepper tree stabbing at the earth with a stick. Tim dropped to his heels facing the boy who saw his sex peeping from his shorts making him stab more vehemently. 'I know. You don't care about me at all.'

Nets of shadows danced over them.

Tim said softly, 'You spied on us last night.'

'I couldn't sleep.'

'Come in to us any time, even if we're, um, busy.'

Don guffawed.

Tim got angry. 'How'd you like it if Sophie spied on us in the showers? You had no right. Aren't we friends?'

'I, er I wanted to be with you. But you don't care. Bonking with Sophie is all that matters.'

'You didn't have the guts to come in, so you wank off outside and punish us. You're a little shit. You know I love Soph, it's no secret. Why shouldn't we sleep together?'

'You fuck and walk away. You don't care. You just take whatever you need.' You don't think what it's like for me, raped and sent to bed.'

Tim was smashed by ghostly accusations wheeling about his head. 'It's not like that. Oh Don, you mustn't say that. Love is a mess, I know. But we love each other. We dared everything. You know I care. It wasn't rape. That happened to me. All this year I have tried to run away from it. I was so frightened. No one has touched me there. Only Sophie, she's been healing me. Only your gentleness gave me courage to let you in. Only you.'

Don gasped. 'Oh shit. You! You're the boy in the papers?'

Tim nodded, white faced.

'Oh Tim . . .' Don fell forward in a hug. Two bent creatures in the shifting shade, curling from the terrors of the world and those welling inside. 'Oh, Tim. I'm so so sorry. I am a shit. Oh, please.'

Tim shook.

'Come.' said Don. He led Tim across the yard and along a track into the fields. They sheltered under a thick stand of trees. The countryside was bathed in the early piercing light of another summer day. Everything shone. A breeze whispered through the drooping leaves. Bird calls hung in the air with the bleating of distant sheep. These first songs of the day soothed them.

Mrs Bayne watched as they returned hand-in-hand. It had looked to her a terrible battle but their faces were calm. 'Growing up is one turmoil after another.' She told herself. Sophie, who had been resting in the living room, emerged feeling better. 'Well, we'd best get on,' Mrs Bayne said. 'And Sophie, take it easy. There's more to us than men, my dear.' Everyone grinned.

It was another long day. The pumping completed, the fields watered; the timber sawn in the paddock and stacked in the farmyard; a beginning made in the kitchen garden. The boys swam. Sophie watched.

Mrs Bayne said. 'It's amazing, so much done. Well then, tomorrow, let's deal with the sheep.'

'I'll do it, with Sophie,' said Don.

'As you wish, son. Then Tim and I'll finish the vegie garden.'

After supper Sophie and Don watched a TV movie in the living room. Mrs Bayne washed up. Tim helped her. Everything was put away. She wiped her hands on her apron, 'Shall we go for a walk, it's such a lovely evening.' Tim shook, grinned, nodded.

It was a breathless night. Stars pricked the sky, trees hung sleepy leaves to a sickle moon, the earth warmed their feet. They drifted beyond the glow of the farmhouse, swallowed by shadow. A fence barred their way. Mrs Bayne moved along to a stile. In familiar territory, she had taken the boy's hand to guide him. She let it go to clamber over but he held it, pulling her back. He put his arms around her, drew her into the press of his erection whispering, 'Dance with me.' Obligingly she started rocking. His heart was beating frantically. He kissed her so passionately she lost her balance in his young arms.

'It was fantastic last night. When you touched me I died with happiness. I thought you'd be furious. Do it now, please.'

He released her. In the space she slid a hand over his shorts and onto his bottom. He shivered with longing.

'Undress me.'

'No, Tim. We mustn't.'

'We both want it. Why not?'

'Because it's wrong'

'No, the rules are wrong.' He kissed and kissed until her body opened, until he had enough courage to whisper, 'I've never known anyone as incredible as you. A wonderful mother – if only – a wonderful boss, a wonderful sport putting up with our nonsense. P l e a s e. I've wanted you all day. I need you to dance with me and tell me about the farm and your life. I really need you. I can't bear it. Please help me, Agnes.'

The woman was flooded with memories of Cliff, her first passion; this pressure was tantalising, like fifteen years ago, before she married. The same sweet lust whose warmth lingered. Once again she weakened. She was giddied by the virility of the boy. Trembling she gently pushed away and knelt down, unbuttoned his shorts and swallowed his erection. It stunned her: its eloquence, so unlike Steve's which was unrelentingly hard (the only other she'd known). Tim's grew under her caress, swelling with desire.

She crouched on the warm earth, flared by his fire. She struggled to her feet; stripped off her slacks and panties; pushed him back onto the lower step of the stile straddling him, lowering herself down. She felt his foreskin ripple back as he entered; she flexed her strong legs to help him. She gasped, fell onto him. Waves of delight washed her beyond the dust, the rank of posts, the twanging wire, beyond the trees, until her velvet universe sparkled. The silence was broken by gasps and sobs.

'I couldn't wait. It just came.'

'Oh, my dear, my dear . . . Will you come to me in the morning, after the children have gone. We can finish then.' She took the weight on her feet and hugged him warmly. He kissed speechless yes's. He had never known such power in a woman, not even with Fran. They ambled back. 'It's like being carried on a wild flood.'

'Better than a dream.'

'Much.'

Tim was reeling. He couldn't face the light or the house. He crept humbly into bed. This victory had defeated him, he was a lone star. He always had been; but with her he wasn't alone any longer.

When Tim emerged in the morning Sophie and Don had already left. He drank a cuppa uneasily until Mrs Bayne suggested showering. She soaped him saying, 'You have the softest skin I've ever known.' Then he soaped her, kneading the muscles and delighting in arousing her. They dried off and she led him to her bedroom to kiss his dribbling erection.

'Are you very excited?'

'Ya, y, yes.'

'Come a little, then we'll last longer.' He flooded her mouth. She loved, above all, his vulnerable testicles' silken juice, 'It's your soft love with a fragrance of blossom.'

Chasing his arousal, she caressed his entire body – every hidden crease, even between his toes. She felt a tremor as she lightly ran a finger down the crease of his bottom. Don had told her Tim was the boy in the papers but she didn't know how to broach it. She had found the scars. She kissed him there (she had never done that to anyone) saying, 'Don told me you were raped. How could those bastards destroy so beautiful a person. Loathsome, evil men.'

He shivered.

'Shall I stop?'

Tim sweated. 'No, go on.'

'It is a neat little mouth,' she said. 'Is it nice eating someone?'

He couldn't answer. He turned and kissed her breasts until the nipples hardened. He moved down her belly, over her thighs, into her vagina finding a strand of twine swelling as he licked.
She gasped, 'That's enough. I'll come.'

'Come. It's all right.'

'No. That'll be it.'

'Please. I'll bring you up again. Really. Come.'

She floated, basking in the ardour of this incredible boy who ran gentle fingers up and down her drooling labia until it became unbearable having him beyond her. She lifted him with strong arms, opened herself and took him in. Greater spasms racked her. A phallus of bliss, it splintered her sight, her expectations, her dreams, demanding total embrace; she was connected to the earth, she was the earth quaking with a towering life-force wanting everything.

Yet Tim was nearly still. The power was in his body tensing over hers, his penis bursting and searching, feeling for ways to prolong her pleasure, allowing her to breathe and flower without the usual buffeting. He managed to ignore his building excitement. They entered a deeper realm. They became babyish; it was simpler now, just thrusting and feeling. She said without command, 'I can come, when you want.'

He felt safe, in an unguarded place, the place of fecundity where he ad started, an ageless, ancient place reeking of humanity, where to thrash and struggle and erupt was right. Sweat ran off his back. Their skin smacked and bubbled. Her vagina farted, his lank hair clung to his brow and neck. He was gasping, she sobbed as he drove faster.

'I'm so close.'

'And me. N o w.' She was gone. She gripped his phallus with strong vaginal muscles and shook him. He hung like a bridge over her until she pulled all the pent-up seed out of his body. He fell onto her. They dozed.

Only afterwards could Tim answer her eating question. Haltingly he told her about Chris who had picked him up at a tram stop and changed his life. 'Making love is different with a man. It's like being bored through, triumphing when it's my turn. There's a unity of being him when he's hard at it, sharing his pleasure and his prick. Not like being with Sophie or you, sharing difference. It's the same unity at the end. Knowing I've given everything and got even more back – it's embedded in love-making. Is this the first secret of life?'

'Well, for a dumb boy you take my breath away. I've never made love like this, ever,' she said softly. 'You say love's made you. Well, it's made you a wonderful person. I'd never dreamed of where you took me this morning, it is a place so precious.'

'So real,' he murmured.

'Yes, real. We were there.'

'Confronting a giant standing stone, dripping.'

'And covered in blossom, celebrating the power of the world.'

'It was like coming home.'

She cradled his head in her arms and kissed his cheeks as he whispered, 'You are my mother, my earth mother. I've found you.'

She cried into his hair, 'You are my earth-son, longed for ever since Don was born, my missing family.'

'And you're my missing family' He shivered. 'Tell me when you decided to let me in?'

'Last night, when your lovely penis parted me. Then there was no way of denying you.' She smiled. 'When did you begin to want a dried-up old farmer's wife?'

'When we were dancing, I told you, when you touched me, telling me it was all right to want. I loved your strength from your first hug. It was like a man's. I always wanted a strong man-mother who'd hold my craziness and stop me destroying myself.'

She ran the backs of her fingers down his chest. 'There's nothing crazy in you. You're wild and wonderful and filled with the life everyone wants to destroy. Don's like you, but confused still. Please help my little wild boy. Don't hurt him. He's very precious, he's all I've got.'

'I would never hurt him. He helped me, maybe I helped him. We fumble in the dark, just wanting something from each other, something maybe we can't give. I don't know, I felt I was like Chris for him. I'll be as gentle as Chris so he'll grow up strong. There's a bit of me wanting to be him. Wanting to be your son. Now I am.' He tailed off. 'And you've made me feel I can live from deep inside, looked after like your abundant land. Agnes, how can I thank you?'

'Did you find a bit of man in me?' she asked.

'Of course. Like all the best people.'

'Mm, I suppose I saw a sweet, submissive creature and found a giant who toppled me.'

She ran her fingers lightly along his crease and pressed his anus until he lifted his bottom.

'Lick your fingers and push them in.'

She prodded and pushed in. 'There you are, a little bit fucked.' She laughed. 'Now we must go out into the garden.'

But he held her back. 'Will you wear a dress and nothing under it?'

'Whatever the Master wants.' She kissed him again on his delicate nipples, his rubbery sex, his sensuous lips. She reclaimed his clothes from a muddled heap. He wriggled into shorts and a tee shirt, pulled on his boots and stamped out into the garden saying, 'I'll pick you an apple.'

She followed with extra gloves, baskets and a bottle of sweet milky tea she set in the shade. For it would be thirsty work. They each devoured an apple, then Tim clambered up the ladder to pick the rest. He threw his hat down because it tangled with the tree, and afterwards his tee-shirt, feeling free and admired, scaling the sky for apples, and then an abundance of pears and a few oranges whose spicy scent echoed in his armpits which she licked dry when they stopped for tea. She pressed a hand over his shorts. He recognised the hunger, 'Do you want . . ?'

She kissed him and stripped him, caressing his flanks. He felt up her dress, discovering pubic hair. 'You've got nothing on.' She laughed, 'That's what you ordered.' He pulled up her dress and pushed into her as she fell back against a tree. 'Just a mo.' She stripped, lay out below him, pulled him into her. They rose and fell and shook, panting towards orgasm, burning with the sun. They gardened again, until the shimmering heat drove them inside.

Don looked in during the afternoon, 'Ah, great, Tim, you've sharpened all the tools. One less chore for me. The bloody sheep are OK. Sophie soon learned to be still and quiet, so the silly buggers didn't rush about.'

His mother smiled. 'Hello, son. I'll make you both a cool drink. Come on, Tim, you too.'

But Tim was tired, 'No, I think I'll take a shower.'

He was still there when Don joined him. 'It'll have to be soap. I forgot the lube,' croaked Tim kneeling down. Marooned in the flooded shower tray Tim moaned, 'Don, I feel awful', and collapsed.

Don hosed them both down, helped Tim to his feet. 'Tim. Come. The house, come!' He led him up the steps and into the house calling, 'Mum, help, Tim's bad. Mum.'

They shepherded him into the kitchen, dropped him on a chair. His head throbbed and spun out of his arms onto the table, his skin was hot and dry, his breathing shallow and swift. 'It's sunstroke. Don, run the bath and put a full measure of those skin salts in the basin cupboard.'

His mother pulled off his damp towel and led Tim to the bathroom. They helped him slide into the water. 'Now, son, sponge him all over. And duck your head under the water, my dear,' she murmured, and hurried away for salt and pain pills.

He was attentively dried by mother and son, led to the rumpled bed in her bedroom where, wearing one of Don's largest tee shirts, he was laid under a light sheet and soon shivered into sleep.

'It's my fault,' she said. 'I let him work out there without his hat or a shirt. I don't know what came over me.' They were subdued that evening. Sleep is the best medicine, everyone anxiously agreed.

Tim was brighter the next day, but not himself. Mrs Bayne declared a holiday. The chores done, they packed a mountain of flasks and baskets and set off for the river. Everyone gambolled in the sluggish water. They wore hats and tops, even in the shade. They wolfed sandwiches, fruit, and slices of rich fruitcake and drank quantities of liquid; they lay back eyeing one another while Tim and Sophie told stories of their bush-walk and Mrs Bayne regaled them with tales of harvesting and shearing on the farms she had known.

Eventually Don wore only a hat and a big smile; his shyness had evaporated, he wanted to be seen, held by all the arms in their eyes, wanted to nakedly embrace them as he stumbled into adulthood. The picnic was balm to the bonds between the four. They threw themselves at the ruffled river and burst gasping for air, refreshed and triumphant.

Yet Sophie was less engaged, as was her way. Wondering as usual, she lay in the circles of need, aware Tim, her delight, shone now with a securer joy. Clinging to a bough of an enormous tree overhanging the water, Tim clutched her with a free hand. She held him with lean legs scissoring his thighs, arms on his shoulders. 'Oh Soph, I'm so happy, with you, here, and everything.'

She kissed him so tenderly his erection flared, as she said, 'We're fruit of this ancient tree, it's our very own love tree. Tim, I'm happy too.'

'Come, you two. Time to go. Last day tomorrow and quite a bit to do.'

They bounced and sang all the way back to the silent farmhouse, took riotous showers, a bubbling supper and then quietly danced before sleep and the last full workday. Then, Tim and Sophie would return for their last school year at Eliza Beach.

Before driving her workers to a distant siding where they could pick up a train, Mrs Bayne pressed a wad of notes into their hands. 'My dears, you did a month's work. Here are your well-earned wages with all my love. I can never pay you what I owe. No, take it, please. And I'll send you our Don in the next school holidays to trouble you with his antics. Remember, you are always welcome here. Always.' She held their fists closed in her strong hands and firmly hugged them goodbye.

Don fiercely flung his arms around each in turn and kissed them, growling, 'Don't go. See you soon. Hey, you promised.' The children leaned out of the train, waved and waved as mother and son shrank, swallowed up by the haze leaving them to face their journey. They were, perhaps, taller, leaner, more bronzed, fit and more striking. Different?

'Soph, next year when we're at university, can we share a room?' Tim asked. 'I've got used to being with you all the time.'

'Don't you need your independence, like now? Wouldn't you rather we were just down the road from one another and met whenever we wanted, Tim?'

'Is that what you want?'

She struggled, slowly shaking her head.

'Me neither. I love you, Soph. I mean, really. I want to be with you. We've learned to be separate as well as together. Please let me be with you.'

Tears shone in her eyes. 'Oh my Tim. That's all I want. I'm silly that way. But let's wait and see. I love you. More than – '.

He stopped her with a lingering kiss whispering, 'We can be together a lot this year, working and playing and going out, and making love – you know I need that all the time. Soph, this has been such a fantastic time. I can't lose you.'

Rocking to the 'Neither can I, neither can I, neither can I' song of the train, she hugged him, holding something deeply treasured. Now, in wildest joy, she held her very own Tim, who had just miraculously given himself, and come home to her, making the everyday a universe. She blinked at the glory. She held him. Delighted.

'They're only kids but they must be on honeymoon. Early starters – what a pair of lovebirds,' the conductor told himself as he checked their tickets. When he returned along the train he suggested they might like a shower. 'You can come with me to First Class. There's no one there. Pity to waste it. Bring your gear, you'll sleep better there. You've got bags, haven't you?' he said eyeing their bush-whacked packs. The two nodded. Smiling they took them off the luggage rack and followed him to the smart car and were shown into a compartment complete with fold-down beds and a miniature bathroom besides.

'I leave the train at Castlemain,' said the conductor. 'If the next chap asks, tell him Reg from Castlemain put you here. You'll be all right. Best lock the door before you turn in. Cheerio.'

'Another little house of our own. For the whole night,' Tim said grinning.

They unpacked their sleeping bags and spread them on a seat where they lay entwined, staring at the landscape and the lilt of wires, up over poles and down again, pulsing past the window. On and on. Tim's erection was rocked to life as Sophie's breasts danced to the bucking train.

'Soph, let's snack and go to bed.'

Sophie got all the packages Mrs Bayne had prepared and they fell to. They let an upper bunk down, clambered in. Wildly aroused and very, very happy, they kissed and erupted, and rocked all the way back.

Arrivals

1:

BACK HOME WAS MUCH THE SAME. Yet Nina saw a different young man: he was leaner, taller, surer, more available in helping her and seeking her counsel. He held his feelings more easily; at last he acknowledged the devotion of Sophie Dean, that gentle beauty who used to hang around the house helpfully expectant, and now came as if she belonged. Nina was gratified to have a man in the house, and his woman too.

Well after term began, Tim, with Fran on piano, played through a bassoon sonata by Paul Hindemith. During the first movement Vic, her boyfriend, slipped into the music room. Finishing the first movement Fran paused and sighed. Looking at her golden boy she said, 'Tim, there's something new here. You've found your feelings. And it's suddenly happened, you know how to channel them. Wasn't it lovely, Vic?'

The burly man nodded, 'You play it well. It's hard to get at Hindemith, Tim you make him speak. You both do. Go on.'

They played the second, slow movement. The room filled with lugubrious honeyed song leaving her breathless. It's our love-making, warm, articulate, longing, she thought, But my Timtim has changed.

She jumped up. 'Vic, you play so much better than I, please finish it for us.' She stood marvelling. 'Now, lovely Tim, take your time. Don't think so much about playing feelingly, in this last movement you need dexterity. Speed alone will take a player through to a great *finale*. Just concentrate on the run of your line, breathing and fingering. Nothing else. And Vic, not too fast.'

But Vic began faster than he might have. It roused Tim. He galloped too until melody tumbled from his instrument, rising to a breathless triumphant end. Vic conceded a nod of real admiration.

'A great performance. I have to say I've never heard anything like it. You have a great teacher, but you have great talent. Fran, he should play it in your next concert.'

She hesitated. 'There's a lot of work we need to do. Playing here is one thing, facing an audience, another. I'm not sure Tim's ready.'

'Well, he's got to come out sometime. Even a half-baked repeat of today would stun them.'

'Perhaps you're right.'

Tim chipped in. 'Luckily the concert date is in the holidays.' There's lots of time to work at it beforehand,' adding, 'After tea, can we play the version of *In Memoriam* Vic arranged for two bassoons and piano? 'He grinned. 'It's perfect for us.'

Later the trio, knitting and twisting loosely, sounded through the house as the players celebrated the dead twin.

They finished. Fran cried. Somehow they had held her grief. It had been a barren stick beating at her heart; now their playing made it blossom into a living twig whose roots surely whispered in the far distant place where Fiona lay.

Tim remembered. '"Music is the food of love", isn't it,' he whispered shyly taking her hand and squeezing it as Vic sat at the piano saying, 'Hey guys, it really works.'

After that Tim found music all around him, even in cheerful greetings and sad farewells. 'Sounds are feelings,' he whispered to the birds, the nodding trees, the sighing sea. He struggled to restate the world and find his inner voice, to make his bassoon utter the words of nature, the treasury wafting around him. Often he would drop his instrument in fury at its dumbness or at the cloaked way it muffled feelings because of its unwieldy mechanism, and the limits of his skill.

'Tim's playing is transformed,' Fran told Vic one afternoon. 'New sounds, a rare intricacy. I'm quite in love with it.'

'Well honey, he's got a gifted teacher. He'll get honours in his exam, don't doubt it. All praise to you both.'

The term galloped by like a train; the wires of periods, homework tasks, swimming and dreaming, rose and fell until everyone stopped for the autumn break. Don was coming. Tim made up the spare bed in his room saying, 'Nina, he's got green fingers. The two of us will soon lick your garden into shape.' Nina had agreed to Don staying for three weeks, 'He must be a special person for Tim to want him here,' she mused. 'I'm looking forward to having a full house.'

And so Don arrived. He, Tim and Sophie tumbled out of the car like silly puppies and into the house, gambolling around an amused Nina who had prepared a small tea party. How close they are, she thought. Good, the holiday will be successful. And intense, of course. Oh well.

Gladly she farewelled them as they cycled over to the Deans' for supper. Jeff was to lend Don his bike while he was away at a scout camp, allowing the three more scope to explore. Jeff was leaving in the morning, so the four children made up wild shrieking watery games in and around the pool, left to their naked selves, 'Without us adults, I think, until Donald feels more at home,' Mrs Dean added. 'No Mum. Dad. His name is D O N,' shrieked Sophie during the barbecue later. Her parents basked in the happiness invading the house.

Jeff was cross to be leaving. 'I really like Don, he's a young Tim,' he decided. 'But at least I'll be sharing a tent with Martin.'

A day came when Tim took Sophie and Don to help in Mrs Brandt's garden. Don, the expert on pruning, showed them how to trim her unruly trees. Gradually they tamed her garden, then were imperiously called in for tea. Over little cakes filled with cinnamon and apple, and chocolate-covered ginger buns, Tim invited Mrs Brandt to Fran's concert in a fortnight's time. 'You can hear her play your husband's bassoon, and me in a sonata by Hindemith.'

'Not his big sonata, dear boy, it's terribly difficult. Of course I'll be there. No, I wouldn't hear of you getting me a ticket.'

'Two complementary tickets, for you and a friend,' Tim said firmly.

Mrs Brandt looked carefully at the three. Fresh, sensitive creatures, she thought fondly. 'And Don, my deepest thanks. You had no need to spend time on my unruly trees. They and I are so happy to meet you.' She watched them ride away. 'They are attended upon by a brightness as lovely as music. I hope there will be no war. We mustn't lose such precious souls,' she murmured. This added to her nightly prayer to the deity who stubbornly refused to take her from the world – 'Take me Lord, what more have I to give.'

Tim's bassoon practice grew frenetic as the date drew closer. Mrs Dean eagerly took over his concert-dressing, taking him to an emporium. 'Now, what you need is this black polo-neck shirt. We must have matching trousers, and then there's the socks to think about,' she rattled on. 'And soft-soled shoes, you say? For walking quietly on stage? How interesting, yes.' Surreptitiously she added two sets of underwear and insisted on a pair of tough cotton shorts, well cut, which he liked. She went with him to the changing rooms; both were unconcerned about his stripping off. He allowed her to stretch and pull at the clothing to see it fitted well, with room for growth. Even in the larger shorts his sex bulged gloriously. 'Get these jeans for the winter term,' she pleaded.

Tim left the store clutching the parcels. 'It's like Christmas.' He kissed Mrs Dean squarely on her mouth and babbled all the way home about the concert, about how Mrs Brandt was coming and how, if it went well, he and Vic would force Fran into playing her *In Memoriam* trio and how terribly happy he was, particularly spending so much time with Sophie and Don.

Mrs Dean finally clutched at a pause to ask, 'And Sophie, are you getting along with her better, after your hike?'

Tim blushed. 'I, um, love, Sophie. I hope that's all right?'

She cast a quick glance at the boy. Ah, puppy love, she thought, putting a hand gently on his knee. 'She has told me she loves you too. I am pleased. You know I care deeply for you. All our times together. You are part of the family, as you have told us, but now you belong in such a lovely way. I'm glad you're such good friends – and I gather it's a little more than that. Just be careful together, Sophie is still my little girl, I'm a silly Mum that way. But I don't want anything to happen to either of you causing the pain we had to deal with after the police . . . after your . . .'

'Rape,' he said evenly.

Sophie was troubled by Don. She felt his need for her welling up, often clouding his fresh face during cycling, swimming, and just mooning about while Tim was busy. She recognised his many unspoken yearnings having met them in her long courtship with Tim. Uncomfortably she knew how they'd lie together; how he'd fumble and shoot. His tenderness and good humour were adorable. But Tim was enough, surely?

Tim must have known. As they all lay on his bed he started undressing her and then Don and lay back crooning, 'Now you must undress me.' Soon they all lay, skin warming skin, chests and breasts heaving, penises throbbing in the dusky glow of a lamp pushed under the bed. 'Kiss her like this,' Tim whispered, and fed from her mouth. 'Go on, Don.' The bashful boy, longing driving him, took his first deep kiss.

To Sophie it felt sweetly passionate. Swimming in the warmth of their triangular embrace she responded by pushing her tongue through his lips, around his teeth and into his throat.

Meanwhile, Tim began to caress Don's thighs and push teasing fingers into his groin, pulling the boy on top of Sophie, positioning him so he lay between her opened legs. Tantalisingly close to his dream, Don shivered, moaned and ejaculated; he lay abashed. Tim whispered, 'Wasn't that great? It's good coming early. We last longer next time.'

Sophie kissed his face saying, 'Don, it's fine. I like your seed.' But he lay inert at her side. Tim started kissing her vagina, as Don had witnessed at the farm. Sophie shivered and cried, shaking with clitoral orgasms. Don knew pleasure; it aroused his ardour.

Tim again helped him onto Sophie, put his stiff member into her vagina so Sophie could wriggle her hips and pull its engorged flesh inside. Soon she was gargling pleasure which ignited Don's lust and drove him to thrusting focusedly. The pleasure Sophie pushed into him was softer, more responsive than Tim's arse. As mysterious, yes. As stimulating, yes. But there was more; something touching life itself, making him whole in ways he'd almost dreamed yet never articulated. Now he understood. Primal sensations carried him into realms of ecstasy, and he cried in blind triumph, distantly aware of Sophie's moans as he slipped out. He lay replete beside his beloved as her mate tensed his buttocks, thrusting, more impassioned with each drive until, she gasping and he panting, they flew and fell, moaning gently and relaxing onto the bed and into a three-fold embrace. Later Sophie admitted to an enraptured Don, he and Tim were the only men she had known this way.

The evening of the concert arrived. Don and Sophie were dazzled. Their tickets put them near Mrs Brandt and her friend, all at the front where Nina insisted on sitting with the Deans, Janet and Max and a knot of young friends from school. The place was packed with the staid regulars and the unkempt young. The word was out, an amazing pupil of Fran's was making his debut. They came to cheer.

It came after interval. The audience hushed as Tim and Vic walked onto the stage. The children were overwhelmed by Tim, so grown up, a slim black star with a glowing mop of hair crowning his gentle face. They clapped wildly for him, tense on the edges of their seats. Vic smiled warmly at him, playing a couple of low A's to which Tim tuned. Then Hindemith breezed out into the vast space of the hall, silencing even the air conditioning.

The new boy breathed such life into the sonata the music students gasped audibly. The regulars loved the lyrical slow movement. Then there was a pause. Tim breathed deeply, slowly turned the page of his music and glanced at Vic who smiled, winked and nodded. The piano rushed away at an impossibly scintillating speed. The audience was aghast; he was so young, so shy. It was so unfair, that bloody pianist. The bassoon jumped in, flowing, weaving, singing and dancing with impeccable precision, on and on. It was such an exhilarating ride, a glorious race of vivacity. With a huge and intricate cadence the two players finished in a flourish of bravado *fortissimo*. The students at the back of the hall roared. The clapping of the rest was drowned by the foot-stamping, cheering rabble at the back, 'Yer, man. That was music as it should be. Yer man BRAVO,' they yelled. 'BRAVO!'

Tim stood up stiffly. He was running with sweat. He took Vic's outstretched hand and together they bowed, twice, three, four times before gliding off, only to return. Vic gently propelled Tim to the very edge of the stage, standing behind and joining in the applause until in panic at being alone, Tim grabbed at his arm and they bowed in unison again and again. 'Encore,' rang out from an old lady standing near the front. Many had joined her in rising and calling 'More.' Then Vic abandoned Tim to the entire hall, vanishing into the bowels of the artistes' rooms. Tim stood as everyone settled expectantly for a solo.

But Fran emerged dragged by Vic to a small ripple of applause. Tim had set two music stands in the belly of the Grand piano so he and Fran could face the audience and see Vic from the corner of their eyes.

Then Tim stepped forward and raised his voice saying

haltingly, 'I have to thank Fran, my teacher, for everything and Mrs Brandt for almost giving me a bassoon. Now we would like to play for you, for the first time, *In Memoriam for Fiona*. Written by Fran for her twin sister who died tragically not so long ago and arranged by Vic as a trio. To lose someone is awful; to lose your twin is the end of half of your life. Fran is terribly brave. It is a wonderful work. Thank you.' The audience stilled and sat silently while the trio tuned and smiled at one another until Fran conducted Tim in to play.

They sang to one another a simple grave melody, two bassoons weaving a love-string of sound. Nothing else was needed. It was masterful. Then the piano was there. Shimmering. The bassoons emerged from and faded into the hovering piano sounds like huge birds wafting through clouds, like two twins playing together, almost identical, yet delicately different. Some of the acute music students imagined Tim and Fran were lovers drifting, meeting, parting.

At the centre of the piece one bassoon drove downward into its deepest register, and snarled with harsh foreboding. The keys of Tim's bassoon rattled in terror as a death knell thundered. Mrs Brandt shivered, the gunfire faint beyond the train, the ditch. The second bassoon, its frightened cheeping wafting beyond the woods, crying its loss, trying to escape, fleeing upward, lightened by losing her mother's pendant, above the dark forest of piano-held muddy chords with the sustaining pedal kept on so the bassoons 'rang' its strings in responding regret. Mrs Brandt wept.

The final section began in a cheerful major key; the three instruments, calm in a chorale-like solidarity, recalled the 'sung' notes the two bassoons had struck in the undampened piano earlier, as if solace and hope could indeed emerge from suffering. The end was like running gently out of breath: a few studied notes, like scattered thoughts, were uttered more and more softly until the bassoons converged into one risky single dying note, while the piano with repeated drum-like notes at its lowest reach heralded heart-beats, or time, or the spirit of life itself, marking - in dread pulsing - the end and the beginning of everything.

The hall remained silent. Many dwelt on lost loved ones, or private agony, or the dignified beauty from three players so well attuned anything they played would be astounding. Then a wave of living, affirming support lifted the hall as one body. Fran cried and hugged Tim so feelingly her own students bellowed. Then she kissed Vic. Tim, turning the tables, pushed the two of them forward to acknowledge their fine composition. Then they swept the boy up to the front of the stage, with trembling release bowed in unison, and hurried away so the rest of the concert could continue.

The Green Room milled with people afterwards. Tim glanced at Fran, saw her blazing, near tears, as sometimes she was after lovemaking. Mrs Brandt shuffled in bent, girlish with joy. He pushed through the throng waiting to see him, to reach her. Speechlessly they hugged until she burst out, 'I think of my Hans when you play. My goodness, it was a fine performance, a very fine performance. Both of you. Alles! Ah, meine Wunderkind. I swore Hans spoke to me from heaven, reminding me of so many sadness and happiness. There is really a heaven on this earth.' Some of Fran's pupils fell back, silenced. 'Wasn't that maestro Hans Brandt's ancient wife?' they whispered. 'Wow.'

Mrs Brandt pushed the boy to arm's length proclaiming, 'You know, Tim, you sound like an angel playing; and you look like one too. My little gardening god. We were right, Miss Fran wrong. You did deserve a fine instrument; you both do. Hans agrees. Now I will go home. Gute nacht, meine leibling.'

The adoring young mobbed him. Sophie and Don looked across amused, a touch envious. 'Would you come to my school and play?' 'Are you going to the conservatorium?' 'Will you record it?' 'Would you sign my programme?' Gently, shyly, he responded. A ramshackle man approached grunting. 'Well, Macknight, this is a surprise. Another secret out of school.' Mr Adamson, his old form teacher with his wife and daughter shook hands weakly, continuing, 'My bemused daughter insists she meet you. She tries to play the flute.'

Tim turned to a pretty mincing girl. 'I love the flute,' he said. 'It's the bewitching voice of nature, don't you think?' She blushed. 'Shall I sign your programme?' She looked helplessly at him, holding out a creased programme. 'Have you got a pen, Sir?' he asked. Mr Adamson fumbled and produced one. Tim said, 'What's your name?' The girl stammered, 'Victoria.' So Tim wrote, *To Victoria, the prettiest flute player in town, with my love*, and pressed her wrist as she tried not to cry. Mr Adamson retrieved his pen. 'You've done quite well since you left us then.' Tim smiled. 'Because I left.' The old teacher coloured slightly, then guffawed, 'Still cheeky as ever, Macknight. Good luck to you.' And withdrew.

One of the music critics cornered Tim, salaciously pressing him about his transformation from a rape victim into a star and asking, 'Has music helped?'

'Yes, music and my friends.'

'And your teachers?'

'Many of my teachers are my friends.'

The little bespectacled man nodded. 'Well Tim, it was an excellent concert and you played in as masterly a fashion as your teacher. I'll tell the world next Wednesday in my review.'

Shivering, Tim nodded his thanks. Surely he could escape now? He looked at Fran, who understood and nodded 'Let's go.'

2:

THE FRIENDS from Eliza Beach rolled triumphantly home. After all the hard work and then the glory, only sleep could soothe their stretched, aching bodies. Tim dropped as one dead. Don, speechless with admiration, saw him to bed and then shyly turned off the light; he lay in the moon-silvered dark seething with images of Tim's concert (as he saw it): how fantastic to have Tim conjure up the vastness of the country, the shimmering stands of dense forest - the pelts on hills and sprinkled in valleys - his own minuteness in the vast sun-drenched spaces, the rich emptiness in the Bush itself, the long meandering life of the river, all the excitement of fucking and fury, of being alive with Tim and with Sophie, and all the things he promised himself he would accomplish. He fell asleep trying to recall them.

The next day the boys were left to their own devices as Sophie went with her father to collect Jeff from scout camp. They rose late, breakfasted and threaded down the steep path over the cliffs to an empty beach, just warm enough for them to strip and swim. They wore togs – 'This is not our own river,' they grinned. They played and surfed, at which Don was very good, beyond beginner's luck, until goose-pimpled they scrambled up the cliffs to a warm shower and joyful sex, wonderingly, as if for the first time.

For Don, it was being god-touched.

For Tim, who had just found a letter addressed to him under Don's clothes in his suitcase, it produced a cyclone of feelings about potency, a sense of the tangible effects of love and of his prick in the real world, as distinct from the floating world of his feelings and dreams. Mrs Bayne had written:

> *My dearest dearest Tim,*
> *Don will give you the news that Steve and I are to*
> *have another child. But I want to tell you myself.*
> *I am sure you understand my agony and my joy.*
> *You are right. It is a repeat. This time I am truly*
> *happy. I hope you feel all right. I mean about this,*
> *and about us. I mean, about all of us!*
> *Steve and I would love it if you would agree to be its*
> *godfather. If it is a girl we want to call her Sophie.*
> *If it is a boy he will be called Tim.*
>
> *I am crying with happiness as I write to you and*
> *remember how we found that ancient, sacred blossom-*
> *clothed dolmen with all the beautiful and sacred*
> *spirits of life. And of my memories of you holding*
> *it with me as we danced together. I can*
> *never, never forget. Please forgive.*
> *You hold all the secrets of my life. Keep them*
> *close to your heart and away from your lovely*
> *gossiping lips just as you promised me!*
>
> *Remember, every child of love is sacred.*
>
> *I hope you are all right and that your concert*
> *goes well. Don will tell me all about you and*
> *Sophie when he returns. Look after him, my*
> *dearest. I know you will.*

Don't worry. I'm all right. I'm truly happy!
I'm resting. I miss you!
All my love,
A.
PS: I hope it has your grey eyes.

XXXXX

'Sorry, I forgot, I thought I'd given it to you,' Don said. 'Sure, Mum and Dad have started again. I've wanted a sister and a brother forever. Now it's a bit late. Anyway, now I've got Sophie and you.' He grinned. 'Oh yes, I'm pleased for them. They seem happy about it.'

Tim, panicking, pressed the younger boy to go exploring on his bike. He was awash, unable to feel anything clearly, with no-one he could turn to. He sat trembling until he remembered Nina and stumbled through the house looking for her.

'My dear, You're shaking. Is it that letter?'

He nodded.

'Give it to me. Make us mugs of tea, bring them to the library and tell me how I can help. Timothy, courage. We can cope. Really.'

Over tea he told her everything: about the mathematics proving Don's conception by her friend Cliff; about the masculine yet deeply feminine mother figure who had taken him in and given him a home-coming lifting him into the world; of the delights; of the striving; of sharing things with no words only echoes of the array of humanity's dream, of his moment of feeling the godhead throbbing in his arms; of a new-found freedom within himself; and of embracing some of the deepest most perfect love he'd ever known.

He stammered, 'I don't know what to do, being a father.'

She caught the rigid boy and drew him to her withered chest. 'Would you agree, my dearest Timothy, you had been struggling up to that moment as much with your past as with trying to define your future?'

Pale and trembling, Tim looked at her. He was so contained by her concern, her understanding, her fierce engagement, he outfaced the demons plaguing him. He nodded.

Nina took his listless hands and held them in hers, warm dry faded yet very able, saying, 'Timothy, remember far back, we read *The Chalk Circle*, where we had Azdak's Golden Age pronouncement like this: "To the committed drivers, let them have the carriages, to the green- fingered, let them become our gardeners, to the motherly (and fatherly) let them have the care of our children – and never mind whose seed made them."' *

Tim nodded. Sweat ran down his back.

'My dear. Think of the little prince at the end of the play. Don too has a loving mother and father. Now there will be another little prince, or princess, whom these loving parents will nurture. Only your silence can make that possible. And your being able to bear this burden, small compared to the gifts coming with it. Only you can help this Golden Age to come about. It's not a question of who made the child – as Azdak says, siring a child does not necessarily make one its parent – rather, it's they who love and care for it.

'If you admit to siring you'll destroy its family, destroy Sophie and destroy a future you have struggled for. This is the time to abide by the rascally rules of that rascally judge, and not convention or law. That is what, in her own inarticulate way, your earth mother is appealing for. And you must do it. Gift to this child what you sought so ardently. Think of this particular secret not as a stone dragging you down but as another tiny beating heart bringing them, and you, a new breath of life, if I can mix my bodily parts. A new innocent heart some of us are privileged to bear as a secret, one emerging from our deepest most humiliating and heavenly struggles. I happily bear a clutch of such secrets, so I speak with insight.'

She was silenced by reminiscences and a tousled head falling into her lap wet-cheeked, shaking, moaning, 'I couldn't lose Sophie.'

'Well, that's it,' Nina tendered, 'Don't you see. There really is no conflict. You can keep everything, Timothy. Everything you have ever wanted. Everything, if you can add a small new heart which, actually you have carried for some time; I have seen it many times shining your eyes, making your body bloom, adding an edge to your laughter and strength to your able hands. Just accept the load, it's light. Go into your own Golden Age, and theirs.'

The old lady looked gladly through her tears at the troubled boy who had turned, astonished, and was looking up at her.

Tim struggled to his feet and very tenderly took Nina in his arms whispering, 'Oh Nina you are the most wonderful person in

---

*   See notes at end.

the whole world. I am such a trouble to you.'

Nina smiled. 'Yes, you are; but Timothy, make no mistake, you bring with you such riches it lifts my old heart. This house glows, as I do, having you here. It has been such a joy helping you to find yourself. I tell you, I could not have coped without you. You have kept the old house and me going with care and love and all the small tasks you undertake.' She stopped. 'Which brings me to something I want to say: From now on, I want you to put your own work before anything needing to be done here. I'll get Maria's nephew Lui to do the lawns and some trimming, if you would show him. I want you to get through this last school hurdle. I have spoken to Chris and we will share additions to your bank account until you are settled at the university. No arguments. Remember, we love you very much and don't want you to fall at this stage. Of course, it depends on your agreeing to silence and a Golden Age.'

In the glowing light in the book-lined library peace reigned. The old lady sat quite still while the radiant, tear-stained young man nodded over and over again as her advice echoed and was answered, thought on thought, until she saw a fervent nod of understanding and conviction. He stood before her, no longer the bruised and abused boy but a man born from struggle and love into a troubling world.

Later, calling for them and slamming doors on the way, Don burst in, taken aback by the quiet. 'Hi. Um, is everything OK?'

Nina looked fondly at this lively younger image of Timothy. 'Yes. Everything is OK. Isn't it?'

Tim took her arm, almost floating. He carefully nodded. 'Yes. And I need your help in the garden, Don. Are you free?'

For a contented hour or so Don helped Tim who said gratefully, 'You're so green-fingered, Don. You are the best.'

'Not really. I'm useless at school. I don't like books. I want to be a farmer like Dad.'

'Hey, you're brilliant at that. I've seen you driving, pumping, wood-cutting and herding the sheep, servicing engines, playing in the river, making love, taking charge when I collapsed. You're no drooling clot.'

The boy blinked, warmly doubtful. 'Only you think that. Perhaps Mum and Dad. And Sophie.'

'Don, you're not the fool, it's the school and the teachers – all

189

the clots who run our lives. They value the wrong things and make us failures because they don't understand what to measure or what's important or what we have to do to get there. They trip us up with fear and judgement – anyway, that's what Nina thinks. I know you're brilliant. You've got certainty, that's more than I've had.'

He fiercely hugged him. 'But if you want to be a good farmer, you'll have to know all the technology of farming: the biology, the chemicals used on the land, about fertility, how water leaches the soil, reading poetry and reports, how to be a sheep doctor and a tractor doctor, a tree doctor, a doctor of fucking, for your wife.'

Their laughter brought Nina to her window, smiling.

'You need to go to university. You must do well at school. So I'll tell you how to do that, I've been through it. Listen, first talk to a family friend. What about your parents' friend Cliff?'

'Uncle Cliff. I like him. I can talk to him.'

'Good. Then you must find one or two teachers you like and ask for extra lessons. Your parents will pay. For, what happens at school is part of becoming a farmer, not a punishment for being a silly little fool. Everyone's a silly little fool at school, even teachers.' He pressed against Don's wiry frame, feeling budding response. 'You're a silly little fool wanting to fuck.'

'So are you.'

'Of course I am. But you know the rewards of working hard at sex. It's the same with books and thoughts, and doing things.'

'But I can't come after reading about geography or science.'

'But it's fun. You'll be horny with everything you learn. It's like sex. Better, because you can go on and on.' he grinned. 'Don, I'll help you. But only if you promise to break your balls trying. Together we can do anything. You know that. And Soph can help with the baby so your mum can make us drinks and snacks and we can dance in the living room and walk under the trees, as before.'

Don's lip trembled. Then he needed Tim to shove and spurt, filling him, sharing life, friendship, hope and the power to do anything. Hurriedly the boys washed and went to the bedroom. In turn, they groaned emptying and filling, sprawling wasted, and reviving on a bed wrinkled with the calligraphy of lust; their miraculous contract made, signed and sealed with signatures of velvet seed on the vellum of themselves.

3:

'AND IT CAME TO PASS . . .' At the end of the year Tim and Sophie were offered places at university. Sophie, near the top in school, would start a Pre-Med course; Tim, with a sound pass and brilliant results in music and science, would continue at the conservatorium; both on full scholarships. Don forged a link with Cliff and began to take his schoolwork seriously. His parents and Cliff were delighted.

Summer returned. The four children planned a bush hike. Don would bring his girl friend. They would retrace some of Tim and Sophie's earlier journey, starting out from Don's farm.

Tim and Sophie began hunting for accommodation; the Deans offered to pay. Nina's Maria had a friend who was letting the top of a terrace house near the university: two rooms, kitchen and shower, with outside WC. 'Someone, almost family,' Nina observed, 'to keep an eye on you.' Sophia and Toni were doing it up. It would be ready for term time. Come with your things before. 'Bellissima, bellissima, mio carissimo,' cooed Sophia. Mrs Dean paid the deposit.

Meanwhile, Chris was expected. Sophie told Tim to do whatever he felt was best – she'd be near if he needed her. When Chris arrived he booked into a hotel nearby. Tim took Sophie to meet him. It was awkward at first, but Chris was delighted by Tim's life and Sophie whose passion for Tim mirrored his own. 'I dreamed you'd find someone like Sophie. You deserve the very best, both of you.' He hugged them warmly, tinged with sadness. Sophie understood: Tim was being offered to her.

'I don't mind if Tim stays with you tonight,' she whispered. 'He's told me everything. I know how close you are.'

Chris was startled by her trust. He looked questioningly at the fresh-faced pair, tempted, so tempted. 'Fantastic, Sophie. But it's up to Tim. We could say goodbye now. It may be easier.'

Tim felt saturated: his two most precious friends; he was so happy and terribly sad. He swayed between them. Helpless. Both essential. He cried and took the man's haggard face in his hands, covering it in kisses. Felt the firm trunk containing so much of the love he had absorbed, so much of the power enabling him to face the challenges of growing up; it was all his important yesterdays, as

Sophie was his future.

Desperate to unite them, with his usual impetuosity Tim dragged both to the huge bed, tumbled over them, pulling off clothes to reach the two bodies where he had found himself. He fell blinded by passion on Chris kissing fumbling for, finding his softest spots. Tim felt strong hands turn him as Chris and Sophie caressed him, kissing desire into him until he lifted his hips, imploring the manly phallus. Hugely it split him. He burned and flickered as it thrust and probed till he was seeded. Both men lay gasping, undone from this striving after a dead dear dream, while the girl aflame with fearful wonder lay watching over them as only women can, weeping for their and her vulnerability.

Later Tim fell into her yearning legs and laboured until they both cried out their youth and love, a victory over doubt and terror, over all the unknowns haunting the inexperienced, what their bodies and dreams laboured for when relinquishing everything.

'I'm glad I saw it' the girl whispered later, caressing the two men. 'You're beautiful. Bound by such a fierce ageless love.'

The three sprawl close. Trancelike. Changed. The girl experiences the power connecting her to everything through her precious boy. The three doze. Chris wakes first. With these children he had ventured into the primal bed-chamber and touched the ecstasy in his own conception. Love shows the way, he thinks, including pitfalls. But now it was time to go. With infinite care Chris rises and dresses. He sadly fills his case and tiptoes from the room, its breathing silence undisturbed.

Tim and Sophie awaken. Rush to the window searching for him. 'Look, is that his car?' Kneeling naked on the ledge they strain their eyes. Somewhere in the traffic below, Chris navigates towards a distant airport. One of those tiny gleaming specks is him, vanishing into the haze, a mirage? The children search vainly, blinded by feelings and by distance and by time.

The heat-burned trees hang their heads as usual. The birds flutter, thirsting as always. The infinite sky, ablaze with blue, stares unblinking on the world revolving as it has for many millions of years; and to Tim and Sophie it's wonderful.

Ageing

1:

IN A COMFORTABLE COLONIAL STREET, the two-storey terrace houses have balconies at both levels with frilly cast-iron balustrades throwing frozen shadows mimicking the trees. There, one Saturday a week before term starts, Tim and Sophie stand outside Toni and Sophia's brightly painted house waving as Mrs Dean and Janet pull away in their empty cars.

The two young ones stomp up the stairs to their first floor flat and continue to unpack. It is a much bigger exercise than arranging their little house on the Bayne farm but they find a place for everything. Tiredly they sprawl in the two huge upholstered armchairs Toni had manhandled up and into the large front room – their workroom – sip long frosted glasses of beer and sigh. 'Well, here we are.'

Tim bends over Sophie, grins and picks her up. She throws her eager arms about his shoulders; he staggers with her along the short passage into the bedroom overlooking the rear yard, nudging the door shut and falling with her onto a large double mattress on the floor. It is covered in a colourful kilim Nina unearthed. Another one in red, purple and brown with strutting birds and deer hangs on the wall behind their heads, a forest extension of the bed.

Joyously she pulls the cover back as he strips first her and then himself. They lie smiling in their new life with a gentle exchange of whispers, then kisses, then lovemaking to the stuttering arguments of sparrows in the eaves until she moans, 'Oh Tim' and he replies after his love gushes into her, 'Yes. Soph, it's so good.'

Waking later on the bed and in their first house, there is so much she wants to say. But the sun drenches them in dazing warmth so all she manages is, 'Tim, we must try to share and to be separate. You need your space. But let's go on being wild together too.'

He leans over and kisses her stomach. 'But no secrets, eh?'

She stretches and kisses his elegant neck. 'Our house will be our refuge where we return from the comings and goings.'

They decide they will make it a soft nest, leaving shoes at the head of the stairs as the Japanese do, and pad about barefoot.

Tim rolls over and looks at her tenderly. She is so beautiful he falters, perhaps for the first time. But she is too knowing, joyful in his hanging back; she rolls onto him nibbling his tiny nipples and chewing at his neck, rubbing his inner thighs and tweaking his sacs elongating in the heat until his erection stands up again and she straddles it. She rises up and down with delicious pleasure until weakening. He turns them over and re-enters. They forget the neighbours. The floor thunders. They erupt. He now basks on top of her, the sun bathing his back, his face dusky in the sheets. 'Never leave me,' she whispers. He shakes his head. 'Never.'

On a following Sunday morning, while Sophie makes breakfast and potters   happily at the back of their flat, Tim practises for a scholarship performance early in the term. He is working on *Canzona*, another piece by Hindemith unearthed by Mrs Brandt. Fran is very excited, for it's an autographed original manuscript given Hans in 1950 by the composer; she insisted Tim photocopy it and return the original to Mrs Brandt, who had a pile of such treasures. He and Fran had been working on it for many weeks, 'You'll have to find a pianist when you're at the Con,' she advised. 'There're lots of able accompanists there.'

Tim and Sophie pull a table onto the sunny front top veranda and perch over breakfast like two chirping birds. They dress and go exploring along their road into the shopping street filled with eating places, a book shop, three pubs, milk bars, and bijou shops selling cheese, coffee, pastries, groceries, and clothes, thronging with students enjoying their last weekend before term.

They wander into *Readings,* a bookshop where Tim discovers in a glossy book on Greek sculpture a reproduction of the statue he was likened to in Greece all those years ago. While he pokes about in the music section Sophie buys it and hides it in her bag. She gets a book on the ethics of medicine and he a set of essays on music by Wilfred Mellors which they open over fruit juice in a nearby bar.

But they can't read, it's too exciting. Tim is speechless, Sophie too. They beam. He pushes her leg with his. She sees such desire shine in his face. She leans into him and kisses him. He shuts his eyes savouring everything.

'Look, those Freshers are so in love.' someone says watching as the two, arm in arm, blissfully saunter back to their flat.

That evening they have their own candle-lit dinner – a mountain of pasta which Sophia insists on, a bottle of wine from Toni, and a plate heaped with fresh summer fruit. Tim finds a present standing at his place, the Greek book with an inscription saying, *My love, my Acolyte of Zeus. Always throw your thunder - bolts at me, yours for ever, Sophie.*

'Have I done wrong?' she asks, seeing Tim blinded.

He shivers. 'Is it possible to be so happy, Soph?'

She hugs him. 'For now. For ever.'

'I'm happy and crying like a silly girl.'

'Stars on your cheeks.'

'It's your fault.'

'It's yours. And mine. Timmy, eat! Here's to us.'

'Wow. I'm famished.'

Freshers' Week was fun, particularly for Tim who knew many of the music faculty already. He would join the choral society, Sophie the art club and the students' paper. She took him to the medical faculty to sort out the science course he was adding to his music syllabus and showed him where she would be studying; they went to a crazy concert by the music students, filled with jokes and wheezes.

Then they hurried home to shower, to lie on their bed and review the day, to share desire before tucking into a bowl of mixed salad using Sophia's olive oil and lemons from her garden.

Later they sprawled in the armchairs listening to CDs. They emptied the last few cardboard boxes, squashed them and put them out for collection with Tuesday's rubbish. Naked in a summer night ringing with sounds from all the open windows glowing around them, they lay together in their bedroom ('our bedroom,' Sophie whispered) until he took her and emptied all his love into her so she sighed. 'Oh Tim. You are beautiful. That was so good.' She drifted into sleep thinking, It's not possible to be happier than this.

The early morning sun blasted off the buildings overlooking the garden. Sophie curled up dazzled in the big bed while Tim warmed up on his bassoon and got down to practise. 'He has no money. He needs the scholarship,' she said to herself. She tiptoed in with breakfast and stood behind him putting her arms about his trunk, kissing his neck and pressing the soft pouch in his crotch until it began to swell.

'I've made you breakfast, when shall we eat?' she whispered.

He put the bassoon down carefully, rose and pulled her to him. 'Can it wait till later?' He led her down the hall to fall onto the bed, feeding off skin, basking in depths until he spouted into her. They showered, bounced into breakfast and gobbled their eggs.

'Tim you look fantastic.'

'So do you.' He smiled. 'We'll have to dash.'

They abandoned coffee and hurried off for the last day before the real work would begin. Just inside the campus gates their paths diverged. He murmured, 'Soph, before you go.' He put his bassoon case down. They embraced shyly; her mouth opened as he planted soft long kisses of farewell; their lips melted. Alan Martin paused on the steps to the medical school, arrested by their tenderness. The long slip of a boy bounded away, the succulent girl, bright-eyed, proudly bosomed with a shining ringlets of brown hair, drifted along the path towards him.

'Good morning. Wasn't that young Tim Macknight?'

She flushed. 'Yes.'

'And you, I think, must be Miss Dean? I am Doctor Martin, the registrar. We have an appointment in a few minutes. I knew you from photos of students we have in faculty. Do come to my office?'

They walked slowly down a sunny corridor through the throng of students and into his roomy office filled with files, books, a jug of flowers on his desk and two bright landscape paintings on the walls. He hung his jacket on a hook behind the door and motioned Sophie into an easy chair by the window, taking a slim file with her name on it from his desk and sitting comfortably in the second chair.

He smiled encouragingly at her. 'How do you know Tim Macknight?'

'We grew up together in Eliza Beach.'

'Ah, so you know Doctor MacKay?'

She nodded.

'He was finishing just as I started medicine. He was the most brilliant student. Did he inspire you to take medicine?'

'He encouraged me. How do you know Tim?'

'Oh, my family and I are fans of Fran and of Tim. We go to their every concert. We're amateur musicians. I play the cello, my daughters the violin and viola, and my wife is the pianist.'

Sophie smiled. 'The Martin Quartet.'

'We don't broadcast it. Did you meet Tim by chance just now?'

'No, we are sharing digs.'

'Ah, I see. How lucky you are. May I warn you about the stress which is inevitable when your work begins to overwhelm you, which it will. Always try to keep some time for your relationship whatever else; work feeds off life as well as enriching it. And remember, I'm always here for every student. So do drop in either for a chat, or if there's something you need to talk over. Don't be embarrassed, it's my job.' He stood up. 'Miss Dean, we are particularly pleased to have you with us, there are too few women in Medicine. We need you.'

Sophie felt more secure. 'Thank you. By the way, would you like to hear Tim play an original piece by Hindemith he's discovered? He'll be playing it in the Con for the scholarship concert in three weeks' time. It's for bassoon and piano, called *Canzona* just as the composer wrote it.'

'And does this mean your missing your lecture here?'

She nodded.

He was charmed. 'I'll try to arrange things so I can come. Let me know the date and time, will you, Miss Dean? Perhaps you should inform your lecturers before you absent yourself. They will probably accept it if it's a rare occurrence.'

They walked to the door, the sun pouring into his friendly office and glancing off his thinning hair. He shook Sophie's hand saying, 'It's nice to meet you. See you soon Miss Dean,' and let her out, graciously ushering in the next student as she slipped away into the melee of the medical department.

Tim was anxiously talking to the music librarian about copying his score and looking for a pianist when they were interrupted by a shambling girl in third year looking at the

Hindemith score as if at a holy icon. She took it from Tim saying, 'Wow. Neat and orderly like his music. Wow.' Her face grew girlish as she stammered, 'Do you know his treatise on composition, it's fascinating. I agree with him, no time for mechanistic composition.'

'Do you two know each other?' asked Sue the librarian. 'Grace Stone, Tim Macknight. Grace, a brilliant composer, Tim . . .'

Grace interrupted, 'Is our famous first bassoon. Yes, yes.' She imperiously shook his hand. 'Wherever did you find this treasure?' They moved their discussion to a corner of the room until there was a 'Sh,sh,sh' from other readers.

'Let's go and have a coffee,' Tim whispered, winking at Sue in apology and ushering Grace out the door.

Grace, plump and ungainly, was direct, her enthusiasms bubbling in her talk, transforming her into someone wonderfully wild and interesting. She felt at home with Tim, who was so intense yet not aggressive, possibly gay. She pored over the Hindemith piece, wondering aloud at its focused energy. 'Is it good bassoon writing, do you think, Tim?'

'Some of it's really difficult. Even Fran says so. But it sounds great. By the way, do you know an accompanist?'

'Oh, let's go and see Robert. He'll do it well.' She scrambled to her feet and dragged Tim to a practice room strewn with music and manuscript paper where a slight tense boy was playing the piano.

Robert looked unwillingly at the composer's scrawl. 'I don't know. There's not much time. I'll have a go,' he said, and blushed. They agreed to try it out that afternoon. Grace inveigled herself in as page-turner. 'I can't stop looking at his hand on the page. Stravinsky is the greatest, but Hindemith tells us how to do it.'

The word got round. Robert, Grace and Tim were cooking up something special for the scholarship concert. The hall was thronged with students, one or two staff and their professor, Dick Maxwell, who hurried from a meeting just in time to acknowledge Alan Martin sitting to one side with a pretty student, as Robert and Tim climbed the steps onto the platform. To Maxwell's alarm, Tim opened the lid of the grand, He'll be drowned, he thought in dismay.

Tim sucked and wet his reed and tuned. The piano stuttered its first bars heralding the lilting uneasy entry of the bassoon. It was a big sound, gloriously filling the hall, the two friends struggling with the giant demands of the score, the subtleties of texture and detail. Between the first and second sections there was a single clap and a clearing of throat from Doctor Baxter, one of the adjudicators sitting at a side table. 'I think that's enough,' he called out. 'You must learn to prepare more thoroughly next time. Too many inaccuracies.'

This was greeted by silence. Slowly Tim rose from his chair, whispered to Robert and turned towards the table saying evenly, ' We are playing what the composer himself has written.'

'How can you say that?' Doctor Baxter barked, 'We have a score here, Breitkopf and Härtel, Leipzig. There's not time for a detailed examination, there are others waiting to play.'

Tim was sweating. 'We have the composer's own handwriting here. See for yourself.' He pulled his score off his music stand and marched over, threw it onto the table and stormed back, pushing the stand to one side and sitting down. He took a deep breath. The people in the front row saw him shaking. He turned slightly and nodded to Robert to start again. There was a gasp of admiration as the music, getting off to a shaky start, again filled the hall. Fran was in tears watching her beloved Tim playing magnificently from memory, a piece he had studied and slaved over. The sound was inextinguishable.

The two boys filled the dismissive silence again with the first movement so full of conviction everyone sat up. There was a pause. They played the second. Then the last. The final chord rang long and clear, then a torrent of applause until everyone's hands ached. Tim took Robert's sweaty hand in his and they bowed. He stalked over, snatched his music from the table and strode out of the hall. I don't give a shit, Tim thought angrily. 'Thanks, Robert. You were tremendous.' He hugged his dazed accompanist. Already the next performance wafted faintly through the closed doors of the hall.

Alan Martin nudged Sophie. 'He's wonderful. Go to him, my dear.' She stumbled out, eyes brimming, and hugged him. 'We all thought you were brilliant, you and Robert. What a pig. Who is he?'

Robert, blazing from the effort and Tim's hug, said, 'Oh, he's Doctor Baxter, head of composition here. No balls and no judgement.'

Grace stomped through the doors shouting, 'Tim Macknight,

you were stupendous. Robert, fantastic playing. The best thing I've heard here. Some real music at last.' She eyed the pretty tearful girl clutching Tim, So, he's not gay then, she mused and shook Sophie's hand. 'We all know music is beyond that dried-up piece of shit.'

Alan Martin left the conservatorium shaking a bemused head. 'That's no way to deal with students. Particularly ones as talented as young Tim. No wonder the students complain,' He murmured as he hurried back to his duties in the Medical School. In a quiet moment he penned a short note to Sophie:

> *Dear Miss Dean.*
> *Thank you for telling me about Tim's concert, which*
> *I thought a triumph. I wonder whether you could*
> *persuade him to join us at home for next month's*
> *music making on the twelfth. We would be delighted*
> *if he would play for us. But would be delighted*
> *to have you both in any event . . .*
> *Sincerely yours,*
>
> *Alan Martin.*

Fran was beside herself with fury. She stormed into Professor Maxwell's office crying, 'So, what are you going to do. Disqualifying Tim is a disgrace. . . Well, Dick?' Dick Maxwell looked up from his cluttered desk, surprised at the vehemence of his wild-eyed gypsy reed teacher, 'Fran, it's up to them. I can't interfere.'

He had never seen her so upset. My God, she's so involved with her students. It's admirable, if a little disturbing, he thought as she crashed out of his office leaving her displeasure ruminating in its corners long enough for him to stumble on a supplementary plan (his ability to calm troubled musical waters was one of his many aptitudes as head of the Department).

Grace disappeared for two days of struggle emerging triumphant to present Tim and Robert with a musical reply to the Philistines, a piece based on Hindemith's opening bassoon theme which wove an intricate and evocative series of cries, of love and of pain from the top of Tim's register to the bottom, and involving him in saying as he played a central theme: 'Baxter, you shit' which was of course unrecognisable but brought comfort to the performers.

Since Tim had given-up on getting the scholarship, Grace's piece was compensation.* Robert and he played it through then offered it to the weekly student lunchtime concert where the ruffled students eagerly pressed them to introduce it with the Hindemith *Canzona*. This world premier was scheduled in two weeks time, just after the scholarship results were to be announced.

The scholarships, three of them, were duly announced by Doctor Baxter to the slightly embarrassed recipients and to a hall of stony students whose anger at the injustice was palpable; until Professor Maxwell came forward to say, 'Ladies and Gentlemen. It's my office to allot the four-yearly Faculty Scholarship in the name of Percy Grainger. As you know it reflects what I and the faculty think a student's talent, seriousness and contribution to the Faculty is likely to be, or has been. Also his, or her need is considered.

'This year the PG Scholarship is again due. After careful thought and due consideration we are pleased to announce the recipient this time round is Mister Timothy Macknight who has already . . .' the rest of his speech was drowned in hooting and cheering and cries of 'Bravo!' as Tim was pushed to his feet and was born on waves of encouragement and pleasure to confront their admired Professor, have his hand shaken and be photographed for the students' paper. Everyone beamed.

The atmosphere in the faculty was transformed into a busy hive of music making bees. After a troublesome beginning the year is now off to a good start, Prof. Maxwell decided. The next appreciation was from Fran who burst into his office and kissed him. 'Dick, I love you.' and rushed cheerfully away to her teaching chores. 'Music is the food of love', she fondly reasserted Tim's quote. 'Papa Shakespeare was right.'

Tim returned to the flat with a bunch of his friends for a celebration. Sophie was as delighted as all of them. Sophia and Toni were invited up. There was much shouting and drinking, many hoots at the expense of Dr. Baxter and his subservient committee.

Sophia cried authoritatively everyone must come down to the garden for a proper Italian pasta, 'Pronto.' Toni uncorked armfulls of Cianti and Vino Verde. It was early in the morning when everyone happily drifted away - rolled might be a more

---

*   see notes at end.

accurate description. Peace descended on the house.

Upstairs in bed Sophie nuzzled up to Tim. 'Tim, I'm so proud of you.' He trembled. The cruel world had been tamed. He unsteadily pushed into his own dear girl. The two lovers slept as they came or came as they slept (it was muddled delight carrying them), discovering their future was secure facing it with friends. They were confident that, as Tim had promised Don (as Chris had promised him), "Together, we can do anything."

Tim and Robert played through Grace's 'protest' soon afterwards. There was much discussion about Tim's idea the recurring theme, hidden most of the time, emerging at the end, be emphasised by another instrument. 'After all, it is firstly doubt, then understanding and then conviction,' Tim cried. 'We need to hear how it grows into a clarion call.' Grace nodded ruffled if grateful for the careful attention. Robert's suggestion of a viola won the day. Grace, who had laboured for so long, wearily went off to re-jig the piece while Robert hawked it around the cat-gut crowd until he caught a willing performer. Fran suggested to Professor Maxwell it be aired at his quarterly concert at home. The youngsters were pleased, 'Our trio has been noticed. Great.'

Tim worried about Robert's tension. He seemed to withdraw rather than unleashing his feelings to underpin his playing. He felt Robert's yearning rebuttals when he touched him; he had either been severely hurt or was terrorised by values and unable to cross the line into sexual activity. Sophie listened to Tim's concerns. Saying little, wondering whether Tim would try to take him to bed, I know my Love meddles with bodies, she thought. I suppose it's his way of dealing with the unspeakable. She was working very hard, overwhelmed as Doctor Martin had predicted, and as usual, stepping back and allowing things to take their course with Tim but with growing confidence it would turn out all right in the end.

One afternoon Tim was sitting beside Robert on the piano stool listening to him playing when he interrupted softly and said to the tremblingly tense young man, 'Rob, it's wonderful. Relax.' Then he turned him, took him gently into his arms and kissed him whispering, 'If you can't give yourself to the music, give yourself to me.' Robert shivered. He drew back. Tim touched his fly pushing at its imprisoned stiffness and brushed his sad pale face with a gentle hand. 'Rob it's OK. Let me in. You must share with someone, before it destroys you. Rob?'

Two students sauntered along the tree-lined avenue from the conservatorium to Ormond College where Robert was staying. They moved through pools of shade darkening their features to fury, then into sunlit spaces where strained expectancy swept them. It was mid-afternoon. The college was deserted.

Tim pulled the curtains of the room. Robert locked the door. Nervously they undressed. Tim led his friend to his bed, pulling back the cover, pushing him down onto it and then straddling him so he could caress and kiss him. Robert groaned.

Tim turned him over and began kissing down the crease of his bottom. Each knew what was to happen as Robert handed Tim a bottle of baby oil and felt the cool liquid drop into his anus preparatory to being fingered and stretched.

'Can I try now?'

Robert half-nodded unsurely.

Tim with the gentlest pressure pushed and inched inside.

Robert moaned. He was frightened, happy, confronted by dreams (he'd held since school) plaguing him so he'd seized-up.

Afterwards Tim lay on his back, lifted his hips and offered himself to Robert who gingerly pushed in, coming instantly.

'Why were you cut?'

'I'm a Jew.' Robert said. 'We have to be circumcised.'

'The bitter scars of belief. It's naked and beautiful.'

Then he pressed Robert into admitting his love for Graham at his old school, a relationship which never developed although Robert longed for intimacy beyond the mutual masturbation they had engaged in.

'Why don't you ring him? Try him now, Rob. He should be home. If he's not interested he'll hang up and nothing's lost. If he likes you he'll agree to meet. Why not go to the pictures?'

Graham was home. He was pleased Robert had rung. Yes, he'd like to go to the pictures. They'd meet at the terminus of the tram the boy would take to the centre at noon next Saturday.

Afterwards the two friends lay easily on the bed. Tim massaged Robert who flushed with exertion. His relief was tinged with gratitude so deep he couldn't help fountaining. Anyway, Tim was all right about the mess; Tim was a bit his way; there was nothing to hide now. His anticipation entangled them as they lay breathing quietly and peacefully on the dampened bed proclaiming a victory of sorts over fear, privacy and banishment.

Tim had already faced that hell. As in the storm with Chris there were ways of coping. No one would approve; but that didn't matter; getting through it was what mattered, and his friend was on the way. Tim dressed, hugged Robert before pulling back the curtains to let the softening light dance into the room; then he left, trudging home to Sophie hoping for understanding. 'I'm up to my old tricks again' he mused in the street to their flat, acknowledging things were different so old habits should be renounced.

Sophie was bent over her desk. She said smiling, 'Supper's waiting in the kitchen when you want it'. He showered and lay on the bed gazing at his body and his floppy sex as if they would explain why his needs were so fulsome and whether it was time to grow-up. He slept before any answers were forthcoming until Sophie fell beside him kissing him back to life with, 'Let's eat Timmy. I'm starving.'

The centre of Sophie's preoccupation was Gray's *Anatomy*, equal to a double dictionary to be memorised. 'I suppose it's a dictionary of the body.' sighed Tim as he sat by her going through its reams of facts; he was intrigued by what seemed an arbitrary system of Latin names, one day venturing into the classics department to fathom the sense of this dead troublesome nomenclature. A dry impatient scholar talked him through some of the underlying sense in the classification and dismissed him 'Every little helps.' he told Sophie later as they struggled to absorb the mountain of medical paraphernalia challenging them. They pinned pages of diagrams and names to every wall. It was impossible to escape.

Tim took a baroque gamba sonata along to the Martin musical evening persuading Mrs Martin to play the basso-continuo part and Alan Martin to play the base-line on the cello, it was much admired by the two Martin girls and their friend Vicki Adamson who reminded Tim of their meeting at his debut concert.

'Oh, of course,' he said. 'I'm sorry. It's hard to remember; it was such a tumultuous evening.'

'Oh, oh yes, it was.' She blushed.

'Have you brought your flute?'

'You remember. Um, no.'

'Let's play something for the next evening?'

'You mean?'

'Good. We'll ask Mrs Martin to accompany us. What about a Handel flute sonata? Do you know Lukas Graff's recording with flute, harpsichord and bassoon? It has a richness I like a lot.'

Vicki shook her head (secretly determined to immediately find the recording). She was so thrilled this wonder-boy might play with her she left her coat at the Martin house when her mother dropped by to take her home. 'It was the best evening ever. I'm playing next time.' She smiled at her mother's sour face.

'Good. Who was there? Come, jump in we're late.'

Vicki brimmed with pleasure. 'Oh, the usual crowd.'

She could have added, that best of all, Tim Macknight had suggested they meet at the Con one afternoon where his friend, Robert and he would rehearse with her.

'How is it possible dreams can come true?' she asked her pillow before hugging it to sleep. Sixteen, and never been kissed; well, not the way she hankered after, not by a god who would trans-form her into a shimmering tree filled with singing birds and bathed in the love-rain of a million kisses embroidering her with jewels so she sparkled and sighed and melted into air.

Some of the love-rain settled over her making her proof against the cynicism of her blue-rinse parents who belittled her joyous wafting around the house until even her elder sister complained, 'Oh sit still Vick, or you'll melt away.' and never under-stood why this was greeted with a peal of laughter until to every-one's consternation she returned flushed and oil stained from Tim's motorbike having been delivered home after a rehearsal.

They chided her. Her mother concerned about her daughter's virginity. 'Mum it's nothing like that. We just play together. That's all.' But her mother distrusted the joy in her daughter's step, the laughter gurgling from her and the flush rising in her childish cheeks every time the name 'Tim' was mentioned. The brute had interfered with her, Mrs Adamson was sure.

But it was impossible to hold her at home; for just as water slips through fingers, Victoria slipped out to revel in music-making. Now she had found something to absorb her, a vessel to put her dreams into, a boy so wonderful the whole world glowed and sang with her, joined her in her amazement at such magic. Tim felt guilty at using such an innocent girl to get back at the Adamsons for all the indignities they represented. 'I'll show them my way is better than theirs' he vowed. But Robert cautioned him, 'Tim, dear Tim, we all had to face the Adamson scourge at school. It ruined you, almost finished me. But don't damage Vicki. That's cheap revenge.'

However, Tim parked his bike, took Victoria in his arms and thoroughly kissed her until she was so weak-kneed she tearfully staggered up her front path and blundered into the house, crying with a helpless joy shocking even her experienced sister.

'You'll see no more of him.' shouted her mother.

'Oh shut-up, Mum; I'm going to the Martins on Saturday to stay-over with Felicity and Joel and to play a trio sonata with Tim and Mrs Martin. It's all arranged.'

'You, playing with Mrs Martin? Well I never. I suppose just this once. With Mrs Martin, you say? Now you behave yourself my girl.'

She would have flipped if she'd witnessed the kissing and groping: Victoria handling Tim's erection until it spurted over her dress; then, her first orgasm as he expertly fingered her clitoris, and the gentle thanksgiving of their embrace afterwards.

'Victoria, dearest, this must not happen again. I'm sorry. You are OK? You know I have a girlfriend. We must stop; if you like me please allow me to go. We can always be friends but not this . . .'

'Friends Tim; we, I. Yes, friends.'

In victory he tried to be magnanimous. Robert accused him of being a hypocrite, Graham, in on gossip, agreed.

Tim was too ashamed to tell Sophie. He said to himself, 'I admire Robert: he has avoided anger. I'm filled with it.'

He missed Victoria's idolatry. Repentant, freed, he was aware his music making was soiled for weeks afterwards. Only the hair shirt of abstinence and fasting on the most gruelling work cleansed him. He sweated; Sophie laboured, pushing shit up-hill with a thin stick (as they say), until the end of term.

2:

IT WAS HOLIDAYS. Tim and Sophie lounged around the house or wandered into the shopping street for drinks. They slept until renewed energy goaded lovemaking. They glowed, lying together, deciding they would go down to Eliza Beach, visit home and consult Janet, Max and Doctor MacKay about their studies.

'You look tired my dears.' they all said. They nodded. It had been the hardest three months of their life.

Doctor MacKay nodded his wise old head. 'Sophie, my dear. Just keep at it. Slow. Slow. Every day a little bit more. Remember, minute ants can build mountains. Medicine is not *that* high a mountain. I'm glad Timothy is helping you. Together you can do anything.' He eyed Tim. 'So, you have followed my advice and nurse Sophie's guidance. I imagine you have no problems. You look as fit as a fiddle, Ah, I suppose I should say, as a bassoon'.

Tim nodded. 'No problems. Only Sophie. She takes up most of the bed.' He guffawed; Sophie looked contrite.

Doctor MacKay nodded. His eyes twinkled. 'Dear me, so life has taught you that small lesson. Now, Timothy, please leave us. I'd like a word with Sophie before you both go.' Tim went out. Then the doctor said, 'Tell me how are you coping with University life? Your periods, diet . . . Well done. Exercise? Good. Italian feasts, good. Finally, How are you both getting along?'

'Our sex is the best medicine there is. You know, Doctor MacKay, I love him more every day.' She blushed.

'It was silly of me to ask, I can see how happy you are, both of you. I'm delighted. Tell me, how is my old friend, Alan Martin?'

Sophie enthused, reporting on his fatherly support and all the fun they were having at the Martin house.

'I'm so glad you're spending time with them. Your report confirms my view he is one of the few humane doctors up there. Now go and get Timothy, I've something to say to the both of you.'

The two ravishing youngsters sat expectantly before the wise bent old man who warned there would be stress during their study periods, that they must not allow the mischief of tiredness, preoccupation and different programmes to kick shit out of their relationship (They were surprised how earthy Doctor MacKay could be). He concluded looking fondly at his patients, 'My dear Sophie, my dear Timothy, just remember to take a break when things are going wrong in order to remake contact. That really matters. Don't let work dominate you at a cost to your relationship, that messes-up love.'

No one had ever used the word 'love' to them before; they were startled. The two tousled students smiled and nodded gratefully. 'He always makes us feel well.' they agreed at his gate.

'They're like Hansel and Gretel in the bewitched and awful wood of the world. But I think they'll win-out.' he mused as the two, hand in hand, danced down his surgery path and away along the road. 'If only all the kids here had the same luck and the same charming talents.' he said to his stethoscope nodding approvingly below his double chin as he made cursory notes on their patient-cards before replacing the files on the proper shelves.

Tim came in from manicuring the garden when Nina called him for tea. They sat in her living room, lined with books; comfortable chairs, a sofa, colourful rugs, and standard lamps standing sentry where she liked to sit and read. She was very frail but as firm in voice and thought as ever.

Nina looked at the trim handsome young man and smiled. 'My dearest Timothy, I have a few things I want to discuss; first, thank you for your help round the house, you have better things to do; I appreciate it. The place looks much better with your care and attention.

'Now, as far as I am concerned: Doctor MacKay has found a nice young nurse who will live here in the guest room and help me. Maria, bless her, is coming with her nephew and her youngest daughter to do all the chores, so you must not worry yourself about me or the house. Only remember this is home and you always have a place here.

'Now then, I got Rudy to overhaul my old car; it's no use to me now. He says it is strong and will go on just like me. But I want you and Sophie to take it back with you. I have changed the insurance and altered the tax certificates; I am exceedingly worried about you dashing about on that blasted motorbike of yours with Sophie and your bassoon. My recurring nightmare is your having an accident. I have left the keys and the papers by the front door; it would be a comfort and a relief if you'd use it. I hope there will be no argument.' She paused.

He sat looking at the floor. She continued, 'Timothy. I want you to tell me – look at me – tell me how the arrangements are working out with Sophie; I know her parents are paying for the flat and I suppose you have no alternative to staying there. What sort of sharing have you?'

Tim's face flickered with emotion. He looked into the keen eyes of his dear old godmother. From an intense silence he managed to say, 'Nina, oh, Nina, of course this is my home. Of course I belong here. I love you so very very much. You must promise me if you need me you will let me know. Promise me.'

She nodded her old face twitching with love and unspoken feelings for this other precious son. Then Tim, ringing with the same firm committed tones she had used said, 'Nina, I love Sophie. More than anyone in the whole world. She's my life. Our happiness is everything. We share so much. And we allow each other separate lives. The flat the Deans provide is our home like here; it is ours, jointly, where we work and play and love; the base from which we get the strength to deal with what's outside, which is not always easy. I carry Sophie in my heart; I can't imagine being without her. I think she feels the same. I've never been so happy. Nina, you know, I've never admitted to anyone but Soph how much I love her. I'm not sure I even knew until after hiking in the Bush and until we began living together. You mustn't worry about us, or about me and money. I have another scholarship giving me lashings of money, more than I need. I am not as rich as her but neither of us care about that. We share everything.'

Nina watching his wild, radiant face gladdened, and straightened in her chair. 'Timothy. All my blessings . . . I fell in love when I was a girl, just like you. It's the only real power propelling us through adversity and through all the arduous years. I could not wish for you more than you already have. I am thankful, nay delighted, much much more than I can say. No wonder you shine here like the sun. No wonder Sophie has become such a strong fine woman. You found love by sharing your lives, by sharing your selves. I know she has supported and probably deeply loved you for years. That you have found each other in this way is everything.

I'll never worry again. But my dear, you too must always come home if anything happens so we can search for solutions. You must promise me this.'

He nodded, smiling. Her concern fortified his spirits.

A tetchy autumn breeze tossed leaves around the garden. The gnarled trees, witness to much in this old house, leaned protectively over the frigid ground sheltering the life nestling underneath which would burst out once again when a stronger sun warmed it. For although the earth withers in arduous winter, its glory is revival.

Tim's pillioned Jeff Dean to Mrs Brandt's house where they dug and pruned and tidied her tumultuous garden, 'in preparation for the winter,' they told her. While she entertained his attentive assistant, Tim leafed through a stack of yellowing manuscripts she'd put out for him. Then, while Jeff gambolled with her new kitten, Tim made careful notes about all the composers and any information she remembered from Hans about the compositions. She insisted he take them, he, promising he'd play through everything, 'To bring to life silent voices. My friend, Grace, will be over the moon.' he said sliding the fat bundle into his pannier bag.

Then he dragged Jeff into the house next door because Max had invited him in to chat about the science subject he was taking at University. Jeff s eavesdropped on their conversation and carried to the motor bike a couple of books Max lent Tim to help with his studies. Jeff was glad of the opportunity to see Max out of school (He's almost human, Jeff thought.)

Then the two boys roared off into the village for a milkshake and a chat. Jeff seemed older. He admitted being lonely now Martin had found other friends. Tim watched him eyeing the girls who milled around drinking and giggling. 'You know Jeff, when you leer like that I don't see a sweet gay boy anymore.' Tim grabbed his sex provocatively. They gleefully laughed. 'And Jeff, thanks for helping me today. I enjoyed your company, as usual.'

'No problem. I enjoyed it too. Maybe I'll do science next year. Max is OK. Don't look so worried.'

'You're getting serious. Hey Jeff, I'm glad.'

Mrs Dean heard the motorbike thunder up the path; the two boys, as happy, wind-blown, cold and demanding as in the old days bounded into the kitchen both kissing her boisterously. 'We're going to swim. Will you make us toasted sandwiches?' She watched them fling themselves into the steaming pool their deepening voices and hairy bodies the only discernible change. She admired Tim's maturing sex, unable to exclude lascivious images of its dallying with her daughter and their tangible love for each other making her shiver with both relief and remembered teenage dreams flooding her when she spied them privately smiling at one another.

'In a funny way we're blessed,' she pondered as her two beloved boys rollicked outside and Sophie tripped down the stairs to see what all the noise was about and calling, 'Daddy, come and have toasted sandwiches with us.' as she passed the little room where he was glued to his computer. They had not asked Sophie or Tim much about their life at the University. Clearly each was doing well academically; their radiance expressed how well their shared digs had turned out; although Tim had hugged them both one evening saying 'The flat is wonderful. Almost as wonderful as Sophie. Thanks a million. It makes us so happy.' The two parents were gratified, three blessed, beloved children, at long last.

During the last week of the vacation Tim and Sophie returned to their flat. Each had work to do; each savoured this free time. One afternoon Robert came over with Graham. They mooched down the road for a hot drink in one of the cafes. While Tim and Robert talked about some of Mrs Brandt's scores, Sophie and Graham wandered into *Readings* bookshop. She caught him leafing through a book of erotic Greek art, countered his embarrassment. 'I'm glad you like it. The Greeks were much more open about love than we are; particularly between men.' Together they poured over illustrations of men and boys tempting one another. There was one picture of an excited man caressing a boy standing between his legs returning the caress. The bursting erection proclaimed the carnal attraction. 'It's beautiful. It is absurd to say Greek love was platonic.' breathed Sophie into Graham's bemused ear.

Gratefully he leaned into Sophie's body whispering, 'It was like that with Robert. But I feel bad about it now.'

'Have you found someone else?'

'Yes, No. It's just that . . . I don't feel comfortable anymore.'

Sophie had observed his appraisal of girls in the cafe. 'Graham, Robert loves you. Don't hurt him. You make him happy. Try to leave him, if you must, gently. Don't just throw him away like other people do. He's a fine and sensitive person who has given you the most precious thing he has. It would be unforgivable to turn him into trash.' She turned him round and looked deep into his eyes. 'Don't let shame drive you away. Or your appetite for things excitingly new.'

'Do you know about Robert and Tim?'

'Of course.' Sophie said, angered by his tittle-tattle. 'They are close friends. Sometimes that leads to sex. And why not? Sex is a way of talking to one another. Haven't you found that?'

The boy nodded slightly.

'Sex can be like music; it allows things hidden within words to be said. Sometimes it's the only way of being together.'

'I just need to come.'

'That's easy. But there's a lot more to lovemaking. Perhaps you should begin to explore Robert and explore yourself. You will find how fantastic your bodies are. I used to be disgusted with mine until Tim showed me the treasures it contains.' The boy looked mollified. 'Don't run away from your feelings. Let them play in you, Graham. So, would you like the book?'

'Yes, but I don't have enough money.'

'Give me what you have and I'll get it for you now. You can repay Robert, or me when we next meet.'

His face unclouded. He skipped out of the bookshop, mixed up between desire for Sophie and relief that all the unspeakable and wicked things he had done with Robert were not unique, in fact they were rather lovely, as his new book demonstrated.

Winter term commenced. Sophie was swept away by the demands of her subjects all clamouring for immediate resolution. She battled with the impossible, determined not to be overwhelmed; becoming increasingly angry there was so little time left, until she decided life was as important, and she should spend time with her friends, and joining Tim as he galloped through his lectures, tutorials and performing. And, he enjoyed sharing her work, revelled in the struggle to master all the science she was confronting. 'I don't know how you do it all.' she cried admiringly one afternoon after they had mastered the intricacies of metabolisms which she then roughed out in an essay.

They were going to the Wattletree Pub that evening where

he, a jazz pianist and bass guitar were playing smooth jazz, for a tidy fee. 'Jazz bassoon?' the publican had queried doubtfully when Tim had approached him. But the catchy tunefulness quickly dispelled his doubts, and the crowd which swelled as the news Tim Macknight was on, cheered him up, no end.

The evening at Professor Maxwell's house drew near. Grace, Tim and Shane a viola player were to perform Grace's revised protest about Philistines, now named BIAS (Baxter is a shit). It would follow after Robert and Tim played the autographed Hindemith *Canzona*.

It was a formal evening; the students were prepared to meet the black-tie standards half-way. For instance, Tim wore his black skivvy, trousers and soft black shoes Mrs Dean had bought for him; Grace, remarkably, wore a plain black dress (She'd never been seen in a dress at the conservatorium).

The same bespectacled music critic who had quizzed Tim at his concert was there; and a number of big names from the Arts. There was general admiration for the students' professional performance. That Wednesday a brief note concluded that week's newspaper concert reviews praising the conservatorium for nurturing talented young musicians. Everyone was gratified.

Tim and Grace became inseparable. She poured over Mrs Brandt's treasures. Excitedly she discussed editing and playing the pieces with both Fran and Tim, 'To give them the life they deserve.' she cried. Fran tried to slow the helter skelter. 'My dears take your time. There is a mountain of work required in preparing a concert of even a few of them. You know each of you must also prepare the list of exam pieces. These works deserve your best. Don't rush into half-baked performances.'

Grace and Tim were also experimenting with expanding the sounds of the bassoon. Fran had encouraged him to investigate circular breathing with an oboist who had mastered the technique. Grace was fascinated with its potential to allow playing uninterrupted by breathing. She and Tim sat for hours as he squeaked and squawked and buzzed and double-stopped and found new high shrieks beyond the accepted range of the bassoon, all of which she began incorporating into her graduation composition he had agreed to perform with her.

He talked to her about antitheses (as Chris had with him),

explaining their Persephone Syndrome, the opposing sides of a ravine and the bridge joining them so Grace began exploring the idea of an argument, between a murderous male authority and a resolute female protagonist; not so much an argument as a battle (yes, she liked that idea.) in which, from near death, her hero would find strength from a vision of a better world and rise triumphant above the slough into a clear bright female heaven.

One afternoon, in excitement, Tim embraced, her holding her for a long time. Dazzled by the visions they were sharing, unresisting, she was kissed, and returned his kisses; she felt his erection spring against her stomach, felt all the power and the tenderness she so savoured in him tempting her, sharing with the only man she had ever fancied what she groped for in women.

She had intimations of the richness of his maleness, of the complex pleasures possible if they were to make love. She was devastated. Yet enraptured. Gently they drew apart, rapt by the strangeness of what simmered, uniting them.

'Can we really be friends?' Grace whispered.

'We are, Grace. We're lucky; we don't need to get into sex. Music is our way of making love.'

Grace looked at Tim, so gentle, so brilliant, so passionate, so right. 'I've never had a friend like you. I always feel alone.'

'Grace, I need you too. You help me speak all those things locked inside clamouring to escape. Your battle is also mine. We're both bruised. It's not a matter of gender. We must protest the violence and speak out about our pain and our anger – you are angry, like me aren't you?' She nodded, looking at him attentively. 'That way we'll cure ourselves, and help others to do the same. And alter the world so others are hurt less.'

A flush lit her pasty face. She smiled, hugged him. 'You've been curing me, Tim.' She broke away with a cheerful yell. 'I'm off to begin our battle, Tim. I love you.' She blundered out of the practice room and thundered down the corridor freed and filled with resolve. Her struggle was worthwhile now she shared it with Tim and with all the others.

Fran laughingly confronted Tim one lesson. 'What have you done to Grace, she's like an excited child with free range at the Fair; she bursts in on me with questions of bassoon technique with scraps of manuscript, raving about you (well on that we agree.)?'

Tim smiled happily. 'She's writing me a sonata as her graduation piece. Fran, I love her. She's a real friend.'

Fran tenderly kissed him. 'My dear Timtim you love so many of us, I can't keep up. Now play me a B-flat minor scale in quintuplets as a warm-up for the Weber piece.'

Later she spoke to Professor Maxwell about Grace and Tim. 'You know, Dick, I think we're in for something phenomenal from those two. From what I've seen, Grace is writing an impossible piece which I have little doubt Tim will master. This relationship between composing and performing, you've been encouraging, is bearing impressive fruit.'

'And thank you for your enthusiastic support of my policy and of the students. No wonder we all love you.' he said squeezing her arm as they made their way down the corridor to a staff meeting.

Tim telephoned Nina. 'Can Grace and I come down and spend a week finalising her *Duet* ?'

'Of course, Timothy. Come. You can have the library. It will be pleasant to have music in the house.'

'Great, Nina. We'll put Grace's electric keyboard on the table, I'll bring my music stand. I'm looking forward to swimming. The sea's better than the mouldy Uni Pool.'

Grace felt immediately at home in the mellow timber house lined with books and strewn with kilims. She responded to Nina's literary interest, talking confidentially with Nina (rare for her) about the ideas underlying her piece, about conflict, dream and something nobler than tawdry values destroying dreamers. Nina, who had discussed with Tim on many occasions his and Chris's Persephone Syndrome, took down a book for Grace.

The next morning, the sun dancing with its mimicking shadows over the windy garden, Grace excitedly waved the book. 'Tim, Persephone is my music. Well, my last section, listen:

> . . . *I and earth, and light and dark are one;*
> *so a tiny candle*
> *shapes the formless black*
> *into ordinary miracles.*
> . . . *Then, like a needy bulb*

I push the clinging earth
search for freedom light and air
burst shy and sure, . . .

. . a frail green lash
loosed in the earth's eye, . . .

. . . The light and you
unmask the other me,
transform my world . .
to see myself in love
with sight and blind
the 'seeming' balanced
by the tangible . . . *

'That's how your solo emerges from the darkness of doubt and oppression; that's how I want you to find and to grasp the dream, searching for freedom, transforming the world so my music can blossom. Do you see?' Grace was beaming. She found music in the poetry liberating her to pull from the depths of herself the agony she struggled to set down. She went on excitedly, 'Listen to this, dark Hades reminds his bride, although it is colourful and delightful up in the light with her mother: . . .*your dreams are here!* 'Imagine our dreams being in hell. Fuck, they are.' Grace cried. 'I agree with Persephone when she says:

> *Sometimes appearances make me gloomy.*
> *I long for significance of introspection.*
>
> *Life is seldom what it seems . . .*
> *
> *Music drops like tears*
> *damps darkness*
> *implores attentive ears*

'Tim I want our music to do that. It must.' She paused in her onward rush. 'The last poem is my inner journey, my cry, listen:

---

* See notes at end.

On the long journey into light
I call to you,
longing for touch
for dark embrace,

the long journey wanting light
and your dark ecstasy
baby-bleating in my arms,
sharing earth's treasures.
I journey with these riches
able to bear bruised body,
mantled in such majesty
bequeathed by understanding.

I am the bridge
linking sight and insight
binding the split soul,
celebrating darkness and light.

Grace was blushing. Tim, pelted by her enthusiasm, smiled. 'For me too. It's been that kind of struggle. My dreams, hellish for a long time, emerging with the encouragement of people like Nina and Fran, and you, Grace. That's why our work's so important.'

He hugged her. She hovered there sheltering, celebrating until with a shout of pleasure she broke from him and settled herself into a flurry of work. She was half condemned and liberated yet she laboured on. 'My "music drops like tears" like Orpheus in poem sixteen, "I smell of pollen and freedom" too. And when I've finished your sonata, I'll set all these poems to music. Wow, me as *Persephone*, what a project.'

It was not simply a flurry of words, Grace was roused deeply. For they acted as a spur, a help to each of them in clarifying what to write and how to play it. Nina watched fondly as the two slaved over writing and scrubbing and altering and copying and arguing and shouting in frustrated delight as they honed sense onto the pages of Grace's sonata.

She watched her tired young man stroll through the garden making his way down to the beach where he washed much of his head-spin away and was refreshed by the sea's winter-chill.

Tim felt welcomed by his beach, and his Nina; she might be failing, but she had made a peaceful oasis whose soothing balm settled his (and Grace's) anxious passions. Nina, like Doctor MacKay, although living in a back-water, was more in tune with the youngsters' preoccupations than most of the crowd in the City.

Nina encouraged long dinner chats about, what they called, "Persephone's Bridge". She tentatively suggested a run-through with a small audience of The Deans, Janet, Max, his wife and Mrs Brandt (Fran was busy dep'ing that week). Actually it was Jeff's idea; he had been haunting the house glad to help, and to join beach expeditions. He wistfully aired the idea one afternoon when preparing afternoon tea to entice the two musicians into taking a break.

The run-through was a bit of a mess; but it showed where the score needed amending as well as special practise. Everyone was encouraging (if perplexed). Mrs Brandt shook her head. 'My dears, I've never heard so eloquent a bassoon. I'm not sure my Hans could play what you are doing. It's lovely, and terrifying. I'm sure it will be a success.'

Summer was early. It warmed the end of swat-vac, tempting students to slip outside instead of pouring over books. The sun shone and danced temptation. Tim wheeled his motorbike out from Toni's shed where it had languished for months. Shirts were removed and tables reappeared on pavements as warm clothes vanished into wardrobes. Jeff had come up with a party from his school to visit the museum and (prompted by Janet about his discomfort at school) had been invited to stay for the weekend. Sophie took him around the medical faculty where he confronted, in fascinated disgust, some samples in jars of formaldehyde, specimens of foetuses and other preserved mammals used for teaching. He examined the coloured charts of cut-away diagrams of the body looking at all the tubes and ducts associated with the penis. So that's what the lumps in my balls are, he thought. Tim explained about the prostate, being close to the rectum so sometimes men came when they were fucked. 'I never do.' Jeff whispered, 'Do you?'

Tim nodded. 'Sometimes.' Then, as Sophie had to finish some revision, Tim took the boy into the conservatorium. The cacophony of everyone frantically preparing for exams amused him. 'It's like a CD gone wrong,' he laughed. Patiently he sat in on a rehearsal of Grace's *Duet*, as she had decided to call it. Jeff was impressed by the intensity of work and enjoyment and without silly teachers interfering. This was so much better than school.

The two went swimming in the University pool. Jeff failed to out-swim Tim underwater, although his diving was superior. In the showers they played with soap until surreptitiously masturbating they climaxed, dressed and cheerfully lounged in the canteen.

'Jeff, tell me about your trouble at school.'

'I've been banned from History because I fool around. But no worse than the others sitting at the back.'

'If you dislike class lessons, why don't you get some private tuition, like Soph and I had? Jeff, it's fun at Uni. You'd love it here.'

'But I hate classroom work. I want to be a farmer like Don.'

'Well then, Don's working hard. He's coming here to study agriculture so he can farm well. Why not break your balls and join him. Wouldn't that be fun?'

Jeff loved Tim (although he couldn't put it this way.) and he admired Don. He was tempted by the dream of being with both of them and with his sister, doing what he wanted. Free, what a dream that was. He agreed to go back and consult Max and Janet, asking his parents to finance extra tuition. He grunted. 'It's worth a try.'

'If you're serious, I'll come down and coach you on the exam-passing techniques Chris taught me; they really help.'

That sealed it. To have Tim help him again, as he had after the sex/drugs debacle, and in the way he worked with Sophie, was a juicy carrot this charming teenage donkey hungered for. 'I promise.' he said seriously. And he meant it.

Sophie and Tim took Jeff to the Wattletree pub for the last evening of bassoon jazz until after the exams. Jeff was delirious in the easy freedom of the bar, seething with fans and friends. He rolled happily home singing and dancing all the way. They put him to bed, undressing him to his giggles of tipsy delight as he slurred, 'That wass the greateshsht night, ever.' and immediately fell fast asleep. Tim and Sophie rocked each other to sleep in their own boat on a sea of pleasures with exam sharks, stirred by anxiety, threatening equilibrium.

3 :

A STORM BROKE over Grace's composition thesis, *Persephone's Bridge - A duet for piano and bassoon.* Dr Baxter growled, 'This isn't music; it's unreadable, filled with your own private marks, and unplayable. You've not researched the register of the bassoon let alone fitted the parts together. There are one or two musical ideas. Take them and develop them into something comprehensible. I'll not accept this travesty of composition. Notation is advice to the player. Performance is key.'

Grace was crushed, Tim furious. He took his friend and her manuscript and angrily confronted the Professor. 'Grace has slaved over this. So have I. So has Fran. You can not fail her.'

The score looked extraordinary; but Dick Maxwell, with premonitions, already had a plan. 'All right. Come and play it for us next Friday at my Music Night. I see you are pushing bassoon technique beyond normal limits; it looks a wild and interesting piece, as far as I can judge. A pre-run before the graduation performance would be prudent.'

He looked fondly at the two crestfallen students (two of real quality, he was convinced), saying gently, 'Remember, those of us who push through the boundaries are bound to get into trouble. You've done that. Now let's see what you have to say. I support your work, dedicated composer and performer. You'll get a fair hearing. But I suggest a short explanation would help us to listen with more understanding.' Tim beamed. Stammering confused thanks the two withdrew.

Grace burst into tears outside the door. Tim gently led her outside, sat her on the grass and held her hand. 'Grace, you know it's a battle. Don't abandon it now.' She looked through her tears thinking, He's so young, so girlish. So naive. The dream has crashed and he can't see it. She shook her head. 'I'll fail.'

Tim was dismayed. 'You weak shit. You won't even defend what we've done. You don't believe in it do you.' He groaned, 'All that work, and you just walk away. All that struggle with Persephone, it might as well have been a fart, for all you care. You don't know about love. That's your problem. You fucking liar, fucking fucking liar.'

Grace saw him crumple. Defeated. The same empty bag of shit quivering, useless, unloved. The same mess, she thought. And it's my fault saying I could do it, saying I loved him. Talk, talk, talk. Bullshit. She lashed this boy with the contempt wounding her - the sweetest, most able person I've ever known. She howled in delusion and despair. 'Oh Tim, I'm sorry. No Tim. No. But we can't.'

Students hurried in and found Fran. She strode over the lawn saying in tones unchallengeable, 'Tim, Grace. You both IMME-DIATELY come with me. IMMEDIATELY.' Meekly they followed her to her room where she confronted them. 'What sort of rehearsal was that? What sort of spineless robots are you? You let one mind-less man disable all our work, just because he doesn't want to under-stand? One man; or the crowd supporting you, a crowd of talented people who know a masterpiece from drivel? You let one single voice silence you? I'm ashamed of you. And you Grace, you allow a man to silence your voice, a clarion call of our freedom as women to express our own unique vision of the world?'

Tim could only love her; she was magnificent; everything. Everything. He nodded. 'She's right. She always has been when she struggled with me over and over again. And I thought I was leading the way.' he said to himself, reeling with devotion.

He suddenly knew Fran was blazing with the defence of everything he sought. In her own way she sought a better world and had battled to help him take his place beside her. Transfixed he looked at her, swept away by admiration. 'I tried.' he croaked.

Grace was overwhelmed by Fran's passion. It was what she dreamed of possessing, something fearless. Irresistible. Here was deep truth, conviction and power blazing, lighting her bemused darkness. She loved this women. Her disdain wounded yet uplifted her. She gasped, 'It's my fault. Tim tried. I didn't believe him. I thought . . .'

Fran waved an impatient hand. 'This is no time for such thoughts. You've got a concert next Friday. Get on with it. Don't let me down or Professor Maxwell. And don't let yourselves down. You are both good enough to win through. Hell, I know you both very well. You can do it, if you complete the work we started all those months ago. That is what you must concentrate on. You've got four precious days. Now go.'

Her face softened. She hugged them both and propelled them towards the door. Trembling, the two friends stumbled away to find an empty practice room. Trembling they set-up stands. She opened the lid of the piano, he a battered bassoon case. Trembling they waited. Grace nodded and the battle commenced.

The last item of Friday's concert at the Maxwells' was *Persphone's Bridge*. One of the chamber groups had sympathetically withdrawn so the night would not be too long. But word had been put about; all the literati, critics and some recent graduates committed to new music packed the long elegant music room and hushed expectantly as Tim rose to introduce Grace's piece:

'Ladies and gentlemen. First we must thank Professor Maxwell for inviting us. Then we must thank Fran who has encouraged us beyond everything. And, Thank *you,* too. *Persephone's Bridge* gets its name from myth and poems about this Greek goddess who bridged the two kingdoms: Zeus' brightness above the ground, and his brother, Hades', gloomy underworld.

'Grace wanted to express the battle (that's how she sees it) between the extremes; the battle we have to engage to find our own lives: the battle with authority to find our individual voices, the battle between the unrestrained new and an entrenched tradition; and the battle with a sick demented world we musicians must win by confronting it by speaking, well playing. Music is the food of love. Its message must be heard.

'The first movement depicts the death of beauty, youth and the dream. Grace has researched many new sounds and a new upper register; the straining you will hear, we are trying to communicate: new sounds for modern feelings.

'The second movement is a requiem for the dead; it looks two ways, backwards to chorales and other sacred music, for instance Bach, Palestrina and Faure and forwards through Messien to another sound-world.

'The third movement is in two parts. First we discover Beauty and Youth are not quite dead. Their insistent life is conveyed by non-stop melody, without gaps for breathing.' (Fran had suggested 'circular breathing' here). 'They revive, and unsteadily begin to dream again until the reality and the power of Right is reborn. The second section becomes a celebration of that truth, and of its ultimate victory over the cruelty, contempt and ignorance driving the world. Grace has asked me to say she conceived the piece, not as a sonata, but as a duet; it is intentional sometimes one part drowns out the other. You should decide at the end which is victorious.'

The audience smiled accomodatingly at the two intense performers. 'What preposterous ideas to sit a sonata on,' they thought, 'As Hamlet says, "Words, words, words." The dears.'

Then, alone, the bassoon begins. Clear, precise, weaving a longing melody growing into so rich and complex a song people sit back relaxing in their chairs. Warmth settles. Then with devastating ugliness the piano crashes in, with short stabbing motives lengthening to cruelly mock the bassoon and thunderously drown it in asphyxiating chains of notes. The bassoon is crying in split notes, thin strangled cries, higher and higher (even more amazing than in *Bias*). Hurriedly Tim changes reeds. Now he is using one of Fran's allowing double-stopping. The bassoon is castrated, screeching until only a wheezing thread of breath remains. The piano, triumphant, crashes its monstrously aggressive triple fortissimo. Then silence.

Only the skilled pick out the chorale underpinning the emptiness haunting the second movement. More, decipher a theme from Faure's Requiem and a troublingly bare Bachian motive piano and bassoon throw at each other like the tree-top baby rocking in the falling cradle; everything seems imprisoned in a chordal structure; cold, dead and hopeless. Many recall a nuclear devastated landscape; war, abandon, loss; some feel the despair in loneliness; some uneasily deny the message for its unpleasantness.

The third movement begins with a recall of the bassoon's earliest motives. But now they are sewn into one another in one long insistent peal of notes, on and on and on. Many of the listeners gasp in disbelief at so impossibly long a breath. It's unbelievable. (The acute, see Tim breathing-in as simultaneously he pushes out air with his throat). The sounds grow thicker, warmer, both instruments weaving together reach a minute pause. Then floating like a gossamer bridge, a pianissimo line of bassoon notes stretches over the abyss as piano-life flows under it. The closing passages, full of contrapuntal snatches of earlier themes, are thrown about joyously over a ground-bass above which all the other parts float twittering like birds. Then a short coda of triumph until the piano seems gently silenced as the bassoon, luxuriating and syncopated, simply flies away into a sky in whose benign silence everyone is blessed.

Fran is weeping, she is not alone ('Oh my dearest boy, such savage majesty we dreamed together, such tenderness. Oh my dearest, fantastic beloved Tim.').

Professor Maxwell unsteadily gets to his feet. 'Bravo! Bravo! There are few in the world, Tim who could play as well as that. Grace, well done. A very moving piece. Friends, we have heard a new voice tonight. Thank you for coming. Now let's have supper.'

Grace slips off the piano stool and joins the drift into an adjoining room with tables laden with food and drink. People begin to talk again. Tim slouches on his chair. Haggard.

Sophie hurries over to him and squats beside him whispering, 'Oh my Tim. It was brilliant: so much cruelty and happiness. You're amazing. Oh, darling.' He looks at her wanly; he is far away and trying to return. Marooned in the far reaches of that space, he sees Fran floating, registers her brimming eyes and struggles back seeing/feeling/touching the two whose love he most harbours drawing him back, like a humming line of oxygen, from outer reaches to a Mothering Earth. He smiles faintly, sharing his inner achievement of having crossed his Bridge of Dread and fallen safely into their arms.

Passion obliterating prudence, Fran says, 'My beloved Tim. I have never heard or even dreamed music could speak to me of all the tangled things which drive and terrorise me. Never dreamed when I let you play my bassoon at the choral camp all those years ago you would lead me on so wonderful a journey. So, finally you have mastered life by being able to express its secrets. I love you. You're magnificent.'

'I must concur.' a soft voice interrupted (it was the bespectacled music critic). 'You have made the impossible tangible. No one else in this city could have played that caldron of chaos. No one could have played it better, anywhere. Young man, I knew you were good. But this good? I salute you and your brilliant teacher,' (Tim nodded in devoted agreement) 'and a department which lets you find your voice in this way. Thank you. Fran is absolutely correct.

You have spoken the unspeakable. I can imagine the months of work you must have undertaken to achieve a new dimension to playing the bassoon' (Fran nodded) 'and the inspiration, something which thankfully litters the history of music, the inspiration you have been to your young composer friend. Seldom have I experienced after a recital the feeling nothing will be the same again. Professor Maxwell tells me this is a dress rehearsal. Well, I can't imagine what further polish the performance needs. I hope you won't mind if I gate crash Grace's presentation? My dear boy.' He drifts away.

Tim is returning. He stiffly rises and hugs Fran. 'Thank you Fran. Thank you for making it possible, for everything.' He puts a weary arm around Sophie and they walk out into the hall and along to where he left his instrument case in the Maxwell's spare room. He sits on the bed and carefully dismantles his honey coloured bundle of sticks, pulls a cloth cleaner through to absorb the condensation, stows the bits in their satin lining and clips the lid shut.

Sophie looks on pensively. 'My Tim, you are not an apprentice now, but the Sorcerer who can make all those bits play properly.' He stands. They embrace. She feels tension oozing away. Then they go down the hall towards the babble in the dining room.

'Let's have a quick drink and say goodbye.' But he becomes enmeshed in an excited argument, about what drives composition, instrumental technique or musical imagination, a knot of recent graduates is having with Professor Maxwell and the critic.

'Surely each feeds off the other.' Maxwell cries. Tim agrees.

Grace is eventually released by propositioning men from a film company and the National Broadcasting Corporation. Fran approaches and says softly, 'Grace. Well done. You see, it was worth the risk, as we told you.' Grace looks uncomfortable as Fran continues, 'You should thank Tim. Without him you would not be here.'

Grace is ruffled. 'He's used me to further his career. He should be thankful.'

Fran is shocked. 'I see. Well Grace, Tim had a career before he came to the Conservatorium. He has jeopardised his exam chances by spending all his time on *Persephone's Bridge*. Remember, you have finished; he has all his exams in two weeks: performances and written papers. He has given up everything for this project. Why should he play for you? No one else, except you will be passed because of a composition performance. Only his brilliance makes your work admissible, and gets you a degree, which you do deserve. But he has his own work to pass, yet he dilly-dallies here for your sake. If you can't acknowledge his commitment then you are a sick, selfish girl.'

It is late. The last guests cheeringly pat Tim's back and exit. Professor Maxwell moves over to Sophie who is talking to Trish, his youngest daughter, a psychology student, and chides, 'Sophie my dear, your wonder boy looks very tired. Take him home. See he rests. It's not over yet.'

The two leave. They walk through the dark deserted campus, along sleeping streets, up into their flat, and tumble into bed. 'I love you, my sorcerer Tim.' 'I love you Sophie. I do.' Sleep's charms engulf them.

Fran is so worried about Tim she telephoned Doctor MacKay. 'As it happens, I'm coming up some time to visit the Medical Faculty, so I can sit-in with my pal Alan Martin on Tim's performance before our meeting. Will that help?' Then Fran drops by Professor Maxwell's office voicing her dismay at Tim's sickly demeanour and the huge stress of the immanent exams.

As usual the wily professor has a solution, suggesting he ask the instrumental examiners to be present at *Persephone's Bridge* and assess Tim's playing for the year on that performance rather than his having to present another clutch of pieces. 'Presumably we may take it he knows everything on the syllabus?' Fran nods. 'Then he has only to concentrate on his written work.' The warmth of Fran's smile quite undoes him.

The conservatorium hall is packed with a throng of students buzzing with excitement about the 'come-uppence' of Doctor Baxter; there is a smattering of curious outsiders who have read the rave notices in the papers about the Maxwell run-through. A long table has been set-up where the adjudicators sit staring in disbelief at copies of the score and shuffling their papers restlessly until Doctor Baxter rises to speak. 'Ladies and Gentlemen. It seems my challenge has been accepted. Grace Stone has found a willing lamb for the slaughter to prove me wrong that her – I must say, much improved – graduation composition can be played. This is an unusual occasion. You are all welcome.'

The doors creak open. Grace and Tim enter and walk down the isle and up the steps onto the platform to rowdy applause. Tim settles himself behind three music stands over which he stretches out many sheets, puts four reeds into a small glass of water on a table beside him and begins masticating another and warming-up as Grace introduces her piece:

'I thought of the gap between my dreams and how I have been treated. These are the extremes I express. It's a battle between good and evil. Good wins in the end, I think. The first movement is *Allegretto viva*. The bassoon and piano fight it out. The piano wins. The second movement is *Adagio expressivo*, a requiem for the dead bassoon's dreams. The third movement, *Allegretto, Vivace*, in two sections: the first the reawakening of hope and life; the second an affirmation of hope, the victory of life over all those stultifying forces oppressing us. This is a duet, for two equal parts, as you will hear. Finally I have to say my piece is dedicated with love to Tim Macknight. He is the best bassoon player in the world.' There is a gasp from the audience. Excitement, pride, wonder, anticipation; most of the students break into applause. Everyone settles for Grace's Impossible Bridge.

The performance stuns them. As the closing notes hang yearningly in the hall, a profound silence remains. The two performers, clad in black, sit like mourners up on the stage, heads bowed, Tim pale, wan and sweating is immovable even to shouts and applause. Grace rises and bows. Then she goes over and drags Tim to his feet, kisses him and joins him in stiff bows.

Together they sweep out of the hall ricocheting to foot-stamping and cries of delight, It was an impossible bridge. Tim, our fantastic boy has reinvented the bassoon so their own voices, their own dreams howling, humming, re-make the world. Awesome, meaning and music.

Tim went outside to the sun. Doctors MacKay and Martin met him, very warmly shaking his limp hands.

Fran and Sophie joined them as Tim was saying, 'Doctor MacKay. You here is the greatest treat.'

The old man looked carefully at him. 'My dear Timothy, I am here as your doctor. I am ordering you to go home and do nothing at all until the exams start. Is that clear?'

Fran reached over and took his instrument case. 'You won't

need this for a few weeks, so I'll get it to the repairers.'

'But I've got all my exams.'

'No Tim. No exams. You did them just now, And I'll hazard a guess you did very well. Professor Maxwell and I decided this could be your exam. Doctor MacKay is right. You must go home and sleep and rest and find enough stamina to tackle your written papers. My dear, you always sail too close to the wind. This has been too close. We have seen you shipwrecked before. You must learn there's a line far too dangerous for you to cross again.'

'Passed all my performing exams?'

Everyone smiled.

'Yes, my dear, with performances all the year which have stunned and delighted us.' Fran looked grim. 'Dear Sophie. Take Tim home. Only you have the medicine to bring our golden boy back to life. Be tough on him. We all think it's either rest, or calamity.'

Sophie nodded, looking expectantly at Doctor Martin.

'Sophie, what does your heart tell you?'

'   'To be with Tim.'

He looked at her fondly. 'Then I think you must. Each of you will somehow pass; too much work has been done to fail. You know Sophie, you're as brilliant as he. If you want anything, drop by.'

The two doctors bowed farewell and wandered away. Fran hugged her favourite two students and gently propelled them towards home. 'He's right. Now go. And at least a week of holiday. See you soon my dears. And Tim, you are the best.'

Fran watched two figures in synchronous rhythm wend away. Love wafted them home. Love would repair and strengthen them. Love and music; music-making, love-making and the calm majesty of the blue summer sky bathing them in visions of many, many tomorrows.

Sophie nursed Tim through the exams. She put in such a good year the faculty awarded her the Terrance Leicester prize for an out-standing student (a pretty certificate and a fat cheque).

Tim was called to an interview with a panel in the Conservatorium his friends judged sadly to be a pass or fail panel for borderline cases. He was invited into the Professor's study. There sat Doctor Baxter, Fran, Miss Roach his singing coach, and Professor Maxwell all of whom smiled and bade him be seated.

Miss Roach asked Tim to sing an alto aria from Purcell's

Dido and Aneas which he half-knew, he sang, "When I am laid in earth, remember me." The ground bass reminded him of the end of Persephone's Bridge. He mentioned it. Professor Maxwell asked him to expand so he said, 'I think a ground base becomes a base melody, as distinct from a base line the harmony rests on, rather, it is a generator, for instance here and in Grace's last movement. It gives the melody a counter melody, a sort of polyphony.' To his surprise Doctor Baxter agreed; asking Tim to try it once more with him playing a different accompaniment to which Professor Maxwell gently objected. But Tim and the Doctor were away. Tim finished, shakily but (again to his surprise) Doctor Baxter's approving question, 'Where did you learn to sight-sing?' 'Fran showed me in our first lessons with her *In Memoriam*.' 'Excellent training.' Baxter beamed. Then they asked him if he would sing a song of his choosing. He selected an aria by Handel. Tim thought everyone was pleased.

'You have a lovely voice.' said Fran encouragingly, 'I remember your unbroken voice. Something of the same rare quality is being developed by Miss Roach, don't you think?' Tim nodded, the teachers nodded and Professor Maxwell asked, 'I suppose you know why you're here?' Tim was uneasy. 'I suppose I failed something.' Everyone laughed.

'No Tim, you are an outstanding student; we are investigating honours. You missed your aural in singing, so we wanted to hear something from you. You put in an exceptional year. Congratulations. But we all feel after such an overreaching start, you should try to go backwards and study more from the past. After all, to understand today, you must know about yesterday; and to deal with the future, you must understand both yesterday and today. So we suggest you immerse yourself in the past during your second year. Now do you have any questions?'

Tim paused, looked at the sun dancing through the trees beyond the window and grinned. 'This has been the toughest year of my life. Also the happiest. Thanks for having me. I'll think about what you've said.'

'Well I never.' said Dr Baxter, 'Mr Macknight, thank you for making it such a stimulating year for the whole faculty.' The Professor wished him a pleasant holiday and he was dismissed. The way Fran was beaming told him it had gone well.

4:

SUMMER HOLIDAYS AT LAST. Sophie and Tim spent a lazy week mooning about in their flat, in the University Pool and the nearby street cafes. In the quiet they found solace and delight, often in bed with lingering love and conversations until Sophia came up from her steaming kitchen thinking they must be sick.

She knocked and entered the bedroom startled as two perfect, naked figures emerged from a tangle of sheets saying, 'No Sophia. We are very bellissimo, is that right?'

Sophia laughed shrilly (to cover her awe) 'Yes my poppets, that's good enough.' She sat gingerly on the end of their bed (it was a long way down for her). They discussed holiday plans. Sophia said, 'Are you giving up the flat?'

'Can we stay? We love it here.'

Sophia beamed. 'Of course mio bambini, mio tresoro.'

They told her Sophie's brother was coming up and they were all going into the country to work on a farm where they had friends.

'Have the fun.' Sophia smiled. 'Toni will do little work here while you are away. But come back to us always.'

'Any time?'

'Si bambino, always.' She struggled up, took a last look at the fecund love birds and pounded downstairs, delighted. She loved them both. Their jollity filled her empty house. 'Ah, if only . . ' she mused, pushing her barren yearning away by preparing another feast, trying not to strain her ears as the floor throbbed overhead.

At the Bayne farm Jeff and Sophie were over the moon. They both enjoyed Don hosting them as he attended to his many tasks. Tim was disturbed by the uncanny resemblance the two year old Tim had to himself, 'Grey eyed, with the same slender penis, well-shaped bottom and straight as a rake.' Mrs B chuckled. One day the baby was playing on Tim who lay sprawled in the vegetable garden, bouncing on his naked chest and bubbling with pleasure until he lay there and fell asleep. Tim carried him inside to bed. His mother eyed them both. 'Tim, he'll sleep for a couple of hours. I kept him up so he would. Come to bed.'

She took his hand and led him to shower, lovingly soaping, leaning and slipping against him until it was too exciting. They hurried to her bedroom where she drew him down and kissed him to such heights of excitement, he soon crashed into her.

Desire lubricated them. He thrust. Ah, such pleasure. It was as if it were yesterday. They lay thrashing in the giant cave raining with petals of pleasure. She was crying, he gasped 'I'm coming. I must.' She closed her mouth on a violent scream. They shook.

He lay on her dripping with sweat. She firmly held his wilting penis with strong vaginal muscles, repeatedly kissing his face, caressing his sticky flanks and rigid back reviving him. Then she relented and let him thrust into her until she was gasping. He quickened his driving. She wept joyously, they lay wonderingly.

The baby's small protests woke them. They scrambled into clothes and hurried to salve the tiny master's ruffled spirits by covering his naked body with sloppy kisses, farting into the crease of his bottom and into his diminutive arm-pits until all three lay in a happy heap on the floor in a love-knot bringing blushes and babbles of pleasure.

'It's hard, having a secret family.'

'Your turn will come, I see it in Sophie's eyes.' Agnes sobered. 'I don't know if I can explain this one.' she looked down beyond her tummy. 'Tim, you are the only one who understands . . . My God I love you.'

Then reluctantly she let him go. Riding far afield chasing sheep, snaring rabbits, setting the tractor to its pumping, collecting wood, laughing and larking until, clothed in dust, the four youngsters stripped and threw themselves into the river, close knit by work. Jeff admired Don, a year older, who was competent at everything around the farm but consoled he was equal with Don in schoolwork, 'Maybe we could do the agriculture course together?'

'Let's try for that. Yer, man. It's a cool plan.'

Tim was suspicious about the time the two took showering and afterwards, their blazing faces. Was it so obvious when Don and I were lovers? he mused.

Sophie still fell back when aware of his preoccupations; this she felt at times during their stay. She had inklings about what was happening; but she loved and trusted him if with growing curiosity.

Sophie was struck by the uncanny likeness of the baby to him. Suddenly she saw the long road to having children; sometimes it looked far too long. But the consolation she found in Tim's arms on many nights in their little house beneath the whispering pepper tree calmed her impatience.

5:

FACING ANOTHER YEAR. They began to pace themselves better, making more time and space for each other as Doctor MacKay had advised. However, as Tim more soberly settled into his second year, Sophie's impatience grew. She felt she was losing herself in all the paraphernalia of medical science; it was not what she wanted. She knew her parents would deny her complaints, so she turned to Tim.

He, adept at doing many things, suggested she carry on, and take-up additional skills which met her interests. So she accompanied Trish Maxwell, daughter of Professor Maxwell, to Psychology lectures. Here, Sophie felt more at home. It was the invisible things which Freud and his followers had pioneered which preoccupied her. She felt she might be able to touch the power driving the world, and had driven Tim beyond danger point, and which had been employed to help drag him back. Music expressed it in glorious if wordless ways, but with Psychology, finding specifics for it, she could be more effective, and importantly, more herself.

Tim had agreed to share Fran's pupils at a time she was away on tour. One Sunday morning, after Sophie left to visit Trish, Scott Trilby turned up for a lesson at the flat. He was around thirteen, lanky with long dark hair, a long face with a cheeky dimple when he smiled. Tim asked him to play some long notes as warm-up. He winced as he took the big breaths; he winced when Tim gently pushed at his diaphragm to show him how to support his playing. Tim pulled up his tee shirt and was shocked to discover weals across his chest and stomach. He took Scott's instrument and laid it on the table and gently stripped him.

Scott stood shaking in his grubby underpants. Tim, without

a word, took his hand and they went downstairs. 'Sophia, do you have any bruise ointment?' She emerged and tut-tutted and hurried to find her *Arnica*. They smeared it over his bruises. Tim removed his underpants discovering cruel welts across his lower stomach, thighs and buttocks which he covered with cream. Scott stood mute. Then, tube in hand (for him to take home) Tim led him upstairs.

In the workroom he sat on the spare bed in the corner and pulled the rigid boy into a gentle embrace. 'Scott, tell me.' Scott shook his head. Tim hugged him, stilled his trembling mouth. 'Was it at home?'

The boy nodded.

'Your Dad?'

Scott nodded and clung. Unthinking, Tim kissed him.

The boy warmed to the caress. His penis stiffened. He whispered his secret. 'Saturday nights Dad comes home plastered and beats me or Mum before crashing into bed. It was my turn last night. No one knows. Don't tell. Ah, that's good.' Tim's hand strayed down Scott's back feeling the welts on his bottom, running down his crease onto his clenched ring. Scott froze, the pole in his underpants in Tim's stomach. Tim took them off hazed with desire.

'Just a minute.' Tim stood up and locked the door. He stripped and pulled the boy onto the bed.

'Have you done this before?'

'No.' Fondling continued.

'Can you come?'

Scott nodded, froze and fountained in tandem with Tim. They basked in more secrets: 'I share a room with two of my brothers, they sleep together. I hide music and things under my bed. Sometimes I dream and wet it. You know, that stuff we just did (he pointed). Is that bad?'

'Of course not. I did too.'

'Oh . . .There's so much shouting and hate. Last night the little blighters cried themselves to sleep. They often do. So did I, sick with the pain. It's dirty. Real dirty, do you know what I mean?'

Tim licked his salty eyes and nodded.

'Most times Mum's all right. Sometimes she goes bananas. Screams and cusses us kids. It's not our fault, I knows that. Its . . .' He tailed off in confusion.

'Scott, Would you like to come here on Saturdays, sleep over and have a lesson on Sunday?'

'Stay here? Me? Oo yes.'

Scott was basking between Tim's legs. Tim pushed him up. 'Can you play for me now?'

Scott pulled on his underpants, picked up his instrument and sat on the chair. Grinning, he played a short exercise. Tim ran a hand through his hair. 'Great. Now play it without any breaths.'

Scott looked doubtful. He managed the second time.

'Fantastic.'

Scott looked up with a yearning smile.

'Now play the next one.'

'But I haven't learned it.'

'Never mind. Play for me, Scott.'

The boy haltingly began, growing more confident.

'Fantastic, sight-reading. Now, the next.'

Scott's eyes clouded. He looked up appealingly. 'I can't.'

'Try.'

The boy shook his head.

'Try, for me?' Tim bent down to kiss the nap of Scott's neck.

The boy took a big breath and played almost note-perfect.

'And the next.' commanded Tim smiling.

'Only for you.' Scott blushed. And played without faltering.

'Scott, you play really well. That was fantastic. They're all very hard. You're a fine player. Well done.'

Scott's penis reared. Tim teased the bulge. 'Now that Norwegian Song Fran has given you, please.'

The boy played it through stumbling here and there. Tim hugged him. 'Good. Now let's look at bars four and fifteen, then you will be able to get it all right.' So the two worked happily until the boy could play it. Then Tim took his own instrument and played along with him until the room resounded with the warm glow of two bassoons. Scott glowed. Tim chuckled. 'Fantastic. Let's stop now.' OK, I'll walk you home.'

Each pulled cleaners through their bulky tubes and stored them away. Ruffled by lusty secrets, they hugged and dressed.

Strolling along the street they arrived at a small house with a broken-down, gateless front fence. Tim pushed through the unlatched front door. The house echoed with the fractious cries of children. He stood irresolutely in the untidy living room. 'Scott, keep an eye on the kids while I have a word with your mother.' Scott looked terrified. Tim hugged him. 'Scott, don't worry.'

The boy went fearfully to the door. 'Mum, can you come? This is Tim my music teacher at the moment. He wants a word.'

'The kids.' prompted Tim pushing the boy into the passage.

It was a terrible confrontation. Accusations of prying; denials, tears until Tim said unsteadily, 'I have arranged for Scott to come over on Saturday afternoons and sleep-over for his lesson on Sunday. That way he will avoid Saturday nights. It's a start. You know if anyone sees his wounds the police will be here and every-one else; you could loose him. You must all be unhappy. If it were me I'd need sex. Do you still have that?'

Mrs Trilby looked angry. 'You can hear the din. Do you think we want any more?'

'Sex is a sort of cure. Why not take the contraceptive pill?'

'We're Catholics.'

'You must decide. You seem to have done your duty by the Church; now you must do your duty by your children. Having them is one thing. Bringing them up is another.'

'Our doctor won't help.'

'There is a good local man called Doctor Wynn who will help. Go to him. Maybe if Mr Trilby felt he was coming home to you it might take the edge off his distress. It's only a start, but the risk of losing the kids is real. I've seen what the courts can do. And anoth-er thing, try to get his wages paid direct into a bank, then he won't have a pocket-full of money to spend in the pub.'

She cried helplessly.

'I'm trying to help. Easy now. Scott is a grand kid. I know what loosing a family is about. It's like being in hell. I've been there. You mustn't let that happen.' His cheek trembled. 'And another thing, why not get a cheap fridge, keep it on the back veranda filled with beer; that way you can watch him and enjoy yourself as well.'

The unkempt woman had a bruise over her eye. She sobbed. 'You're a brave man coming here and saying all that. I'm at my wits end. It helps to share it, even with a music teacher. You know, those are all good ideas. May the Lord forgive me. I'll try them all. Please stay and have a cup of tea with us.'

Tim joined the melee of children in the kitchen, robustly

coping with their rumbustious advances. Mrs Trilby was worried by the admiring chagrin her eldest son regarded this grave, handsome young man with, wondering, Maybe a good teacher cares for his pupils beyond the music-room? I pray he's not hurt. Anyways, thank God someone cares for him, the poor little blighter.

The next Saturday Scott arrived with his father. Both were washed and brushed. With clean underpants? Tim smiled to himself. Mr Trilby was a big shambling Irishman with huge hands. Sophia showed them upstairs where Mr Trilby cased the joint. 'I don't as see hows one as young can teach.'

But he and his bright-eyed son were charmed by Sophie's retort, 'Tim's been in the papers, he's one of the best in the world.'

'Anyways,' he concluded as he backed out, 'You're grand friends for the boy, even if his music is a waste of time. What boys need is a trade. God save us but the school insisted.'

From what she had been told, Sophie had expected a battered waif. She was relieved to see a thin, fresh boy who seemed to adore Tim. Scott burst with pleasure sharing a meal with them and then promenading for an exotic fruit juice in a cafe in the main street before bedtime.

He beamed at them sitting on the end of his bed where he lay shyly wearing a tee shirt and underpants, relaying some of the gossip about the local crowd. Then Tim, following Sophie's example kissed him good night (although he was probably too old for that kind of thing). He lay smiling in the darkened room the windows open to the hum of the night, the lace curtains wafting lazily in a tired breeze, feeling safe, falling lightly into a deep and restful sleep as in the next room the mattress trembled under flexing bodies.

After breakfast Sophie left to study with Trish Maxwell. The boys cleared-up and lay about eyeing one another until Tim asked, 'Were you OK afterwards?'

'I was guilty, nothing new. But OK.'

'Let's look at your bruises. Hey, that's better.'

'The cream was great. Thanks.'

They fondled their erections. Tim began kissing down Scott's chest, through his legs and into his anus. Scott forgot everything.

'Let's take it in turns,' said Tim. 'You first?'

The boy nodded. Tim licked the small tight glans and rubbed

the length of his slim phallus, increasing the speed as Scott's excitement grew. Scott, carried away by pleasure, stretched to Tim's lips.

Tim sucked at the soft hairless face leaving snail-trails of saliva dripping down Scott's chin. It was wonderful, this fresh young boy blushing with lust, bursting to shoot. 'Are you getting close?'

'I'm nearly there. Oh my God, oh Tim, I'm coming, oh.' Scott wilted. It was impossible anybody could give such pleasure. Impossible that two guys could do this. Neither he nor Tim were quite sure whether it was tears or sweat which Scott wiped from his streaming eyes. He shyly reached for the bouncing manly prick wondering about the power in his hands transfixing his teacher.

With an indrawn breath Tim ejaculated. Streams oozed down Scott's stomach and thighs like scalding rain.

They collapsed on the bed, hectored by judgmental voices. Scott groaned, 'Tim, it's really bad, what we're doing.' Tim knew the voices. He turned and kissed his face. 'Nearly everyone, probably your God, would say so. Afterwards you feel guilty, but during, isn't it great.'

Scott remembered every feeling. 'But we're not supposed to.'

'It should never be denied. It's all we have. The cost can be terrible. You have to be strong to face the consequences. Scott, we made love, you know it's between us, made by me and equally by you. Whether you can own it I can't tell. You're right, it's heaven but also hell. The best things are. It can be better than this.'

'I'll go to hell. And I don't want to be gay.'

'Can't you love me without being gay; I love you but I also love Sophie. Or do you think I'm gay? You love your mum and dad, so why not your girl friend and me? Trust your body Scott. Listen to what it says. Forget the rules.' He teased the small snail until it awoke and pushed longing into Scott's thoughts.

'I do feel guilty.'

'Frightened?'

Scott nodded. 'But I feel so good, about lots of things.'

'And about music?' Tim rolled him off the bed, reaching for a box of tissues to wipe their clotted skin, throw him his clean underpants and a tee-shirt and point to his bassoon case grinning, 'Let's see.'

Scott stood and played, his breath blowing like a fully-fledged breeze through the length of his bassoon, Tim's arms around his waist, approval cooing in his ears. He was sweating from exertion. Tim pushed him beyond his limit, further and further. He felt dizzy and sick, his arms ached, his body tensed like a constricted spring. Over and over. Further and further. Until with a groan the boy lowered the heavy bundle, tears in his eyes, head spinning, he collapsed on a chair.

'That was truly magnificent.' cried Tim. 'You see, how well you can play.' He squatted in front of him, pushed the heavy instrument to one side and kissed Scott's lips. 'It's so hard to play well. It involves all of you. Scott you'll be a great player.'

Surprised and proud, Scott shone with the praise poured on him. Suddenly he cared more for Tim and for sharing music with him than all the fear, all the accusing voices, all the incense, prayers and confessions constricting him. Not only his body bloomed in Tim's lusty arms, he discovered a dream of solidity.

Radiant, he later played duets, finding in their joined voices another limit they pushed through (using his ears which best teach musical skills). Eventually Tim stopped. 'Dear Scott. Stop now. It's too much strain. You must take care of yourself. Come, we'll have a drink.' He took the boy, down the passage into the kitchen. They stood at the window watching Sophia playing (trying to play) ball with a little boy.

'That's my brother.' cried Scott. He'd been sent to bring Scott home for lunch. 'What's this about?' asked Scott, 'Something at home's changed.'

The following Saturday evening Tim and Sophie were going out. Sophia, still upset by the boy's damaged body, gladly offered to baby-sit. Warily Scott put his bassoon case down and followed the beaming woman into her kitchen bathed in steam from a multitude of pots simmering on the cooker. 'We will eat, manjare, when Toni comes.' Sophia cooed, sitting the boy in front of the TV with a cool drink and a special Italian cookie. 'Then you take-away a bath.' She left him to channel-hop for half an hour.

The bath water smelled faintly of pine and tar. Sophia had added a skin cure, 'To make you bellissimo'. Tenderly she undressed him. Scott stepped embarressedly into the water while Sophia appraised the condition of his body, moaning over each bruise and welt. 'Now, Scotty, you lie there it will make you new.'

'I'm too old for this', he told himself, yet he basked there, until Sophia pulled the plug and with a huge soft towel tenderly dried him and rubbed a camphor cream into his wounds, giving the boy the jar and pointing to his sex. 'Beam-down Scotty, you better do that a bit yourself.'

They laughed as she dressed him. Then supper. Mountains of food, silly talk, laughter and Scott's first taste of wine with a dash of lemonade, 'I don't like beer.' he answered with Toni's approving grunt, 'Si. Si. Vino puts a sparkle in your eye and a lead in your pencil.'

Then the three of them watched a TV film. Afterwards Sophia shepherded the sleepy boy upstairs, carrying his bassoon case and tucking him up with a hug and a kiss and a whisper, 'Now you just come on down if anything bothers you, sleep well my treasure, my beauty.' and she pounded down the stairs, her kitchen bustle audible as Scott lay calm, secure, filled with attentions which carried him into sleep.

Scott awoke suddenly. Someone bumped his bed. He curled away from blows. More fully awake, he remembered. It was Sophie who had come in to get her things ready for the next morning's psychology work with Trish. Seeing him staring fixedly at her, she sat on his bed brushing a lock of his hair off his brow. 'Sorry, did I wake you?' His hands were still outside the covers (The priest had ordered him to sleep that way).

Sophie bent and kissed his forehead. He hugged her. She smelled of cigarette smoke and booze. She reassured him (not like Dad), took her things and tip-toed out shutting the door. He lay in the dark watching the curtains sinuously dance in the wind with lusty suggestiveness. He overheard the two lovers, clumsy from drink, engage in drumming antics until he forgot all priestly advice and comforted his erection. Then Sophie let out a stifled cry of ecstasy; Tim shook the house for a little longer, heralding silence.

Scott was overpowered by very recent memories of sounds of his parents coupling. His mother seemed beaten. Her strangled cries still trembling in his head, he'd looked unbelievingly at her serene face in the morning and at his relatively benign father. 'Is peace possible from such demented belabouring?' he wondered. was it the same for Tim and Sophie? He drifted into sleep asking 'Does God know what terrible things we do to find peace?'

The next day Scott acceded to Tim's pressure to couple which was discomforting. Scott was scared. Tim grateful. They shared ecstacy and guilt. Yet imperceptibly each pulled back, aware of other priorities. The lesson was filled with gentle argument representing a distance between them. They were moving from a united view to distinct views each craving recognition, manifested in the final half-hour of duets.

'Is that all for today?'

'Let's stop while we still have energy.'

'I'm tired, but I.'

'Scott, wonderful, wonderful music, let's finish on a high. It will echo all the week.' Packed up, they went down to collect Scott's brother who had been invited by Sophia to play in the garden again.

'Look, at her Scott, she should have children.'

'Then, who'd look after us?' said Scott enjoying the quiet.

The following Saturday Tim was playing jazz with Jango Petersson in the Wattle Tree pub. All three went along. Scott began to see where music might take him, as it had Tim. They gambolled back and fell cheerfully into bed. The two boys made arms-length love the next morning. The lesson was a struggle with technique. Scott collected his younger brother and they dragged home for lunch which had become, surprisingly, quite fun.

During the week Mr Trilby visited Tim. He was angry. 'I know your game: musos, leadin my son astray, drinkin an fooling in pubs when he should be home. I know. My mate saw you an' all.'

'Hang on. Scott drank juice all night. You know he doesn't like beer. He was there for the music, we all were. He behaved very well. Everyone said so. Don't mistrust him. You are the one who should be home. Give your son a break.'

'He'll turn out like the rest. A useless drunk.'

'No, Mr Trilby. No. Give Scott a chance. He has real talent. It'll take him far. His teacher is the best. I can see him up on the concert platform with her with me. Your own son. Help him up!'

The rugged man was silent.

'And, why not help yourself? Some training, to have more say and more fun, like the bosses have. More for you at work and at home. Break the rules – sex is just a start. You're talented; where do you think Scott gets it from?'

The man's huge hand enclosed the arm of the chair. His forehead pulsed. 'This guy is serious. He cares. He's a fighter, I like that. Scott admires him, the wife agrees. Certainly things are on the up just now. Maybe a pufter muso could be right. Me mates are pretty hopeless. So, they went for the music and not the booze. Funny thing, I believe him, and the boy,' He told himself. Then he nodded. 'I'll chew over your advice. And well, OK. I was wrong. Thanks for teaching Scott while his real teacher's away. He seems happy.'

'He's welcome here any time. Tell him.'

The man ground Tim's hand into pulp and thundered out.

6:

ONE AFTERNOON SOPHIE found Sophia in tears. 'We try so much for a baby. Nothing happens. What can I do. You are a doctor. Help me. I am angry with God; he never listens. I try hard; and Toni.' She wept. Sophie was distressed, this cheerful woman was so distraught. 'Sophia, dearest Sophia. I'll ask Doctor Martin. He'll help us, Sophia. Leave it to me.' Sophie hugged her, the tears were stanched by a faint smile, 'Mio tresoro, Grazia, mille Grazia.'

Alan Martin listened carefully to Sophie's report, then gave her the name of a specialist in the city called Timothy Gray, advising, 'I'll ring him. Go with her Sophie, and take her husband, I hope he has money for quite a big fee. There is no one better to sort this out. But remember, adoption is sometimes the only option.' Then he enquired about her studies noting a blemish in her enthusiasm. 'My dear, keep up the good work; your insightful approach to medicine is an essential part of our profession. Let me know how the fertility matter develops. I do enjoy our meetings. And by the way, the children are clamouring to see you and Tim. Do come and see us. Ring Pru and fix lunch sometime, please.'

Sophie took Toni and Sophia to the grand building shimmering with brass plates where they found Mr Timothy Gray, Gynaecologist, on the ninth floor. He was a small kindly man who, appraising the Italianate anxiety, carefully outlined the first steps, of looking at the womb and testing the sperm. Sophie unravelled the matter with Sophia and Toni. He was abashed at having to masturbate into a plastic container; she, afraid of inspections and ultrasound examinations. Mr Gray suggested he demonstrate the ultrasound imaging using Sophie as a guinea-pig. Sophia gratefully watched as a configured womb shimmered on the monitor. 'You should have no trouble conceiving.' commented Mr Gray. 'Now Mrs Ligetti, would you like to try?' Sophia lay on his narrow couch and watched her own image emerge while her husband argued with his unwilling erection until his body took over.

Eventually the three sat again in Mr Gray's office with a sheaf of prints of a womb and the results of the sperm test. He looked thoughtful. 'First, let me say each of you is healthy and functioning. Your sperm are numerous and frisky, however, your womb has a curious configuration. I think we've found the problem. You see, one needs a curved penis, which no one possesses, in order to place the sperm near the ova. I suggest you take these forms away and for the next two months fill them in, Miss Dean can help you. They will show us when you, Mrs Ligetti, are fertile and when we should inseminate you with a curved replacement penis-syringe, using your husband's seed for the purpose. I can see no reason why you shouldn't become pregnant during this year.'

The Ligettis bundled Sophie into a nearby Trattoria and treated her to a sumptuous lunch. They were so, very very happy. 'Ah, this Signor-gay, the university and our own Sophie and Timmy, such fortune smiling since you move in. For ever we grateful.' Sophie was happy but nervous. 'Let's wait and see.' Soberly they clasped hands. 'You will make it work; and Tim will play symphonies; we are lucky.' They beamed as the tram trundled homewards.

Scott, his brother and a sister visited regularly. Sophia had insisted. She made many delicacies for them, filling the children with love. Such clamour in the house strengthened her resolve.

7:

MEANWHILE, TIM WAS BUSY at the conservatorium. One morning Professor Maxwell invited him into his study. 'Tim I want you to look at this.' He held out a batch of letters and sat him down.

'It's about a music club for children?'

Maxwell nodded. 'The local council asked me to find a team to run it. We did a little work and insisted the budget be doubled, to a minimum amount. This has been promised. Now I want to recommend a director and a team. Would you be interested in taking on the job? Fran reports you are becoming an excellent teacher, you get on well with children and parents. I think you would be a good choice; it will involve both music and the politics of persuasion about financing music in a deprived area. Finances are derisory, but you and your friends might succeed.'

Tim looked doubtful. 'Let me talk to Robert and some of the others. Can I get back to you?'

Dick Maxwell smiled. 'Of course. Do talk it over. I need to answer them by the end of the week, if that's possible.'

Tim took the correspondence and description of the event and asked Robert: 'It could be fun. You in charge of keyboard, Shane in charge of strings, he's a good violist. Sue from the library might help with the flutes and singing. I'll do reeds, Jango Pettersson, folk and jazz. Come on Rob, don't look glum. It'll take your mind off Graham, and there's some money too. Rob you're the key. Accompanist, friend. It's impossible without you.'

Robert finally smiled. He needed a diversion and musical friends just now. He sighed. ' Of course. Put me down Tim.'

Shane was enthusiastic, Sue touched to be asked, 'I'd love to help but having a salary already don't need paying.'

'You're staff; everyone's paid.'

'Well, bless you, Tim. Perhaps I can help in other ways, by being librarian and helping you find and copy music; the children will be helped that way, if you agree?'

'Brilliant.' Tim bounded off to see the Professor. 'Look. I've got most of the team, except Grace Stone. We'll do it. Tell them.'

'Well done. And I'm glad you are involving Sue. She's a very fine player, too shy to cope with professional life but an excellent team member. And the department will help in any way we can.'

Grace was easily enticed with the chance of composing for such a variety of ensembles, singers, recorders, strings, wind and keyboard. The publicity would reinforce her credentials with the film and broadcasting fraternity (wolves, as she described them).

When Tim visited the Council he received a cool reception. 'Sending us a kid to run a kids' event. Typical. Absolutely no idea, these musicians.' But Professor Maxwell's letter of recommendation was so authoritative they grudgingly responded to all Tim's queries and demands, except their providing a canteen. Brushing aside his pleas children need stoking up during the long day they replied, 'At other events catering is leased out; food and drink sold to cover costs. We suggest you do the same. The school kitchen may be used.'

Sophia was incensed. 'No food for all the day? Impossible! Tim, I will feed you ALL. Leave it to me. Toni will help. Sophie and Scott also, while you make a de musica.'

'I want Scott to play.'

'Niente probleme. You are not worried. We maka manjare.'

One evening the team gathered at Tim and Sophie's flat. Tim's idea of starting with everyone singing was approved, Sue volunteering to unearth suitable music for so mixed a group. There was a list of sorts which Grace took saying she would produce a piece for so rag-bag an ensemble for the last day's concert, 'Which each of you will have to teach in your sections.' she said regally. A plan was agreed. 'Let's not call this a school. I hate that word.' said Tim. 'Let's call ourselves, "Family Tree". 'Yes.' cried everyone, 'Family Tree.' Then they trooped down to sample Sophia's cooking, which amply filled the rest of the night.

Tim had bitten off far more than he could chew; Fran resignedly excused him from work and lessons for the few remaining weeks of term on his promise he would fit in a couple of lessons with her during the vacation. 'This is a bad time to let your work slip.' she murmured. To his amazement Doctor Baxter suggested he delay his composition work and concentrate on 'This teaching experiment', catching-up in the term-break. All the Faculty was sympathetic.

Tim was very happy. "Family Tree" now included the whole music department. 'It's fun having so large a family,' he told Sophie one evening in bed.

'Let's have our very own, some day my Tim.'

'LOTS of little Sophies and Tims and trees sss,' he gasped as his seed flew into her.

'Us and babies, babies and music. Ah, my Tim mmm.'

Each dreamed the same dream: of chasing charmed little people about an eiderdown world and singing and crying and laughing in and out of every soft hollow, and over every breathing ridge until they stumbled into sleep and loved happily ever after.

8:

THE FIRST MORNING of "Family Tree" was set by Tim. 'We may be your teachers, but please call us by our names, I'm Tim; this is Robert, Shane, Grace, Sue, Sophia and Toni, Felicity (Martin) and Vicki (Adamson). Jango and my Sophie will come tomorrow.'

The rag-bag collection of youngsters murmured, grinned and settled. A little girl whispered, 'This is going to be fun.'

The eaves-dropping Tim replied, 'Let's all have fun. That's why we're here. Music is fun. Now let's sing. Remember to come here first every morning for choir.'

Robert held the group together. Everyone joined in.

While the rehearsal was underway Sophia hurried to the kitchen to unpack morning snacks. These turned out to be a problem because few of the children had money. So Sophia cheerfully waived payment, saying, 'They must eat.' So a much reinforced clientele tackled the mid-morning master classes scattered throughout the building. Quite soon Sophia decided because so many of the children were too thin, she would feed them free lunch as well. 'How can Tim's bambini work on empty stomachs?' she cried to Toni who, looking a trifle nervous, nodded.

There was a glut of flute and recorder players. Tim had drafted in Vicki to help. She met Patrick, a fifteen year old, who played weakly, 'Because you haven't discovered your diaphragm,' said Tim. He put Patrick's hand on his own tummy and demonstrated, inviting the boy to say "H" until he found how to use his muscles. Then the three marched round the room to a rhythm of H's until Tim approved. 'Now Vicki, get him to play scales with H's rather than his tongue Tomorrow, simple pieces with only H's until he can support every note. Pat, we'll have you playing like a man in a week.'

Victoria was bemused. She felt so comfortable with the boy. Patrick was gorgeous. And responsive. Fine fair hair, blue eyes, a compact body (like Tim), sensual lips (like Tim) and a soft voice which caught her off-guard every time he spoke.

'Touch him, show him how to use his body. Don't be shy. Our bodies make the music.' Tim told her later. He was amused to see Vicki so disorientated. 'It'll do her good.' he said to himself. 'And that beautiful boy needs a fuck. Who knows. Lucky Vicki.'

The strings were mostly at first position, so Grace had to revise the string parts. Felicity and Shane asked everyone to play; nerves lessened as enjoyment grew. Then to fill some of the remaining time, the tutors played a duet for violin and viola, then all the strings danced off to beg Sophia for food they knew she would cheerfully give, before the farty wind players mobbed the canteen.

Tim saw the value of that duet. It was decided playing to and with the kids must be part of the day. Tim named this "the Felicity Syndrome" winking at Shane who approved.

He later drove Victoria to the tram terminus to prod her about her 'beautiful pupil'. She blushed. 'Vicki, use your feelings. They are the root of music, a love-bridge for making music. Don't be ashamed. You can help him if you share everything. You know what I mean about feelings? Of course you do. But you must lead him. He doesn't know what to do, you can see that, can't you?'

She nodded. 'I'll try, yes, if that's what you think.' She threw Tim a radiant smile from the tram rolling relentlessly towards her judgmental home.

The friendship blossomed. Some days later Tim offered Patrick his door key and a couple of condoms. 'Take her there. You both want it. Be gentle, talk and play with her lovingly. Don't thrash around, you'll come too quickly.' Vicki was contrite. Music, Tim, Patrick held her in thrall. Initially it was messy, but delirium blossomed.

Tim introduced Scott about half way through. He gladly joined in. The kids admired someone almost their age who played with their super director. Tim wanted to push Scott further to show his parents something they'd support. He included a bassoon duet in the final concert, Scott promising to drag along at least one of them.

The children enjoyed themselves. "Family Tree" was a place without cruelty or competition. Everyone contributed. Even tears were something to be proud of; breaking down with the intensity of the work, feeling the beauty music liberated, searching to express the inexpressible; and the anger, usually at oneself, for fluffing or missing the point. All feelings were shared sympathetically without rancour. Often, individual rage or tears represented the group's feelings, as joy did. Joy in particular shimmered within and outside.

"Family Tree" became a haven. Parents flocked there, curious about the magic transforming their children; it made no sense, this group of big kids playing with their children. "Six or eight Pied Pipers bewitching children like so many eager rats, drawing them to that musty school, then long afterwards playing their childish hearts out all over the Borough." That's how the local paper presented it. A national paper picked-up the tale adding, "of course with stars such as Jango Petersson, Tim Macknight and Grace Stone, it made a sort of sense, if somewhat a waste of talent."

The final concert was packed with curious admirers and worthy local councillors who wanted to be seen. Bemused parents, ordered to come by their children, made up the bulk of the audience.

The babble in the hall ceased as The Director and his bassoon rose to speak. 'Hello, everyone. I want to thank you for lending us your talented children for two weeks. We've all had such fun. That's what music can do, you know. This concert is made-up of items from every section. But we will start with everyone singing, and finish with our massed orchestra. So it is a sandwich. Which brings me to an urgent matter. Food. The Council was unwilling to pay for the canteen. They said we must run it and charge. Well, Sophia who provided all the food felt everyone should be properly fed, you know the way Italians are.' There were chuckles. 'Well, no one had any money but she fed them anyway. We are heavily in debt. No doubt your roads and dustbin clearance and all the rest are important. But we agree with Sophia, your children are as well. We have nothing left, so the staff have offered a concert here this evening to try to cover food costs. Please go out and drag your neighbours along if you agree your kids are worth the trouble. Sue has printed leaflets at Uni and Sophia promises to provide snacks and drinks, available free after the first part of the concert. We hope the second part will be a sort of cabaret. Jango Petersson's trio will play during supper. Everyone is welcome. Adults pay five dollars or what they can afford; kids are free. I hope you'll help. Now the choir will welcome you all with some songs. Thank you.'

The children sang their hearts out; the hall filled with song. It was a delicious sound; free, heartfelt, joyous. The children smiled and giggled at the applause and retreated to their seats. Afterwards smaller items were performed. Then, with a noisy flourish, everyone played Grace's bouncing rhythmic piece called *Family Tree - an exercise for instruments*. Afterwards knots of adults collected offering to canvas, angry with their councillors, angry how under-valued their kids were, angry about the world, and grateful to the young people who had made their children so busy and happy and proud and important.

Some stayed later to clean-up and mollify the caretaker who would have to be in attendance until the end (Sophia and Toni had already bribed him with food and drink). The Trilbys thanked Tim for everything. They were taken aback their stripling could stand-up and play in that way; one of the best kids? Unbelievable. They took Scott home both vowing to attend the evening concert.

The concert was another triumph, so was the cabaret. No one wanted to stop. The caretaker was dancing after the crowd had gone. He agreed with Toni that wine washed the music down 'just perfect.'

Music+Food+Love, it really works, Tim mused as he straightened the love-rucked bed where Patrick and Vicki had been, remembering Scott's ravishing smile that afternoon, and the frantic welcome he had found in Sophie's body when finally they were united very very late that same night.

9:

STUDY THE PAST, Tim had been advised; so he did. He studied and played music from the fifteenth to the nineteenth centuries. Shawm, viol, horn, cello, even flute and violin music was shared with Robert, Shane and Fran. Doctor Baxter was consulted about Gregorian plainchant, Duffay, Kromer, the English Madrigalists (Tim arranged a group of Elizabethan madrigals for wind much to Baxter's approval). When he played bits of a Beethoven cello sonata,* Doctor Baxter laughed. 'It's outrageous, but most interesting; I'd like to have a public debate over parallel performances with you and the cellist, Miss Barnes, on one of our Friday matinees; there'll be outrage arising from your poaching string music, all right?'

Tim rang Mrs Brandt asking her if she would come up and support the bassoon lobby in what was likely to be a heated exchange, enticing her with a promise of a lift back to Eliza Beach where was going to see a very frail Nina that weekend. It was a long and troublesome journey for her, yet Mrs Brandt cried, 'Timothy, you are incorrigible. Of course, I would be delighted to join your lovely war.'

Baxter rearranged the hall so the performers were located on the main floor, their backs to a side wall with chairs arcing around them. He felt it best for Tim to play first, followed by the proper cello version. Robert accompanied both performers. Doctor Baxter welcomed the unusually big audience, saying that this was a discussion-recital and all should participate. Lyn Barnes and Tim were friends, they turned the pages, in turn, for Robert smiling warmly at each other, marooned in no mans' land.

For the atmosphere was electric. Doctor Baxter had ways of making war out of musical events and this one promised lots of blood.

There was a hush at the end of the two performances, who would fire the first shot? Then the quavering voice of an elderly lady at the front said firmly and carefully, 'Very interesting. May I raise a few questions about how to read a score and about musicianship?

---

*   See notes at end.

Firstly, as an accompanist, I was struck how different Robert's approach was with each instrument; he is telling us there are differences which bassoon and cello highlight - helping the players to voice them. Did you notice how he 'breathed' with the bassoon – so essential with all wind instruments? That responsive support is the foundation of chamber music, in fact any music-making.'

She paused beaming at the sweating trio. 'Let me just mention the first repeat of the last movement, diddle diddle dee da da dee da, da dadi dadi dadi dadi dadi dadi dadi da . . . I noticed Lyn rushed the first run, as if they were all grace-notes leading to the longer note, as an introduction to the first note of importance. Now this fits well with the usual approach to this composer, reinforcing the manic; for Beethoven is overrated but misrepresented by performers adopting this stance. Whereas Timothy, with his wild communist ways played every note of the run as if each had an equal right to musical space, in fact, I noticed he reached the top of that little run with decrescendo, a daring way to introduce this brilliant rushing song-like movement. I saw, for the first time, how important that run is, for it heralds so much of what is to come.' She ignored Baxter's nods trying to stop her.

'But we cannot say one is right and one wrong, can we? Both heartfelt, both legitimate interpretations. Each tells us something about the music; it also tells us about the performer. All vital. This difference Robert sensitively responds to making each rendition a delight.' The attentive warmth in the hall was tangible. Somehow this once acclaimed lady had reminded them, that when engaged in sharing, differences were ideas, not bullets. Eventually it was judged the most exciting matinee of the year.

Mrs Brandt was touched by an invitation to tea in Professor Maxwell's study with staff and senior students. Several of them challenged her division of music leaving Beethoven as an outsider: 'Well, in a way that's how his music, brilliant though it is, strikes me,' she cried. 'Whereas there is fragility in Ravel, Prokovief and Warlock; Joy in Stravinsky and Mozart; thought in Bach, Ives and Hindemith; humanity in Haydn, Schumann and Britten; and what I call an unselfconscious brilliance in Monteverdi, Schubert, Janacek and Vaughan Williams, Beethoven shows his manic streak which probably suits our manic preoccupations, don't you see?'

One of the students said, 'Perhaps the big difference between today and earlier is a banishment of madness from life, for it has been institutionalised; in spite of our new awareness from Freud about those inner aspects of man, the split remains. Beethoven reunites the two; which is why we honour him.' Mrs Brandt looked seriously at him. 'But the battle in music must be with the universal, not with the self. We musicians, composers and performers, are nothing. We must think deeply about interpretation; asking ourselves how much we are projecting into innocent music.'

Doctor Baxter nodded. 'I must say I think Western music reached its peak in the seventeenth century. Perhaps extending up to Haydn; but the Classical era is already in decline.'

Mrs Brandt shook her head. 'That also is an interpretation we should examine carefully.'

Professor Maxwell took her arthritic hands. 'Mrs Brandt, thank you so very much for visiting us. We warmly remember Hans. You brought a lifetime's experience to share with us today. It was much appreciated by old and young.'

Shortly afterwards Tim brought the car to the front steps and helped her in.

They talked merrily all the way. Mrs Brandt told Tim how her leibe Hans had once been a doctor from the Sudetenland and given it up because it was ideas distilled from music, not bullets and blood he sought for the world. She sat laughing inside a waterfall when Tim eased the car through a garage car wash, so it would look presentable for Nina. He dropped her at home. She waved gaily before letting herself in.

The day-nurse was leaving as Tim arrived. 'She's very frail indeed, but is eagerly waiting to seeing you. She made me get her up so she could dine with you. The dear never takes no for an answer. Don't be too shocked; remember she really is old. A wonderful person.'

Tim found Nina sitting in the dining room in a day housecoat talking to the night nurse and to Maria's daughter who had been prevailed upon to cook and serve supper which, as usual, they ate early. Nina keenly probed Tim about his studies and about his future with Sophie.

He laughed at the mention of children.'Yes, of course we will marry and have children. No it won't be that long. Sophie is broody now Sophia is pregnant. But we want to wait a little until we're more settled, maybe when I finish at the end of next year, or when she's a doctor in three.' Nina listened to Tim's account of Mrs Brandt's views on bullets and ideas. 'But Timothy, medicine is also about ideas rather than bullets; has not Doctor MacKay shown you that?' With that she was helped to bed quavering, 'My own dearest boy, I am so proud and happy. Your struggle is not in vain. Look at you. Go on turning your ideas into bullets. We will win the war against the philistines in the end. Sleep tight my angel.'

The night nurse shook Tim awake as the sun was fingering the tops of the trees. 'She's gone Tim. Come to her.'

She helped him up the stairs, through the hushed living room awash with books and papers, pictures and kilim colours, and into Nina's bedroom where she lay, thin and grey, straight as a frond of grass under her sheet, her sharp eyes already closed, but with a smile as bright and eradicable as the sun arching over the roof.

Tim sat by her until hours later Doctor MacKay led him, stiff with loss, to Nina's living room where they drank tea. The old man sighed. 'Timothy, she loved life as she loved her husband, as she loved you, fiercely, joyously. It is a miracle she survived so long. I think she was waiting until she knew you'd be all right.'

Then the living room splintered through Tim's tears. He had lost the love of his life; his homing power; his fearless companion facing ideas, dreams and terrors; the only one who had loved him completely, true, honest, with vision; greater still, the only one who really felt with him his anger at the betrayal in a self-seeking world trampling on the innocent and unwary, careless of everything. Then, there was nothing left; he saw nothing beyond the waterfall of tears.

Then Doctor MacKay spoke. 'Timothy. Tim. We all mourn her passing, and will for a long time. But we must follow her spirit to celebrate her life. We need to reflect on how much she has bequeathed to us.' He looked shrewdly at the young man. 'Now it is up to us to carry her torch. Tim, the greatest problem for the living is not grieving, but going on with life. Actually there is nothing else to do. You know Nina expects that of you, my boy, don't you? Her vision of a decent world must not die with her.'

The sun arched over their silence, until Tim nodded. It had

taken an age dealing with memories, the requiems for his life with Nina, laments which wrung him then pulled him back to his beloved house which he must now leave as she had, and to the careful doctor, her friend and aid as he was, Tim's. He nodded saying softly so as not to wake her, 'Yes. You are right . . . and I must tell Sophie . . . and Chris.'

Sophie spent the last night with him sharing his room and his bed, sharing his distraught farewells, nursing him (more or less as Nina would) until like a tiny new bird he slept in her arms. She wept for grief and love determined somehow they would see this through, and everything else as well.

Never again would nothing matter. He mattered. They mattered. Everything mattered. In the faint light of dawn they made love; it was shorn by grief into a simple joining; his seed splashed into her as she shivered. 'Oh, Love. My Tim, I love You.' Waking late, they packed the car with his possessions, shut the house – it was her family's now – and sadly went for a very late lunch at the Deans where Jeff spoke for them all when he farewelled them in the early evening. 'Come back soon, this is your home now.'

Yet however much Tim managed to ride his grief, his old sense of immortality had seeped away; his vulnerability kept him close to tears which tended to break when he played; for the well feeding his musical strength now contained this grief. He managed all his written exams and then turned-up for the performance audition commencing with ear-tests and answers about theory and history related to the pieces he was about to play.

Then he embarked on a clutch of works he and Fran had prepared in which she accompanied him. The second work was an adaptation of a Vivaldi sonata which reminded Tim of the evening he had introduced Sophie to the *Four Seasons* on Nina's ancient steam-gramophone. His mouth filled, his eyes brimmed until he faltered and stopped. Fran looked up in alarm. 'It's OK Tim. Take your time.' Turning to the adjudicators Fran murmured, He has just lost someone very close.' Tim tried again but the well was filled with grief. It silenced him until the chairman said, 'Why not take a break. Come back when you feel better. We can continue with the next candidate.' Fran led him out. The students waiting were appalled, 'Had Baxter been at him? He's so good.'

'Is it really my turn now?' someone stammered.

Fran took him into the courtyard within the conservatorium. Unconcerned about gossip, she embraced him caressing the hair frothing off his brow and kissing it. 'There-there, my Timtim, there-there. Remember Syrinx, you told me about her?* Nina is here. Can't you hear her railing against injustice and singing about the Family of Man, her encouraging smile, her energy, all her songs you and I hold forever inside; songs that never die, music that will always be played. Just as Pan lamented and remembered Syrinx on his pipes, we'll play Nina's songs.'

'He is so, so beautiful grieving', Fran acknowledged shivering with the power her feelings and memories evoked.

Tim looked gratefully at her. A shadow of a smile lit his leaden face. 'Oh, dearest Fran. Yes, we *will* play her songs. She will never die.' He finished his drink loudly slurping the dregs up the straw. 'I'm OK. Fran, thanks. What would I do without you.'

She sent him to wash his face and meet her outside the exam room 'So we can play Nina's songs together.'

10:

THE EXAM ROOM WAS THE SAME. But Tim's grief metamorphosed it. Just as music transforms the ugliness so often breeding it, Fran the musician had shown her bassoon ward how to transform his loss into majestical song. From a tentative start Tim's performance blossomed stunning the jurors. He sat tiredly at the end while the chair unprecedentedly responded, 'Thank you very, very much Mister Macknight.' He and Fran then departed. Fran's sparkling eyes reflected his honours. He didn't care much about the exam; she had granted him the real honours.

Sophie's exams were as praiseworthy, in fact she again won the exceptional student award. Something of the same transformation seemed to have effected her. Her involvement with Tim and his frantic life and her incursions into the social sciences had sharpened

---

*   See notes at end.

her medical knowledge not diffused it. Perhaps it was propelled by the intensity with which she lived. However they got their results with relief before planning how to holiday.

Tim's idea of going back to the Black Dolphin Motel (where Chris had taken him) for swimming, sailing and beach combing sounded perfect, although laughingly she cried, 'But no shitting in the bath, my darling.'

'Why not? If we want, to.'

'Only if we really, really need.'

He held her hips and slid a finger round to poke her bottom.

She whispered, 'My love, I am waiting for you there.'

His erection sprang up hungrily as he said to her left breast, 'I'm not sure I want to wait that long.'

After this loving, banqueting seaside time, they spent a happy fortnight with Don and Jeff at the Deans mooching about, as they had so often done in the past, their antics and good humour filling the house, swamping the yard.

Then Tim and Sophie returned to their flat to prepare for term and to help Sophia, who was finding her morning sickness a trial. Actually there was nothing the two could do for her, but Sophia having two such adorable extra mouths to feed became so busy, quite suddenly the morning unease mattered less. As time passed her biliousness decreased. However, she attributed her growing into parenthood to the magicians' spells drumming above.

During the next term, Tim's graduation year, he received a long formal envelope in the post. It was from Nina's solicitor:

> *I am sorry for the delay, but it has taken some time to*
> *sort out challenges to the enclosed will, to clarify details.*
> *However I am now in the position to inform you that the*
> *family house in Eliza Beach has been left solely to you, the*
> *deeds of the afore mentioned have been amended and are*
> *enclosed herewith. Further, her open letter addressed to*
> *you of which I have apprised the family is also enclosed.*
> *Please call on me at this office when I will be pleased*
> *to acquaint you about further details and hand-over*
> *all the keys and the balance of documents.*
> *Yours truly . . . . . .*

Nina's letter, in a spindly clear hand, read as she would have spoken it:

My dearest Timothy, and my dearest family,
After much thought I have decided that you, Timothy
should have the house. What is inside, allow the family
to have as each wishes, but the structures and land
I earnestly wish you to take for three reasons:
> *firstly, because you have nothing and deserve*
> *this sort of start;*
> *secondly, because you have worked diligently for*
> *years maintaining it;*
> *and thirdly, because I love you as a son.*

Do not let the house hinder you. It has served me,
and you, and other generations before us. Now it is,
I am told, largely only of value as real estate. It has
nurtured life happily flown elsewhere;
it is otherwise a dead thing. Use and dispose of it freely.
It is yours. As you know, it is your dreams, not your
memories, which must always guide you.

Remember, all of you, that your father and I always
deeply loved you. Please be happy in your life and
remember all of you are one family.
All my blessings, my dearest children,
Nina.

Tim blanched. 'Soph, I think I'll go for a walk.' He returned vowing, 'I don't want it.' But he visited the solicitor who reported how fervently Nina had made her decision, how just she had always been, and prompted, 'Go away and think about it. Talk to your close friends.' Sophie was troubled by his disquiet and rang her father. 'My God, it's a gold mine. Of course I'll discuss it with him, or you both. Over dinner? Good. Meet me at seven at the *Groucho* next Thursday.'

They found him inside looking the successful business man, seated in a private corral where they could more easily talk. After cocktails he brushed aside Tim's objections. 'Just listen to me, my dear Tim. First look at Nina's letter; it contains the following: "your start in life, your deserving repair-work, her love for you; its real-estate value, solely yours to use or dispose of." Is her understanding of your life and her message not clear? Tim, she has a better understanding of life than you. But then in her own peculiar way, she always had clarity.'

Both children nodded.

Mr Dean ordered, then waved the waiter away. 'Tim, where will you live without a house? How will you support a professional life? How can you live without capital behind you? How will you support my daughter in the way to which she has become accustomed?' (The children frowned, he could see he was onto a looser with both of them). 'But seriously in this regard, as a family man you must have the means to provide. Tim, think of this as a legacy from Nina, the equivalent of your scholarship, your fees, a daily income – call it a pension. Can't you see it as a basic necessity?'

Tim nodded uncertainly.

'It is what any parent would give to any son. Sophie and Jeff will get the house when we go. It's a natural way of helping them.' He stopped. Tim was near tears. Not because he spoke too rudely about life. But suddenly Tim realised that indeed, Nina had been his family and, in the face of opposition from her own children, she had demonstrated a deeply held belief in him and in their relationship, and that he held the same view. It was inconceivable not to accept her love, and the house representing it. Nina's love, never controlling or binding, had fed him all these years and was still feeding him.

'So you agree with me?' Mr Dean asked timidly.

Tim nodded, smiling through his tears, He held Sophie's hand. 'It's hard to be loved, isn't it? It's like Soph. Her love is the same you know. Thank you for letting me steal her from you. And thank you for everything. I'm glad you are both here to help me when I muddle things up.'

Mr Dean's throat tightened. Oh, how he loved this boy; oh, how happy his darling girl was and how successful; such beauty; beauty for him to savour. He shuddered with discomforting delight. Dinner was transformed.

He rang a few days later. 'Tim, I've been thinking, you don't need Nina's house. When you visit, you stay with us; so why not let it through the local estate agents. Actually, there's a chap in my office who wants to move into the area; he wants a place for a year or two until he finds something to buy, so why not settle everything in this way? Yes? Good. Then let me lend you the money to refurnish the house now the family has taken most of Nina's possessions. You can repay me when the rent monies start coming in.'

'You will? Can I? Tim gasped. 'Perfect, yes, oh hang on, Sophie thinks so too.'

At the end of the term Sophie announced that she wanted to quit medicine. Nina's death had made her finally realise how important finding her own life was. She was beginning to see her interests lay in the social sciences. She begged Tim to accompany her to confront an understandably angry Doctor Martin. Their appointment, made with his secretary, was first thing the following Monday.

Autumn bullied the lifeless leaves and threw squalls of rain at them as they scurried up the steps of the Medical Faculty.

Doctor Martin greeted them warmly, a touch apprehensive: they were so formal. Sophie broke the silence. 'I don't want to go on with the course. Medicine is not for me. I am truly sorry. Please.'

He'd dealt with bright students before. He was calm. 'Tell me how you arrived at this position.'

Sophie sat shame-faced so Tim helped. 'Sophie feels she has different skills. Medical ones are more about engineering than feelings and. . .' Sophie continued, 'I think I'm better with people as thinking and feeling things rather than as bags filled with hearts and spleens, stomachs and genes, the stuff we deal with here. I'd prefer to be a social scientist.'

Doctor Martin looked at her fondly. 'You prefer egos and ids and social dynamics and family structures? Perhaps first you should visit the Psychology Department; I can arrange that.'

'Oh, I've done that. I've been studying psychology with Trish Maxwell for a year now, and attending a few lectures when there's time. That's how I know where I should be.'

Doctor Martin smiled. 'Well, my dear. I congratulate you on your initiative. The Faculty will miss you. But may I advise you?'

Sophie nodded.

'I suggest you go on working in both places and finish your

year's study here. There is a minor qualification of Medical Assistant you will gain by doing so. The Psychology department will credit you with that and so shorten your course, prevent you getting bored, repeating what you already know.'

'I am sorry, Doctor Martin. You've been so good. I feel I'm letting you down.' Her face trembled.

He leaned forward and squeezed her hand. 'Dear Sophie. Of course I'll miss you here. But your happiness and fulfilment mean more to me than having you run round the medical racecourse and finish. I take a wider view of society than a medical one. I have no doubt at all as a social scientist you will be a boon, but I am sorry you felt you needed Tim to protect you from the ferocious medical faculty.'

She blushed.

Tim started. 'Actually I wanted to see you, with Soph here, um, about something.'

Both looked at him.

'I'm having a ball doing music. I've begun thinking about graduating. I don't want to teach or play that much anymore. Sophie and I were very struck by Nina's death: it set us both thinking. Music has been my essential therapy. I feel I'm reaching the end of it. Just having pleasure in my life is not enough – it's not enough for either of us. The poverty and deprivation of the kids who came to "Family Tree" upset me. I began thinking how I could help.

'I often think about Doctor MacKay. I want to be like him. He saves lives both in medical and in psychological ways. I remembered Nina saying once that we should try to leave the world a smidgen better than how we found it. My dream is to work beside Sophie and to help those kids. I have learned a lot from her textbooks and from Doctor MacKay and from you. I've been doing the science course too. I um, wondered if it would be possible to become a doctor?'

Tim, accustomed to being greeted by silence, waited.

Sophie recovered first. 'It's true, you know almost as much as I do. We study together, he helps with scientific mumbo-jumbo.'

Doctor Martin's heart sank. More gifted problems, he thought ruefully.

Tim blurted, 'Would you help me to catch-up. It's really important for me?'

Alan Martin gazed out of his window as the wind ripped all the useless leaves off the trees in preparation for winter. He meditated, 'Autumn makes me realise we too must slough off our dead leaves of habit, tradition, prejudice and prepare for spring seasons of promise and dreams and new-growing ideas and skills. Just as you both remind me. Now what can we do?'

Sophie took Tim's hand; they waited.

Doctor Martin slowly began, 'Tim, in three weeks there's a pre-med exam, for those wishing to join the faculty well beyond their matriculation year, as you are. If you have the time, Sophie and I could prepare you for that, assuming she has correctly diagnosed your medical knowledge. For the rest, leave it to me. I'll move heaven and earth to get you admitted. But you must complete your first degree. Is it a deal?'

The youngsters were dazzled.

'No, no my dears, I am just doing my job. Let's meet tomorrow evening here so we can start grooming our new doctor.'

Pensively the Registrar watched the buffeted trees. At the lower corner of his window he saw his beautiful young friends embrace and kiss farewell for the day. 'Ah, such tenderness' he reflected. He couldn't hear what they said, only imagine it: 'So, with a bit of luck we'll have a doctor in the family, anyway.' 'Only with your help.' 'I love you - love you - love you . . .' The wind blew their words away, driving them like leaves to dance and scurry to their studies, blooming with a delight never found in leaves.

11:

SOPHIE HAD DIAGNOSED Tim's medical knowledge accurately; as it turned out he knew a great deal. Doctor Martin was able to persuade the faculty not only to admit him into the first proper year of the course, but to credit him with almost half of the first year's course. The Registrar was concerned Tim had time to earn the money to cover first year until the Faculty was able to offer scholarships. And he was tempting Tim to continue with his music.

Providentially Mrs Brandt intervened, getting the chairwoman of a Jewish support group to see Tim who won the committee's hearts, even though he wasn't Jewish. His references reaffirmed their opinion. Here was a deserving case; yes they would support him for the duration of his course, provided he repaid half the money within ten years of graduating. Gleefully he accepted.

He reported this, and that he'd soon be a landlord, to the Registrar who chuckled at his delight. 'Well Tim, now you will have absolutely no excuse next year for not studying *and* playing, and of course keeping up with Sophie. Plus coming to see us. I am getting sick of trailing along after my talented women. We need a bassoon to keep us up to the mark. You must both come to dinner regularly.'

Tim, although embedded in his preparations for the graduation concert, was very grateful indeed. He shyly plonked a box containing two special bottles of wine on the desk and said (almost) what the card said: "Doctor Martin, Thank you. Love Sophie and Tim"

Rather abashed, and late for a tutorial, he hurried away. Prucilla, Alan Martin's wife and his two daughters said approvingly that evening, 'Daddy, Dear, you deserve it. You worry too much. So Tim and Soph will keep a doctor in the family. Great. Let's hope music-making continues.'

Singing was Tim's other instrument. His tutor, Miss Roach had accepted his programme, including Doctor Baxter's suggestion of settings of four poems Tim had made in class, 'They show admirable skill and an understanding of their lineage.' said Baxter, 'We should support the composition and performance of new music.' he added. 'These are noteworthy.'

The rest of his programme consisted of a set of Brahms songs, (adolescent yearning), songs by Charles Ives (landscape and war), Vaughan-Williams (folk stories), Peter Warlock's Shakespeare settings of ribald love and sleep, finishing with two by Schubert: *The Dwarf* and *The Erl King*. (Tim wanted the triangular love of the deranged dwarf to lead into the devilish death of a hapless boy).

For his settings, Tim chose poems from the book* Grace and he had poured over during work at Nina's:

1 Realisation   *(for Nina)*

In that night
that is our day,
that terrible dark
of being alone,
there, I miss you.

There, is my dream
which I cannot touch.
There only is
my love deepening.
In that awful
hole of want
I see your shine
like the only star
with lovely light
faint, fragile and unique,
a light which reaches me
far, far at the end of space
at the end of wits end
in the darkness of alone.

There, lights meet:
we meet, and all the
loneliness of want spills:
all the wasted dreams
break like waves
about my head until I drown
willing, washed, unwilling
tossed lifeless, screaming
as if just born.
The wind wet with want
the sea, restless

---

*   See notes at end.

as my empty arms,
beating against
an unheeding shore.
Beyond streaming spume
there, we meet at last,
son and moon, one loveliness,
one joy, in the great emptiness
of space which cries,
"I alone am nothing without you!"

2 Reflections   (for Chris)

You dive into the pensive sea
gleaming at first light,
an arch of skin evoking wonder:
a playful dolphin?
Although less nosy, floppier
you reflect such grace.

The magic eye of the sea
is tinged with green of weed
and ochre rock in clear depths;
sky is lush on its mischievous face.
I soar dreaming, nodding
in unison on our boat.

Awoken by your shout,
deer, gulls, dolphins eclipsed
you wave me in;
a breeze scuffs leaping nakedness,
light dances in opened arms.
Breathless I am embraced.

3 Tempest (for Fran)

Lion night,
roaring,
claws incising,
humid wind
of hot blood
red wet faces,
livid hands,
slimy rubies
underfoot,
gasps of
the drowned,

the prayful prey,
only whites
of stilled eyes
shriek
in this
red night.

4   Overtime   *(for Sophie)*

The clocks
strike twelve:
a new day!
Is this the day
you will come
come back, come
into my arms
into my life,
is this the
new day?

I need to embrace,
need to love
completely,
need to forget
myself in you
rutting breathless
wonder found.
All that love
unfound, lost love,
loneliness,
all the alien
world cried in,
all that loss
payed-off:

I would give
you nothing
visible or valuable
but a small thing
(perhaps unvalued):
my devotion, myself
all of myself,
with joy chiming
in paradise.

Tim set *The Tempest* for voice alone; it had echoes of Grace's piece, with grating savage threat. The others had a piano accompaniment which Robert played. *Overtime* included a viola chiming like a clock throughout until the final 'paradise', a quiet, quick joyous figure ornamenting the singer's whispered 'paradise'.

Doctor Baxter smiled at his pupil's appropriation of Renaissance lyricism which suited his unquavering early-music voice with its disturbing thread of suffering. When the *Erl King* had vanquished the boy at the fleeing father's side, Baxter allowed a tear to course down his cheek as Tim brokenly whispered the last words with bewitching agony, "in his arms the child was dead."

'He's not such a shit, after all.' students murmured.

Trish Maxwell accompanied Sophie to the concert. His voice stirred her. 'It was such a moving program, Tim. But tell me, should I be sad about the death at the end?' Trish asked carefully.

'Did you feel sad?'

'No. Relief. The last songs seemed more a sort of farewell after celebrating friends, love and war.'

'Trish I think you're right.'

'Death in dreams, and probably in poetry, is often an ending, like leaving childhood or losing a lover. You sang appreciations of friends and life, ending with a farewell to triangular love and to needing a father's arms. Now free, you're moving into another life. Is that approximately correct?'

Tim shivered. 'I see what you mean. Um, yes Trish.'

Sophie grinned. 'Timmy, you sang for us both, finishing and starting. No wonder I cried.'

'So you're happy, Soph?' He grinned. 'She cries when she is.'

'Feelings belong with tears.' Trish murmured.

Sophie clutched his arm. 'Yes, I am.'

The following week was Tim's final bassoon recital, which was also Robert's accompaniment exam. It consisted of some of the unplayed and unpublished music Mrs Brandt had given the library. A thoroughly prepared recital won distinctions for them both. As his citation put it: "Performances of distinction crowning an excellent course of studies."

Professor Maxwell asked to see him. He was shocked to hear Tim would pursue medicine. What a wasted effort, he thought looking distressedly at his star pupil. Tim understood his

265

disappointment. He wanted to explain.

He started haltingly. 'Being with you all has been the best years of my life, playing-up and playing around, and just playing. It's been paradise here, and at your house, all over the city. I needed the therapy of music to help me grow up. But now I know I want to do more than enjoy myself.

'I suppose it's partly my past, partly the courage you have given me, and partly the terrible savagery of the world I glimpsed living and teaching in Sophia and Toni's poor district, also my experience in "Family Tree". Those deprived children, cheated of a decent future by everyone, including their battered parents.' He was encouraged by the kindly face. 'You see Professor, I was a child like them; then I stumbled upon love and music and a skilled determination to help me, enabling me to get here. Fran was one of those. I love her more than I can say'

Professor Maxwell nodded. 'Tim, I love her too. I think I understand . . . but it was her music?'

Tim shook his head, 'Much, much more than that.' The Professor nodded. It really is love, he thought and was hit by the connection Tim then made, 'Music is the food of love. But I think I have other food to give.'

Dick Maxwell looked admiringly at his student. 'Tim, I have no doubt you have. You brought much to the Faculty. I must say in some ways it doesn't surprise me. It only saddens me we won't be closer colleagues. I remember a brilliant doctor, Boyd Neel, who directed a string orchestra with great distinction. Perhaps Doctor Tim Macknight will do the same. My boy, my warmest wishes. Please come and see us. You will always be welcome.'

Sophie's year was meretricious, marred only by the disapproval of some of her teachers that she was leaving to pursue the quasi-science of Psychology. She packed her bags gladly; she had done her duty. Now it was time to do what she wanted.

There was nothing wrong with change, in spite of so much dissent (parents, teachers and friends); anyway Tim agreed with her! 'Do what you must, fuck the consequences, it's your life.' He was rasher than she. A trifle disconnectedly, they saw their flat with new eyes, yet reassured by its familiarity.

12:

ONE WEEKEND SOMETIME LATER, Toni and a very pregnant Sophia go visiting. Tim and Sophie are alone. Like energetic brumbies they prance about, galloping naked into the shower then around the flat until they gleefully fall onto their bed and teasingly devour each other, putting off the delicious moment of penetration, feinting, giggling sweating with desire until she pulls him in.

She holds him tightly, lifting to let him in further, stretching hungry, gasping with excitement. She moans as he moves, cries as he thrusts and thrashes wildly, whimpering weeping with ecstasy as he finishes. She shimmers; tidal waves carry them onto a counterpane-shore their skin stuck by sweat, their arms wrapping, until they can lie on their sides and regard each other.

She adores the sharp set of his shoulders the saddle pushing his hips up, his elegant legs. He wonders, again and again, at the fullness of her breasts, the vitality of her body, until he whispers, 'Will you marry me now?'

Sophie looks deep into his feather-grey eyes, two lustrous wishing-wells finally granting her life's dream. 'Now?'

Tim nods and kisses her mouth so gently their lips hardly part. She cuddles up bursting into tears so joyous her face sparkles with diamonds. 'Oh my Tim. Is it really time?'

He looks far away beyond the now into the past and into the future, measuring their many changes. 'Don't you think it is?'

She rolls him onto his back kissing him ferociously saying more and more loudly, 'yes, Yes, YES, YES!' Then she stops. 'Tim, are you sure?'

He smiles his engaging irresistible smile. 'Only if you want.'

She sobs. 'I do, I do. Oh my Tim. I do.' She mobs his body with lips, hands, thighs, shaking legs; feet tangling with his.

Stomachs collide; lips merge; breasts squeeze his beating chest so fervently he gasps for breath, gasps for more as he thrusts into her with equal ferocity until the house drums and rattles and sings, 'YES, YES, YES, YES, YES, for always and always YES!'

The sun, dipping over the roofs beyond the garden, slyly slides in to wake them. 'You'd better ring your parents.' Tim murmurs. They cover their nakedness and bound downstairs to Sofia's phone.

'Darling. I am delighted. (sob) Oh, darling. Here's Daddy.'

'So he's to make an honest women of you at last eh? Congratulations.'

Jeff screams, 'WOW. About time. Come and see me. Come now.'

'We'll have a barbecue next weekend, OK?'

So, it is agreed. A few close friends are invited. Mr Dean pulls back the rugs so they can dance. Mrs Dean's salads are the talk of the party. The pool area is awash. Everyone is delighted.

Tim and Sophie make love late that night for the first time in her old room, in her bed, their bed, for the room has been refurbished to accommodate them now that Nina's house is let.

'Everything is changing, we're changing, Soph, aren't we?' he whispers. 'I'm home at last.'

They lie watching the dark trees nodding.

She kisses him. 'Changed, oh my own Tim. Not really.'

Sleep weaves them smiling together.

*

Notes on some of the texts cited

p14   Ned Kelly was an Irish desperado, a bushranger in
             1870's Australia, who robbed banks and pubs in
             country towns, and made a last stand at Glenrowan
             against the police, wearing iron head and body
             armour; captured when his legs were shot away.
             See: *Ned Kelly* by R. Melville and S. Nolan,
                   Thames and Hudson, Lond: 1964.

p20 ff   Greek Myths:

             Robert Graves *The Greek Myths* Penguin.
             Carl Kerenyi *The Gods of the Greeks* Penguin.
             H.J.Rose *A Handbook of Greek Mythology*
                   Routledge.
             A.Baring & J.Cashford *The Myth of the Goddess*
                   Penguin.

p47   Charlotte Bronte *Jane Eyre*
p52   Jonathan Swift *Gulliver's Travels*
p54   George Orwell *Animal Farm*

p109   William Shakespeare, "Twelfth Night"
                   in *Complete Works* OUP 1991:

             ORSINO   *One face, one voice, one habit,*
                          and two persons, a natural perspec-
                          tive, that is and is not . . .
             ANTONIO   *How have you made division of*
                          yourself? An apple cleft in two
                          is not more twin than these two . . .
             OLIVIA   *Most wonderful!*
                                                   (5.1.213ff)

p118   John Donne, *The Undertaking* :
             Janet took minor liberties in writing out the poem for
             Tim, yet her version is faithful to Donne's meaning.
             Some early MS versions were titled *Platonic Love*.

p154   A catch by Thomas Ravenscroft in a play called
             The Knight of the Burning Pestle by Beaumont.

p188	Berthold Brecht *Caucasian Chalk Circle* Methuen 1979: . . *[then] Azdak disappeared and was never seen again. But the people of Grusinia did not forget him and often remembered his time of judgement as a brief Golden Age that was almost just . . . [maintaining] that what there is shall belong to those who are good for it, thus the children to the maternal, that they thrive . .*
p201	All music alluded to exists except the works attributed to Paul Hindermith, the Bassoon Sonata and *Canzona*, which, like Grace Stone's and Fran's compositions, are imaginary.
p216ff, **263**ff	F. Oeser *But, Persephone and other poems.* The Sicnarf Press, Lond: 1996.
p249	L van Beethoven, Sonata for cello and piano No. 3 in A major. Op.69. The discussion centres on the third movement, second part, *Allegro vivace*, its opening.
p254	*Syrinx grazed a contented flock because she sang to them; sang of the winter gales striking bell-like ice-clad branches; of the lazy summer buzz of bees and nodding grass, the carolling brook gambolling down the valley in spring; of the calm majesty of larks' chorales in airy space.* *Passing one afternoon, Pan was enchanted by her songs, for they were of his godly domain. He grew over-rapturous when he spied so beautiful a singer! Syrinx fled in panic down the valley to splash into a lake at its margin. But she could not swim.* *With Pan hot on her heels she appealed to Zeus. He reciprocated with the smallest of thunder bolts which, as Pan clasped her, transformed her into a sinuous stand of reeds. But when the wind blew through them, her songs resonated again.* *Pan sadly fashioned the reeds into 'pan-pipes' and played them, so skillfully it is said, the winds ceased and stones gathered round him - as circles of stones attest in Greece to this day.* Another version is contained in Longus' *Daphnis & Chloe* Book 2 ss 34. Penguin Classics, 1956.

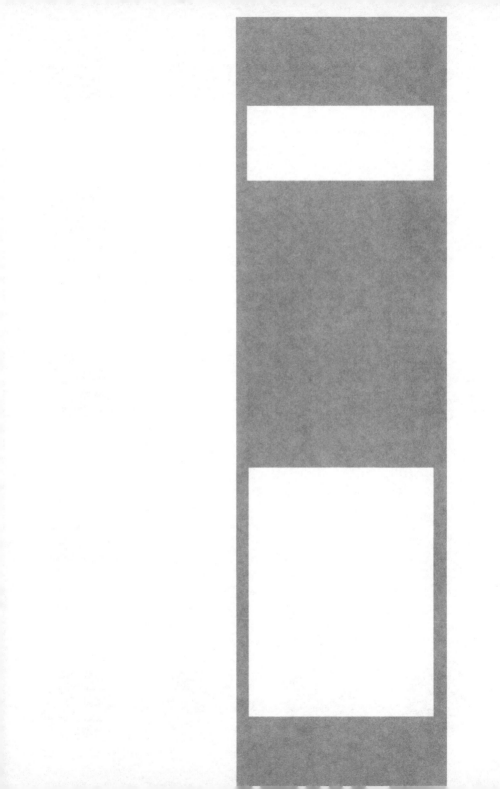